"Margaret." He took a deep breath. "Will you marry me?"

"Yes," she said softly, still in a daze. "Yes."

A broad grin spread across his face, and his sun-bronzed cheeks flushed with delight. He leaned down to kiss her once more, but she halted him abruptly with her hand.

"Ash!"

He stopped, his countenance suddenly unreadable.

"What's the date?" she asked.

His eyes narrowed as he stared over her shoulder, and again she was astonished by how magnificent he was, a face of hard and even planes but such expressive eyes and mouth.

"Let me see," he muttered. "Today is Thursday, October 22, 1863."

"Oh." She swallowed, swaying slightly in his embrace.

"Is anything wrong?"

She closed her eyes for a few moments, then brightened and gazed straight into his face. "Ash! Your birthday is in three weeks."

"Margaret," he said softly. "I have to return to my command. Do you want to marry me now, or on my next . . ."

"Now," she cut off his words, shudder coursing through her body. This birthday would be his last. For she knew that sometime next summer, General Ashton Powell Johnson, C.S.A., would be killed by one of General William T. Sherman's crack sharpshooters.

Unless, of course, his wife could prevent it. . . .

Books by Judith O'Brien

Rhapsody in Time
Ashton's Bride

Published by POCKET BOOKS

Ashton's Bride

Judith O'Brien

POCKET BOOKS

New York   London   Toronto   Sydney   Tokyo   Singapore

This book is a work of fiction. Names, characters, places and incidents are products of the author's imagination or are used fictitiously. Any resemblance to actual events or locales or persons, living or dead, is entirely coincidental.

An *Original* Publication of POCKET BOOKS

POCKET BOOKS, a division of Simon & Schuster Inc.
1230 Avenue of the Americas, New York, NY 10020

Copyright © 1995 by Judith O'Brien

ISBN: 0-671-87149-8

First Pocket Books printing April 1995

10 9 8 7 6 5 4 3 2 1

POCKET and colophon are registered trademarks of Simon & Schuster Inc.

Cover art by John Stephens; stepback art by Jeff Cornell

Printed in the U.S.A.

To Allen and Seth,
who endured weekends of third-rate movies
so I could write this book

and to Aunt Grace,
who had the forethought to save a bundle
of yellowing letters from the trash can.

CHAPTER
1

Although she had fallen into a deep sleep, an unpleasant odor assaulted Margaret Garnett's nostrils. First, her nose twitched, then her mouth tugged into a grimace, and finally, her eyes opened, startled and blue.

Her face, even in distress, was more than pleasant. It was a wholesome face, slightly round, with neat features that were very close to pretty. She was not wearing makeup, but even without artificial enhancing Margaret had an all-American, Norman Rockwell sort of face. Her hair, light brown and straight, was cut into a sensible, no-nonsense page boy. She looked much younger than thirty, yet something in her eyes, a fleeting darkness that sometimes appeared, made her seem much older.

It had taken Margaret two full hours on the ancient bus to fall asleep, two long hours of trying to forget her ultimate destination, a place so remote and godforsaken that the only way to reach it was by car or by

Rebel Line bus. This was not a journey to be made impulsively. It took extensive planning, since even old Rebel Line would only venture there once a week. Weather permitting.

And the way Margaret had been feeling lately, with moods so bleak that other New Yorkers passing her on the street urged her to cheer up, she didn't trust herself behind the wheel of a rental car. It would be too easy to turn around and flee—to do a simple U-turn back to Nashville, hand in the car keys at the airport, and catch the next plane back to New York.

The stench that awakened Margaret was more powerful now, an aroma of salt and grease and something indefinable and animal-like. She turned her head around, the little piece of paper towel clipped to the headrest sticking to her hair.

A man in the seat behind her, the one with the green mesh baseball hat and low-slung belt, was happily munching on something from a cellophane bag. It rattled every time he dipped his reddened, moist fingers into the bag to retrieve a morsel. Earlier on the trip Margaret had watched as he chewed tobacco, explaining the worn patch on the back pocket of his jeans. It was circular, the exact shape of the red tin of snuff. At the time she had been curious about the Royal Crown Cola bottle in his hand. It kept on getting fuller, a dark line rising to the bottle neck. Then she realized, with open-mouthed horror, that he was using the bottle as a cuspidor, spitting tobacco juice into it as he chewed. It was at that point she decided to find refuge in sleep.

He gave her a lopsided grin and held the bag in her direction. Margaret didn't realize she had been staring at the man, but of course she had. Now she could see the writing on the bag—Uncle Bo's Bar-be-que Flavor Pork Rinds. She shook her head and tried to smile, but only managed to bare her teeth. He shoved a

2

crackling mouthful into his grin and nodded toward the window.

"Pretty country," he crunched.

Margaret glanced out of the window and had to admit he was right. They were beginning to wind up a twisty mountain road, and the ragged gray rock of the mountain was softened by patches of brilliantly colored flowers, wild and magnificent and unexpected. From the opposite window was a picture postcard view of the valley, the lush green of the grass, the weathered red of the rough-sided barns, vague outlines of split-rail fences marking property lines.

The bus groaned with the effort to climb the spiraling road, gears grinding madly with little result. They were traveling at a snail's pace, with the grating commotion of Le Mans.

Before reaching this stretch of road they had passed rustic farms and small towns with names like Muggin's Pass and Smileyville. It hardly seemed possible that this was the same America she had grown up in, the same country that had given the world New York and Chicago and San Francisco.

But this was different. This was the Deep South.

"Where you headed to?" It was the man with the green hat and pork rinds.

Margaret folded her hands on her lap and tried to sound cheerful. She was getting quite good at it, having had plenty of practice declaring her destination to her fellow graduate students at Columbia University in Manhattan.

"I am going to Magnolia University, a small, fully accredited liberal arts college located in the heart of the beautiful Smoky Mountains of Tennessee," she replied.

"Hey, ain't that something? So am I!" A fleck of pork product shot out of his mouth. Margaret tried to

3

keep her face blank, but a sudden thought pierced her tortured mind. What if this man was a student? Or a professor of English? Or even a dean?

"You a student?" he asked.

"No. I'm going to be an associate professor of English literature."

He whistled, obviously impressed. This was the first positive response she'd had to her new position, and it was coming from a man with a mouth full of fried pig skin. Still, it was better than what she'd received from her pals at Columbia.

At first everyone thought she was joking, her peers who clutched envelopes containing plush job offers from Yale and Duke and Penn State. Margaret had been the star of her group, the only one whose doctoral dissertation was going to be published as a book. And this was her second Ph.D., the first being the one she earned right out of college in American history. That dissertation had also won praise. The topic had been on Sherman's march through Georgia during the Civil War, as told from Sherman's viewpoint. It, too, had been published, under the title *He Did What He Had To*.

Margaret's only failing had been in her procrastinating. Sure, she could whip off a publishable paper in a matter of days, could write a master's thesis in a few weeks. But when it came to real life, to balancing a checkbook or applying for a job, she was hopelessly, chronically late. When everyone else was applying for grants and teaching positions, Margaret ignored them, rationalizing that she wouldn't need a job for a year, so why rush? There were books to be read, wonderful historical facts to learn. Why get all bogged down with the boring details of real life when you can revel in the past?

Then suddenly it was spring, and everyone else had jobs, and Margaret had nothing but a stack of student

4

loans to pay off and a forty-dollar advance from the university press that was publishing her dissertation.

A flurry of application writing was followed by a steady rain of carefully worded rejection letters, all stating that she would have been perfect, but the application arrived too late. All of the good positions were already filled.

So Margaret Garnett grabbed the only job she was offered at small Magnolia University. She knew the name of the school simply because it had been destroyed during the Civil War by a Union regiment from Massachusetts. As a native of Boston, Margaret had been especially proud to hail from the noble state that had tried to erase Magnolia University from the face of the earth. Unfortunately, they rebuilt.

It wasn't that she hated Magnolia University for itself. She had never been there, had never even seen a photograph of the place. Until she applied for a job there, she had scarcely been aware of its existence.

But now everything had changed. Magnolia University was a physical symbol of her worst failings. She herself was to blame for her predicament, for she was the one who waited too long to send in the stupid paperwork. Clever Margaret, brilliant Margaret, was forced to call mediocre Magnolia her employer. Margaret, who had always scorned anything southern, would be sharing her hard-won northern knowledge with a bunch of kids from south of the Mason-Dixon.

It was so outrageous, so unthinkable, it was almost as if the Confederacy had decided to avenge itself after her glowing dissertation on General Sherman. If that was the case, the South truly had the last laugh.

"I'm a local," said the man with the green hat, jolting Margaret out of her musings.

"A local what?" she asked without thinking. The man laughed, a deep chuckle that was, surprisingly, not unpleasant.

"Just a local, born and raised in the town of Magnolia. My daddy and my daddy's daddy worked here, and so do I, in the cafeteria." He said this with such obvious pleasure and pride that Margaret smiled.

"It's nice to meet you. I don't know anyone yet, just some voices on the phone. My name's Margaret Garnett."

"Good to meet you, too. I'm O.B. Willy Thaw, but everyone around here just calls me Willy."

"What an interesting name. What does the O.B. stand for?"

Again he laughed. "Don't know. It's been a family name for longer than anyone can remember, and my great-great-great whoever forgot to write it down. I suppose they never thought this far ahead. Anyway, we just ignore the O.B. most of the time."

He crumpled the empty bag and stuffed it into his shirt pocket. Suddenly he stood up, touched the ceiling of the bus, and sat right back down. He saw the wary expression on Margaret's face and raised his thick eyebrows.

"You probably wonder what I just did."

Margaret nodded slightly, a little worried now. She wondered if he had a psychological disorder, a strange syndrome that might compel him to do weird things, like fondle bus ceilings or abuse small animals.

"I just put back my angel."

Margaret's back straightened, and she glanced over to the bus driver. Could she get his attention in a hurry if she needed to? The bus was almost empty, so her only hope was the driver.

"It's a legend, you see," Willy continued. "They say Magnolia is just like heaven, so you don't need any special help from angels while you're there. But when you leave those old stone gates, better grab your angel, 'cause you might need it in the real world. So I just put back my angel, since we just passed the stone gates to Magnolia." He shrugged his shoulders. "I've been doing it so long now, I don't even think about it except when I'm with someone new to the mountain. It's kind of a nice story, isn't it?"

"Charming," she replied, wondering what other little bits of fantasy awaited her. Perhaps they all believed the South won the Civil War or that Magnolia University was actually considered an adequate place of learning.

Willy pushed up his cap, revealing a deep, reddened crevice on his forehead where his cap had fit too snugly.

"Here we are, Miss Garnett," he announced as the bus gave one last explosive rattle before wheezing to a halt.

With great apprehension, she turned her head to see out of the window, to view her new home. The other riders slumped off the bus, and Willy stood behind her, waiting for some sort of movement on her part. But Margaret was unable to move, transfixed by what she saw.

There seemed to be no actual town of Magnolia. In her mind she had pictured a little village of the Mayberry ilk, the only southern town she was familiar with, other than the nightmare hamlets created by William Faulkner and Flannery O'Connor. She had been secretly hoping for a Mayberry, a place with a wise and gentle sheriff and a large-bosomed Aunt Bea to bake lattice-topped pies.

Instead Margaret saw a store, a single store. The sign above it was hand-lettered, the first few words in red paint, the last in brown. It said Magnolia University Book Store/Post Office/Supermarket. In her mind she added, Bus Stop/International Airport/

7

Cultural Center, and when she saw a well-dressed young man exit the store eating a candy bar, she slapped on Restaurant.

Willy was still waiting, shifting his weight from one leg to another. So she stood up.

"Holy sh—uh, excuse me," Willy stammered.

Margaret looked down at Willy, sympathetic and amused. The poor guy. Little did he know when he offered her the pork rinds that she was six feet tall.

One would think that when a woman reached her full height of six feet by the age of fourteen, she would be accustomed to gapes and stares. But Margaret had never really adjusted. Even at the age of thirty, there was a secret corner of her mind that was used exclusively for thoughts of what it would be like to measure in at five foot three.

And even after all the years of basketball jokes and total strangers cupping their hands to their ears and asking how the weather was up there, she was still at a loss for how to prepare people for the initial shock. Perhaps when Willy first offered her a tidbit from his bag, she should have declined with a sweet smile and an explanation. "Pork rinds? No, thank you. I'm six feet tall."

When she accepted the job at Magnolia over the phone—there been no time for an exchange of formal letters—she should have said, "Although I'm clearly overqualified for the position of assistant professor of *anything* at your little school, I will gladly accept because I am six feet tall." And when her last boyfriend dumped her for a diminutive cocktail waitress, Margaret—if she had any sense at all—should have been more understanding. "Of course, dear. It's only natural that you would trade a two-year relationship based on mutual interests for a three-week fling with a girl who is almost half your age. Not to mention I'm six feet tall."

Willy, still gaping at Margaret, whistled through his teeth. "You sure are tall." He shook his head. Margaret laughed at his refreshing honesty. Most people would look embarrassed, hem and haw, then change the topic when they first realized how tall she was.

Margaret handed Willy his luggage, which was hanging in an overhead mesh shelf. He thanked her, and she pulled down her own meager luggage, two duffel bags and a PBS tote filled with books. The rest of her possessions were being shipped in the mail. She was beginning to wonder if the postal service, which, according to their advertisements, could locate a tent in Nepal, would be able to find Magnolia.

Willy offered to escort her to her new home, a cottage named Rebel's Retreat. She had a ten-month lease on the place for less money than the monthly rent for her apartment share at Columbia.

The bus screeched away the moment she stepped through the door, and she assumed the driver was as eager to leave Magnolia as Margaret was. The driver, however, did not have college loans to repay. He was a free man.

Since it was the end of August, a few students were milling about on campus. They were, without a doubt, the best-dressed group of college students she had ever seen. There were no torn jeans and bandannas, no pierced noses or leather jackets. At Columbia the students took pride in their grunge. This group looked like a Republican youth convention, or a retreat for unshakable Osmond fans. A vague fragrance of Ivory soap was detectable only when one of the students swept by.

Now that Margaret had a better view, she could also see that the university buildings were made of heavy Victorian stone, sprawling and squat at the same time. They were all of a uniform buff color, but each structure managed to maintain a unique character.

"Excuse me, are you Dr. Margaret Garnett?" A slender, middle-aged man stood before her, delicate features behind round, horn-rimmed glasses. He wore a blue blazer, a button-down oxford shirt, and neatly pressed khaki slacks, the ensemble of favor, she surmised, judging from the other males on campus.

He was a few inches shorter than Margaret, and she noticed that he glanced involuntarily at her feet. It was a natural reaction, one she was used to. Men seemed to assume she was wearing either platform shoes or standing on a box when they first met her. She was, instead, wearing flats.

"Hello." She extended her hand.

"Welcome to Magnolia. I'm Chester Dick—we spoke on the telephone. I'm the head of the English department." They shook hands; his was a firm, dry grip. "I hope you had no trouble getting here. We're famous for our fog, which sometimes isolates us. You missed real pea-souper by about twelve hours." He seemed pleased by the foul weather, similar to the way New Yorkers boast about fending off muggers.

"No trouble at all, Dr. Dick." She flushed when she said his name, like a gawky junior high student. Struggling to think of something to say, she turned to Willy, who was still standing next to her. "Oh, do you know Willy Thaw . . ."

"Of course," he said jovially, clapping Willy on the shoulder. "How was your fishing trip, Willy? Did you catch the big one?"

"Nope, Dr. Dick." Willy shrugged and held up his bag, and for the first time Margaret noticed a spreading wet stain seeping through the canvas. "But I gigged me a few frogs."

"Mmmm." Her new boss nodded sagely. "Good eating."

Willy grinned. "Especially with Mama's hot sauce. I tell you what—I'll fix up a plate for you, Dr. Dick, but

10

don't tell no one. I don't have but two dozen legs, and you know how fast they go."

"I'd appreciate that, Willy," said Dr. Dick, genuinely pleased with the prospect of eating frog limbs. He then took Margaret's luggage. "I'll show you to Rebel's Retreat. And Willy, we sure missed you in the cafeteria."

Willy turned red with pleasure and winked at Margaret. "Good luck, ma'am." And he lugged off.

"Willy's a real character." Dr. Dick smiled. "There are a lot of them around here."

"I would imagine," she replied, as noncommittal as possible.

After a short walk they were at the quadrangle, an impressive square surrounded by more stone buildings. "The stone is all from a nearby quarry in the valley. We only used local materials in building the campus. That's why it's almost impossible to tell if any given building was erected last week or in the last century."

Margaret took in the sights with a mixture of surprise and irritation. There was no denying that the campus of Magnolia University was nothing short of magnificent. And it bothered her that a college with absolutely no academic reputation should be housed in such a glorious setting. The quadrangle was a stately fortress, no higher than three stories, anchored by a majestic bell tower. The solemn lines of the structures were tempered by lush bushes and brilliantly colored flower beds. The floral fragrance was clean and fresh as the warm breeze jostled the plants.

This was the ideal backdrop for a world-famous university. Oxford or Cambridge came to mind, yet this was a mountain in Tennessee. If there were any academic justice in this world, Magnolia's campus would be made of corrugated tin lean-tos and rusting mobile homes jacked up on cinder blocks.

11

Dr. Dick was watching Margaret, his eyes narrowing as he saw the play of emotions on her face. She was aware of his curiosity and offered him a completely artificial smile.

"How old are most of these buildings?" she asked, brightening into her best tourist impersonation.

"Most are from the late eighteen sixties or later. The university as well as the town of Magnolia were destroyed during the Civil War." Although Margaret knew this, she felt suddenly, and ridiculously, guilty. She stared straight ahead as he continued.

"Only a few of the buildings around here date from antebellum times. You're lucky, Dr. Garnett. Your new home is the oldest surviving structure on the campus."

"Rebel's Retreat?" Now Margaret was unintentionally fascinated.

"Yep. It was built by one of Magnolia's original professors. He later became one of the South's most prominent generals. Have you ever heard of Ashton Powell Johnson?"

Margaret thought for a few moments. In truth, her studies had centered on the North. She could rattle off the name of almost every general and high-ranking officer who served for Lincoln. By contrast, she spent little time and effort studying the Confederacy, only viewing the short-lived nation in terms of how it impacted the North. And she had been so focused on literature for the past few years, the names of famous battles and their heroes now seemed foreign and remote.

But everyone had heard of General Ashton Johnson, a commanding figure with the startling mixture of moderation and audacity. He had fought against Virginia's succession, but once the deed was done, he became one of the Confederacy's most daring leaders.

It was Johnson who came the closest to halting Sherman in Atlanta, and without Sherman's victory in Atlanta, there would have been no March to the Sea. And without Sherman's devastating march through Georgia, Margaret would have had to select another topic for her first dissertation.

Another by-product would have been the prolonging of the Civil War by another few years and, perhaps, a cost of life so great on both sides, the Union may have never recovered. With a nation so weakened by internal strife, the United States could have become an easy harvest for more powerful nations such as France or England.

Had the admittedly brave Ashton Johnson been successful, there might not be a United States of America.

"General Ashton Powell Johnson." Margaret nodded. "He organized the Virginia cavalry, and only Sherman could stop him."

"Sherman and two dozen Yankee sharpshooters," corrected Dr. Dick, a thatch of his wispy brown hair ruffled by the wind.

"What was General Johnson of Virginia doing in Tennessee?" She tried to keep the tone light, noting the passion with which Dr. Dick had defended the general.

"He was trying to provide the South with a university based on his ideals of education. And it would have worked, too, had the war not pulled him back to Virginia. Who knows what Magnolia would have become if the general had survived the war?"

Margaret frowned, pondering the fate of a Confederate general. It was a compelling story, but common. The guy picked the wrong side to back, and that was his fault.

Now Union officers, that was a different matter. A topic she could warm to, those gallant men in blue.

Just the thought of how many northerners suffered misery and disease and death for the cause of justice was enough to bring tears to her eyes.

"Well, here we are." Dr. Dick's voice startled her for a moment, then she looked at where they were.

Before them was a good-size house, covered with vines and wisteria and a strange-looking, lovely climbing plant. The roof was gabled, and there was a long, wraparound porch, complete with a white gliding swing and dozens of potted plants, all in full bloom.

"This is it?" she gasped, stunned by the size and beauty of the so-called cottage. After sharing a two-bedroom flat with three other women for the past few years, Rebel's Retreat was positively palatial.

Dr. Dick climbed the four steps to the porch and smiled at Margaret's obvious pleasure. "I think you'll like it here, Dr. Garnett. Everyone who passes even a single night at Rebel's Retreat falls in love with it. Some say it's the ghost of General Johnson that makes the guests feel so welcome. He's the eternal host, you might say."

"I was expecting a cottage, Dr. Dick, not an estate."

He laughed and reached in his blazer pocket for the keys. "Well, it's your home now. And by the way, please call me Chet. I'm fully aware that the name Dr. Dick is hell to utter with a straight face."

Margaret beamed, comfortable for the first time since she accepted the job. "I'll be glad to call you Chet, but only if you promise to call me Margaret. Somehow Dr. Garnett sounds too prim and spinsterish."

They shook hands, both grinning, and he opened the door. She stepped into the front hall cautiously, as if afraid that the inside of the house could not possibly live up to the promise of the outside. Her eyes,

ASHTON'S BRIDE

accustomed to the dazzling sunlight outside, slowly
adjusted to the cool dark hallway, little spots dancing
in front of her before she could finally see clearly. Chet
crossed into a room to the left and threw open heavy
velvet drapes, bathing the room in sunshine softened
by the hedges outside.

The room, a large parlor, was filled with heavily
carved Victorian furniture. It was a style she had
always abhorred, preferring instead the simple, clean
lines of earlier furniture. But this room was a revelation. Rather than emitting a feeling of self-conscious
formality, every piece of furniture seemed to welcome, beckoning with soft chintz cushions and time-
warmed wood.

There were two large sofas, both with darkly carved
backs and brightened by fresh pillows scattered in the
corners. A marble-topped table, slightly too high to be
called a coffee table, stood between the sofas, offering
an array of yellowing magazines and a selection of old
beverage rings staining the marble, testimony that this
was a table to be used, not just admired.

Bordering the room were a pair of wing chairs
upholstered in a pale green brocade, both with foot-
stools underneath, separated by a round, tilt-topped
wine table. On the other side of the room was an
enormous buffet with weirdly carved feet. Margaret
noticed the legs of the buffet right away and moved
closer to examine them.

They were cabriole legs with ball and claw feet.
What made the feet so odd was that they were webbed
like a duck's feet, so realistically carved that it seemed
as if the buffet could waddle away.

"This is great!" she exclaimed, touching the wood,
almost expecting the claw to pull away at her prodding.

"Glad you like it," said Chet. "It unnerves some

15

people. There's a matching table in the dining room, but there wasn't enough room for both the buffet and the table together. There used to be a dozen or so chairs to complete the set, but they disappeared years ago."

"I've never seen anything like this." Margaret straightened, shaking her head. "How could anyone not like them? They're wonderful."

"I think so, too. They're from General Johnson's estate. Apparently he had a somewhat quirky sense of humor, along with a rather fanciful idea of what a home should be. You'll come across his stuff all over the campus. If it's strange and funny, it's bound to belong to the general."

Margaret smiled. "What did his wife have to say about animal feet on the furniture?"

"Oh, he never married. The one true love of his life died a few months before he was killed." He looked at the buffet with sympathy. Suddenly he brightened. "Anyway, I'll let you settle in. There are two small bedrooms upstairs, you can take your pick."

Chet walked toward the door, turning as he reached for the knob. "I almost forgot—there's a reception tonight for new faculty members. It's in Johnson Hall, the big building next to the bell tower on the quadrangle. It's scheduled to begin at eight o'clock, but we're pretty casual here. Drop by any time. And Margaret?"

"Yes?" She glanced up from the buffet table.

"We're delighted to have you here at Magnolia. I'll see you later." He gave a little half wave and left.

An odd feeling came over her, a sense of vague guilt. It was the way one feels after trashing another person behind their back, only to discover that same person has heaped your name with praise. Magnolia was delighted to have her, and she was a nasty guest.

Margaret went back into the hall to retrieve her bags, noting the lush Oriental carpeting as she walked through the parlor. It was slightly worn in spots, but still lovely and obviously very valuable.

Pausing in the hallway, something caught her eye—a glittering light. She turned and saw a mirror, her own face reflected through the age-spotted glass.

The mirror was utterly fantastic. At first it seemed to be a normal, if intricately carved mirror, the frame large and glossy with sweet-smelling wood polish. Upon closer examination the real design was revealed, and Margaret couldn't help but laugh aloud.

The frame was one continuous bar scene, with comical figures leaning over the straight-edged wood in various states of intoxication. It reminded her of one of those riotous Hogarth paintings of peasants, every cluster of revelers was a self-contained vignette. Some were tipping drinks, others had their mouths wide open—and from the expression of the people beside them, they were singing loudly and off-key. A few men were slumped with tilted hats, and one woman, clearly of dubious virtue, had a shapely leg thrown over the bar.

"General Johnson—I love your taste in furniture!" she said. At once she stopped smiling and gazed at herself, a sadness creeping over her.

Odd. Of course she had not been thrilled with the idea of coming to Magnolia, but since meeting Chet and seeing her new home, her mind had been free of the depressing black thoughts that had been plaguing her for the past few weeks. Now she felt something more than self-pity. It was a sense of crushing sorrow, brief but almost unbearable.

In a moment the feeling was gone, evaporated as quickly as the morning dew. She looked more closely at her own face, surprised—in a detached way—at

17

how good she looked. In spite of her exhausting, emotionally draining journey, her blue eyes looked bright, her usually lank hair hung not in clumps but in gentle waves.

And strangely enough for Margaret, the thought of attending a reception that evening was not at all unappealing.

CHAPTER
2

Johnson Hall was easy to find. Not only was it exactly where Chet said it would be, but it was lit up like a Las Vegas casino; the sounds of laughter wafted over the quadrangle in stark contrast to the somber bearing of the bell tower.

Margaret paused for a moment before opening the heavy oak door, giving her loose hair a reassuring pat before entering the party. She hadn't been sure what to wear, especially since the few people she had seen around the campus seemed to be dressed more formally than most weddings she had attended in Manhattan. What, she wondered, would they wear to a party if their everyday clothes were so stodgy? Tuxedos and ball gowns?

Playing it safe, she opted for a calf-length embroidered skirt she'd picked up in a Greenwich Village secondhand store and a jade-colored silk T-shirt. She sincerely hoped there wouldn't be any more receptions for a while, for this was her one and only evening outfit, and only one of two skirts. The rest of her wardrobe consisted of jeans and sneakers and rugby shirts. No one had ever accused Margaret of being a clotheshorse.

She even applied a touch of makeup for the occasion, something she rarely bothered with. It usually didn't matter how her face looked once she stood up, but tonight, for some reason, she wanted to look her very best. Standing in front of the strange mirror at Rebel's Retreat, fumbling with her ragtag assortment of drugstore cosmetics—all zippered into the same quilted makeup case she'd toted since high school, she felt an unfamiliar sense of excitement. This was going to be her real introduction to life at Magnolia University.

So why was she anxious? Earlier that day, on the creaking bus, she wanted nothing more than a one-way ticket back to New York City. Now she felt a weird, fluttery sensation in her stomach, as if she was about to meet someone very special.

Once she defined the feeling, she could almost laugh out loud. Imagine, six-foot-tall Margaret Garnett, Yankee through and through, finding romance in the hills of Tennessee. It was absolutely comical.

Still, she hadn't been able to shake the notion. And as she clasped the oversize brass doorknob to enter Johnson Hall, her hand was shaking and her throat was suddenly very dry. Taking a deep, fortifying breath, she entered the building.

Bourbon. The moment she opened the door, the brackish scent of bourbon blew over her, tangy and brisk. The smell reminded her of a freshman dorm party or a bar at happy hour. She hated bourbon.

Breathing through her mouth, she scanned the room and was stunned by its size. The entire building was one single gallery, large and open, with a high ceiling that arched in the center, held up by solid beams that made the ceiling look like an inverted ship's bow. Lining the walls were elegant bookshelves packed with leather-bound volumes, hundreds, if not thousands, of them. There were a few oil paintings of stern-looking gentlemen, all in dark clothes and serious-looking poses. They looked damn proud to be hanging on the walls of Johnson Hall.

The crowd was conspicuously well-dressed, just as she had imagined they would be. The men wore blazers or suits, the women were clad in cocktail dresses of silk and pale chiffon. The crowd was older, most seemed to be about forty or fifty, although there was one man seated under a painting who appeared to be in his early hundreds.

A few people glanced at Margaret with fleeting smiles and a young man in a white apron raised his eyebrows and pointed to a gallon of Jim Beam. He was behind a card table, the makeshift bar, and was manfully plopping chunks of ice into plastic cups, adding a few splashes of water and generous glugs of Jim Beam, and placing them on the edge of the table. The moment they were deposited, a hand would pluck them away.

Margaret was suddenly aware that she was being watched, and felt that thrill of anticipation course through her, making her fingertips tingle and her stomach knot. She turned her head and saw a man—very tall and very handsome—staring at her. He nodded a silent greeting and walked toward her with long, graceful strides.

He was blond. That somehow surprised her. She had a small, ridiculous twinge of disappointment, and a ludicrous pang in the back of her mind—the small corner that harbored her girlish, romantic notions. She just wasn't expecting a blond. Almost immediately she snapped to her senses. She was no starry-eyed girl but a solid, well-educated woman of thirty. But still . . .

"Are you Margaret Garnett?" His voice was pleasant, perhaps a little too smooth. This was a man who was used to getting his way with women. She wondered how he knew her name, and had a momentary flash of the Magnolia University gossip mills spreading the news of the Yankee giantess stalking the campus.

"Yes, I'm Margaret Garnett." Her voice was a little more frosty than she had intended, but it didn't seem to put him off. He continued to smile.

"I'm Brad Skinner." He shifted his bourbon into the other hand so he could shake her right hand. "You and I constitute the only new faculty members here. Welcome."

She took his hand, uncertain. He continued to speak. "I guess we're both after the same tenured English position, eh?"

"Huh?"

He laughed. "It's Magnolia's policy—for every tenured slot that becomes available, they hire two applicants and let them teach for a year or two. The winner gets the job."

"I had no idea! That's positively barbaric!" Margaret was truly stunned. Why hadn't anyone told her this was only a trial position?

"That's because these positions only open up about once every twenty years or so. See old Dr. Taylor over there?" He pointed to the ancient man on the chair. "He's been teaching here for about sixty years. He's an expert on the Civil War, or—as he calls it—the War of Northern Aggression."

"An expert?" she harrumphed. "He probably fought in it." She blushed, suddenly aware of how malicious she sounded, but Brad Skinner merely laughed.

"Actually, his father was the one who saw active duty."

"You're kidding! His father was in the Civil War?"

"Absolutely. He was only a drummer boy, and married very very late in life, but it's the truth."

"Next you're going to tell me that his father lives just over yonder." She cocked her head, waiting for the answer.

"To tell you the truth, he's buried just over yonder, in the Magnolia cemetery."

"How do you know so much about Magnolia?"

"Ah. I'm an alumnus—college class of 1980."

Great, she thought. Her only competition is with an alum of the school. Not that it really mattered, she shrugged.

"Can I get you a drink?" He placed his hand under her elbow and gestured toward the bar.

"Sure. Uh, do they have anything other than bourbon? Maybe some white wine?"

He grinned. "I wouldn't bet on it, but I'll check."

And once again, she was standing by herself. She surveyed the crowd for Chet, but couldn't find him. She wanted to ask him more about this tenure situation.

Her request for white wine had caused a commotion at the bar, and both Brad and the young bartender were looking under the card table, rooting through a cardboard carton that said Jim Beam in large red letters.

Suddenly, Margaret felt a chill run through her, as if a door opened and a gust of frigid wind swept through the room. But she hadn't heard the heavy oak door open, and even if it had, it was a warm night. Her short-sleeve blouse had seemed too confining as she walked over from Rebel's Retreat.

Her hands were trembling, and she clasped her arms together for comfort and warmth. No one else seemed to notice anything, the party sounds remained the same, with the clinking of ice and disjointed giggles. There was a dry lump in her throat, and she could feel the downy hairs on the back of her neck bristle. There was someone behind her.

Slowly she spun around to face the person, but there was no one there. Then her eyes focused on an oil painting hanging on the wall. And against her will, she gasped.

It was a portrait of the most handsome man she had ever seen. He wasn't simply good-looking, for a painting of a good-looking man can be found in any museum. This man was drop-dead spectacular.

Margaret walked toward the painting, her legs seeming to move involuntarily. The man in the painting seemed to watch her, an optical illusion that happens frequently, she thought. But this was different.

He was young, perhaps thirty or thirty-five, which immediately set him apart from the other paintings, all of white-haired gentlemen with musty gazes and blue-veined hands. No, this man was vital, alive. His clothing, a plain cravat peeking from billowing academic robes, was simple and seemed to be the style worn in the middle of the last century.

But his face—his expression—could have been painted last week. Instead of the self-conscious countenance worn by the other men, his face was amused, a slight smile playing under the light brown mustache. His eyes were an extraordinary hazel color, not really solid brown, but the artist had painted flecks of green in his eyes. The overall shape of his face was slightly square, and his features were regular enough to be called chiseled, but that couldn't really describe his handsomeness. Perhaps it was his hair, slightly long and sun-streaked, that gave him such a modern look, or his sensual smile.

Margaret stepped closer, her hands clenched. This was he, she thought. This is who she wanted to meet, who she had been looking for, the reason she wore makeup . . .

Then she began to laugh at herself, at the absurdity of her bizarre feelings. Margaret Garnett, six-foot-tall Yankee giantess, wears makeup for oil painting on Tennessee mountain. It was ludicrous, insane. Maybe the altitude had made her crazy. But still she couldn't turn away from the painting, those compelling eyes, the smile.

"So I see you've met your host." Brad Skinner was at her side, offering her a plastic cup with an inch of bright yellow liquor. "We're in luck. There was some wine."

Margaret took the glass mechanically, without taking her eyes from the painting. "Who is he?" Her voice sounded strange. She had been looking for some indication of who he was. Even the artist was anonymous—no signature in the corner to indicate who painted the piece.

"Don't you know? That's General Ashton Johnson, C.S.A., the builder and first occupant of Rebel's Retreat . . ."

But Margaret didn't hear any more. She simply dropped her plastic cup and ran for the nearest exit.

The courtyard offered no relief from the suffocating feeling that had so swiftly washed over her. It was too warm, too sticky. Even the foliage seemed to radiate heat.

Brad had not followed her outside, and the still-functioning part of her mind realized he must be wiping her spilled drink off the marble floor in Johnson Hall.

None of that mattered. The only thing that seemed important was that painting, or rather, the man in the painting. Never had Margaret felt so completely drained, yet exhilarated. Part of her wanted to rejoice, to revel in the newly found sensation of finally falling in love. The other part of her was already laughing at those feelings with complete disdain. It was comical —Margaret Garnett falls in love with an oil painting of a dead man.

Just the thought, the disjointed knowledge that this man was dead, was almost overwhelming. But of course he was, for more than a century. Perhaps she simply felt this strange emotion for an equally dead artist, but even as the thought formed in her mind, she realized that was not the case. It was not an artist's rendering that had caused this tumultuous effect. She was certain that it was the man himself. She had felt it earlier at Rebel's Retreat, and now she knew why.

Suddenly her arm was touched, and she jumped. It was Brad Skinner, grinning at her as if her abrupt departure had been the most natural action in the world.

"You were right to run," he murmured, casually wiping his lapel with a wadded-up napkin. It left streaks of white paper crumbs on the dark blue. "The wine ate through three layers of marble when it hit the floor, and there was a hole in the plastic cup. Take my advice—stick to bourbon. It's safer."

Still trembling, she managed to smile. "Sorry. I suddenly felt ill. I must be more exhausted than I realized."

"It was the picture, wasn't it?"

Margaret stared at him, her face blank. She didn't want him to know how very right he was. "The picture?" Even to her own ears, she sounded inane.

"The portrait of Ashton Johnson. Women love it; they seem to find the old guy more fascinating than any of the living men in Magnolia." He shrugged, carelessly tossing the napkin into the bushes. "Do you know how demoralizing it is to have a dead Confederate as your competition?"

The party inside was still in full swing, but Margaret felt as if it had ended long ago. "I think I'll go home now, uh, I mean back to Rebel's Retreat." She felt self-conscious in front of Brad, as if he knew how unnerved she really was.

"Would you like me to walk you back?" The offer was noble but halfhearted.

"No, but thank you. I'll be fine."

"Well, it was nice to meet you, Margaret. I'd better get back to the reception." He motioned inside with a nod of his head. "I'll explain to everyone that you're exhausted from the trip. They'll understand." He smiled and ducked back into the hall. The courtyard was illuminated by light for the few seconds the door was ajar, and she could see the courtyard was open. The path that led her to Johnson Hall was visible from where she stood.

Before she left, she reached into the bushes for the napkin Brad had pitched earlier. For some reason she didn't bother to analyze, the thought of trash outside Johnson Hall was particularly disturbing.

CHAPTER
3

The next morning was a revelation to Margaret. To awake without the city sounds of bleating car horns, whining alarms, garbled curses, and the constant crunching of garbage trucks was an experience she had not enjoyed for twelve years. Twelve years.

She rubbed her eyes, willing the memories away, but they refused to vanish. It was a little over a dozen years earlier that her life had been forever changed, yet there were still times she was able to forget what had happened on that July day.

Hugging a pillow to her chest, Margaret fell back against the heavy mahogany headboard, heedless of the harsh sting when her head hit a sharp edge. The pain was good, reassuring. Because for so long she had felt only numbness.

It was the summer after she had graduated from high school, taking the Hawkins English Award and a partial scholarship to Columbia University. Her father treated the whole family to a trip to Martha's Vineyard.

For as long as Margaret could remember, she had wanted nothing more than to visit Martha's Vineyard. She badgered her parents every spring, hoping against hope to talk them into vacationing on the island, but the answer was always the same.

"I'm sorry, Margaret." Her dad would ruffle her hair affectionately. "It's just too expensive. Maybe next year."

This was the first family event that was completely Margaret's doing. Without her years of begging, they never would have planned the trip. Without her pleas, her father would not have managed to find a place in the exclusive Gay Head section. The owners needed a spot in Boston for a week, and the Garnetts simply swapped homes with them. It was perfect.

And it was all to celebrate Margaret's graduation from high school and her scholarship to Columbia.

Her brother and sister, both already out of college and working, came along as a surprise. She could still see the pleased grin on her mother's face that evening during supper, toasting the Garnett clan with chipped glasses filled with bourbon. They had forgotten to buy wine, and the only liquor in the house was a half bottle of inferior bourbon left by the previous renters of the cottage. So they each took a few sips, her brother nudging her all through the seafood dinner, teasing her about the torments that awaited her at college. But she could tell he was proud of her. They were all proud of her.

Margaret never knew whether it was the fish or the bourbon that caused her to become so ill during the night. Since she'd only had a few sips, she assumed it was the fish, although no one else in the family got sick. It didn't matter what caused her to stay in bed the next day. The only thing that mattered was she was unable to go on the fishing trip. Her dad could rent the boat only for a day. With long faces and plenty of sunscreen, they left the next morning. Her mother wanted to stay with her, but Margaret insisted she go.

"Well," her mother had said uncertainly, brushing a strand of hair off Margaret's forehead.

"Come on, Mom. There's plenty of ginger ale and crackers here for me. I'd rather be alone anyway . . ." Those words always came back to haunt her, but at the time—as they hung so innocently in the air—no one gave them a second thought.

"Are you sure?"

"Absolutely. Just don't expect me to eat the catch of the day."

With that her family left. Her sister opened a window to let in some fresh air, and her brother tossed her a baseball cap. "Hold on to it for me, Sequoia. It's a genuine Red Sox cap. Puke on it, and you're dead meat."

It was the last time, she recalled later, that anyone ever called her Sequoia, her family's name for her once she reached her full height.

Margaret sat up in the bed, running her fingers through her tangled hair. It was never determined how exactly the little boat flipped over, or how her family, each member an expert swimmer, could have perished so swiftly. Her uncle, who became her guardian until she was twenty-one, launched an investigation, demanding answers that were better left unknown. Margaret didn't care how they died, if there were enough life preservers, if they hit a rock or another vessel's wake.

Instead of becoming her closest relative, her uncle became her most vivid reminder of the tragedy. And he could never forgive Margaret for not joining his crusade. Her uncle wanted to sue everyone, to point accusing fingers at the entire state for the death of his brother and the family.

Margaret buried her grief in her studies, making friends slowly, delighting in English literature and history. Dwelling in the distant past became her refuge. Her uncle had been furious that she spent her small inheritance on education, then continued to study on loans and additional scholarships.

And now she was in Tennessee on a remote mountaintop. A wonderful fragrance filled her new room, subtle and green and fresh. It was late summer, and still this place smelled better than springtime.

She stood slowly, stretching, arching her back and extending her arms. She had slept surprisingly well after last night's reception, slipping into the soft bed. It was an old piece with carvings of griffins and unicorns on the headboard. This was surely one of Ashton Johnson's beds, strange and fanciful. Right before she fell asleep, she had a fleeting thought.

"I wonder," she murmured aloud. "Did he actually sleep in this bed?"

And from some faraway place, perhaps a whimsical corner of her mind she hadn't reached in over twelve years, she heard an answering voice, male and drowsy and touched with a southern drawl.

"Yes. But I do believe they have changed the linens since then."

She managed to find some coffee in the old kitchen at Rebel's Retreat, a discolored tin with a few scoopfuls of coffee so stale she doubted there was any caffeine left in the grounds. Using a tin stove-top coffee maker, she doubled the amount to compensate for the advanced age of the beans, and ended up with a cup of musty, elderly brew.

Padding around the kitchen, barefoot and in a

faded, crumpled sundress, Margaret explored the near-empty refrigerator shelves and the crooked drawers. There was a half bottle of Major Grey's Chutney, the cap askew and caked with dried brown crust, and some pickled okra. The flatwear consisted of three bent-prong forks and a tarnished serving spoon. One shelf contained some mismatched plates, and another held a can of Le Sueur Peas and a sticky baby bottle nipple.

Somehow this struck Margaret as funny rather than sparking her fury. She was in a strange place, knew virtually no one, and had no idea what to expect, yet still she felt the unfamiliar stirrings of optimism. Before she had sought comfort in the vastness of New York City, where no one knew her past and there were no side glances at Margaret Garnett, survivor of the boat accident. Now she was in a small community where intimacy would be impossible to avoid. And she wasn't terrified.

Perhaps this would be good for her, she mused, staring out the window at a beautiful drooping tree. Maybe this absurd place could herald a new beginning.

A sudden rap at the front door caused her to jump. It wasn't a loud sound, simply unexpected in the vast quiet of the kitchen. As she walked to the door she couldn't help but smile. It had been a long time since she had been comfortable with silence.

Peeking through the curtains, she saw a woman about her own age carrying a stack of papers with a white bag balanced on top. Without hesitation, she threw the door open.

"Hi," said the young woman, pushing her sunglasses on top of her head. "I'm Emily Ryan, school librarian and fellow northerner. I've come to ease your culture shock."

Margaret laughed and let her in. "I hope those papers are crib sheets on how to decipher southern accents. Please, come in—and by the way, I'm Margaret Garnett."

"I know that." Emily dumped her papers onto a chair in the hallway. "That's why I've come bearing drinkable coffee." She opened the paper bag, which contained two paper cups with plastic covers, and handed Margaret one.

"Let's see." Emily wrinkled her nose, which was sprinkled with freckles. "If I know my Columbia students correctly, you take your coffee light with no sugar."

"How did you know?"

"I went there, too—for Library Science." She glanced into the parlor. "You're so lucky to have this place—we're all in love with it."

"I can sure see why." Margaret led the way into the kitchen, and they both settled into sturdy, ladder-back chairs. "There's a wonderful feeling to the cottage, isn't there?"

Emily nodded, sipping the coffee. "How do you feel?" she asked after a slight pause. "I mean, this is such a big change from Manhattan."

"Weird," she admitted. "It's been so long since I've been out of New York that I feel like an alien here. How long did it take you to get used to Magnolia?"

Emily laughed and put down her cup. "I wasn't in Manhattan as long as you were, and before that I was at my parents' farm in Iowa, so Magnolia seemed more normal than New York. Still, this is a unique place, to say the least. And you, Miss Margaret Garnett, are just about the biggest thing to hit the mountain since *Gone With the Wind.*"

"Huh?"

"And so articulate." Emily grinned at Margaret's

startled response. Reaching into the paper bag, she handed Margaret a paper napkin to wipe up the coffee she had just spilled.

"You see," explained Emily, "you're the first female professor they've ever hired here. The school was a men's college until twenty years ago, but they've been hemming and hawing about female faculty members. To tell you the truth, some of the male alumni could barely stand the thought of women students, so the idea of a woman professor made them positively nauseous."

"So why am I here?"

"They couldn't resist you, my dear. They had set impossibly high standards for female applicants. The dean claimed it was so that the first woman professor at Magnolia would be a scholarly example to us all. When your application came in, they couldn't come up with any more excuses. They never dreamed you'd accept."

"In other words, I'm not really wanted here." Margaret looked out of the window, the same view that earlier offered such hope now seemed to taunt her with its serenity.

"Not true. Every female within five hundred miles is delighted. I sure am. It was lonely being the only woman who is neither student nor faculty wife." Emily leaned forward, cocking a perceptive eye at Margaret. "How do *you* feel about being here? It's not exactly Ivy League."

"I'm not sure." She shrugged. "Yesterday I was completely ticked off about the whole situation. Today I'm disappointed that some people up here may not want me. To tell you the truth, I don't know how I feel. I'm just in a sort of unreal limbo."

Emily nodded. "I know what you mean. Magnolia is a strange but wonderful place. Once you get used to it, I think you'll enjoy it. Especially living here in Rebel's Retreat."

Margaret welcomed the opportunity to change the topic. "Isn't it terrific? I saw a painting of General Johnson last night . . ."

"Great-looking guy, wasn't he? Too bad he doesn't come with the cottage."

"I'm not so sure he doesn't," Margaret said softly.

"Excuse me?" Emily shot her a curious look, but Margaret just shrugged.

"Do you know anything about him?" Margaret continued. "I mean, are there any books about him, memoirs, that sort of thing."

"Funny you should mention it." She tucked a strand of brown hair behind her ear and leaned back in the chair. "The university was just willed a whole stack of his letters. There's some mystery surrounding them—the donor requested anonymity, and everyone assumed that letters from Ashton Johnson would have surfaced years ago. I have them under lock and key in the library vault, if you'd be interested in looking at them. There's some talk of publishing them, but who knows."

"I'd love to see them." Margaret tried to keep the excitement out of her voice.

Emily glanced at her watch. "Yikes! It's after ten. I have a dozen students waiting to learn how to stack and file." She stood up and walked to the front door. "Oh, those papers are your bible—past teachers' plans for the courses you'll be teaching."

"Thanks. And the coffee was a godsend."

Margaret waved as Emily crossed the lawn with long, athletic strides, looking like an adolescent tomboy rather than a university librarian. It wasn't until Emily left that Margaret realized with startled certainty why she felt so comfortable with Emily.

The librarian was at least an inch taller than Margaret.

She spent the morning wandering about the campus, exploring the cool stone buildings and peeking in empty classrooms. The rooms could have been plucked straight from the last century, whether they were small, cramped offices smelling of leather and decades of crumpled paper, or the vast lecture halls, wrapped in chalkboards so old they were pale with the ghosts of forgotten lessons, chalked long ago onto the blackboards by gowned professors.

Some of the classrooms were furnished with ancient-looking desks and chairs, others were arranged in straight lines, with medieval planks stretched across the room to serve as the students' desks. She looked closely at one of the planks, thick and smooth to the touch. On a corner of the board was an ornate carving with the date. The initials had been scratched by a student in the year 1873.

Only after flipping through the stack of papers Emily had left did Margaret realize that she, too, was expected to wear an academic gown while teaching. And according to the pamphlet on the history of Magnolia, professors expected their top students to wear the black robes in classes. That bit of information was something of a relief to Margaret. She had seen an absurdly young-looking pack of kids wearing flowing academic gowns, and had been racked with the fear that they were her fellow professors. They were simply upperclassmen, swooping down on the campus a few days early.

More students were arriving, some looked frightened, casting anxious glances at their parents. Others drove alone, unloading their luggage and stereo equipment into the airy dorm rooms. Most were in groups, laughing, whooping hellos to classmates they hadn't seen since the spring.

And like the students she had seen earlier, they were remarkably well-dressed. Some of the young men wore ties and button-down shirts; the women wore dresses, skirts, and slacks that were so well-tailored they looked positively uncomfortable. Some of these rich kids, she thought grimly, would soon be her students. She would face them each day, sharing with them her hard-earned knowledge.

They didn't have the pinched, earnest look of Columbia students. They may have catalog-perfect clothes and spiffy cars, but these were not scholars. This was going to be like teaching at a resort.

"Ah, Margaret." Her elbow was caught, and she turned to see Chet Dick smiling at her. "I was hoping to see you. Sorry I missed you last night."

Margaret stopped and looked down at the man, slender and clearly harassed. "I'm afraid I left early— more exhausted than I realized."

"Sort of jet lag without the glamour of transatlantic flight, eh? Not to worry. You didn't miss much, except for Professor Taylor's attempt at replicating the rebel yell."

"You're kidding! I missed that? Remind me never to leave a party early. How did it sound?"

"Who knows. He said he couldn't do it with false teeth and a full stomach, so it was more like a wheeze than a yell. Anyway, I'm gathering the English department for an informal meeting. Care to join us?"

"Sure. When is it?"

"Now. This is a spur-of-the-moment meeting, just to go over some of the developments of the summer, including your own arrival."

"Oh, that reminds me, Brad Skinner said my position was only on a trial basis . . ."

Chet turned to her, the casual, friendly expression on his face replaced by a look of unwelcome surprise.

"He what? Brad said that?"

"Well, eh, yes, he did. Is something wrong?"

"Damn. Excuse me, Margaret." He shook his head and continued walking, motioning for Margaret to follow.

"I'm afraid Brad Skinner is a little on the conservative side in respect to Magnolia. You see, he's one of the hard-liners who believes the campus would be better off without women. He's threatened by you, Margaret. You have the education he lacks, the impeccable scholastic record that he can only envy. Brad was always a solid student, but football and fraternities were more his style."

Margaret stopped walking, and Chet turned to face her. "Is what Brad said true? Is there only one tenured position?"

"I'm afraid so, Margaret."

They continued walking together in silence, Chet waving greetings to passing students. But by his subdued tone, his attention was focused on Margaret.

"Chet," Margaret said at last, "I feel as if you weren't completely honest with me. I believe you meant well, but to tell you the truth, I'm pretty disappointed."

His face fell, and she could tell she had struck his guilt chord. "Margaret, what can I say? How can I make this up to you."

They were just entering the main office building on the quadrangle, and Margaret was aware of other voices drifting down the hall. She had to make this good.

"Well," she began softly, "Emily Ryan, the librarian, mentioned the newly aquired letters of General Johnson and that there was some talk of publishing them in book form."

Chet nodded uncertainly.

"Could I index them? I have a lot of experience, and my history dissertation was on Sherman's march, which would be the perfect tie-in with General Johnson, and . . ."

"Enough! You win!" Chet said with a relieved laugh. "To tell you the truth"—he flushed as he said the word *truth*—"this is not actually my jurisdiction. It would be a joint project with the history department. But I can't think of anyone more qualified. You've already been published. This might add some academic weight to the project." He extended his hand. "I think I can safely say it's a deal."

She accepted his hand, and together they entered his cluttered office for the meeting.

Throughout the entire session, Brad Skinner stared at her with unblinking, hostile eyes.

CHAPTER
4

The letters were bound in three volumes, pasted into old photo albums covered in cracked leather. Margaret placed them on the dining room table, ignoring the fanciful notion that the letters were finally home. The writer of the letters had chosen the table carefully, with its unusual legs and beautifully smooth top. Now the letters had come full circle, back to Rebel's Retreat.

It was impossible for Margaret to concentrate on the next day's lesson plans. All she would be doing was explaining the freshman English semester, which offered little room for variation on the set curriculum. Gone were the glorious dreams of teaching an enthralled class, of adjusting the reading list to the students' own interests. This was the first semester survey course, and it had been set in stone decades ago. She outlined a brief speech on the importance of *Beowulf,* glancing at the patiently waiting letters as she jotted down the major points she wished to make.

In a worn canvas tote bag emblazoned with the Channel 13 logo, a premium she had received six years ago by making a ten-dollar donation to New York's public television station, were five books with biographical information on General Ashton Johnson. Margaret resisted the temptation to page through the books. Instead, she would read the letters through without knowing anything about the man. It was a system one of her professors at Columbia suggested, so she might be able to see information clearly without being swayed by preconceived notions. Later, after one or two read-throughs, she would research his life and military career, then return to the original letters. Sometimes previously overlooked clues popped out, vital data that had been there all along but had been passed over by researchers who hadn't expected to discover anything new.

The one notebook she had opened contained the barest facts of the general's life—birthdate, where he was raised—nothing to sway her in her studies. She already knew his date of death—the summer of 1864. Yet she would try to forget even that information, preferring instead to read each letter as it was written during wartime, the receiver never knowing whether it would be the last. That was another one of her research tricks—whenever possible, she would attempt to replicate the sense of uncertainty the original readers must have felt.

But no matter how strident her methods, a few dates filtered unwillingly into her mind. The general would die during the summer of 1864, struck in the head by one of General William T. Sherman's sharpshooters. And, according to the thumbnail sketch provided by Emily's staff, Meg or Mag, his fiancée or girlfriend, would die of lung disease in the fall of 1863.

With the calm deliberation of a surgeon, she washed her hands, making sure they were fully dry before handling the letters. She filled a chipped kettle with water for tea and placed it on a gas burner. It was almost dusk, and she switched on the dining room light. Although there was plenty of afternoon light now, gently illuminating the room, she didn't want to be disturbed later.

Her hands were trembling as she slid the first volume into her lap. She had handled old documents before, hundreds of rare papers written centuries ago, yet this was different. There was an unsettling sense of anticipation, an excitement she had never before experienced.

Swallowing hard, she ran her hand over the table, in case there was an invisible damp spot on the glossy wood. These letters had survived over one hundred and thirty years; she did not want to be responsible for placing them in a puddle of diet cola.

Opening the book, she was enveloped in a musty sweet scent, the unmistakable fragrance of decaying paper and fading ink. On the first page was a small scrap of embossed paper and a brief note written in a strong, childlike hand. The date in the corner was November 10th, 1840.

This is a specimen of my writing with my new gold pen, which was a present from my mother as a token of respect and friendship to her son. I do highly esteem this present, and intend to be studious, correct in my language, clean in my habits, and respectful in my manner in the future.

Ashton Johnson

She stared at the paper for a few moments, slightly taken aback by the note. There were fold marks on the paper, as if the scrap had been preserved in a small place, such as a tiny jewelry box, or slipped into a locket. These were supposed to be historical letters covering the general's exploits in the Confederacy, not the childish scratchings of a little boy. Flipping open the notebook with information on General Johnson, she discovered the date of his birth. The note had been written on his tenth birthday.

A sudden vision came to her mind of a small boy proudly handing his mother his work, and her delighted response. It must have been very precious to her, a tangible reminder of the child he had been.

The next letter was written in the same hand, but the penmanship was bolder, more confident.

St. Louis, May 25, 1847

Dear Mag,

Please excuse the brevity of this letter, but I have just learned of my acceptance to the military academy at West Point. As I am expected to arrive there before June 10th, I will not be coming home to The Oaks first. Therefore I must bid a hasty good-bye to my St. Louis cousins and forgo many pleasures they had planned for their Virginia relation. One pleasure I did not forgo, my little Mag, was buying you the doll I promised. She has black hair like yours, although her face is not nearly as fair. You must give her a name and tell me how I am to address her, for ladies deem it a high insult for a gentleman to address them by the wrong appellation.

Tell your brother Tom that the entrance examination for the military academy was simple, amounting to little more than proof of an ability to read and do basic mathematics. The examiner was startled at my ability to read French, and I am thankful that he did not realize how poorly the Virginia accent serves that grand language. The physical exam was even less arduous, consisting of little more than proof of all four limbs. I confess I was tempted to attach an artificial limb, just to see how valuable *five* sound limbs would be to the military academy for bearing arms.

I will miss you, dear Mag, for it will be two years before I am granted a "furlough" of two months to go home. I have asked your doll, name unknown, what she thinks of a military man, and from the shine in her painted eyes, she must approve. I only hope her owner will approve as well.

My mother will have my full address soon and give it to you and Tom. Until then, I am your obedient friend,

Ashton Johnson

P.S. Cousin Lizzie Giles sends best love and wonders why you don't answer her letter.

The sudden wail of the tea kettle jolted Margaret out of the chair, and she looked around self-consciously, as if someone had been there to witness her surprise. Smoothing her hair with a deliberate hand, she walked slowly into the kitchen and fumbled with a bag of herbal tea, unwilling to admit how glad she was to get away from the letters.

There was something about these letters that she found disturbing. Perhaps it was the tone, so warmly casual, as easy as an old friend ruffling her hair. Margaret didn't have any old friends. She deliberately let friendships slide after the accident, unable to face familiar faces, the worried looks of well-meaning neighbors carrying casseroles and banana bread.

She picked up the tea kettle, careful to use one of the pot holders that looked like a fourth-grade craft project. Her mind was on the letters, and she tilted the kettle too far, splashing scalding water on the hand holding the chipped teacup.

"Mag!"

Margaret jumped, the kettle clattered into the sink.

"Who's there?" she shouted, her own voice high-pitched and unnatural, the sound of someone who had not spoken for a couple of hours. A man. It had been a man's voice, deep and rich and urgent.

But there was no answer, no noise other than the soft whisperings of a branch against the kitchen window. Her heart was slamming against her ribs, and she saw her reflection in the window, stupid and frightened. The sight made her laugh, and she stared at herself, giggling and smiling as if sharing a joke.

"I didn't want tea anyway," she said defiantly to the reflection. She ran her burned hand under cool water for a few moments, then wiped up the spilled water with a paper towel.

Part of her wanted to pack the letters away and give them to Brad. But it was only six-thirty at night, and she had read just two entries. After fighting hard for the right to index these, it would be ridiculous to give them up so easily. With confidence she didn't feel, she grabbed a pen and notebook, and began to index. West Point. Entrance examination. St. Louis. The Oaks. Lizzie Giles. A friend named Tom.

And Tom's sister Mag.

Margaret left blank dashes next to their names, for she had to do a little research to find out what their last names had been. She looked over the letter again, and wondered, fleetingly, if he had been using his gold pen.

"Yes."

It was the same voice, but soft and close, right next to her ear. A strand of hair ruffled. Her arms were suddenly covered with goose bumps in spite of the sultry evening breeze.

She sat very still and stared at the letters, their faded ink betraying nothing.

"Why are you doing this to me?" she pleaded quietly, her eyes still focused on the open volume before her. But there was no answer, no response.

Straightening her back, the very picture of strident efficiency, Margaret lifted the book. A piece of cardboard fluttered out of the leaves, twirling to the floor before she could capture it. She stared at the card before picking it up, for there was writing on the back. It was in Ashton Johnson's handwriting, a few brief words scrawled in haste.

Mr. W.T. Sherman of St. Louis, class of '40, who wrote me a letter of recommendation for West Point.

A.P.J.

Margaret flipped the card over and gasped. It was a photograph of a young man with searing eyes, a face that would, in maturity, grace the pages of newspapers and history books both North and South. Her hand clasped over her mouth.

"Oh, my God," she said out loud, stunned by what she saw.

It was Union General William T. Sherman, still in civilian clothes, the man who devastated the South, staring benignly into the camera. It was Sherman who recommended Ashton Powell Johnson to West Point.

And it was Sherman's own sharpshooters who killed General Ashton Johnson.

Margaret stood before the freshman survey class, wondering how they could look so fresh at the ungodly hour of 8:00 in the morning. She hadn't been able to continue working on the index after the photograph of Sherman came tumbling out of the volume, too disturbed by the knowledge that General Johnson had been educated at West Point and had been killed through the efforts of the same man, the very same individual that Margaret had studied and revered.

The young students gazed at Margaret with expectant eagerness, and she smiled at their willingness to learn. From what she had seen of Magnolia, that eagerness would soon be replaced by an overwhelming desire to party.

"The first work of literature we will be studying is called *Beowulf,* and it was written . . ."

Margaret frowned, noticing the class exchanging wary looks.

"Is there something wrong?" she asked, trying to hide the irritation in her voice.

One brave hand shot up, a young man with a clip-on tie. She nodded and he began.

"Well, you see, Dr. Garnett." He glanced at the other students as if looking for support, "most of us have already read *Beowulf.*"

"You're kidding?" she said, and by their nodding she knew he was right. The semester outline seemed like a joke now, and she grinned at the class. "Okay, I'll make you guys a deal. I want each of you to write me a paper on *Beowulf,* on its importance to literature, on the story, anything. Just let me know you've read it. If I'm satisfied you have a grasp of *Beowulf,* I'll let you off the hook, and we'll study something fun. Deal?"

There was unanimous applause, and Margaret adjusted her academic gown, surprised by the enthusiasm of the class. They seemed so, well, intelligent, she mused. Let's see how they can write. She dismissed the class and ordered the papers in at the next session on Wednesday.

They were chatting excitedly as they filtered out of the room, and Margaret had a brief twinge of regret. She hated the thought of actually grading their papers. It would be a shame to break their spirit.

That night, with no class to teach the next morning, Margaret returned to the letters. After a sunny day and no teaching blunders, she felt refreshed. And instead of a lonely dinner in the cottage, she had gone to the student pub for pizza and beer with Emily. They shared a delightful meal, with Emily giving her a complete rundown of the available males on campus.

Surely the weird feelings she had experienced the night before, the detached voices and creepiness, had been due to simple exhaustion. After all, she was in a strange place, with strange people, away from the security of the Northeast for the first time in her life. It was only natural that her mind would become distracted. She was facing reality for the first time in twelve years.

"Okay, Garnett. Let's get to work," she said aloud, slipping off her sandals. The floors at Rebel's Retreat were smoothed to a silky gleam from years of footsteps and careful polishing, and it was a delight to feel the wood under her feet.

The letters were still on the dining room table, the photograph of General Sherman marking her place in the volume. She was jittery, as if she'd polished off a half dozen cups of coffee, yet she knew caffeine was not to blame. Absurd though it was, she was nervous about the letters, frightened at the prospect of getting to know General Ashton P. Johnson, C.S.A.

Roughly pulling up a chair, she sat down, clipping her hair back. This time she didn't wash her hands. These were simply old letters, nothing more, she angrily tried to convince herself. They were of little historical value and would probably reveal no startling insights into the Civil War.

The third letter. Pen poised on notebook, she began to read.

> Camp Cummings, near Mobile
> March 13th, 1862

Dear Mag,

I just received your letter of the 2nd inst., and decided to use you as an excuse to delay ploughing through the regimental paperwork. Should Mobile fall to the enemy, the Confederacy will point to the lovely Mag, who distracted this general from the dull duty of war.

Your visit is still the talk of my men, who found your presence more beguiling than three weeks' leave. My young aide-de-camp, Sam Walker— formerly a student of mine at Magnolia—seems especially smitten and walked into a water trough last evening. He confessed that he was staring at the lace handkerchief you left at headquarters, handling the cloth with the reverence of a sacred relic. I removed it from his person, simply to avoid further danger, fearing he would march into the Gulf if he became more distracted. It is now firmly planted in my own pocket, and I am determined to return it to you in person. Your fragrance still clings to the delicate cloth, my dear Mag, a soft scent of flowers and springtime.

We have several dozen new recruits, fresh-faced

boys who should be in school, not training for battle. They were on review for the first time, each very aware of the young Mobile ladies watching them from under bonnets and parasols. Unfortunately, they were so intent in impressing their rapt audience, the fledgling soldiers failed to take note of an early hornet's nest on the field and marched directly into the angry swarm. The ladies were hardly reassured as to the future of their country when they saw the bold men in gray drop arms and flee for no apparent reason.

"General," asked a young woman from behind fluttering lashes. "Is that sound the rebel yell?"

I maintained a composed expression until I reached headquarters, followed by Colonel Morris and Captain Delancy, where we were at last able to give way to laughter. It was good to see Colonel Morris smile, as he has worn a sour expression ever since some anonymous but steady-nerved individual shaved his horse. It's difficult to appear commanding on top of a maneless mount with a naked tail.

Write soon, my dear Mag. If you only knew how much your letters mean to me, how I cherish each one, you would put pen to paper twice a day.

Your affectionate,
A.P.J.

Odd, thought Margaret. This did not seem to be the letter of a general, there were no hints of coming battle, none of the bravado seen in other military missives, especially given the flowery language of the nineteenth century.

Instead, this letter seemed to be from a man more interested in people than in campaigns. She jotted down items to index. Camp Cummings. Sam Walker. New Recruits. Colonel Morris. Captain Delancy.

And again, Mag.

Curious, Margaret flipped slowly through the remaining pages in the volume, each page smelling of age and stale air. And each letter was written to the same person. Mag. There were no envelopes to give her last name. Chet mentioned that they had been pilfered long ago by some stamp enthusiast eager for the valuable Confederate stamps.

Margaret carried the book over to the living room and curled up on one of the old couches. She left her pen and notebook in the other room, for she was no longer in a mood to index. She simply wanted to read, to lose herself in the letters of Ashton Johnson.

> Near Williamsburg
> Yorktown Road
> May 7th, 1862

Dear Mag,

I am told you were recently ill, and have been quite concerned. On many occasions I have myself witnessed the disorder that overtakes you, and am convinced that if you could somehow remain calm, the attacks would be less severe. How I wish I could be there to help you, my dear one. But I do not write to scold or advise you, only to tell you how you dominate my thoughts. Any wishes and prayers on this quarter concern your own well-being.

There was a battle here two days ago, and we rode close to the College of William and Mary. That beautiful place was well nigh deserted, and I could not help but stare at the very walls where Jefferson received his knowledge, wondering how different my life might be now if I had been educated there rather than at the academy. Little did I realize what an important decision that was, Mag. I realize now the academy was my first choice mainly because of the smart cut of the cadet uniforms.

General Jubal Early reluctantly spoke to me, mostly on matters concerning battle and procuring provisions. As you know, he has little use for the cavalry, feeling we are but small improvement over cutthroats and thieves. He is a surprising character, stoop-shouldered with the voice of an irritated schoolmarm.

"General Johnson," he said in his reedy tone. "A rascal tells me you are courting Miss Mag of Seven Pines." I admitted that I was indeed the fortunate fellow, and he looked at me with undeniable annoyance. I could not take my eyes from his hat, which was a wide-brimmed crushed felt thing with the most ridiculous plume I have ever before seen. He spoke well of you, having met you some years earlier, and asked if you are as beautiful as you were as a young girl. I admitted that you more than fulfilled your early promise of beauty, and he sighed.

My aide-de-camp then appeared with my horse, curried to a high gloss, and he expressed admiration for my mount.

"What is this fine animal's name, sir?" he asked.

I mumbled the name, hoping he would not ask me to repeat the unfortunate appellation. You know, Mag, how I have tried to change the beast's name to something more suitable to a warrior's horse, but he stubbornly refuses the change.

"What did you say, General?" he repeated cordially.

"His name," I confessed, "is Waffles."

And then young Sam Walker, ever helpful, added, "But he also answers to Daisy."

The general's mouth dropped opened, as if convinced this must be but a poor jest at his expense. But when I said "Waffles," my gallant horse nodded and whinnied, as if unwilling to be left out of the conversation. Then General Early began to laugh, a hardy, infectious chuckle, and we have been on friendly terms ever since. When I saw his action on the field before he was wounded, I was mightily impressed.

My dear Mag, this letter must end, as it is time for us to leave this place. Please write to me soon.

Love as always,
Ash

The other letters had a similar tone, very little battle information, personal accounts of men and places, but no talk of the war itself.

As she read on, she became used to his easy words, lulled by his calm humor, savoring every word. Margaret began to forget that these were the letters of the enemy, a Confederate general who had been dead for over a century. They seemed to speak directly to her, to Margaret.

By six the next morning she had read two of the three volumes. Her fingertips were darkened with flaking dust from the paper, but she didn't care. She had discovered the most wonderful of men, and the hours flashed by with astonishing speed.

She saw a man of unfailing good humor, who found himself in a position of military power he had tried to avoid. The letters to Mag touched briefly on his childhood, and she gathered that Mag was five or six years younger than Ashton. His family's plantation, The Oaks, was in Petersburg, Virginia, although he spent much time with his cousins in St. Louis, where his mother's sister lived. Margaret became familiar with the names of Ashton's cousins, old names such as

Giles and Peyton and Branch came to life with fresh vigor.

He had been against war, arguing that the election of Lincoln was not cause for secession but for compromise. He left his position as an English professor at the newly founded Magnolia to plead for Virginia to remain in the Union; and he left eight weeks later a reluctant colonel in the Confederacy and was soon promoted.

From what Margaret could garner, his dear Mag wasn't much of a letter writer, but was something of a first-rate flirt and a tease as well as a hypochondriac. Letter after letter asks for her to write, with humorous but increasingly sarcastic references to other men. There must have been an understanding between the two, for he mentions keeping a promise about glancing at the moon at a specific time each night, knowing she is doing the same and thinking of him.

But by 1863 the letters became slightly angry, as if even-tempered Ashton could keep his cool under enemy fire, but not under Mag's silence. The last letter Margaret read was different in tone from the others.

> Richmond
> April 28th, 1863

Mag,

Under the circumstances it is appropriate for me to return the enclosed. They are the letters you have written to me these past years, and for once I am pleased by how paltry they are in number, as it will save me considerable postage.

Good luck to you, Mag. And remember, should you ever require friendship, if you are in need of a hand, I will come directly to your side. My pride lies in shreds, but never my love for you.

> Ash

Margaret blinked at the brief note, only vaguely aware of the early morning sun streaming through the window. What had happened? What had Mag done or said to cause such a response?

Rubbing her eyes, Margaret thought of the importance of the date and place of the last letter. That was about the time that Jefferson Davis called his leading military men, including Robert E. Lee, to the Confederate capital to discuss Lincoln's new commanding general, Ulysses Grant. So, Margaret mused, Ashton must have played a vital enough role to have been called to Richmond.

With no class to teach until the next day, Margaret was free to read the final volume of letters, but she was unable to concentrate. An uncomfortable mixture of feelings, from rage at the foolish Mag to anguish for Ashton, filled her thoughts. In a daze, she stumbled over to the dining room table, her legs wobbly from being tucked under her for so long. What she was about to do was ridiculous, but she was compelled to follow through on her instincts. She would never be able to get through the day unless she completed this one task.

Grabbing her notebook and pen, she returned to the sofa, still warm from where she had sat all night. She flipped to a clean page, free of indentations from writing on the previous page. Not allowing herself time to think it through, she began writing.

Magnolia University
August 28th

Dear Ash,

It seems impossible to me that I am writing you from so far away. I've read your letters, the wonder-

55

ful, warm letters to "Mag." Forgive me, but she was not worthy of your affection to have thrown it away so carelessly. She was a dimwit.

Perhaps I write from loneliness, for I am lonely, or through some mad corner of my mind. But I feel I know you, and I want to reach out to you from my place, from my safe and distant refuge.

I am frightened, Ashton. I am away from home, I have no familiar face to turn toward. For the first time in years I miss my family so much it hurts. Not a single person here knows what happened, and I can't bear to tell them. The thought of their pity keeps me silent.

How I wish we could talk. But that, of course, is impossible. Here at your home, Rebel's Retreat, I feel your presence. It's everywhere, in the furniture, seeped into the walls, and throughout the very floors upon which you paced. I treasure the absurd notion that perhaps, if life were fair, if there were a compassionate being in heaven, we could communicate.

Strange as it may seem to you, there is a comfort in knowing that, at one time, you did exist.

Love,
Margaret

Feeling very foolish, Margaret reread the letter. Yet she did not throw it in the trash can in the kitchen or crumple it into a ball. Instead, she placed it inside of the final volume of letters, the ones she would read tonight. And without a backward glance, Margaret indulged in a luxurious stretch and lumbered to the bathroom for a refreshing shower.

She had a delicious inkling that it was going to be a glorious day.

* * *

Twelve hours later, trudging up the front lawn of Rebel's Retreat in the pouring rain, limping on a broken sandal, her glorious day had turned into one prolonged disaster.

After her brisk morning shower she walked to campus to check her mailbox, where she found a large envelope. It was a wedding invitation from Andy McGuire, her last serious boyfriend. Although she hadn't seen Andy in over two years, she still thought about him on occasion, wondering how he was faring in Alaska, where he had been sent to do research on Arctic wildlife. There had always been a comforting feeling in the knowledge that if she ever really, really wanted him back, she could hop on a plane and head straight to Anchorage. He had declared undying, if uninspired, love to her. If worse came to worse, she needn't be alone.

But old faithful Andy had somehow gotten himself engaged. She checked the date of the wedding and realized he was already married—the invitation was for the middle of July. Whoever sent Margaret the engraved invitation was clearly trying to let her know that Andy was no longer available.

Then Margaret ran into Brad Skinner, who told her, in clipped tones and no uncertain terms, that the Johnson letters would eventually be published with the name Brad Skinner as editor. She was an interloper, with no right to even handle the letters; and as soon as Chet realized the truth, the work and the tenured position would go straight to Brad.

Something Margaret ate at the faculty dining hall didn't agree with her, and she began to feel ill just as she was informed by Emily that there was a required ceremony to officially open the university. Margaret was forced to sit motionless while the dean and the chancellor made welcoming statements to the new students, returning students, and faculty members.

That's when the rain began, a downpour unlike any Margaret had ever experienced. Then she learned the rest of her luggage had arrived and was waiting for her on the muddy, wet lawn of Rebel's Retreat.

The heel snapping off her sandal wouldn't have been a problem, except that the only other shoes she brought with her were sneakers and a spiffy pair of Payless vinyl pumps. They were a dark shade of purple, which was fine, since they matched the chiffon bridesmaid's dress she had been forced to wear at her classmate's wedding.

The rain had caused the luggage on the front lawn to dissolve, which wasn't surprising considering that the luggage was composed of flimsy cardboard boxes from a Manhattan liquor store. The entire time she had been at the opening ceremony, there had been five large cartons on her lawn stamped clearly with brand names such as "George Dickle" and "Captain Morgan's Rum." No wonder she had been on the receiving end of some curious stares on her way back to the cottage.

She was able to drag the boxes inside, cursing softly as the corners pulled off in her hands. By the time they were all safely, if soggily, inside, she didn't care. Yanking some of the clothing out, she hung the dampest items in the kitchen and bathroom, the rest she draped on the banister. The interior of Rebel's Retreat could now pass for a Hong Kong junk.

Margaret folded herself into a soft terry cloth robe, hanging her dripping clothes alongside the rest of her newly arrived wardrobe, and went downstairs to make herself a cup of hot tea. Her mind traveled unwillingly to Brad Skinner and his ambition to get his greedy little hands on Ashton's letters.

"They're mine," she whispered, surprised by the intensity in her voice. She was not ready to give them up. Not yet.

The hot tea bathed her face in moist steam, and she held the mug still while she closed her eyes to the mist. She walked into the dining room, remembering the silly letter she had written that morning, akin to a grown woman sending a wish list to Santa Claus. Margaret, who was known for her clear-headed, unimaginative pragmatism, had written what amounted to a love letter to a long-dead Confederate. Smiling, Margaret picked up the third volume of letters, where she had placed her note, and turned to the first page. There was nothing but the old letters in Ashton Johnson's now familiar hand.

"I must have put it in one of the other books," she murmured, slightly rattled. She clearly remembered putting the letter in the last volume. She was sure of it.

The letter was not in the other volumes, the ones she had read through last night. The canvas tote bag held nothing but the library books, and it wasn't stuck between the pages, or back in the lined notepad where she had plucked the paper to write the letter. On her hands and knees, she searched the ground floor of Rebel's Retreat, throwing open drawers, rustling through old magazines and bookshelves.

It was gone.

Margaret choked back a gnawing desire to cry. The thought of Brad Skinner finding the letter flashed through her mind, a triumphant Brad, the campus version of Eddie Haskell, holding the letter in front of Chet, proclaiming Margaret's mental instability to the entire English department.

Too stunned to think clearly, Margaret slumped into a chair in the dining room. In front of her was the third volume of letters, and she opened the cover slowly, hoping to see her own white sheet written in ballpoint pen. Instead it was a letter from Ashton.

It was another letter to Mag.

Momentarily forgetting her own search, Margaret

was overwhelmed by curiosity. It was like an addictive soap opera plot. What could have caused him to write to Mag after his last and, she presumed, final letter to Mag?

The Oaks, Petersburg
September 12, 1863

Dear Mag,

What in the blazes are you doing at Magnolia? There is neither student nor faculty remaining; all have been called to arms. I just received your letter and immediately sent a note to my housekeeper there, Mrs. Thaw. She is instructed to open the house and to make my home as comfortable as possible for you.

To say your letter was a surprise is to undervalue its impact. There is much for me to tell you.

I am presently at home recovering from a wound I received during the July battle at Gettysburg. On the second day I received a note from your brother Tom, and it is enclosed here for you to keep. He was with my old friend Lawrence Chamberlain—you remember me speaking of him—he was my equivalent at Bowdoin College in Brunswick, Maine. Our parallel lives continue. He is now a colonel with the Union Army, the 20th Maine, and has proved to be one of their most gallant leaders. I cannot think of firing upon the likes of Tom and Lawrence, as I will lose all heart.

Your brother survived Little Round Top, Mag, but that is all I know.

Your words confuse me. What do you ask? You wish to see me, yet when last we met you offered nothing but scorn and anger. You discarded me. You beg friendship, but you laughed when last I offered my love.

I remain unchanged, Mag. Unlike you, my tenderness cannot be altered. If you are true in what you say, I can only rejoice at the change in you.

I know how difficult it is for you to speak of your family and what happened so many years ago. But I firmly maintain that if you speak of the events, you will eventually be free of the anguish that has crippled you for so long. Tell me about it. Write me of your emotions and confusion. I am here for you. Always.

Soon I return to my men, so address me thusly— any letter will be immediately forwarded.

Also let me know how I am to address you. You signed your letter *Margaret,* a name you profess to have disliked from the beginning. Does the new name mean a new Mag?

I am, as always, your obedient,

Ash

P.S. The name you gave my cottage, Rebel's Retreat, is ideal, although I trust you mean "retreat" as in "refuge," not in reference to the late events at Gettysburg.

Margaret stared at the letter, afraid to move. Was it possible? Did this morning's impulsive note find its way through the years to Ashton?

Her hands trembled as she retied her bathrobe. This was crazy, nothing more than a strange, one in a million coincidence. She felt dizzy, light-headed, and more than a little spooked.

"I'm going nuts," she stated, but her voice was clear and unwavering. She reread the letter, slowly this time, with careful attention to details that might betray the truth. But upon the second reading, the tone seemed even clearer, more definite. Ashton was speaking to her.

61

She scanned the page but could not find the note from Mag's Union brother Tom. What had it said? Whatever the message had been, it was now lost.

Opening her spiral notebook, Margaret turned to a clean page and grasped her pen. This would prove it, she thought. This letter would be impossible to answer.

Magnolia University
Rebel's Retreat

Dear Ash,

I was alarmed to hear you were wounded at Gettysburg, but trust you have by now recovered. Could you tell me what happened? What the battle was like?

I hope you can forgive me for my behavior. But you are right—the events of my past have haunted me for so long, I no longer feel like the same person. There are mornings I awake and expect to see my mother and father, to hear the laughter of my brother and sister downstairs. Then I remember what happened and long to return to my dreams, where everyone I love is alive and well. Have I gone mad?

Magnolia is a quiet comfort now, except for the treacherous Brad Skinner. His one goal in life is to make my life miserable, and he is quite good at it.

How tall are you? What is your favorite dinner? Please excuse my questions, but I would appreciate an answer.

I still wish I could see you and speak to you. Perhaps one day we'll meet.

Until the next letter . . .

Love,
Margaret

P.S. You may call me whatever you wish (as I'm sure you already have), but I do prefer Margaret now. I believe she's a kinder person than Mag.

With calm deliberation, Margaret placed the letter in the third volume on the second page. Before class the next morning she would check the volume and see what the letter said. She knew not to check until the morning for one simple reason.

The letter from Ashton wasn't ready yet.

CHAPTER
5

Her eyes were playing tricks on her.

That was the only explanation she could come up with, the only reason for the odd sights dancing before her eyes. For the next morning, after sleeping through her alarm and bumping into a quilt rack in the bedroom, she could have sworn she saw a blue-and-white pitcher and bowl on the dresser. Margaret blinked, and it was gone—there was absolutely nothing on the dresser other than her plastic hairbrush and a tube of lip balm.

When she bent down to retrieve a pair of sneakers from under the bed, there was a brief flash of white on the wall. But when she stood up, the wall was covered with the same yellow flowered wallpaper she had always seen, tiny blossoms with small green stems. For a moment, when she was on all fours, it looked as if the wall had been whitewashed.

The whole time she stumbled through the motions of getting dressed, her mind was on the volume downstairs, wondering what she would find. By the time she was brushing her teeth, she had convinced herself that all the strange events were the product of an exhausted, overactive imagination. The letter she read yesterday, the one that seemed to speak directly to her, was simply a coincidence.

Margaret even managed to smile at herself, wondering how such a pragmatic individual could lose touch with reality. Luckily no harm had been done; she didn't tell anyone she had heard voices or become pen pals with a dead man. She had managed to go temporarily insane in the comfort and privacy of her own rented cottage.

"I'm simply overwrought," she said as she plucked some of her now dry clothes from the shower curtain rod and placed them in the bottom drawer of the dresser. Before she shut the drawer, she saw the blue-and-white pitcher again, fleetingly, just within her peripheral line of vision. This time she even saw a small chip along the edge of the bowl. And again, it was gone before she straightened—vanished, and replaced by the hairbrush and lip balm.

"I am simply overwrought," she repeated emphatically, squaring her shoulders and trying to think of the class she would be teaching in another half hour.

"I will now have a cup of coffee," she mumbled, walking down the stairs to the kitchen, anticipating the weak state of the instant coffee she bought the day before. She made a calculated effort to turn her back on the dining room while she filled the kettle with water, placed it on the burner, and slowly pulled down a mug and the small jar of instant coffee. Behind her were the letters.

There was an odd sense of anticipation pulsing through her, like a child waiting for permission to open Christmas gifts. Had anything happened during the night?

With a suddenness that caught her by surprise, Margaret spun around and walked toward the letters. She had to know. Although she had tried to convince herself that she had simply imagined everything, there was an overwhelming compulsion to find out for herself. Now.

She placed her hand on the volume, then opened it. Her letter was gone.

A whooshing sound swirled around her, a pounding in her ears as she read the second entry from Ashton Johnson.

> Near Fredricksburg
> October 5th, 1863
> Monday evening

My dear Margaret,

Your last letter has rendered me speechless; and for that favor, my aide-de-camp, Sam Walker, wishes to thank you. I have addressed you as "Margaret" for you are no longer Mag to me. There is a warmth to you now, either I was blind ere this, or you have changed.

You have asked my details of battle, specifics of how I was wounded. Yet you have told me, in person and pen, on countless occasions, how vile and abhorrent you find such matters. So I will tell Margaret. And if Mag interlopes, she may give way to her distaste and ban my further company, for I no longer speak to Mag but to Margaret.

Words fail me at describing in a coherent fashion the events of July. I recall those three days as a series of detached scenes, as in a nightmare, of screams and wails, the buzzing of minié balls, the stench of death and acrid, choking clouds of dirt and gunpowder and sulphur and heat. My voice, hoarse and unfamiliar to my own ears, rang out commands, but was inaudible in the chaotic hell. I don't know when I was wounded, for I continued upon my horse, riding the lines, trying to show our men a confidence in our position that I had not felt since the first day of battle.

I remember issuing a command to push forward, and the world began to tilt for me, and at once I could not distinguish sky from earth. I am told I slid off my mount, and I do recall a raspy voice in my ear, crazed and desperate.

"The South will whip! The South will whip!"

Another voice called "The general's been hit!" and I tried to ask, which general? Lee? Pickett? Longstreet? But no sound issued from my throat.

A surgeon was called—and this I was told, for I do not remember—and it was ascertained a ball had passed through my right leg, about five inches below the back of my knee. By sheer luck, and the thick leather of my boots, the ball missed both bone and artery, but bled profusely nonetheless. The surgeon wanted to amputate my leg—this I do remember—but I managed to talk him out of it and said a tightly bound bandage would serve me better. He was slightly disappointed, but I knew the wound wasn't serious. Even after a considerable loss of blood, I also knew I outranked him.

Do you remember, Margaret, I once told you I could survive anything, save a direct hit in the head? I still believe that is true.

My height, by the way, is still six feet and three inches, unless the perpetual ducking of bullets has decreased my size. It is still safe to call me "Too Tall Johnson" and "Sequoia." And my favorite meal remains Aunt Hattie's chicken and dumplings, although I now survive on hardtack and cornbread. I keep on trying to throw the hardtack away, but the vermin within causes it to crawl on back, so I am obliged to eat it.

I know not how you will react to this letter. I have been frank and honest, perhaps for the first time. But I feel lighter in spirit than I have for years, sharing with you, even on paper, some of these events.

Do you know what I was thinking this morning, before your letter arrived? About your parents. I don't know if you ever understood how very proud they were of you, how your father's eyes would shine at the mention of your name, how your mother would straighten her shoulders and tell the neighbors of your latest award in literature. In a hundred ways they told the world how their youngest child, their little Maggie, was their bright star. And wherever they are, dear Margaret, you still are.

Yours always,
Ash

P.S. Please tell me how you are faring at "Rebel's Retreat." Has Mrs. Thaw made the place comfortable for you? Although I still have no earthly clue as to what you are doing there, it no longer bothers me. For I have given up trying to read the changeable mind of Margaret.

How long the kettle had been whistling, Margaret didn't know or care. And she wasn't aware she'd been crying until the second time she read the letter, when a word, penned in ink over a hundred years earlier, became blurry with her freshly shed tears.

There was a small sentence on top of the page, and she stared at it for a few moments before the impact of what it said hit her full force. It was clearly jotted down as an afterthought, for there was no room on the bottom of the page.

"Who on earth is Brad Skinner?" it asked, in the bold, precise hand of General Ashton Johnson, C.S.A.

At least she'd had the presence of mind to call in sick, three minutes before she was due to teach her second class. Chester Dick had been able to substitute Brad Skinner, who was only too glad to help out.

She sat motionless for over an hour before her teeth began chattering, and she numbly wrapped an old throw rug around her shoulders. She knew it was hot out by the smell of sun-warmed grass and the vibrating hiss of crickets, but she was unable to stop shivering.

There was a sharp knock on the door a little before noon, and Margaret, still in a daze, still wrapped in a blanket, shuffled to the door. It was Brad Skinner, with her class essays on *Beowulf.*

"Hey, you look like hell!" was his greeting.

Margaret could only nod.

"You know," said Brad, "the freshman survey class is supposed to read *Beowulf*—it's on the schedule. You have to teach by the book, Margaret. Are you listening to me?"

Again she nodded dumbly as a fresh bout of shivers overtook her.

"You weren't faking it, eh? You're really sick." He reached over to feel her forehead, and she ducked. An uncertain look passed over his face, swiftly dissolving back into the bland mask he usually wore, but Margaret—even in her trancelike state—saw it. Anger? Defiance?

"How are the letters coming?" His voice oozed sarcasm. "How far have you gotten?"

Margaret's eyes snapped to his. "I'm on the final volume. I've read the first two and have begun indexing already."

"Fine. Good work." He began to walk past her, striding through the front parlor. "Where are they? Chet told me to give you a hand. Why don't I just take the last volume . . ."

"No!" she screeched, startled by the venom in her voice. "You can't have it," she said more calmly. "What I mean is, I've already started on the third volume."

Brad stared at her for a few moments, and he spotted the first two volumes. "Have it your way," he said softly. "But I may as well tell you Chet has finally given me permission to work on these. Since you were too sick to teach, you're clearly too sick to work on the letters." He picked up the first two books and began to walk toward the front door.

"I'll be back later, Margaret, after I speak to Chet. We'll both come back for the rest of these. They belong with me, not you." The door slammed behind him.

She managed to walk back to the dining room before her knees began to weaken, and she slid into a chair. The third volume, open to Ashton's last letter, lay before her. She reached for her notepad and pen, and began to write.

Magnolia University
Rebel's Retreat

Dear Ash,

Please excuse the shakiness of my writing—I must be coming down with the flu.

I received your letter this morning, and I cannot tell you what it means to me. My first thought was that I must get to you somehow, to help you recover

70

from your injury, but I now realize you have already been mended without my help.

I have read of battles, seen statistics, understood the meaning of a casualty list. But your description, so vivid yet without self-pity, makes me feel as if I was there. I'm not thinking very clearly now, forgive me. I want to shield you from the nightmare of war, but how can I?

By the way, your housekeeper, Mrs. Thaw, is a treasure. I hardly know she's here.

Margaret stopped for a moment and looked over what she had written. It was gibberish, and she knew she should take an aspirin and lie down for a few hours, but she needed to write to Ashton. They might take the letters away from her.

Something flashed by the corner of her eye, but she ignored it and began writing again. She had to finish this letter. She coughed, slightly surprised—did she have a cough before?

"What you said about my parents," she continued. "Were they really proud? Have you seen them where you are? Sometimes I wonder if I could have done something, but really . . ."

Her head was pounding, and it was becoming difficult to breathe.

"I shouldn't say this in a letter," she wrote, her handwriting almost illegible. "I think I may have fallen in love with you. When I first saw you, the painting in Johnson Hall, I so longed to communicate with you. And then these letters . . ."

Margaret dropped the pen and began to cough, a bone-racking cough that shook her entire body. Did she fall asleep? Someone was speaking to her, and she recognized Brad Skinner's voice, and he was speaking to someone. Chet. They were carrying her upstairs.

"No!" she shouted. "He's trying to take Ashton away from me! Stop!"

Nobody seemed to be listening to her, and they were hazy, shifting in and out of focus like a crazy student film. There were hands and voices and hands, sounds like a train rushing past.

Then there was one voice, a familiar, soothing voice in a strange, soft accent. She was aware of large, sure hands on her forehead, and someone held her up when she began to cough, speaking the whole time.

"I'm here, Mag. Hold on to me, come back. You can't leave me now . . ."

The words flowed like a warm caress, and she felt herself relax against a heavily muscled shoulder. This isn't Brad, she thought briefly. This person's much bigger, and he smells of horses and leather. She leaned into him and sighed, and whoever he was, she heard him laugh, a wonderful, rich sound.

Then she fell asleep, the deepest, most satisfying slumber she had ever experienced. She slept straight through the night, and only the sunlight in the window alerted her that it was once again morning.

Cold. She was freezing, but only her face was cold. There was something heavy across her chest and shoulders.

The sunlight. It was coming from the wrong angle— as if it were winter instead of late summer. She reached a hand from under the warm blankets and touched her index finger to her nose. It was cold.

Her eyes began to focus, and she saw the blue-and-white pitcher and bowl, and the walls were a startling shade of pure white. She squeezed her eyes shut and opened them, expecting to see the yellow wallpaper and her plastic hairbrush.

The walls were still white. The blue-and-white bowl had a small chip.

And it wasn't a blanket keeping her so warm. She

looked more closely. It was a jacket, a worn gray coat with yellow stars at the collar and brass buttons. The buttons were embossed with three large letters. C.S.A.

Her mind whirled, and then it came to her— impossibly and undeniably. Confederate States of America.

She tried to sit up but wasn't able to gather the strength. Her leg, encased in blankets, pushed against something large and warm, and she gasped.

Peering down at the foot of the bed, she saw the figure of a man. He was in a chair, but he was slumped over the bed, his head cradled in his arms and his face turned away from Margaret. All she could see were broad shoulders under a white shirt and thick auburn hair, streaked light at the ends by the sun. She knew, without a doubt, who he was.

"Ashton," she whispered.

And slowly, he turned to face her.

CHAPTER
6

The oil painting in Johnson Hall failed to do the man justice.

Margaret's hands clenched the gray wool jacket as he rubbed his eyes, and she saw a momentary flash of disorientation on his features as he faced her. Then he smiled, a small, hesitant smile.

This Ashton was too thin, with prominent cheekbones that gave his face a harsher appearance than in the formal painting on the campus. His clothing was hanging loosely on his large frame, and she could see the angular collarbone jutting from behind the white cotton shirt.

No artist, no matter how gifted, could have captured the barely restrained energy that was apparent with his every move, or the brilliant color of his eyes, brown with green and gold flecks. There was an incandescent intelligence in the eyes, and she watched with fascination as they swept over her, taking in every detail.

From under the golden brown mustache, neatly trimmed, his mouth still held an uncertain smile. He glanced at a glass of water by her bed, and Margaret noticed how long his hair was, well past the snowy collar. The hair was reddish brown and curled slightly at the ends, defiant as his gaze.

"Would you like some water?" The voice was the familiar, gentle tone she had heard before, with a strange accent softening the hard vowels with honeyed warmth. The "r" in "water" rolled away smoothly, like silk gliding over velvet.

She nodded, afraid to take her own eyes from the apparition in case he should vanish. His arm reached over her, and up close she could smell his spicy masculine scent. He stopped before picking up the glass and placed his large, calloused hand over her forehead.

"Your fever's down," he murmured. Again the "r" melted into oblivion as he spoke. Before removing his hand, he brushed her cheek with his knuckles, with more tenderness than Margaret would have thought possible from a man of his size.

Without thinking, she grasped his hand, surprised by the strength and warmth she felt as the hand instinctively folded over hers.

"Ashton," she said, her voice sounding strangely low to her own ears. He reached for the glass of water with his free hand and offered her a sip. Her eyes were glued to his as she drank, holding tightly on to his hand.

"Ugh!" she pulled back as soon as she tasted the water. It had a flavor of dirt and metallic grit, as if someone had sifted sand into the glass. She ran her tongue along the inside of her teeth and gasped. Something was wrong.

"I've lost a tooth!" she exclaimed, but it didn't sound like her regular voice. The words that spilled from her mouth were spoken in a lower register. But that didn't bother her as much as a missing tooth. She could feel a gaping hole in her mouth, one of her bottom molars was gone. It didn't hurt, but it was alarming nonetheless.

"Which tooth?" he asked, and suddenly Margaret smiled at this bizarre scene, discussing her dental health with a ghost.

"In the back—a molar." Her words were garbled, as she was exploring the site with her tongue as she spoke.

"Margaret, you had that tooth pulled when you were sixteen. Don't you remember?" His searing eyes seemed to envelop her, and she frowned and shook her head. "I took you to the dentist in Richmond, and you were quite a handful. He gave you nitrous oxide, and you were telling everyone on the streets that you were a cloud. Remember? I was accused of getting you intoxicated . . ."

"No. I really don't remember. Have I ever been to Richmond?" His hand tightened over hers, and he looked away.

"Ashton, how did you get here?" Her voice was soft.

"I received a telegram from Mrs. Thaw that you were ill. General Lee gave me a seven-day pass." His thumb stroked her wrist as he spoke, but he seemed unaware of it. "Lee is more terrified of the wrath of Mrs. Thaw than most anything." Again his mouth quirked into a small grin. "Including 'those people.'"

"Who are 'those people'?"

"The Yankees." Ashton leaned back in his chair and pulled his hand away from hers, folding his arms across his chest. His presence seemed to fill the room, as if his very being consumed space. He took a deep breath, his eyes burning through her with molten intensity.

"Margaret," he said at last. "I believe you're ill."

"Ashton. I believe you're dead," she replied as gently as possible, her hands once again clutching the phantom jacket in her lap.

Whatever reaction she had anticipated, it wasn't explosive laughter. His head tilted back, his shoulders shook with mirth, and he laughed—a deep, rich, glorious sound.

"Ah, Mag," he said at last, wiping a tear from under an eye. "I never know what to expect from you . . ."

"No, Ashton. I'm afraid it's true. You're a ghost. I'm sorry to have to break this to you, but it's 1993, and you've been dead for well over a hundred years . . ."

Suddenly, with startling force, he jumped to his feet. The chair skidded on the wooden floor, and he stood to his full height, enormous and powerful. With a distracted hand, he pushed the thick hair out of his face and walked to a window. As he walked, she noticed a slight limp, the firm sound of his boots on the floor.

"I thought you had changed," he said softly, but there was an unmistakable edge of menace to his voice. "But you haven't. You still delight in your childish games. You were simply teasing me with those last two letters, weren't you? Watching how many hoops I'd jump through for you."

"No! No, please," but she couldn't seem to catch her breath, and there was a pressure on her chest such as she had never felt, as if a vise were tightening around her, preventing her from taking in air. She tried to sit up, and the effort made her dizzy, the jacket slid to the floor—brass buttons clattering against the wood.

Ashton turned on his heels with lightning speed, the anger on his face dissolving to alarm. He was back at the bed in two long strides, his large hands pulling her roughly by her upper arms. She felt her hands flay helplessly against his shirt, as if that would somehow help her take in air.

The only sounds she could hear were the painful pounding of her own heart and a dry, wheezing sound. Part of her mind was whirling in startled curiosity. Had she somehow developed asthma? Ashton was speaking to her, and she tried to listen, but she was still fighting to breathe.

"Margaret, listen to me. Relax and breathe—hold on to me. I'm here. I'm not angry at you anymore. Listen!"

He sounded very far away, as if he were speaking from the end of a long, hollow tunnel. She felt her hands go limp, and she tried to touch him again. Her arms dropped heavily into her lap. His words seemed to have more urgency now, and she heard her thumping heart slow down, slower and slower and . . .

"NO!" She was frightened by the voice, a harsh, loud command. Margaret was aware that her head lolled back, and she tried to straighten up, but she simply didn't have the strength.

"Margaret! You will not leave me! God damn it . . ."

Suddenly, as if she were watching a movie, she had an aerial view of the room. There was Ashton, looking large and impossibly handsome, holding the most beautiful woman Margaret had ever seen. The woman's hair was long and dark and scattered all over a lace pillow, but she was very still and pale. In Ashton's arms she appeared tiny. But even her unnatural pallor and blue-tinged lips could not betray features of almost eerie perfection. Her eyebrows arched delicately over half-closed eyes, and her nose was small and fine, but more aristocratic than cute. Even the shape of her face was a flawless oval, tiny ears revealed under the lush raven mane.

She was wearing a loose camisole, but Margaret could see full, rounded breasts under the fabric. And crumpled beside the woman's bed was a gray jacket with yellow trim.

Margaret felt an unfamiliar passion surge through her, a wild-eyed hatred such as she had never imagined. She was jealous.

"NO!" Ashton roared to the woman, in a voice teeming with shattering anguish.

Margaret was now aware of another person in the room, a thin, pinch-faced woman in a faded calico dress and a severe, graying chignon.

"General." The woman's voice was brittle. "General Johnson. She's gone."

And then Margaret witnessed something truly extraordinary. Ashton pulled the beautiful woman into a sitting position and, taking a deep lungful of air, he breathed over the beautiful woman's mouth. He did this again and again until the woman in the calico dress began yelling to stop, she's already dead, it's indecent.

But Ashton ignored her, and Margaret marveled that a ghost could perform mouth-to-mouth resuscitation on a scantily clad, undeniably beautiful woman.

In the blink of an eye the scene was gone, replaced by whooshing darkness. Margaret felt the tops of her arms being clamped with bruising force by a pair of powerful hands. And she also felt the light, but not unpleasant, tickle of a mustache on her lips.

The sun was still streaming into the window when she awoke, filtered through lace curtains, giving the room a surrealistic quality. She immediately knew she wasn't alone, and her eyes searched the room for her ghost. And he was still there.

Gingerly, she raised herself, propped up on her elbows. Ashton was asleep, his face soft and gentle in slumber. Under his eyes were dark circles, as if he hadn't slept for days.

Margaret's chest hurt, every breath was painful, and her upper arms were mottled with blue and purpling thumbprints. Still watching Ashton, she drew her hand slowly over her chest—and gasped.

His eyes flew open, and in an instant he was at her side. "Margaret, how are you?" His voice was filled with an aching tenderness.

She tried to speak, her hand still rubbing her chest. Beneath her hand she felt the soft beating of her heart, and large, perfectly shaped breasts. Margaret had always been flat-chested. Her mind worked furiously as she moved her hands in a circular motion over the breasts. And she could feel ribs—something Margaret had not been able to feel on herself for years. Breasts and ribs. Had she undergone breast implant surgery and managed to forget all about it?

"Ashton," she whispered, her low voice filled with awe. "I have large breasts."

He was suddenly overcome with a suspicious fit of coughing, his head turned away, and she could have sworn she saw him laugh behind his rolled fist. Within a few moments he had composed himself, but his eyes were still bright with humor.

"Excuse me," he managed to sputter, standing up abruptly. "I'll get you something to eat."

Again, she was startled by his height and breadth, shoulders wide in spite of his leanness. He opened the bedroom door, and with a brief wink at her, he called down the stairs.

"Mrs. Thaw." His voice was clear and buoyant. "May we please have some of that broth? Miss Mag is sitting up."

He came back into the room, and Margaret was

aware of his limp as he pulled a chair right next to the head of the bed.

"How's your leg?" she asked, embarrassed that she had forgotten that he was wounded at Gettysburg. He sat down hard in the chair and shot her a dazzling grin, white teeth and deep dimples at the side of his mouth.

"Why Mag, you *do* care!" She had the distinct impression he was not completely serious. Are phantoms sarcastic?

"Of course I care," she harrumphed, with more anger than she had intended. "But you're so busy giving mouth-to-mouth to beautiful women, you probably didn't notice . . ."

There was a clatter of silverware as Mrs. Thaw, the woman in the calico dress, appeared. Her eyes never left Margaret, and she scooted into the room with her back to the wall. In her hands was a large covered tray, and she plopped it onto the floor, still staring unblinkingly at Margaret, and pushed it toward Ashton with her foot. Margaret noticed she wore small boots that laced up the front.

"What's wrong?" Margaret asked Ashton as she left the room, her hurried footsteps clattering on the steps. "Hasn't she ever seen a ghost before?"

Ashton's startled eyes snapped to hers, and he began to laugh. "You know, that's exactly what she thinks you are!"

Margaret giggled, clamping her hand over her mouth. "I didn't mean me. I meant you!"

They both began laughing as he reached for the tray, each unsure of exactly what was so humorous, but both relishing the shared moment. On the tray was a single bowl, a steaming, brown-colored broth. Ashton moved closer, stirring the soup, then offered her a spoonful.

"Aren't you having any?" Margaret asked, and for a moment Ashton seemed surprised.

"Oh, no. I'm not hungry. I, eh, ate while you were asleep." He didn't look at her eyes and seemed suddenly very interested in the spoon. "Here we go . . ."

With an astonishing delicacy, and before she could move away, he pushed a spoonful of broth into her mouth. It tasted awful, pungent and gamey and slightly tainted.

"What is this?" She nudged his arm with her hand. He looked at her, genuinely perplexed.

"Why, Mag. It's your favorite—mutton soup."

"Lamb? Little cuddly lamb?"

Ashton's face remained impassive as he dipped the spoon back into the bowl. "Margaret, believe me, this was never a cuddly lamb. In fact," his eyes flashed to hers, and the green flecks seemed to sparkle, "I have it on good authority that this animal was the most hated beast in the Confederacy." She began to protest, but he silenced her with another spoonful of broth. "This, my dear, was the infamous Murdering Mutton of Magnolia."

"The wh—" but her voice was cut off by more broth. The soup did not taste so strange now, and her attention was on his story.

"It's true," he said solemnly "This very animal took cruel delight in tormenting the other lambs in the pasture." He kept spooning broth into her mouth as he spoke. "It all began in 1859, when a pack of frightened sheep was seen fleeing from a large, galumphing creature."

"Galumphing?"

"Galumphing," he repeated with a nod. "He would nip their little legs, and block their way to the pond. Some even say he poisoned the water . . ."

And by the time he had finished with the ridiculous

story, she had eaten the entire bowl of broth. She couldn't help but grin at him.

"You know, you're very good at diversionary tactics." But all of a sudden she was exhausted, and her eyes began to flutter shut. "Please don't leave me," she whispered as she fell asleep.

"I won't, Mag. Ever." His voice was heavy, and he stared down at her perfect, slumbering form.

A gray head peered through the doorway.

"Did she eat the broth, General?"

He nodded. "Every drop, Mrs. Thaw. How much laudanum did you put in it?"

"Oh, about three drops, just as the doctor said." Mrs. Thaw couldn't drag her eyes away from the general, the way he tenderly brushed the raven hair from Margaret's face.

"Very good, Mrs. Thaw," he said in dismissal, without turning to face her. "That's enough to stop a galumphing sheep."

"Sir?"

"Never mind, Mrs. Thaw. Never you mind."

In her sleep she resembled an angel, an ethereal being placed on earth to soothe a man's soul. Ashton leaned back in the chair, wondering how such perfect beauty could coexist with such treachery.

A soft sigh escaped her parted lips, and he bent over her, placing the back of his hand on her forehead. She was cool to the touch, the fever was gone. Just as he was about to remove his hand, she grasped it in her own, a grip of surprising strength. Her other hand moved slowly over their clasped hands, as if to ensure his presence, and she settled the entwined hands on her breast.

Ashton looked behind him, aware of what a damned awkward position she had him in. Mrs. Thaw would positively seethe if she witnessed this, but Mrs.

Thaw was terrified of Mag now, the woman returned from the grave. Ash pulled the chair closer to the bed, making as little noise as possible without disturbing Mag.

Mag. Could he remember a time when she hadn't been a thorn in his side? He could see her now as she was as a child, petulant, always tagging behind Tom and him, managing to keep up with their every move. She was lovely even then, but his mother had never been able to warm to Mag.

"Too much beauty hardens the heart," his mother said once, watching Mag and Eddie, Ashton's younger brother, play blindman's buff. Ashton said nothing but was always careful to avoid discussing Mag in front of his mother.

When Mag's parents died, his mother softened a little toward Mag, but she still made it clear she preferred Tom, sunny, easygoing Tom.

It was during the years Ashton was at West Point that Mag blossomed into a stunning woman with all the wiles of a panther. Ashton fell in line behind other cadets and young officers, but Mag remained an enigma, a quick-witted, well-read tease. He had asked her to marry him so many times he lost count. She never said yes, but she never said no either, always leaving open the possibility, tantalizing his dreams.

He had been with other women, lovely creatures, a few who genuinely seemed to love him. They would have made good wives, ideal mothers. And just when he made up his mind to marry Annabelle or Rebecca, he would receive a letter from Mag, a few funny, short lines, and again he would lose his heart. She always managed to coax a smile, to make him laugh. But deep down he knew she didn't love him. Perhaps she was incapable of love.

Finally she was out of his system. After a series of

scathing letters and a miserable visit last spring, she told him to leave her alone. She hated him, she vowed. Her brother Tom was a Union colonel, and Ashton would no doubt kill him. Mag was convinced of Ashton's desire to personally shoot Tom. It was an irrational, almost insane, notion, but she refused to listen to reason.

Then, out of the blue, he received the warm, pleading letter. At first he doubted his eyes, for the handwriting was different from Mag's. But there was no doubt—it was his Mag, now calling herself Margaret, worming her way back into his heart. In truth, she had never left.

Had she truly changed? He didn't know for sure. There were a few moments when he saw something new in her eyes, a tenderness he had never seen before. She asked about his leg. The old Mag never asked about anyone, never thought beyond her own, perfectly shaped nose.

He leaned down and rubbed his aching leg—it was painful to be in one position for so long. As he bent over her, he caught her scent, a heady fragrance of blossoms and sweetness. In time he might live to regret coming to her side, breathing life back into her, watching her as she slept. But in truth, he thought with a wry curve to his mouth, this was the only place he wished to be.

Margaret was aware of the large hand she held, and smiled at the warmth and comfort it seemed to offer. She was dreaming, a wonderful fantasy with a dashing Confederate general and a ravishing brunette; and the best part was that Margaret, tall, ungainly Margaret, was the lovely brunette.

Filtering into the dream were bits of unwelcome information. She had a class to teach. Brad Skinner was taking the letters away. Her clothes were becoming moldy in wet boxes. She struggled to the surface of awareness, but still she held the large hand. She could even feel the calluses where he had held a horse's reins, the hardened palm where he had wielded a sword in battle. She smiled, and a puff of warm breath was on her forehead, followed by the soft bristles of . . .

His mustache.

Her eyes flew open, and there he was. Her ghost.

"Hello." His voice seemed to rumble from deep within his chest.

"Hi," she replied, still holding his hand. Odd. It was so very warm, so alive. Her thumb moved over his wrist, and she felt a distinct pulse. "How are you feeling?" she asked.

His face registered surprise, then he laughed, and she again noticed how very white his teeth were. "I'm feeling well, and thank you for inquiring," he said at last, his eyes betraying vast amusement. His rolling accent made the words purr with smooth sensuality.

For a moment she was transfixed, their eyes locked in unspoken silent communication. His lazy smile faded, and he moved his free hand toward her face.

"I have to go," she announced suddenly, shattering the aura between them. She sat up, and his hand slipped to the small of her back, where it seemed to encompass her entire waist.

"Where?" His voice was husky, and he cleared his throat. "Where do you have to go?"

"Oh, hell . . ." she whispered.

"You're going to hell?" He had regained his composure, eyebrows arched in surprise.

"No." She swung her legs over the side of the bed, letting his hand drop. "I have a class to teach. *Beowulf.* Will you be here when I return, or do you have to go to the light at the end of the tunnel, or whatever?"

"Margaret, what in the blazes are you talking about?"

"I'm going to get fired if I don't teach the freshman survey class, Ashton. That's the way things are here on earth. I have student loans to repay, an overdue credit card bill, all sorts of mundane worries. Will I see you again?" There was a sudden note of regret in her voice, unmistakable and heavy.

"Margaret, listen to me." His voice was low but commanding, and it demanded her complete attention. She stopped, her head cocked slightly, marveling at how solid he appeared. He continued. "You have been very ill. Indeed, you came within a hairsbreadth of dying, but you are going to get better . . ."

"Oh, Ashton. You still don't realize that you're dead, do you?"

"I'll admit, if anyone can complete the task, Margaret, you're the one. But no, for the time being we're both very much alive."

Margaret sighed, then had an idea. "Ash, is there a mirror around here?"

He nodded once and, then shaking his head in bewilderment, stood up and reached for something on the dresser, next to the blue-and-white pitcher. Margaret saw a flash of light on the ceiling as he handed her a magnificent silver mirror.

"Hey, this is beautiful," she murmured, running a finger over the ornate design on the back of the mirror. "Okay, Ashton. Take a look." She held the mirror to his face, and he leaned closer.

He frowned and rubbed his chin. "You're right, Mag. I need a shave."

"You can see your reflection? Impossible!" She flipped the mirror over, and all color drained from her face.

It was the beautiful woman, mimicking Margaret's every expression.

87

"Margaret?"

There was a buzzing sound, and she felt her chest constrict, that tightening vise again. This couldn't be!

With a shaking hand, she reached for a thatch of dark hair, the lustrous curl reflected in the mirror. And she felt it in her hands, smooth and heavy, attached to her own head.

She was the beautiful brunette.

The wheezing noise was back, and her eyes darted around the room. The walls were white. There was an opened door where the bathroom should be, and she could see clothes hanging in it.

Was *she* the ghost?

"Margaret! Look at me!" The mirror slid from her hand and shattered on the ground, and she looked at his eyes, intense and compelling. His voice became softer but no less urgent. "Margaret, you have to calm down, relax. When you become frightened or panicked, the illness overtakes you. Hold on to me, Margaret. I'm here."

Her arms reached up for his neck, and at once she was folded into his embrace, pulled against his powerful chest. Her head rested on his shoulder, and she could feel the muscles work as he rubbed her back with soothing, hypnotic circles, around and around, until she was unconsciously following his own slow breathing pattern.

"That's a good girl," he murmured into her ear. And she gave a weak laugh.

"I'm not a horse," she said softly, and she felt him swallow hard and pull her even closer.

Margaret became aware of the hair tumbling down her back and onto her bare shoulders, and saw arms that were slender and very white wrapped around Ashton's broad shoulders. With the world suddenly gone crazy around her, she held on to his solid form, feeling very safe and cherished as long as he clasped her.

They were both unwilling to end the embrace. His head slowly lowered, and she felt his warm lips pressing kisses against her ear, her neck, at the base of her throat. She pulled away to face him, and a fleeting darkness shaded his eyes. Reaching up to his face, the hard, chiseled features she had so admired in a lifeless painting, her fingers combed the hair away from his temple. But her eyes became fixed on his mouth, generous and expressive under the mustache. And with exquisite tenderness, she tilted her face to meet his mouth.

Margaret had been kissed before, many times, but nothing could compare to his searing touch, a completeness she had never in her wildest dreams imagined. It was the most perfect of moments, and she could feel his breath quicken and . . .

"General!"

Margaret jumped back, but Ashton held her firm, his arms like iron bands. There was a softness in his expression, and he, too, seemed startled by more than just the housekeeper's voice.

"Mrs. Thaw," he said in reply without turning to face her. "I'll be with you directly, Mrs. Thaw." His voice was strained, and Margaret saw Mrs. Thaw shake her head with strident disapproval and stalk out of the room.

"Margaret." He took a deep breath. "Will you marry?"

"Yes," she said softly, still in a daze. "Yes."

A broad grin spread across his face, and his sun-bronzed cheeks flushed with delight. He leaned down to kiss her once more, but she halted him abruptly with her hand.

"Ash!"

He stopped, his countenance suddenly unreadable. "What's the date?" she asked.

His eyes narrowed as he stared over her shoulder, and again she was astonished by how magnificent he was, a face of hard and even planes, but such expressive eyes and mouth.

"Let me see," he muttered. "Today is Thursday, October twenty-second, 1863."

"Oh," she swallowed, swaying slightly in his embrace.

"Is anything wrong?"

She closed her eyes for a few moments, then brightened and gazed straight into his face. "Ash! Your birthday is in three weeks!"

"Margaret," he said softly. "I have to return to my command. Do you want to marry me now, or on my next—"

"Now," she cut off his words, an involuntary shudder coursing through her body. This birthday would be his last. For she knew that sometime next summer, General Ashton Powell Johnson, C.S.A., would be killed by one of General William T. Sherman's crack sharpshooters.

Unless, of course, his wife could prevent it.

CHAPTER
7

Night came swiftly, and with it flickering candles and the strange noises of darkness. Never had Margaret experienced such complete blackness. There were no car headlights, no wavering house lights in the distance, no streetlamps or blinking airplanes in the sky. There was nothing.

"What time is it?" she whispered to Ashton, who was reading a book in the dim light cast by two candles.

"The downstairs clock struck ten a few minutes ago." His voice was warm in the chill of the room. She was wrapped in two blankets, he wore his gray jacket —at her insistence. The cold did not seem to bother him in the least, yet Margaret was frozen to the bone.

"It's a bit nippy in here," she said, moving her finger between her teeth to keep them from chattering. Ashton closed his book softly and smiled, his face illuminated by the candle's warm orangish glow. He stood up, placing the book on the chair, and lifted a candle, cupping his hand in front of the flame to prevent it from blowing out as he walked.

In a few muscular strides he was beside her, sitting on the bed, resting the fluttering candlestick on the small table beside her. Wordlessly, he took her in his powerful embrace, wrapping the wool jacket around her, placing her arms between his coat and his chest.

There she found warmth, the heat radiating from his body vanquished all of her chills. She snuggled closer, her hands roaming over his back, her head tucked in the crook of his neck.

And for the first time she could remember, Margaret felt completely safe.

"I apologize, Margaret." His eyes shot to the empty, cold fireplace. "We're woefully short on firewood here. The trees and branches outside are too damp to burn. Tomorrow I'll chop up a few of those chairs you hate so much . . ."

"Do they have webbed feet?"

"Those are the ones."

"Don't you dare touch them! They're fantastic, Ash. It's not worth it to burn them just for a few moments warmth. No way."

He shook his head. "You are a changeling, Mag."

Her hands moved up his back, and between his shoulder blades, just to the left of his spine, she felt a scar, a ridge that seemed to extend the width of his back.

"What happened?" she asked softly, her voice wavering.

He didn't answer for a few moments, and then she felt his voice against her ear, his breath caressing her cheek.

"That was a gift from a Union saber at Chancellorsville."

"Ouch," she murmured, stroking the scar gently.

There was the soft rumble of his laugh. "I believe I said something along those lines at the time," he chuckled.

At once she pulled back and stared into his eyes, potent even in the faint glow. "Were you there when Stonewall Jackson was killed?"

His gaze raked over her, and he gave a single, swift nod before pulling her against him once again. Suddenly Margaret felt a hard, bitter lump rise in her throat, and she closed her eyes against the tears that were stinging like a thousand needles.

She had always been so cocksure of who was "right" and "wrong" in this war. In her studies she had gloried in the triumphs of the Union, admiring the determination of the South, but she knew who was going to win the war—it was a fact she had known since she was a child.

And here was a man, sheltering her from the cold, who was on the other side, who had witnessed their brightest hope—General Jackson—fall in friendly fire, by the musketry of their own Confederate sharpshooters. The man who held her close had been wounded, had faced defeat, and would see his cause stumble before he himself would fall.

Her arms began to shake with silent sobs, and she buried her face in his chest. He stroked her hair gently and tilted her face toward his own.

"Mag?" He was stunned by the tears flowing so freely from her face, dampening his shirt, leaving her long black lashes luminous in their wake.

He had never seen her cry.

"How?" Her voice was a shattered whimper, and she swallowed and began again. "How can you possibly go on?"

He glanced away uncertainly, resting his lean cheek

against the top of her head. "How can I not?" he said simply.

Margaret took a deep breath, trying to compose herself, to get her fragmented emotions under control. And she closed her eyes as Ashton inhaled her scent, his large hand moving along her neck, the roughened thumb settling on the base of her throat. He felt her sharp intake of breath, the quickening of her pulse.

Just as he lowered his head to claim her mouth in a kiss, the deep silence of the night was broken by the sound of thundering, galloping hoofbeats.

An excited voice pierced the dark. "General Johnson!"

Ashton smiled sadly at Margaret, detaching her arms from under his jacket. A chill licked her bare arms as she felt the cold air once again.

"I'm sorry, my love." His voice was thick with regret.

He stood up and walked to the window, the slight limp more pronounced, buttoning his jacket.

"Scouts," he said softly. Then he turned to her, and even in the indistinct light of the room, she was awed by the sight of the man before her.

He was, quite simply, the very ideal of a Confederate officer, of any officer. He was broad and defiant, commanding even in silence. The beautifully cut uniform, although slightly loose on his lanky body, was nothing short of splendid. He emanated power. She had an absurd desire to salute.

"I'll be back." And then he was gone.

Although she knew exactly where he was and could hear his booted footsteps on the staircase, then on the porch, she felt an aching sense of loss. The room, without Ashton, seemed very big and cold.

Still wrapped in the blanket, she stepped out of bed, halting against the momentary dizzy spell. She then continued to the window, where she saw Ash in deep discussion with four other men in ragtag uniforms. He clapped one of the men on the shoulder, and although the face was indistinct in the moonlight, she could tell by the man's posture that he had just been commended.

A bit of extraneous information flashed into her mind, and she recalled an account of General Johnson by one of his men. The quote came to her complete, word for word, as was often the case when she did consuming research. A piece of information would reveal itself, something she had read and somehow memorized. This had been in a green book at Columbia's library, published in the early nineteen hundreds, called *Recollections of a War Long Gone.*

"He was always quick with a word of praise, and tempered criticism with a smile or a soft joke. On the field there was none more gallant, and his example brought out the best in those around him. He was much beloved by his men."

An unfamiliar feeling swept through her, intense and poignant. And Margaret, the Yankee scholar, realized she was proud, to the point of exploding, of her Confederate general.

The scouts brought information that had Mrs. Thaw up and packing by dawn the next morning: The Yankees were coming.

The Federals were still at a distance of some fifty miles, but they planned to pass through Magnolia within the next few days.

Ashton had slept in the other room, and Margaret awoke a dozen times, disoriented, wondering where she was. The coarse linen sheets and the frosty air around her were a sharp reminder. She was in 1863 Tennessee, engaged to a Confederate general, and inhabiting the body of the most beautiful woman since—or until—a young Elizabeth Taylor would hit the scene.

All in all, she mused, it beat the hell out of teaching *Beowulf.*

There was a soft knock on her door just as a hazy new sun gleamed off the dark furniture.

"Come in," her new voice purred, and Margaret wondered if she could sing.

Ashton grinned when he saw her, wrapping a large arm around her shoulder as he kissed her forehead.

"Good morning, love," he said.

"Morning," she returned, aware that she was probably smiling like a besotted idiot.

"Do you feel well enough to travel? We could probably wait a day, but I do believe it would be best to clear out as soon as possible. And I need to telegraph General Lee about the troop movements."

"I feel wonderful," she sighed, and meant it. Whoever had been sick, Margaret or Mag, was apparently completely well.

Ashton began to leave the room. "I fear you won't be able to take much, Mag." He gestured to the massive closet packed with clothes. "There is a chance the Yankees will loot this place, so choose what you want with care. We'll bury anything of value in the backyard under the big elm tree. I would burn the house down, but there's no need to announce our location."

"They won't find it," she said with certainty. "They'll destroy the campus but leave 'Rebel's Retreat.'"

"Who can tell?" he shrugged, looking around the room. Margaret knew by his expression exactly what he was thinking—this was the last time he'd be there in the home he had built. His eyes snapped to hers, and his features softened. "Do you need help getting dressed? I'll send up Mrs. Thaw if you wish."

"I'll be fine. I think I can handle a few buttons."

Half an hour later, Margaret wondered if she had spoken too soon. It was one thing to read about the layers of undergarments and petticoats and another to actually try to wear them. There were drawers filled with springy hoops and stays, corsets that looked like medical devices, lace chemises, a paper box filled with gloves, short and long, kid and cotton.

Margaret finally selected a dress, a plain wool gown of indigo blue with two dozen jet buttons down the front. Or the back, Margaret wasn't quite sure. She pulled out a pair of black leather half boots, some cotton stockings that had seen better days, but looked warm, a lace chemise and a tie-at-the waist pair of drawers that had a slit in the crotch. The hoops and crinolines were hopeless, some completely round, others flat in the front.

At last she was dressed, but there were a few serious problems. From the way the gown fit, it was supposed to button down the back, but that would be impossible without someone else to do the buttoning, so she reversed it. Now, however, her breasts were flattened, the buttons pulled taut to the point of erupting. And there was a definite billowing in the back, where breasts should be. So Margaret improvised, wrapping a fringed, paisley shawl around her shoulders to cover the top. Fine, she thought.

The length of the gown was another problem, about four inches too long to walk on even flat surfaces without hiking up the hem. She supposed she needed to wear a hoop, but it was like a massive Slinky, ready to twist and flip on its own. She decided to simply hold up the skirt.

Brushing her hair was fun, long, luxurious black

tresses unlike any Margaret had ever seen, much less grown on her own head. She could find no hairpins—a relief, since she wouldn't know what to do with them if she could locate them—but she knew that she couldn't leave the hair loose. In a drawer she found what she assumed was a blue velvet snood. At least, she prayed it was a snood and not some form of exotic underwear.

Since she had broken the mirror the day before, she was forced to tuck her hair into the net blindly, feeling for stray curls and wisps, tightening the snood with the silk drawstring.

"There," she said with finality, glancing down at the small booted feet, the full skirt, the shawl barely concealing a generous bust and an impossibly tiny waist.

She made the bed and straightened up the room, folding the blankets neatly and fluffing the down pillows. Running a finger over the carved unicorns on the bed, she, like Ashton, wondered when she would next return, if at all.

The steps downstairs were troublesome to negotiate. Not only was the heavy skirt a hindrance, but everything seemed so large. The last time she had gone down these stairs, she had been over a foot taller and barefoot. The railing was higher, the thickness of the banister made her new hand seem all the more childlike. Slowly she descended the stairs, her eyes narrowing as she saw the mirror on the wall.

Instinctively she went to it—it was exactly where she had seen it last. But now it was much higher to her. Instead of seeing her full face and shoulders, Margaret could barely view the upper portion of her head.

The face she saw was, indeed, extraordinary. Her eyes were startling, a violet-blue she had once seen in an advertisement for tinted contact lenses. Yet these eyes were real, surrounded by lashes so thick and black, they would put any self-respecting drag queen to shame. She couldn't tell if the eyebrows had been plucked, but they were delicately arched over the eyes, set into a brow of smooth, pure alabaster.

The nose, too, was flawless, but completely natural, straight and fine. Tilting her head back, heavy with the thick hair, she could see the mouth, full and red and slightly parted to reveal white teeth, small and perfect.

Only Margaret knew Mag was missing a back tooth. Margaret and, of course, Ashton.

She stepped back, regarding the lovely face with detached admiration, the way one studies a painting or a piece of jewelry. This was who Ashton loved, not Margaret.

Her hand crept to her throat, the movement graceful, reflected in the mirror.

Suddenly she was aware of laughter in the kitchen, and she followed the sounds, trying to ignore the awful feeling of despair that threatened to overtake her. This is who he loved, she thought, glancing down again at the beautiful woman she had become, the female perfection she had borrowed.

"Hi." She smiled, stepping into the kitchen. Mrs. Thaw spun around and stared at Margaret, her eyes growing wide with disbelief.

"Miss Mag? You dressed yourself?" Mrs. Thaw's mouth hung open.

The four scouts were in the kitchen drinking coffee, although Margaret couldn't detect the scent. They sprang to their feet, young men all, nervous as colts.

"Ma'am," one mumbled.

"Howdy, hello, ma'am," another with a garish plaid vest under a gray-green jacket croaked. The other two stood in respectful silence.

"Good morning. I'm Margaret." She extended her hand to each of them, and they all grinned back,

reddening and shifting on their feet. She noticed they
all had hardened hands like Ashton.

"The general's out getting your horse ready, ma'am.
He'll be back presently."

Her horse. Damn, she thought. She was terrified of
horses, ever since a circus pony named Pretzels had
bitten her when she was twelve. He was a nasty,
mean-spirited animal; and she could never again face
a horse without experiencing an awful sense of doom,
which made her, of course, the perfect choice for a
cavalry general's wife.

With difficulty she managed to straighten her shoulders and turn to Mrs. Thaw. "May I help you?" she
asked.

Mrs. Thaw's hand shot to her chest, and she backed
away. "Why no, Miss Mag. I'll get you some coffee."

"Great! I could sure use a cup . . ." Her voice
trailed off as she saw the brownish-beige liquid Mrs.
Thaw poured from a pot. There was virtually no
fragrance to the brew, and Margaret sipped it slowly.

"This is the best peanut shell coffee I've ever had,
Mrs. Thaw," said one of the scouts. And Margaret
suddenly felt like a fool—of course there was no real
coffee. These people probably hadn't tasted genuine
coffee since the war began.

The back door opened with a brisk gust of wind and
dried leaves, and Ashton entered, dwarfing every
other figure in the room. His eyes settled on Margaret,
and he smiled and approached her, cupping her elbow
in his hand.

"Men, I don't believe you've met my intended
bride, Miss Margaret . . ."

The last name was cut off by whoops and congratu-
lations, and Margaret realized she hadn't the faintest
idea what her surname was supposed to be. But she
accepted the good wishes of the young scouts, and the
icy glare of Mrs. Thaw, who clearly felt Mag wasn't

good enough for General Johnson. And she was probably right.

The smell of burning bread suddenly filled the kitchen, and Margaret, who was the closest to the iron stove, grabbed the handle of a frying pan filled with cornbread.

She gasped and the pan clattered to the wooden floor. She had anticipated, lamely, a heat-resistant handle.

"Mag!" shouted Ashton, and a chill traced her spine. It was the exact voice she had heard before, in her other body, when she spilled the hot tea on her hand.

Her hand began to redden, and Ashton pulled it toward a red, long-handled pump that was where the sink would be in a hundred years. With casual but obvious strength, he began to pump water into the sink, bathing her blistering hand. Everyone else remained silent, staring at the sight of the general calmly attending to the minor burn of his fiancée.

"I'm fine, Ash," she said at last. "Embarrassed out of my wits, but fine."

The cool water eased the sting, and with a gentle pat with a soft towel, Ashton looked down into her face. "Are you sure?"

She nodded, still mortified, and bent down to pick up the darkened cornbread. Ashton immediately joined her, carefully placing the crumbled bread back into the pan.

Holding a small crumb between his thumb and fingers, Ashton paused and smiled at Margaret. Their foreheads were almost touching.

"Do you know what we call this in the army?" he asked, easing back on his haunches. He glanced to the scouts and Mrs. Thaw, all waiting expectantly to hear his words. "Ten days' rations," he said, and they all laughed.

Except for Margaret. Her eyes slowly rose to Ashton's, and he stopped laughing, stunned by what he saw there. Her violet eyes had never held anything more than annoyance or acceptance for him. Now there was something else, a gentleness and compassion that made her features even more exquisite.

Slowly, she reached up, oblivious to the others, and placed her small, white hand on his bronzed cheek. Her fingers stroked his temple, then with aching tenderness, touched the thick, sun-kissed hair, but her eyes remained fixed on his.

"I love you," she said so softly that only he could hear.

The smile faded from beneath his mustache, and she could hear his breath stop. His own hand drew to her face, and he brushed his knuckles against her cheek, and she closed her eyes in response.

One of the scouts cleared his throat, and Ashton, startled, returned to picking up the scorched cornbread. Margaret placed another chunk into the pan, and Ashton eased her to her feet. His thumb stroked her elbow, lingering there before he spoke.

Clearing his throat, he offered the pan to the men and Mrs. Thaw. "We'll leave immediately after breakfast." And they ate, without a single complaint, the burnt bread.

They had to. It was the only food left in the house.

Within an hour they were ready to leave. Ashton had grown silent as he made one last pass through his home, making sure there was nothing that could be of material value to the Yankees.

The air outside was crisp but warm in the sun. Her booted feet crunched on the leaves, and Margaret glanced at the house, amazed at how little change the next century would bring to Rebel's Retreat. The biggest changes she could see now were wrought by the season, not the years. The leaves were spectacular shades of brown and yellow and fiery red, the shrubs, mini versions of what she had known, caught the brilliant leaves, reminding Margaret of a child wearing her mother's jewelry.

Ashton walked beside her, carrying a large leather saddlebag, which contained most of their luggage. There was something strangely intimate about her clothes mingling with his. It was quite nice.

She looked up at him, and he smiled from beneath his hat, a gray felt hat with a wide brim and a Confederate flag insignia on the band. He had also quietly strapped on a tassled sword and a heavy pistol. From the way he handled them, she could tell he was an expert with the weapons. There was an informal yet respectful grace in his treatment of them, and she shuddered, aware of the injury and death they would bring.

"Men," Ashton called to three of his scouts, "Miss Mag here is one of the best horsewomen in Virginia. Watch her, and I dare say you'll learn something."

The scouts looked at Margaret with new respect, and her heart sank. One of the scouts then appeared with a horse, the biggest one she had ever seen. If Pretzels the circus pony was enough to frighten her, this gray speckled beast was the stuff of nightmares. The horse snorted, a powerful cloud of steam flying from its nostrils. Even the muscled scout seemed to have difficulty controlling the animal on its lead.

"Ah, here we go. She's looking good, Mag." Ashton took her arm and began to lead her to the horse. Surely this was a mistake. This animal couldn't be meant for her. But then she saw the sidesaddle. And, almost on its own, a curse escaped her lips.

"Mag?" Ashton looked truly shocked.

"I said, 'grit.' There was some grit on the ground.

See?" She held up her foot and tried to conceal her rampaging terror.

The horse seemed to sense the difference in Mag. She suddenly began scratching the dirt with her hoof, snorting and swinging her head. She wanted her real mistress, not an imposter.

"You're trembling," Ashton said as Margaret pulled the shawl more tightly around her shoulders.

"To tell you the truth, Ash," she began, her voice reaching a higher pitch as she spoke, "I'm having second thoughts about this man versus beast thing. I mean, how do we know they don't resent us for climbing on their backs? They might be more intelligent than we are, and one day they might turn on us and . . ."

With that, Ashton lifted her effortlessly onto the saddle. The horse took two steps forward, and Margaret gasped. Shaking uncontrollably, she pulled on the reins.

Ashton calmly reached up and patted the mare's flanks. "Atta girl, Pretzels," he murmured.

"What's her name?" Margaret shrieked. But her voice faltered as the horse began to trot forward. The movement caught Margaret unprepared, and she grabbed onto the pommel, the shawl slipping off her shoulders and onto the mare.

"Well, I'll be damned," one of the scouts muttered softly. "I do believe she is wearing her dress backwards."

The shawl draped over the animal's rear, fringed and bountiful, giving the overall impression of a horse wearing a skirt.

"Whoa." Margaret tried to keep her voice calm, but fear made it shake. Trying to get a balance, she pulled up on the reins. Pretzels, confused by the command, began a backwards prance, head held high. Margaret began to list to the right, which caused a thoroughly perplexed horse to perform a backwards trot in a large, perfectly executed circle.

"WHOA!" Margaret shouted, her voice vibrating with every step. She leaned to the front, and the horse launched into a bold gallop. Part of her was relieved— at least the horse was going forward now. If she could only stay on the horse.

Then she saw the fence.

Hanging on for dear life, Margaret yanked back sharply on the reins, and the horse halted several feet before it would have leapt over the weathered fence. In one awful moment, the mare calmly paused to survey the scene. Margaret swiveled in the saddle like a drunken top and, with ladylike grace, tumbled over the horse's head and into a pile of leaves.

Ashton stood in silent shock for a moment. He had never seen Mag even tilt in the saddle, much less fall.

Her slender back was toward him, her black hair loosened from the snood and falling riotously about her, covered with leaves. And her shoulders were moving convulsively, as if she were gasping for breath.

Ignoring the searing pain of his wounded leg, Ashton ran toward her, with each stride feeling his alarm rising. Even over the sound of his own ragged breathing, he could hear her telltale wheezing.

"Mag!" He was at her side, his powerful grip pulling her toward him, his hands entangled in her silky mane. With his palm he tilted her face to his, and his mouth dropped open.

She was laughing.

A single tear slid down her cheek as she faced him, her expression contorted in hysterics.

"I . . . hope . . . your . . . men learned something." She giggled, slumping against his broad shoulders as a new wave of laughter consumed her.

It took several moments for Ashton's mind to register what was happening, that the ever-haughty

Mag was actually laughing at herself. Then he, too, began to chuckle, plucking the twigs and leaves from her hair.

"They will replicate your maneuver on their next drill." He grinned as she began to hiccup. "Complete with skirted horses and rolling dismount."

Margaret, who had been unaware of the location of the shawl, craned her head around to see Pretzels and was again thrown into a fit of hysterics. The horse snorted indignantly and walked a few steps away.

Their laughter faded into brief spurts, and Ashton rose to his feet, bending down to help Margaret. She swept the leaf-covered snood into her hand, suddenly self-conscious as she flicked the debris from the velvet netting.

"What happened just now?" Ashton's voice was steady and serious.

"I fell off a horse." Her eyes flashed to his, but he wasn't smiling. "I don't know." She took a steadying breath and returned to the snood, intent on removing every particle of leaf and twig.

He remained silent, waiting for an explanation. His eyes didn't leave her face as he reached over and snapped the shawl off Pretzels' back, gently wrapping it around Margaret's shoulders. His hands remained on her, and he turned her toward him.

"Your dress is on backwards, Margaret, and you're not wearing your usual corset and half dozen petticoats. You've been kind to Mrs. Thaw and the scouts, then you fell off a horse as if you'd never ridden before. Something's very wrong."

Her smooth brow furrowed, and she finally looked at his face, taking in every detail as the breeze ruffled the ends of his hair. "Something has happened, Ashton. I just don't know what." She swallowed, and he watched the delicate column of her throat move as she continued. "The other day when you helped me. Do you remember?" He nodded, and she paused for a moment before speaking again. "Please don't think I'm insane, but I believe Mag died, and I—Margaret —took her place. I'm not the same person, Ash. I'm the one who wrote the last two letters, but I'm not the same woman you have always known."

Instead of disagreeing with her, his eyes focused just over her head, as if mulling over what she had said, weighing her words. "But just before it happened." His voice was a harsh whisper. "You were different then, too, when you woke up and saw me."

Margaret nodded, hoping he would believe her. "Yes. Then I seemed to have an asthma attack, and Mrs. Thaw came into the room and said I was dead, and you breathed life back into me, and she told you to stop . . ."

"You remember that?"

"Yes," she said softly. "Do you believe me?"

In the moments before he answered she heard the scouts talking to Mrs. Thaw, and the clip-clop of more horses being brought from the back of the house. An animal, perhaps a chipmunk or a rabbit, scurried through the bushes nearby.

"Margaret," he said at last, "I believe what happened the other day indeed changed you. It's happened before on battlefields. Wounded men recover and are never the same. That is what happened, love. You came as close to death as anyone I've seen ere you. As a result, you are a different person."

As if that settled the matter, he brushed a kiss on her forehead and began walking to the horses. "You'll ride with me on Waffles, and Pretzels can serve as our porter."

Margaret watched his broad back as he returned to the men, the hilt of his sword glinting in the morning light. She shrugged, tucking her hair back into the confines of the snood. His explanation would just have to do. For now.

They made their way carefully down the mountain, a rugged path so narrow they were forced to ride single file. The main road was far too dangerous, with enemy troops everywhere. It was peculiar for Margaret to view Union soldiers as the enemy. But for the moment, as long as she inhabited this body and time, her own nation's army was the enemy.

Margaret had been heartily impressed with Mrs. Thaw, who appeared wearing a heavy brown divided skirt and jaunty hat, and rode her horse astride, like the scouts. She had complimented her with such lavish sincerity, Mrs. Thaw actually smiled back.

The scouts, too, were remarkably good-natured, especially considering her humiliating display of riding. The one in the plaid vest, whose name, she discovered, was Ethan, shot her a sympathetic grin and flushed when she returned the smile.

She leaned against Ashton's chest and sighed, his arm instinctively tightening around her waist. The horse Waffles was a massive animal, a glossy chestnut stallion, and her legs were sprawled like a child's in the large saddle. She was held so closely that every jolt was cushioned by Ashton's body. He absorbed the shocks while she simply enjoyed the physical closeness, one of her hands resting on his powerful thigh, the other clutching the saddle.

They rode in the front, and she was aware of some danger to this position. But Ashton alone knew the path, and she watched in fascination as his eyes scanned the foliage and trees that bordered the twisty trail, noting every movement and detail in his piercing sight. She turned to face him a few times, and his eyes would flicker to hers and mellow, and his mustache would quirk over a fleeting smile before his gaze returned to the path.

A thought occurred to her after one of those warm smiles of his. No matter how focused his attention, how riveted his well-honed senses were to the task at hand, Margaret—by just being there—was a distraction. In all probability, Mag should have died a few days ago after that asthma attack. It was Margaret's interference that caused Mag's shell, the exquisite body, to continue living.

Margaret had been confident with the knowledge that she had until next summer to prevent Ashton's death, but maybe that was not the case. Perhaps Ash would become distracted and they would wander into an ambush. Perhaps by spilling the breakfast that morning, Margaret had delayed them, and the timing would be deadly for Ashton and Mrs. Thaw and the young scouts. Maybe, if there had been more food to share—without Margaret's extra mouth—the five men and Mrs. Thaw would be able to concentrate on their surroundings.

Without warning, Margaret felt the now familiar constricting in her chest. No, she thought angrily. She will not have an asthma attack. Ashton's hand moved above her waist, and he could feel her mounting struggle, but he said nothing, gave no indication that he noticed. There was something in the set of her shoulders that told him she wanted to be alone.

Her balled fist slid from his thigh to the pommel, so both of her hands were grasping the saddle. She closed her eyes, remembering a girl she knew in high school who had asthma. The girl was able to control it to some degree by using a form of meditation. Whenever she felt an attack, she would shift her mind to a soothing image, something restful and pleasant.

A beach. She thought of a long stretch of beach in the summer, of walking barefoot in the surf and feeling the foamy water lick her toes. And wet sand, the feeling of sinking when you stop in one place and allow the waves to roll over the tops of your feet.

Warm sun and cool water, the laughter of children racing with the surf. The lone piercing whistle of a lifeguard perched on a white chair, zinc oxide on his nose and reddened shoulders.

And suddenly, the clawing feeling in her throat was gone, her breathing steady and even. Her palms were damp, and she wiped them on her skirt before returning her one hand to Ashton's thigh, the other to the saddle, no longer in a white-knuckled clench.

Ashton said nothing, but Margaret felt him swallow hard as she settled back into his embrace. Just before she drifted off into an exhausted sleep, she also felt his heart drumming hard and fast against her back and wondered what he could have possibly seen in the woods to cause such a reaction.

She awoke with a start just over an hour later, Ashton's finger lightly touching her lips.

"Hush, love," he whispered into her ear.

They were stopped, and Ashton's other hand was up in the air, a silent command to the other riders to halt. The hooves behind them stilled instantly, and Margaret felt Ashton's arm shift, his hand slipping to the pistol while he still held her securely.

At once, from both sides of the path, came a clattering of riders, branches splintering in their haste. Before Margaret had time to blink, they were surrounded by six men on horseback, all brandishing pistols or rifles.

And they were all wearing dark blue uniforms.

"Well, well," said one of the Union men. From the way the other Federals glanced at the man speaking, Margaret knew he was in charge. "Johnny Reb and his fair ladies," he sneered, staring at Mrs. Thaw. Then his eyes came to rest on Margaret, and he licked his lips. Margaret's nails dug into Ashton's thigh.

"You have no quarrel with the ladies, Lieutenant," Ashton said, his voice cool and in smooth control.

"*I* have a quarrel with these men, General." It was Mrs. Thaw, her voice hard as flint. "They killed my husband and my boy. I have a quarrel."

There was a moment of studied silence as the opposing sides eyed each other, taking their measure.

"Gentlemen." The Union lieutenant tossed his head in the direction of the other soldiers. "We have ourselves a Reb general and Reb soldiers. They're surely scraping the barrel if they hide behind the petticoats of their women . . ."

The Union soldiers laughed, and Margaret closed her eyes and pressed herself into Ashton's chest. She whispered something to him, and his arm closed protectively around her. But his eyes never left the Union men.

The young lieutenant suddenly looked furious and leveled his pistol at Margaret.

"What did she say?" he demanded. "General, raise both of your hands away from your pistol and tell me what she said."

"Her words, Lieutenant, are of no importance to you," Ashton's tone was again full of authority, even though they were outnumbered and outgunned. He made no move to surrender.

The Union officer glared at Margaret and raised the pistol to Ashton's head.

"No!" shouted Margaret. "I'll tell you. I said 'I love you, Ashton Johnson.' That's all I said. . . ."

The lieutenant blanched and lowered his weapon, his mouth slack before he spoke. "You're General Johnson, sir?"

Ashton nodded once, his gaze full of rage.

"Sir." The lieutenant's posture and tone were meek

and apologetic. "Do you remember Norman Hale, sir? You taught him at Magnolia, sir. Rhetoric, I believe, and Greek translation."

"I remember him." Ashton's voice was tight. "I failed him for not reading *The Iliad.*"

"I know, sir. He's my brother."

"How is he, Lieutenant Hale? I believe he took the oath and signed up in New York. Does he fare well?" Ashton's tone was honest and compelling, as if chatting with an acquaintance at a tea party.

"Well, sir." The lieutenant dropped the pistol to his side, and Margaret held her breath as Ashton's hand crept again to his own pistol. "Old Norman came down with the camp diarrhea, then the mumps. They sent him home, sir. Back to Westchester."

Ashton actually smiled then, his white teeth flashing in the fading light of the afternoon sun. "Please give my regards to your brother, and tell him to read his Homer. When this cruel war is over, there's going to be a test."

The young lieutenant made a small bow and turned to his soldiers. "Men, forget who you saw here today. General Johnson's just about the most decent fellow on either side, and if we don't win, we'll surely need him to give us all a hand."

He motioned for the men to retreat, and they did, with perplexed shrugs and backward glances, as if forced to pass up a memorable meal. The young lieutenant approached Ashton and Margaret, trusting the enemy not to shoot him.

"Sir?" he said to Ashton. "I hear you were wounded in Gettysburg. I trust you are recovered."

"Almost, Lieutenant Hale. I thank you for your concern." Margaret swallowed as the lieutenant began to whisper.

"Sir, my men don't know this, but there's a price on

your head. Keep low, General, because any Union officer would sell his soul to get a potshot at you."

Ashton's expression remained bland. "Again, Lieutenant, I thank you."

The lieutenant then gave Margaret a small smile and nodded. "I apologize, ma'am," and then he was gone.

It wasn't until they began riding again that Margaret realized Ashton's hand was still gripping the fully cocked pistol. He would not have hesitated to blow the life from the chatty young lieutenant had the need arisen.

CHAPTER
8

The travelers paused for the night several miles north of Chattanooga. After running into the Yankee patrol, Ashton determined it was far safer to rest away from the town, which was still reeling from the Battle of Chickamauga the month before. There were a few homes Ashton could have taken them to, but he didn't want to endanger either the homeowners or themselves. Without any means to communicate, it was impossible to tell which homes the Yankees were using as quarters, which farms were occupied by the enemy.

For Margaret, the realization that there were no telephone lines was startling. Of course she was aware, once she understood where and when she was, that most of the modern conveniences she took for granted were not in existence. But not to be able to flip on a radio or television for news, or to simply pick up a phone and call, seemed absolutely primitive.

The men and Mrs. Thaw were busy tying the horses

for the night and opening saddlebags to retrieve their belongings. Margaret wandered to a rock and plopped down, massaging her saddle-sore thighs and, for the first time in her life, feeling absolutely inadequate.

A stinging phrase, "worse than useless," kept on dancing through her mind. For that's exactly what she had become, a burden and a complete drag on these brave people. They knew how to make do in the wilderness, ingenious ways to survive without so much as a gas grill. Margaret had camped out once, with twenty-five pounds of freeze-dried food, a waterproof tent, and a fully functioning Coleman stove. At the time, Margaret and her friends had felt like real pioneers, heating up their beef stroganoff without a microwave, listening to a portable radio and the creepy sounds of the woods. But they returned to civilization after two nights, feeling bold and grungy after not washing their hair or taking a steaming shower for almost forty-eight hours.

She couldn't even ride a horse. How much had Ashton risked by carrying her in his lap, the helpless prima donna? For all those thousands of hours she had spent studying this era, she truly believed she understood their minds and souls. She would read quaint words, lose herself in the surface charm of a bygone era, and then flick off her electric light, snuggle into her Sealy mattress under no-iron sheets and an electric blanket, and dream of the past.

Sure, she could book an airplane flight and load an instamatic camera, but she couldn't explain how they worked if her life depended on it. She could reprogram her word processor in a flash, just don't ask her to change a simple typewriter ribbon or build a ballpoint pen or even a pencil sharpener.

Without the benefit of vaccinations, she, too, could

fall prey to lockjaw and polio; smallpox could disfigure her; she could keel over with yellow fever or cholera. And no matter what illness she might develop, she couldn't even reach for an aspirin unless she could hold out for another thirty years.

"Aw, Miss Mag, why the long face?"

It was Ethan, the vested scout, and something in his cheerful, matter-of-fact tone struck her as funny. She shot him a beautiful smile and shook her head.

"No reason, Ethan," she announced as she rose to her feet. "No reason at all."

She took a deep breath and stretched, her arms high above her head, glancing around for Ashton. He was talking to one of the scouts and suddenly threw his head back and laughed at something the young man said. Several hours earlier he had come within an inch of being killed by a trigger-happy Union officer, had learned that the United States was willing to pay his assassin, and now he was behaving as if he hadn't a care in the world.

"I'm going to the woods. Would you like to come?" It was Mrs. Thaw, and it took Margaret a few blank seconds to catch her meaning.

Margaret gaped, then nodded. "Oh, you're going to the ladies' room, eh? I'd love to go, Mrs. Thaw."

The older woman led the way, turning once to Margaret. "It ain't so much the ladies' room as the bears' room and the wolves' room . . ."

"And the owls' room and the raccoons' room," Margaret added, and Mrs. Thaw giggled softly, an unexpectedly girlish giggle.

"I'll keep watch first, Miss Mag," she said.

"No. You can go, Mrs. Thaw. To tell you the truth, I've been holding it in for so long, it's going to take my body a while to realize it can be relieved without disgracing the general and Waffles."

"Why, Miss Mag!" But there was pleasure in her voice, and Margaret heard her scratching out a place behind a tree. In an instant she was back at Margaret's side, buttoning up her slit skirt. Margaret smiled and ducked behind the same tree, holding the cumbersome skirts as high as possible.

"Please don't let there be any poison ivy," moaned Margaret, and again Mrs. Thaw erupted in a startled laugh. When Margaret emerged, Mrs. Thaw stared at her a few moments.

"Miss Mag. I mean no offense, but why are you wearing your dress backwards?"

"To tell you the truth, I didn't want to bother you this morning," she admitted, and began to walk back to camp.

"Would you like me to help you now?" The offer was not made grudgingly, but in friendship. Margaret shot her a grateful smile.

"Oh, Mrs. Thaw, would you mind? This dress is so tight in the front . . ."

But before Margaret could finish the sentence, the capable hands of Mrs. Thaw were flying down the buttons. Lifting the gown over Margaret's head and smoothing out the bodice, Mrs. Thaw gave a few motherly clucks and rebuttoned the dress in the back.

Margaret was silent for a moment, and just as Mrs. Thaw finished the buttons, Margaret grasped her hand.

"Mrs. Thaw, I'm so sorry about your husband and son. Please, if you wish to talk about it, or if I can do anything at all, I hope you won't hesitate to come to me. I'll be here for you."

The older woman's mouth parted slightly, and she returned her gaze to Margaret's face. Her expression was one of softness and sorrow, and she brushed a wisp of Margaret's hair back into the snood.

"I thank you kindly, Miss Mag."

And with a brief squeeze of their hands, the two women returned to the camp.

One of the scouts had captured two rabbits and a squirrel for dinner, and they were roasted over a small flame, to be eaten along with cornbread and a few squares of hardtack.

Margaret avoided looking at the animals. There was no way she could possibly eat any of the meat, especially after seeing their little paws and the bright button eyes of the brown rabbit. Even the scent of the roasting flesh was making her nauseous, and she concentrated on her hands in her lap, rotating her thumbs over each other and staring down as if it were the most fascinating sight on earth.

They were all seated in a circle around the low fire, careful not to let the flame get too high in case there were more Union patrols exploring the side of the mountain. The scouts were laughing softly with Mrs. Thaw, but they each glanced over to their general, who sat in silence with Margaret.

"You'll feel better after you eat." Ashton leaned over Margaret, placing his hand over her forehead. "No fever. Good. Can I get you a piece of squirrel or rabbit?"

"Nothing. I'll just have some bread . . ."

"Margaret, look at me."

She took a deep breath and faced him, his features hard in the flickering glow of the campfire. His hat was off, and his gray jacket was unbuttoned, revealing the white shirt beneath. He was, she mused, astonishingly handsome.

"What ails you?" As he spoke he placed a small, charred animal leg on a tin plate.

"That bothers me." She nodded toward his plate.

"The plate?"

"No. The meat."

He stared at the plate, incredulous. "My dear, I apologize for the humble fare. I was hoping to prepare a piquant fricassee, but that would require a fine red wine to complement the flavor. . . ."

"That's not it at all," she began, realizing how ridiculous it was, but unable to stop. "It's the animals. They were so, well, cute and furry. I just couldn't eat an animal so helpless. The bread is all I want."

"Margaret," he said softly, and she could tell what an effort it was for him to control his temper. "I don't know when we will be able to eat next. In all truth, we have very little bread. You need to regain your strength, even if that means you must eat a 'helpless' animal. The alternative, my dear, is that you will become a weakened, helpless animal yourself. Please curb your distaste and eat while there is still food remaining."

Seen in that light, she knew what a fool she was being, jeopardizing everyone in the party for the sake of her pseudo-yuppie mentality. With a small smile, she nodded, slight embarrassment in her eyes.

"Fine." His tone was clipped as he reached for another plate. "Would you prefer squirrel or rabbit?"

Margaret closed her eyes and swallowed. "Surprise me," she whispered miserably, unaware of the brief smile that flitted across his strong features.

"Cornbread or hardtack?"

"Either one." She opened her eyes, gazing at the plate. Her eyes met his tawny gaze, sparkling with the fire's reflection. "I hate to ask this of you, but the paws. Uh, could you do something with them?"

"Of course." His voice was full of warm understanding. "Would you like them to wear mittens, gloves, or shoes?" He grasped the piece of meat on his own plate. "Of course, with his partner here, we could perform a number of popular dances . . ."

"Thank you," she snapped, and pulled the plate into her lap. The meat, thankfully, was charred, so she could not easily reconstruct the full animal in her mind. Instead, she pretended she was at a cookout, and that she was eating a piece of chicken previously wrapped in cellophane.

After one bite, she realized how ravenous she was. The food was gone all too soon, leaving her to gnaw in silence on the bone. Ashton said nothing, but he did grin when he caught her licking the tips of her fingers.

"Would you like anything else?" he murmured into her ear and, ever so slowly, she turned to face him, her fingers curled in front of her, still damp.

There was a moment of silence before he began to laugh, a low, rich chuckle. She joined him in the laughter, and all of the tension that had built up between them seemed to melt away in an instant.

With a graceful nod, she removed his empty plate and helped Mrs. Thaw clean up after the meal. The men remained around the fire, all leaning back as if they had enjoyed a sumptuous feast rather than a few meager bites. If she was still hungry, they must be famished. It was all playacting. Behaving as if one was relaxed and well-fed was the only way to maintain sanity, to give an air of normalcy and to fight the gripping knowledge that at any moment they could be killed or captured.

When the plates were scraped and wiped clean, Mrs. Thaw prepared a pot of peanut shell coffee and placed it in the dying embers. The women then resumed their places around the fire, and Margaret settled a little closer to Ashton.

"Does anyone know any ghost stories?" asked the freckled scout, his eyes darting hopefully around the circle.

"Oh, I do," said Margaret, remembering the classic tale of the lovers' lane couple and the maniac with a hook for an arm. She swiftly made some adjustments in the story, changing it from a 1950s setting to an 1860s scene. With her voice low and menacing, she began.

"What I'm about to tell you is true, and it happened not too long ago right in these mountains."

The scouts exchanged eager looks and moved closer to catch her every word. Ashton leaned back, propped up on his elbows, and watched her lovely profile in the fading light.

"There was once a couple who were very young and very much in love. Unfortunately, their parents were against the match, so they had to meet in secret, away from their strict families.

"One night the young man managed to get the family carriage without their knowledge."

"How'd he do that?" asked one of the scouts. He turned to his friend. "I swear, if I had a penny for every time I tried to sneak out with a carriage, I'd have bought myself a substitute to fight this war." His friend hushed him, and Margaret continued.

"Anyway." She gave a pointed look to the young man. "The lovers decided to go to the top of one of these mountains at night to look at the scenery and spend a few precious moments alone."

Ashton cleared his throat, and Margaret took a deep breath. "Yes, sir?" she asked without looking at him.

"Nothing, Mag. Really it's nothing." Margaret remained silent, and he finally spoke. "What were they going to see from the top of a mountain at night?"

Of course they would be able to see nothing, absolutely nothing. This was a time before battery-operated headlights, car radios to hum "Teen Angel," and, more importantly, town lights. All her lovers would be able to see was blackness.

"Well," she improvised, "they really just wanted to be alone. So they crept up to the mountain with the carriage, but what they didn't know was . . . Yes, Ethan. What is it."

"Who drove the carriage?" Ethan asked reasonably. "If the young man's coachman drove, well, they would hardly be alone. And if the young man himself drove, wouldn't that leave the young lady all by herself in a dark carriage?"

"They both rode on top. Okay?" Margaret took a deep breath and began again. "Well, here they were, all alone at last. But what they didn't know was that there was a crazy man in the woods, escaped from a home for the criminally insane. He was a desperate murderer who had been hacked away by his victims, so all he had left was an arm with a hook in it . . ."

One of the scouts laughed, and Margaret again paused, with all the amusement of a substitute teacher. "What's so funny this time?" she asked.

"Well, ma'am. You say this fellow was crazy and all, and that he was hacked away. I beg your pardon, but this man sure sounds like General Hood."

The scouts and Mrs. Thaw all chuckled, thinking of the Confederate general who was so beset by war wounds, his arm was useless and one leg had been amputated. He was so crippled that he had to be strapped into his saddle before each battle. In addition to his physical infirmities, Hood was known for his recklessness, taking risks in battle that most felt were imprudent, to say the least.

At once the scouts stopped laughing, aware that Ashton was unusually quiet, and the scout remembered that General Johnson was a friend of Hood's. Ashton's head was bent, even Mag could not see his expression, and she was suddenly afraid for the young scout.

Ashton's voice was steely. "Private, as you know, I am well acquainted with General Hood." He then glanced up, revealing a broad grin. "And as far as I know, General Hood was never an inmate in an institution for the criminally insane."

They all laughed again in camaraderie and a shared joy that their general was a man like Ashton.

The laughter dwindled to chuckles, and Margaret saw Ash shift his wounded leg to a more comfortable position. She reached out to touch him in the darkness, and his strong hand clasped hers, pulling her softly to him. His arm then rested on the small of her back, and she found it hard to concentrate on the story.

"Back to my gripping tale of horror," she said wryly, and they leaned forward again, smiles on all their faces—even Mrs. Thaw. "Now, here our lovers were in the wilderness, unaware that a madman lurked just behind the bushes. Suddenly, on top of the carriage they heard a tap, tap, tap . . . All right. What's the problem now?"

It was the freckled scout. "Miss Mag. Why didn't the horses hear the madman? I swear, most horses I know would hear such a sound well nigh before any human . . ."

"Because the horses were eating. They had feed bags on and blinders, and both animals were partially deaf from the infernal questions of their masters."

They were quiet again, but Margaret could tell they were all on the verge of hilarity. "Well, they suddenly decided to leave the place . . ."

"The horses?" Ashton didn't attempt to hide the glee in his voice.

"No, General." Her teeth were clenched now. "The young lovers decided to leave. And it wasn't until they got home that they found something on the roof of the carriage. Something strange and sinister and terrifying . . ."

"The new Confederate paper money?" offered another scout, and they all laughed heartily as Mrs. Thaw handed out mugs and poured the peanut shell brew.

"No, you've ruined it all! The hook! They found the crazy murderer's hook! You see, the man was about to murder them both, but they left and . . ."

"Paper money would have been more frightening," proclaimed Ashton, and they all applauded, except for Margaret. After a few moments she, too, began to giggle, and she leaned closer to Ashton, resting her head on his expansive shoulder.

In the still darkness, one of the scouts began to sing. Softly at first, then his voice—sweet and plaintive and without artifice—rose slightly. The song was "Somebody's Darling," about the body of an unknown soldier who was a cherished son, a lover, a husband, or a brother or friend. It was a song of unabashed sentimentality, the words overlush, the tune simple.

Yet Margaret's eyes were suddenly brimming with sharp tears, and she dashed them away with her palm, embarrassed at how the song had moved her.

Ashton ran his hand up her back, a gentle gesture, but he stopped. What he felt made his smile fade, for under his hand—prominent even beneath her heavy wool dress and shawl—he could feel each of her delicate ribs. He knew she had lost weight, but when he had embraced her at Rebel's Retreat it had been under blankets. Even holding her when they rode, he had not realized how wasted she had become.

Then he recalled the last time he had seen her in that indigo blue dress. She had been tightly corseted, and still her generous figure had made the dress appear bewitchingly snug. Now the dress was loose. No corsets. No stays.

The song ended, and conversation turned to food. They discussed lavish feasts of country ham and roasted turkey, fried chicken, and savory vegetables. Potatoes crackling with sage and cheese, fresh corn roasted in butter. Wine and champagne and sweetmeats and luscious fruit tarts.

But all Ashton could think of was Margaret. She was starving to death before his eyes, and there wasn't a damn thing he could do about it. His finger traced her spine, and he could feel the sharp edges there.

"General?"

Someone had asked him a question, but Ashton didn't hear a word.

"I said it's beginning to rain, General." It was Mrs. Thaw. "Shouldn't we turn in for the night?"

"Yes, yes. Of course."

Slowly they all rose from the fire, sputtering now with the large, cold drops of rain.

He stood up and reached down to help Margaret. "Where did you put your india rubber blanket?"

She gave him a blank look, squinting against the increasing rain. "My what?"

"Your waterproof rubber blanket," he repeated gently.

A sudden image came to her mind of an ugly brownish sheet of rubber and some scratchy blankets. She had left them all back at Rebel's Retreat.

"Oh, Ashton. I feel so stupid, but I left it back at Rebel's Retreat . . ."

Instead of scolding her or giving her the tongue-lashing she so richly deserved, he quietly wrapped his arms around her. He wanted to protect her from the weather and the cold, from hunger and danger, from soldiers on both sides. But this was the best he could do.

"I thought we'd be staying at a hotel," she admitted

weakly, her arms around his waist and her cheek resting against his chest. He laughed and put a finger under her chin, tilting her face toward his.

Even in the black, moonless night, she could see the emotion in his eyes, and her breath caught in her throat. "You may use my bedding, Mag." He brushed a kiss on top of her forehead. "I am accustomed to sleeping in the open . . ."

"No, Ash. Absolutely not. You'll catch your death out here." She swallowed. "Maybe I can double up with Mrs. Thaw."

Just at that moment Mrs. Thaw brushed by, scurrying about the camp like a frenzied housemaid. Margaret stopped her and asked gently if she could sleep with her. Mrs. Thaw opened her mouth, her eyes softening on Margaret when she heard that she had left the bedding back at Rebel's Retreat. Then she stopped, putting one hand on her hip.

"Well, Missy," she began, "this will teach you to pack for yourself. No. I sleep alone."

"Mrs. Thaw, if you please . . ." Ashton began.

"When are you two getting married?" she asked abruptly.

"Why, as soon as possible," Ashton said evenly. "When we reach Petersburg in a few days."

"Well," began Mrs. Thaw, "you keep each other warm, and I won't tell a soul." She then gave Margaret a comically broad wink and bustled away.

Stunned, she looked up at Ashton, who was smiling. Without another word, he retrieved his own bedding, stopping only to speak to the scout assigned to the first shift watch. Within minutes he fashioned a makeshift tent with part of a fallen log and the rubber blanket, and he beckoned her within.

There wasn't much room for one person, much less two. And the interior was not dry, just less wet than the outside. But they were alone.

He took off his jacket and folded it into a pillow, then leaned back and motioned for Margaret to follow. With gentle fingers, he loosened her hair from the snood, combing the silken tresses with his splayed hand.

"Come," he said softly, gesturing to the small space between the log and himself. She slid into the space and, pulling down her bunched-up skirt, settled herself beside him.

His arm immediately closed around her, and with the other hand he smoothed a rough blanket over them both. She was on her side, her head resting on his chest, her arm slowly moving up his shirt. She could feel the crisp hairs there, light brown and clean-smelling, and the steady beat of his heart throbbed against the length of her whole body, encompassing her completely.

Without realizing what she was doing, her hand slid up to his face, and she could feel the new sharp growth of whiskers, the softer texture of his mustache. He kissed her hand lightly, and she gasped at the shock that seemed to flash down her arm. He smiled in the darkness and pulled her closer.

"Ashton?" she said softly.

"Mmm?" he replied, too aware of her body resting so very near to bother with words.

"That man today, the Union lieutenant." She felt him stiffen, but she continued. "Do you think he was telling the truth when he said there was a price on your head?"

For a moment he held his breath, then he exhaled harshly. "Yes. I believe it is the truth."

The only sounds were the plopping of raindrops on the tarp, and Margaret swallowed. "Ashton?"

"Yes." His voice was wary.

"What happened to my parents?"

Again there was silence, and Ashton's hand slid up

her side, resting on her bare neck. "You don't remember?" His voice was so tender, she was almost unable to speak.

"No. Ever since the other day . . . I seem to have forgotten more than just how to ride a horse."

He took several deep breaths before speaking. "When you were eighteen, your parents and your brother and sister were killed in a boating accident."

Margaret suddenly felt as if she, too, were drowning. "It can't be," she whispered, her voice unsteady. "Oh, my God," she moaned. "How can it happen twice . . ."

Ashton suddenly rose, propping himself up on an elbow, slipping his jacket under her head. But she didn't seem to notice.

"I'm a freak here, too. Everyone must look at me and wonder why I'm still alive . . ."

"Margaret, stop." He was still gentle, but his voice was a command. "It was a terrible tragedy, but not a single person thinks ill of you. Mag, listen. Everyone has had their share of tragedy—especially since this damned war."

She stopped crying and lay very still, waiting for him to continue. "Look at Mrs. Thaw—both her husband and son and two of her brothers have been killed within the past eighteen months. Mike Norris, the scout with freckles, why he's lost his father and three brothers, two of whom fought for the North. Aside from the war, Mag, everyone's faced death. I myself have lost my father, two sisters, and a brother . . ."

"Oh, Ash. I'm so sorry."

"We're not talking about me, Mag." But she could hear the smile in his voice. "It is normal to mourn, but it is not normal to blame yourself."

"Ah. Survivor's guilt—I know all about it." She reached up to touch his face, but placed her hand on his throat instead, feeling him swallow as she stroked him.

"Maybe," she said, more to herself. "Maybe that's why I'm here. In this time I'm not so unusual—people seem to forget and accept family tragedies more readily. Perhaps it's because death is so common here, and—"

His mouth was on hers, soft and gentle at first, then strong and demanding—and all thoughts of psychology vanished from her lips.

Gently, he rolled over, cradling her on his chest as his tongue entered her mouth. She fleetingly cursed the rearrangement of her dress—the many small buttons were now in the back rather than the front. Her breath was coming quicker now, and she felt Ashton's hand on her breast, teasing through the cloth of her gown.

"Ash." She breathed and backed away, hoping to see his magnificent face in the darkness.

But her head moved the rubber tent, and instead of getting a full view of him, the tent deposited several cups of very icy water onto his surprised face.

It took him a few startled seconds before he realized what had happened. And then he began to laugh his wonderful laugh, gently pulling her against him as he readjusted the tent. She, too, laughed, wiping his face with the edge of her shawl.

"I think," he said at last, "that was a message from above. In spite of the permission of the powerful Mrs. Thaw, an even higher authority wants us to wait."

With a remorseful sigh, they took up their original positions, her head on his chest. And both slept contentedly in each other's arms until the first light of morning.

CHAPTER
9

Robert Edward Lee was looking old. Acquaintances who had not seen him since spring hid their surprise at his appearance, muffled the exclamations, and averted their widened eyes. There had been a change in him brought on by illness and disease and by watching the army he so passionately loved march irrevocably toward defeat.

Still handsome, maintaining a serene dignity and grace even under news of disaster, there was a slight stoop to his shoulders now. His hair, still a startling white, seemed limp, the dashing beard a little less stiff. His aristocratic face was turned downward, contemplating the telegram that lay in his lap.

There was a single sharp knock on his door, and Lieutenant General James Longstreet, Lee's second in command, entered the room.

"General, sir?" Longstreet moved softly, not wanting to jar his commander. Longstreet, brusque and battle-hardened, loved his general very much.

"Have you seen this telegram from Ash Johnson?"

"No. Has he returned to his command, sir?"

General Lee tapped the rectangular slip of paper and glanced out of the window, squinting against the bright light. "He's just reached Petersburg, The Oaks. He's reported some troop movements. Accurately, I assume."

Longstreet was silent for a moment. "Why, sir, is he in Petersburg? Is it his wound?"

General Lee's eyes snapped to Longstreet, his voice low. "He's going to marry her, James. He's going to marry that woman, then return to his command."

For the first time since the defeat at Gettysburg, Longstreet was struck speechless. "May I sit down, sir?"

Lee answered with a nod, and Longstreet eased himself into a Chippendale chair.

"We should have told him, sir," Longstreet said at last. "We should have told him of our suspicions. There is evidence against her, sir. Once he realized it, he would have—"

"No."

"Sir?"

Someone outside was shouting, and there were sounds of hooves and wheels. But those noises seemed distant, and there was the measured click-click of the pendulum from the wall clock.

"I've known Ashton since he was a boy," Lee said at last. "I urged him to attend the military academy. He learned to ride a horse with my nephew. And I've always known he loved that girl, even as she grew into a woman. After his own father died, Ash looked up to me. He became like another son." Lee's finger smoothed the telegram. "Did you know that it was I who urged him to join our cause? I spoke of Virginia and honor and duty and finally told him it was what his own father would have wished."

Longstreet was about to speak, but Lee hushed him with his black gaze. "I cannot in good conscience interfere with the one fragment of joy he may receive from his marriage."

"But, sir—"

"He's a brilliant man. If something is amiss, Ashton will perceive it soon enough. He will not endanger our cause. He will not risk the lives of his men, even for her."

"He loves her. She is his one blind spot."

"We will wait and see. We will post a man to watch her after he returns to his men."

The air was thick with silence until Lee spoke again. "Ashton," he uttered in a half moan. "I pray to the Almighty that we are wrong, but half the Confederacy knows your bride is a spy for those people."

The faces.

Never had Margaret seen such faces as on the road to Petersburg. The men, mostly clad in some sort of makeshift gray uniform, had long shaggy hair or short-cropped or medium length, with faces clean-shaved or whiskered. But beyond the hair were the most extraordinary faces she had ever passed.

Every one of their life's experiences seemed to leave an imprint on the men. Childhood illness was remembered with pock marks; an adolescent fall left gashes that, when healed, traced the path of the wound. And now, in early or middle or even late adulthood, their faces bore the marks of suffering, of witnessing death, of escaping themselves only to be tormented by the loss of others.

The only uniform feature to the men was their leanness, no extra flesh to pad the features, to soften the glazed expressions. It was as if they had been given a physical truth serum—they could not hide what they had become. Their very beings told the tale before they could utter a word.

They passed a home with dozens of men sprawled on the lawn, some with bandages over empty sleeves or trouser legs, others simply lying very still. The stench as they passed was almost unbearable.

"Hospital," Ashton said in a soft, emotionless voice. Women were tending the men, not the hoop-skirted belles of her imagination, but strong women carrying buckets, with hair plainly dressed and wearing old, mottled clothing.

Margaret said nothing in response. The four-day trip had left her more than exhausted, even her bones felt weary, a heaviness that seemed to weigh her down at the shoulders.

"The road to The Oaks is just ahead," Ashton said a little while later. She simply nodded.

The closer they came to Petersburg, the more formal he had become with the scouts. They were preparing for life in the military, where the general does not tell ghost stories around a fire with privates, where officers are separate and stiff-backed and approachable only for reports and commands.

She fell asleep for a while, and when she awoke they were following a lush, tree-lined path, and she could tell Waffles knew the way. His ears were up, and there was an eagerness to his gait that she had not noticed before.

There was a widening in the road, and then Margaret saw it. The Oaks.

It was smaller than she expected, made of a deep red brick with columns bracing the wide front door. There were two wings branching out from the center building, and the windows were framed by shutters, some opened wide, others closed. The house was surrounded by trees and bushes, and Margaret could see a distinct similarity between the landscaping at The Oaks and that of Rebel's Retreat.

There were noises coming from within, a second-floor shutter was flung open, and a female voice shrieked with joy.

Suddenly Margaret realized an awful truth: she would know absolutely no one at this place. From what she could tell, Mag spent much of her childhood here at The Oaks and was close friends with Ashton's younger brother Eddie as well as his cousins.

"How does it feel, Margaret, to be back at The Oaks?" Ashton was beginning to dismount, and Margaret's mind darted frantically. What should she say? Should she pretend to know everyone or ask them to wear name tags until she could refresh her memory?

He reached up to take her off the horse, and she turned to him, her eyes a reflection of wild panic.

"I don't remember," she murmured.

"I beg your pardon?"

"I don't remember this place or anyone in it. I only know you." She was holding on to the saddle as if she could simply ride away, escape from all she should know so intimately.

Ashton rubbed his eyes with his palm, a gesture of fatigue and disbelief.

"I am not joking, Ashton. I've never seen this place in my life."

Finally he looked at her as his hands clamped around her waist. "You recall nothing? No one?"

Miserably, she shook her head, her hands planted on his shoulders as he lifted her off the horse.

"This is The Oaks," he said tightly. "Presently you will meet my mother, Eliza Branch Johnson. If I am not mistaken, her sister, my Aunt Eppes, is also within. Aunt Eppes was married to William Giles, who died five years ago. Their daughter is Lizzie Giles. Does that name ring a bell?"

She was about to nod, and hesitated. The name Lizzie Giles was familiar, but simply because she had been mentioned in one of Ashton's early letters to Mag. How could she explain recognizing a name from a letter that was fifteen years old now, but deny knowing anything else?

Ashton saw her waver, the uncertainty playing on her brow, then she shook her head. "No," she said. "I do not know the name. Do I like her?"

Fury welled in him, an anger so intense he turned his face away, not wanting her to see his expression. She's doing it again, he thought. Playing her games, teasing him to the very brink of madness.

But she had seen his features twist in fury. He started to walk away.

"General," called one of the scouts, and he stopped. For a moment Ashton had forgotten the others were even there.

In spite of her horse-sore legs, she reached him before the scout, her hand on his bent arm. The scout, seeing the expression on their faces, stopped at once, hanging back until he could again approach the general.

"Ashton, help me," she pleaded, her voice harsh with agony. "Please."

At last he turned to her. He was about to shake her by her shoulders, to demand that she stop this nonsense. As his hands slid over her too-slender shoulders, he stopped. Her face was raised toward his, confusion and even a little fear marring her features. Her gaze was searching, open, and so very unlike Mag that his anger ebbed.

Was it possible that she had no memory of the quarrel last summer between Lizzie and herself? Although he had not been there to witness the scene, his mother had gleefully reported the incident to him through a detailed letter. Apparently, the two women attended the same party in Richmond, and their benign conversation turned toward Ashton. Lizzie, ever protective of her cousin even though he was older by over eight years, stated plainly that she felt Mag had been misusing Ashton and should either discard him altogether or play him fair. Mag responded in equally plain terms that Lizzie's time would be better spent finding her own beau rather than in meddling with others. The exchange soon escalated into a near hair-pulling joust, stopped only by Aunt Eppes's frantic intervention. Since then the two had studiously avoided each other.

"Do you like her?" Ashton repeated Margaret's question, and she gave a little, hopeful smile and nodded. "Well, I suppose it would be fair to say that you two are like . . . sisters."

Margaret responded with a sigh of such blissful joy that Ashton immediately felt a stab of guilt. She must not remember, he realized.

Suddenly the front door of The Oaks flew open, and Lizzie ran down the slight slope of the lawn, arms opened, her gaze fixed only on Ashton.

"Ash!" she cried, all exuberance and airy delight.

Margaret stared at the lovely young woman with wide-set eyes and a slightly square face, like Ashton's. Lizzie's beauty was perhaps a little ahead of its time. She had clear, fresh good looks when the ideal of feminine beauty was more the soft, helpless type pictured on a candy box. This woman was strong and athletic and utterly natural, and Margaret liked her immediately.

"Lizzie!" exclaimed Margaret, throwing her own arms open to receive her, blocking Lizzie's path to Ashton. Margaret fought back her tears—how wonderful it would be to have a sister again!

Locked in Margaret's enthusiastic embrace, Lizzie's startled gaze flew to Ashton, who stood in open-mouthed, mute bewilderment, a slight shrug to his broad shoulders.

"Oh, Lizzie! How splendid to see you!" Margaret sobbed.

Lizzie pulled back slightly, wondering what the trick was. Perhaps Mag had just wiped something unpleasant on Lizzie's last decent day dress or planted a fistful of lice in her hair. But Ashton would have seen it and halted the mischief.

"Hello, Mag," she stammered at last, stunned by Mag's lovely eyes brimming with genuine tears of warmth. "We weren't expecting you . . ."

"Oh, I do hope this isn't an inconvenience. Ash." She turned to him, her delicate hand resting lightly on his forearm. "Ashton, please. I can't impose—let me find someplace else to stay. The last thing I want to do is cause extra work."

"Inconvenience?" Ashton shook his head swiftly, as if trying to jostle sense into his own mind. "No. I mean, Lizzie." He finally grinned at his cousin. "Margaret and I are going to be married. As soon as possible."

Lizzie turned to glare at Mag, but it was impossible. Margaret was staring at her with damp eyes and a quivering lower lip. "How delightful," she finally muttered, watching as Ashton pushed up his hat and scratched his head.

The front door again opened, and a thin woman in a black dress swept down the lawn. Margaret knew at once this was Ashton's mother.

"Ashton!"

Margaret stood back as Ashton gave his mother a gentle hug. She was tall—much taller than Margaret —and wore her dark hair coiled around her head in a single braid. At her throat was a brooch made of human hair, glossy light auburn, and Margaret recognized it as a mourning brooch. The hair was probably from her husband or dead children, and Margaret was unable to repress a shiver.

After stroking Ashton's cheek fondly, she looked over at Margaret and nodded politely.

"Hello, Mag."

"Hello, Mrs. Johnson," Margaret responded, suddenly feeling very out of place.

"Mother, Margaret and I are going to be married."

Eliza Johnson looked up at her son and was about to say something when Lizzie jumped in.

"Aunt Eliza, didn't you say there was some tea in the parlor? Why don't we all go inside. The scouts and Mrs. Thaw can make themselves comfortable, too."

Ashton's mother shot Margaret an unreadable expression and turned toward the house.

"Maybe I'm paranoid, but I don't believe she likes me," she whispered to Lizzie.

For the first time since she could remember, Lizzie had an urge to hug Mag. "No, Mag," she said softly as Ashton unloaded the saddlebags from the horses and led the scouts and Mrs. Thaw to the back of the house. "She's just been under a great strain with both Eddie and Ash in the war, and her husband gone."

"The poor woman," Margaret said, watching after Ashton's mother with unfeigned sympathy. Lizzie stared at Mag for a few moments, disturbed by the compassion in her voice. Had something happened to change Mag?

Taking her arm, they followed Mrs. Johnson into the house. The interior of The Oaks was quiet and subdued, not the gaudy flamboyance Margaret had somehow expected. Most of the furniture seemed to date from the last century, solid dark wood with graceful curves, more like colonial Williamsburg than antebellum Petersburg. It was just the way Margaret would have decorated the place, if she had the money.

They entered a parlor, where tea things had been laid, small bits of bread and cornbread, several biscuits, and some apples. Margaret averted her eyes, fearing her wanton expression of hunger would be unseemly.

Settled into a wing chair, Margaret folded her hands, very aware that she must smell of horses and dirt, and that her dress was filthy at the hem and her hair disheveled. Ashton's mother and Lizzie were chatting about the weather and Ashton's return, each eyeing Margaret as subtly as possible.

Margaret smiled just as her stomach rumbled, a loud squishy sound that everyone tried to ignore.

"So, Lizzie," she shouted, trying to cover up the next abdominal growl. "How the hell have you been?"

Both Lizzie and Mrs. Johnson gasped, and Margaret cringed, realizing the gaffe. Even soldiers seldom used the word *hell* except in reference to a sermon. Then the next stomach growl clamored from under her fist, and Margaret cleared her throat to blanket the sound.

Suddenly, Lizzie's mouth began to twitch, and soon it dissolved into a smile.

"I'm doing well, Mag. Would you perhaps like something to eat?"

"Something to eat?" Margaret swallowed, trying not to salivate. "Oh, perhaps . . ."

"What would you prefer?" Lizzie offered a delicate plate of thin china with minute rosebuds dotting the border. Her hand was visible through the plate, fanned out in a clearly defined shadow.

They leaned over the tiered tea table together, and Lizzie whispered. "You must be famished." Then, in a louder voice, "A tea biscuit might strike your fancy."

"So would a side of beef," she whispered into Lizzie's ear, and Lizzie errupted into a spasm of giggles. "Yes, I believe that would be most pleasant," Margaret announced in a resounding tone.

There was an uncomfortable silence as Lizzie placed the tidbits on Margaret's plate while Ashton's mother did her best to busy herself with a teapot. Margaret glanced around the room, noting family oil paintings, a cluster of botanical prints, and a carefully arranged set of children's silhouettes. There were five of them, and Margaret remembered Ashton telling her he had lost three siblings. The silhouette of the oldest child must have been Ashton, a long-lashed profile of a boy holding a ball. And Margaret knew that somewhere in this house was a sample of Ashton's handwriting with his gold pen, a gift on his tenth birthday.

Lizzie spoke as she handed Margaret the full plate. "Mag," she began, clearing her throat and shooting a cautious gaze at Ashton's mother. "You have finally decided to marry Ashton. I do hope you will be very happy."

Margaret was about to take a bite of biscuit, wondering if she could possibly get away with cramming the whole thing into her mouth at once. She paused for a moment, frowning slightly but never taking her eyes from the biscuit.

"I think," she said softly, "the more important concern is that I make him very happy. There is no doubt in my mind that he will make me happy." She then took a bite and looked up at Lizzie and Mrs. Johnson.

They both stared at her as if she had sprouted a flower pot on top of her head. And she chewed self-consciously, wondering if something ghastly had trickled from the corner of her mouth.

The sound of footsteps in the hallway captured their

attention, and Ethan the scout, with an ear-to-ear grin, poked his head into the parlor.

"Miss Margaret, ladies." He then turned to Margaret. "Ma'am, the general wanted me to tell you that he rode into town to telegraph General Lee. He will be back within the hour, and he asks that everyone be ready for a wedding. He said he was going to grab anyone he could find with a collar, begging your pardon."

Mrs. Johnson was immediately on her feet. "My word! Lizzie, there's so much to do! I'll go to the kitchen and see if I can help Hattie. Gracious! We're out of white flour, and there's none to be had in town. Please, eat no more of the cakes—they will have to do for a wedding cake. Lizzie, do you know where your mother is?"

"Yes, ma'am. I believe Mother went to visit Mrs. Barksdale over at Laurel Hill."

"Well, that can't be helped, I suppose. There's no time to fetch her now," Mrs. Johnson murmured.

"Mrs. Johnson," said Ethan, "I believe Mrs. Thaw is already in the kitchen with your cook, and I would be happy to get anyone you would require, ma'am."

Mrs. Johnson smiled warmly at Ethan, and together they left the room. Ashton's mother did not so much as glance at Margaret.

With a sudden wave of uneasiness, Margaret placed the plate on the tea table, all traces of hunger gone. She scanned her dress, torn and dirty, and the frayed stockings and scuffed boots. What a fetching bride she was going to make, she thought miserably. The dress would count as something old and something blue, and her body could certainly be considered something borrowed.

"Mag, would you like me to help you freshen up?" Lizzie asked gently.

Margaret could only nod. Poor Ashton, soon to be married to a woman who looked as if she'd slept in her clothing. And she had—for the past three nights. The least she could do was brush her hair and wash her face.

"I'd appreciate that, Lizzie," she said at last, trying to sound more confident than she felt.

As they left the parlor to go upstairs, Margaret paused to look at the silhouette of Ashton as a child, touching it lightly with her finger, a whimsical smile playing on her lips. Lizzie watched in fascination, again marveling at the genuine difference in Mag.

"We'd best get you ready," she said. The old Mag would have required a month to prepare for her wedding and would have preferred a large church filled with the cream of society.

Margaret turned to her, the soft smile still on her face. "Oh, of course."

In the hallway the sounds of a house suddenly coming to life were heard, the laughter from the kitchen, plates and silverware rattling. Upstairs, in a small bedroom to the front of the house, Margaret sat before a mirrored table and couldn't help but laugh at her dirt-streaked face.

"Lizzie, it's hopeless!" She giggled, framing her face with her hands. It was so strange to see such lovely features returning her gaze, in spite of the grime. Lizzie stood back, a quizzical expression on her own face.

"Did Ashton tell you about my trousseau?"

Margaret closed her eyes for a moment. "I'm not quite sure . . ."

"Well, Mag." Lizzie's wide eyes twinkled. "You know when I was engaged to General Quarles?"

Margaret nodded, as if she had more than the faintest idea of what she was talking about.

"A few months ago I managed to smuggle my trunks from St. Louis, all of the gowns I bought in Paris last year—right under the Yankees' noses!" She clapped in delight at her own exploits, and Margaret could only gape—fully aware of the danger that must have been involved. "I have them here. Nothing for everyday wear, of course, just fancy gowns and such. Would you like to wear one of them?"

"Oh, Lizzie, that would be wonderful!"

Lizzie handed Margaret a damp towel with which to wash her face and hands, then ducked into the next room. Margaret could hear the sound of trunks being dragged across the floor, then some rustling of tissue. Within a few minutes Lizzie returned with what looked like an armful of cream-colored satin, small white shoes, and billowing underskirts.

A half hour later they were both staring in astonishment at Margaret's reflection. The gown, yards of satin, seemed to envelop her in its luscious froth, fitting her to absolute perfection. The gown was expertly cut off the shoulder with delicate gathers, revealing the gentle swell of perfect breasts. The only color other than the subtle ivory was a wide peach band at her corseted waist. The skirt was lavishly gathered over hoops and petticoats, with a light ruffle at the hem similar to the shoulders. The shoes, fine white kid, seemed impossibly fragile, especially paired with the white silk stockings.

Margaret had never seen anyone so exquisite. She leaned closer to the mirror, examining the beautifully symmetrical features the way she once admired a butterfly collection: It was indeed lovely but did not seem entirely real. This was someone else, she reminded herself. Yet it was also, miraculously, her.

Lizzie put her arm around her shoulders, eyes narrowed in thought. "You know," she said, her gaze wandering to Margaret's hair, brushed and pinned into a glossy ebony twist at the nape of her slender neck, "we are missing something . . ."

At that moment the sound of galloping hooves could be heard growing closer, and they peered out the window to see Ashton and one of the scouts, with a frightened-looking man in a black frock coat balanced on the back of Waffles.

Ashton's mother knocked on the door and quietly entered. Lizzie met her at the door, whispered something, and they nodded, glancing at Margaret. Lizzie scurried out of the room, patting her own hair.

"Mrs. Johnson," said Margaret, somehow feeling as if she should curtsy, but not wanting to risk it in the treacherous hoops.

"My dear." His mother moved toward Margaret, one arm extended. "Please forgive my earlier behavior. You see, Ashton has always been so special to me." She stopped, frowning for a moment as she gathered her thoughts before she continued. "He is my firstborn, and without him, I fear I would not have survived the loss of my other children and my husband. I've only wished for his happiness. And while I was downstairs, Mrs. Thaw told me how kind you have been, how you seem to genuinely love my son now." As she spoke she reached for Margaret's hand. "Please, Mag. Just be good to him and love him with all of your heart. That's all I can ask of you."

Margaret squeezed the older woman's hand. "Mrs. Johnson, I will do my very best to make your son a good wife, whatever that entails, whatever he needs. And if I ever fail, it won't be from a lack of love." Margaret smiled at Mrs. Johnson, and the woman's face softened, eyes misting, and Margaret saw something terribly familiar in her face. With a pang, Margaret realized that Mrs. Johnson wore an expression much the same as her own mother wore the last time Margaret saw her, full of love and hope and worry.

Lizzie entered the room holding a circular object wrapped in tissue paper. She unwrapped it carefully, and it wasn't until the last layer that Margaret could see what it was, and she gasped.

It was a glorious wreath of fresh orange blossoms, as flawless as any flowers she had ever seen. But it was the end of October.

"Where did you ever . . ." Margaret began, and both Lizzie and her aunt laughed.

"It's paper." Mrs. Johnson smiled, gently placing the flowers on Margaret's head like a crown. Even up close it was impossible to tell the wreath was anything but freshly woven. "This was my sister's," she said as she pinned it into place.

"Oh, Aunt Eppes?" Margaret asked.

"No. My other sister—we called her Pink, but her real name was Martha. She wore this when she was married in 1841."

"Did you ever know her, Mag?" inquired Lizzie conversationally, smoothing the satin on Margaret's skirt. "She died in about 1854."

Margaret tried to hide her surprise. How weirdly gothic, she thought. Death was everywhere here, a constant presence, even during a wedding.

Suddenly a fluttery slender woman entered the room, a somber specter, wearing a pitch black dress and a flat little hat covered with black ribbons.

"He's ready! Oh, heavens—Mag, how absolutely exquisite. Lizzie, you must do something about your cheeks—too pale. Oh, Mag. Lizzie, look at Mag as she marries our dear Ashton. That could have been you in that dress with the noble General Quarles. It's not too late, my dear. I'm sure he'll have you again if you just telegraph. Telegraph. Oh, yes. Ashton's downstairs with Parson Jones. The parson's in a hurry, he has a funeral to give; that little Harper girl finally wasted away with the fever. Oh, yes, and our Ashton looks so dashing in his uniform, the noble buttercup and gray." She stopped for a few hasty breaths, then turned to Mag. "How lovely! You're wearing our sweet Pink's wedding crown! Lizzie, you could wear it, too. Think about it."

"Mrs. Giles, I . . ." Margaret started to say.

"Oh, heavens, girl! I'm now your aunt Eppes!" And with that she flew from the room. Margaret bit her lip to avoid laughing, but her eyes met with Lizzie's— already brimming with mirth, and they both dissolved into gales of laughter. Mrs. Johnson, about to scold at first, was unable to keep a straight face.

"Our dear Eppes." She smiled. "She's a great admirer of the telegraph." She gave Margaret's hair a final pat, her hand lingering on her face. "What a lovely bride my Ashton has chosen. Now, Lizzie. We're all ready in the front parlor. Mag? Are you ready, dear?"

Margaret swallowed and nodded once. With a brief hug of both women, she was alone for a few minutes before she was to follow them downstairs. Again she turned to the mirror. The faultless cheeks were now stained with a becoming blush, and she stepped away, still slightly surprised when the beautiful woman in the mirror did the same thing. She felt giddy and terrified and elated, all at once. It was time for her to go downstairs, and she smiled to herself, a radiant creature now, in the mirror.

"Eat your heart out, Andy McGuire," she whispered in the air to her old boyfriend, a man whose grandparents hadn't been born yet.

She maneuvered down the staircase carefully, swishing and swaying like the lead float in a parade. It was late afternoon, and the hallway was flooded with circles of light from gas jets on the wall. One door was open, with the hushed, expectant whispers of an eager matinee audience. Margaret knew she was the show, and only one thought prevented her from locking herself in an upstairs bedroom.

Ashton was waiting.

That simple thought erased all others, made every petty fear and bout of self-consciousness seem insignificant. She was in a strange time and place, yet the one thing she was sure of was Ashton. With a deep breath and a swift mental prayer, she entered the large parlor.

All heads turned toward Margaret—the scouts, Mrs. Thaw, Aunt Eppes, Ashton's mother, Lizzie, and the drably dressed parson, looking very much like an emaciated version of the character on the Quaker Oats label.

She heeded no one except for the tallest man in the room, an impeccably attired Confederate general. She halted for a moment, and he smiled, a warmth that melted away any lingering doubts, and she walked toward him.

Ashton knew she would make a lovely bride—it had been in the back of his mind ever since he was in his teens watching his friend's little sister play with her dolls. But never could his imagination have conjured the vision now before him. She was a stunning mixture of contrasts, her raven hair shining with the soft glow of the satin gown, her bold gaze and the tremulous, almost shy, curve of her lips. Yet her violet stare never wavered. She looked directly at him, and he beckoned her with his own intense eyes.

His open hand was stretched out to welcome her, and she placed her own petite hand into his palm, and the ceremony began. It would be over in a few minutes, swift words that would tie them together for life.

But was it Margaret or Mag he was marrying?

Margaret felt a sudden wave of nausea, heavy and clawing at her throat, and she shut her eyes. She had gone along with the bizarre reality of where she was for the better part of a week. As far as she could tell, nothing she had done so far had made a substantial difference in history.

Now, however, she was taking an active part in rewriting the past. Mag should be dead. And Ashton himself should die a bachelor general within the year. She had fully intended to do everything in her power to prevent his death, and that, too, would change history. She pushed the thoughts out of her mind, willing them away, biting her lip to squelch the scream she could feel rising in her throat.

The parson said something to Ashton, but Margaret couldn't hear. He slipped a wide gold band on her finger, and she briefly wondered where he had managed to purchase a wedding ring.

It was her turn to speak, and her voice was flat as she repeated the vows. And then the service was over. Ashton held her by the shoulders, his eyes searching hers.

"Margaret, are you ill?" he whispered.

She shook her head, and his lips grazed hers with a light kiss. There was polite applause, and for a moment she was startled—she had forgotten the scouts and everyone else in the parlor.

The room was suddenly filled with the soft buzz of conversation, and Mrs. Thaw was busy arranging a refreshment table. A line of poetry floated into Margaret's mind: "The center cannot hold, things fall apart."

It was a famous line. Who said it? Was it Yeats? "The best lack all conviction while the worst are full of passionate intensity." That was by the same poet. William Butler Yeats.

Or was it T.S. Eliot?

She couldn't remember.

"Margaret." Ashton took her elbow and led her to a window. "Here, is that better? You were looking very pale back there." His voice was low but full of such concern that she blinked, trying to banish the dread that was beginning to overwhelm her. She was forgetting her favorite poets, the writers she had been able to quote since childhood.

"Ashton, I can't remember things," she said finally.

"I know," his thumbs toyed with a wisp of ruffle at her shoulder. "Perhaps this is good—a new chapter for both of us. You've changed, Margaret, in such a marvelous way. Perhaps this is good."

His face was very close to hers, and she noticed he was shaved, his mustache trimmed, and the worn uniform had been brushed, his boots polished. How had he managed to do all of that in less than an hour?

Then another thought entered her mind—he had done it for her. For his bride.

"Ash," she murmured, mesmerized by the piercing intensity of his handsome features. "We're married."

A smile played on his lips, softening his expression. "You remembered. I'm flattered." And his hand slipped from her shoulders down her bare arm, grasping her left hand, the one with the plain gold band. Slowly he drew her hand to his lips and stroked a lazy kiss on the top, then, with a gentle flip, another slow kiss on her palm, and then on her wrist.

Her eyes closed and she leaned into him, unable to speak or even to think. She inhaled his scent, of rough wool and leather, clean skin and his own familiar fragrance.

There was a clattering in the hallway, a metallic clank of a sword being thrown down in haste. And suddenly a man entered, a slender Confederate officer in an elaborate gray uniform with gold braiding on the cuffs and down the ornate buttons.

His gaze combed the parlor and rested on Ashton and Margaret, fury radiating from the otherwise cool expression. Mrs. Johnson immediately hastened to his side, looping her arm through his.

"Why, Eddie," she said in a warning tone. "How delightful, you're just in time for the reception. Unfortunately you have just missed your brother's wedding."

Eddie shook free of his mother and marched over to Ashton, who had the beginnings of a vague grin on his face.

"Mag," Eddie said in a clipped tone, taking her in with one swift, disapproving glare. "Ashton." He nodded toward his brother. "I need to speak to you. Immediately."

Ashton's grin faded. "Major, I request that you address me as 'General' or 'sir' when before my men." He gestured curtly to the scouts, who had stopped chewing long enough to watch the spectacle before them.

"Then, General, sir. I wish to speak to you on a matter of the utmost importance, sir." The younger brother's jaw was twitching in barely restrained rage, and Ashton smiled at Margaret, his eyes dancing.

"My dear, would you please excuse me? Your brother-in-law wishes to congratulate me on my marriage. Clearly, his emotions are so joyous he cannot contain himself."

And with that, the two brothers left the room, one in stiff-backed anger, the other with one eyebrow arched in curious amusement.

CHAPTER

10

How could you?" Eddie rasped as soon as they were in the small parlor, away from the guests. He ran a distracted hand through his short hair, a few shades darker than his brother's. Like Ashton, Eddie wore a mustache, neat and carefully trimmed, but he was not quite as tall, nor was he as broad in the shoulder. His eyes were a flat gray, but seemed deep blue in contrast to his uniform. He was in the engineering corps, with the rank of major, yet his jacket was far more elaborate than his older brother's.

"It's good to see you, too, Eddie." Ashton clapped his brother on the shoulder, and Eddie jerked away.

"How could you marry that scheming, deceitful . . ."

Ashton held up a warning hand, and Eddie stopped, biting back an urge to spit a more accurate string of adjectives.

"Margaret is my wife now, Eddie. Remember that."

"Margaret?" Eddie sneered. "You call her Margaret? She hates the name, Ashton. Oh." He executed a crisp salute. "I beg your pardon. General, sir."

Ashton took a deep breath and rubbed his eyes. "Just in front of other soldiers, Eddie. You can call me anything you want when we're alone. . . ."

Eddie's eyes widened in delight, and he was about to speak, when Ashton suddenly smiled.

"Anything within reason, that is," he amended. "You may remember you have had rather bad luck when it comes to calling me by certain names."

Eddie's shoulders suddenly slumped, and he looked at his older brother with a combination of exasperation and genuine concern. "Ash, how could you? You know what everyone says her, yet you married her. Why?"

There was a moment's beat, and Ashton shook his head. "She's changed. Something's happened to her, she's not the girl you know."

"Mag?"

"She was very ill, and I believe that has made her review her life, how she has always behaved. Even Mrs. Thaw has altered her view."

"Now *that* I find hard to believe."

Ashton shrugged, then returned his hand to Eddie's shoulder, smiling to himself at the stiff epaulettes and fanciful braids on the uniform. "Reserve your judgment, Eddie. Talk to her, get to know her again without prejudice, and I think you'll understand."

Eddie glanced down, struggling with his emotions. He had always looked up to Ashton, his older brother, who could perform any feat, from breaking a wild horse to memorizing Shakespeare, with an effortless grace. Everything Ashton had ever done had made the entire family proud. But this?

"She's a spy," he spat. "She is a spy, out to destroy our cause. . . ."

"Oh, Lord." Ashton sighed. "Not the cause again."

"I'm serious. Everyone knows it—her brother Tom sends her notes. Don't you realize . . ."

"I'm not an idiot, little brother." Ashton's tone was so low, Eddie had to lean closer to hear. It was a trick Ashton used with defiant students and now with mutinous soldiers. "I know what is said, the rumors. For God's sake, this war is full of rumors—if we believed half of them . . . well. Did you believe the reports of my death at Gettysburg?"

"Of course not, but . . ."

"Did you believe that Jeff Davis had surrendered Richmond? Or that he fled to England with his family?"

"Nobody took that seriously . . ."

"Did you think General Lee was a coward for digging trenches? Did you call him the King of Spades the way the newspapers did?"

"Now come on, Ash. You know how angry that made me."

"So why are you so willing to think the very worst of Margaret? Has she ever been anything but your friend?"

Eddie's face flushed, his ears reddening the way they did when he had temper tantrums as a child.

"I've heard about her with others."

"You've heard." Ashton's hand clenched into a tight fist. "Eddie, listen to me. I love her, she is now my wife. But I am not unaware of rumors and innuendos. I'll keep an eye on her, Eddie, just to prove to the rest of Virginia that Margaret Johnson is no spy for the Union."

Eddie glanced up hopefully. "Really? You'll really watch her?"

"I really will." Then Ashton leaned over and ruffled his younger brother's hair. "She's Margaret Johnson now." He grinned. "How very strange."

Finally Eddie smiled. "How about that? My big brother's married." Then he cuffed Ashton on the arm, and together they rejoined the party. Yet, in spite of Ashton's assurances, even as they entered the gaily lit parlor, even as he watched the look of apparent adoration on his new sister-in-law's undeniably radiant face, he was unable to quell the feeling in the pit of his stomach, heavy and dead, that his brother had just made the biggest mistake of his life.

At last they were alone.

Ashton closed the door softly, the sounds of the party downstairs still audible through the thick wood and walls, muffled slightly by the plump carpets.

He glanced over at his wife, who was leaning heavily against the mahogany wardrobe, her eyes closed in exhaustion. Her face was drawn and pale, her shoulders rounded, slumped forward, and without the furniture for support, Ashton knew she would simply tumble over.

"Margaret, why don't you lie down? You must be fatigued—I noticed you didn't sit down once during the party."

For a moment he thought she had fallen asleep standing up, a trick he thought only soldiers could manage. But the corners of her mouth curved slightly.

"I couldn't sit down." She smiled, her eyes still closed.

"Why ever not?" He began to unbelt the saber and pistol, still watching his wife. He wanted to memorize her, every angle of her face, the errant strand of hair that twisted in a silky spiral against her slender neck.

"The hoops." She sighed.

"Excuse me?" He laid the cumbersome belt on a table, coiled and menacing, and untied the yellow sash underneath.

Suddenly her eyes opened, and he was startled by the vibrant color, almost lilac, the sparkle in the depths.

"The hoops. I can't get the hang of these things. I was afraid I would sit down and knock myself out with the flying hem."

The sound of raucous laughter below punctuated her comment, and they both smiled.

"The parson finds you amusing," Ashton concluded.

"Why is he still here? I thought he had a funeral to conduct." She reached behind her, fumbling with the tiny buttons and hooks that ran down her back. Ashton walked silently to her, turning her back to him with his strong hands, and began to unbutton the gown. Her head leaned forward, the soft hair swirled at the nape of her neck, and he stared, longing to kiss her there, but not sure if it would alarm her. How much did she know of wedding nights? Her mother and older sister had probably not told her about it before they died, and it was unlikely she had discussed such an intimate subject with another woman. But she did not seem frightened or even apprehensive.

"Ash?" Her hand reached behind her, and she placed her fingers on his forearm.

"Yes." What would she ask? For separate sleeping quarters? For him to leave her alone?

"Had the parson been drinking?" She turned to face him, a playful smirk wavering on her lips.

"As a matter of fact, he had indeed been drinking," he answered, his hand smoothing up the gentle curves of her arm. "Uh, Ethan was able to procure some whiskey. The parson had a few shots and told me in confidence that the funeral could wait. He hadn't performed an enjoyable ceremony in so long that he fully intended to have a good time."

As he spoke she had stopped smiling, her fingers unfastening his own buttons, her eyes transfixed on his face. Even in the dim flickering of the oil lamp, his features were extraordinary, almost harsh because of his leanness, but composed of such even planes and angles that it took her breath away.

With unsteady hands she pulled the jacket over his shoulders, and he wordlessly rolled the heavily muscled arms forward to assist her, his eyes searing into hers. She ran her hands along his chest and unfastened the white shirt, becoming increasingly clumsy with each button.

His hand clamped over hers, and she blinked. "Margaret, my love. Do you know what is going to happen tonight?"

Her gaze was one of befuddled stupor, and he continued. "When a man and a woman are, well, married, they do something, something very beautiful . . ."

But her giggle cut him off. How could she explain that she had understood the 'married' thing since elementary school sex education, and that although she had never been married, she had experienced her first wedding night in her freshman year of college?

With supreme control, she managed to assume a more sober expression. "I know, Ash. I understand all about the birds and the bees."

He cleared his throat, momentarily averting his eyes, staring with false interest at a chair in the corner. "It's very different with people. You see, it's more comparable to other warm-blooded beasts. For example, your barnyard animals, such as the bull and the cow, or the pig and the sow, or the . . ."

"Moose."

"Pardon me?"

"I saw a moose once. I believe it was his wedding night, too. So it's all very clear to me." With that she slipped the cotton shirt over his shoulders and let out an involuntary gasp.

Never had she seen a more glorious body—beautifully shaped muscles sculpted over the lean form. There were small scars on the bronzed skin, but those imperfections, evidence of the rugged life he had led thus far, simply made him even more appealing. Tentatively, she touched his chest, the smooth skin under the brittle amber hairs, and his iron grip clasped her wrist.

"My dear." His voice was husky and low. "I am not a moose. I fear you will be"—he swallowed heavily—"disturbed and perhaps offended by the, eh, natural course of . . ."

But her unbridled gaze silenced him, and before he could form another word, she reached up, raking her hands through his hair, and forced her lips on his.

"Margaret, I . . ." but his voice trailed off as her hands slithered down his back, kneading the tightly sprung muscles.

With a force that left them both stunned, she pushed him backwards, toward the large four-poster bed in the center of the room. His arms banded around her satin-wrapped waist, lifting her up as their kiss vanquished all reason from their fevered minds.

His mouth clamped on hers, her head tilted back, held firm by his powerful forearm. She leaned into him, senseless now, only aware of the pounding need that had turned her knees to liquid, of the tantalizing sensation of his chest hairs pressed into the bare skin above her breasts.

Her shoes dropped off her feet; her toes, still covered in white silk stockings, curled as he hoisted her effortlessly in his arms, rocking backwards and onto the expansive bed.

At once her hoops flipped up, like a rubber dinghy suddenly inflated, with a will of its own. The skirt sprang up so quickly, Ashton—his attention focused so completely on Margaret—was struck between the eyes with a ruffled ring of steel.

Startled and breathless, they simply stared at each other in shock for a few moments. Margaret reached up and gently rubbed his forehead, and they both began to laugh, a skittish, self-conscious chuckle.

Wordlessly, Ashton reached behind Margaret and completed the task of unfastening her gown. He carefully laid it on the bed beside them, his eyes never leaving her flushed face. He then tugged on the corset ties, and with a sigh of relief, Margaret was finally free of the confining whalebone stays.

The hoops slid unceremoniously to the floor, followed in quick order by three petticoats, and Margaret was at last clad in nothing but the light chemise, lacy drawers, and the delicate white stockings.

He watched in astonishment as she untied the ribbon at the collar of the chemise and shrugged the slender white shoulders, the blousey fabric tumbling airily to the floor, on top of the shoes.

With a sharp intake of breath, he allowed himself the languorous pleasure of simply gazing at his wife, the flawless breasts, rounded and full, quivering with each of her own rapid breaths. Slowly, almost reverently, he reached out his roughened hand and cupped one of her breasts, his thumb stroking the nipple, his palm savoring the feel of her heart beating madly in an answering frenzy.

"Margaret," he groaned, pulling her toward him. But she was unable to reply, an astonishing surge of desire welling within her abdomen, reverberating throughout her entire body.

Somehow his trousers were hastily pulled away, her drawers and stockings joined the ever-growing pile of flimsy white fabric on the carpet by the bed. The oil lamp illuminated their bodies, slick with wanton perspiration, their skin glistening under frantic hands and lips. They couldn't seem to move fast enough; there weren't enough hands to delight in each other's feel, the salty taste of skin.

Margaret felt his need, urgent and molten as her own, and guided him to her.

He tried to speak, but again she stilled his voice with her fiery lips, his fingers running lingeringly along the nape of her neck.

"Please," she murmured, her voice cracked and compelled by the most primitive of wants.

Tenderly, he eased into her, braced by her clinging arms, and then he thrust forward. Margaret gasped at the pain, mingled with an absurd desire to laugh. She was perhaps the only woman in history to endure the indignity of losing her virginity twice.

"Margaret, forgive me . . ." he whispered, now moving with her in exquisite rhythm. Then, with shattering beauty, they exploded together, holding on to each other as one, the indescribably magnificent joining of a man and a woman.

They were both incapable of speech, completely absorbed in the astounding sensation of simply being together, a closeness neither one had ever imagined possible.

They lay together for a long time, an eternity of shared moments that truly united them as one being. Margaret's hair lay across them like a wild tangle of seaweed, and Ashton closed his eyes, rolling a silken strand of her hair between his thumb and index finger.

Her shoulders began to shake gently at first, and Ashton tilted her face toward him.

"Are you well?" he asked gently, then realized she was giggling. His own mouth bent into a grin before he asked, "What, my dear one, is so funny?"

"Perhaps next time, Ash," she whispered, "you could remove your boots."

And downstairs, Mrs. Thaw and Aunt Eppes, clearing away the last of the wedding dainties, exchanged perplexed shrugs at the unmistakable sound of the general's laughter.

Margaret awoke with a slow stretch, her arm lumbering over the sleeping form of her husband. He was solid and warm, his arm clamped around her.

The fluttering eyes of slumber played over his closed lids, and she marveled at the beauty of the man asleep. A lock of sun-brightened hair fell lopsidedly over his eyes, and she brushed it aside, breathlessly, tenderly.

A painful knot welled in her throat. He was her husband. This was her fate. She ran a delicate finger along his mouth, so well-formed, so beautifully cut. Part of her wanted to cry—was such beauty possible? Was such happiness allowed? He swallowed in his sleep, a deep, comfortable motion, absolute ease.

She slid out of the bed, momentarily bereft of his comforting warmth. The carpet was cold, heartless, and she walked, wrapped in a fragment of her gown, to the window.

It was a brilliant day, the sun striking bold patterns of yellow and scarlet on the fading green of the lawn. On the table beside the window was his saber and pistol, the heavy leather belt twisted like a drowsy snake.

The sword seemed a relic of another era, glinting in a sinister sneer of defiance, smiling in reptilian triumph. So forbidding, so foreign.

But it was the pistol that fascinated her. She had never seen one before, a cavalry revolver, an actual weapon. It was enormous and oddly weighted, top-heavy and awkward, like a musket that belonged to the Pilgrims. She was not able to hold it upright; it had to weigh at least fifteen pounds, all shiny wood and brass, all flash and power.

"Hold the weight in your elbows." Ashton's leisurely drawl slid over her, goose flesh forming on her skin. She faced him, her eyes questioning, and he moved in a liquid vault toward her, powerful yet utterly unthreatening.

"Lean it back there," he whispered when he reached her side, naked yet unself-conscious. "It's too heavy to hold with just your wrist."

"How on earth can you shoot this thing?" she wondered.

"There is usually some form of inspiration, such as a charging brigade of Union soldiers, all pointing a similar weapon."

"I think I'd just throw it," she concluded, and he gently pried the pistol from her hand and returned it to the table.

"It's terrible but beautiful," she whispered, unable to ignore the weapon. "This isn't at all what I thought it would be like."

"What isn't?"

"This war." Margaret said nothing else, but could not pull her mind away from her thoughts. From the safe distance of one hundred and thirty years, this war had seemed a glorious event, filled with enough triumphs and tragedies to fill thousands of books. The people who had actually lived through the war, the witnesses, were all long gone, and their memories and recollections had proceeded them to oblivion, muffled by decades of retelling and exaggeration.

The reality was a petty brutality that made everyday life miserable. There was constant hunger, far more potent than fear or any noble ideals. Worn shoes were uncomfortable, but most of the Confederate soldiers she had seen were barefoot.

She had yet to see a battlefield, still everything around her reeked of war, a peculiar stench that seemed to cling to people no matter how often they washed. Unlike the black-and-white photographs of Brady and Gardner, images of frozen formality, there was color to the Civil War, but it was muted shades of earth and mud, vivid spots of scarlet on filthy bandages and seeping through clothing.

"None of us really understood what it would be like, not at the beginning." Ashton's voice startled her. His potent gaze shot to hers, a weariness there she had not seen before. "You know, Margaret, I wasn't one of those gadflys who thought this would be over in a month. I thought I was a realist, flattered myself that I knew we were in for a long haul. But I never imagined this. Never in my darkest nightmares."

Downstairs they could hear the sounds of a household awakening, the clatter of pots, drawers being opened and closed, someone talking in the yard. Margaret and Ashton remained silent, and his arm tightened around her shoulders, and he leaned his cheek against her hair.

While the rest of the house was waking up, Ashton and his bride softly, but urgently, returned to bed.

CHAPTER
11

Nothing could delay Ashton's return to his command. Margaret watched as he prepared to leave, brushing invisible dust from his now-pristine uniform, folding the extra cotton shirts with his scent still lingering and placing them into the saddlebags.

There wasn't much for her to do. The scouts had cleaned and oiled his sawed-off rifle, the weapon of choice for the cavalry, and cared for his pistol and sword. The hilt of the saber was visible from its sheath, hardly used now in favor of the more deadly guns.

Her balled fists were tucked under the generous folds of a simple light burgundy gown with a small collar piped in black silk. There was a question she longed to ask, she needed to know the answer to, before she could watch him leave.

"Ashton," she said softly, and he stopped at once, his hand pausing as he buckled the leather bag. "I need to know something."

163

His face dissolved into a brilliant smile. "Are you going to ask me what my favorite dinner is again?"

"No. This is serious, Ash. I need to know what you think of slavery. I am absolutely serious." Her hand patted a strand of hair beside her ear, but her gaze never wavered.

"Margaret," he began. "You know how I feel. The truth is that I am against slavery, and I always have been."

"Then why are you fighting?" She was unable to give into the relief that had washed over her at his answer, not yet. She needed to know why he was so willing to risk his life for a cause he was partially against. Somehow, she knew this was the very key to her husband.

"Why, I'm fighting for states' rights, of course." His voice was full of disbelief, as if explaining a very basic and simple truth to a dull child.

"States' rights?" she repeated mechanically.

"I believe, Margaret, that Mr. Lincoln is riding dangerously close to a complete dictatorship. Now isn't that what our own grandfathers fought against? Why, Lincoln is no better than King George if he . . . Margaret, what's wrong?"

"Do you really despise slavery?"

He stiffened. "I always have. It is the most evil injustice on the earth. No man can own another."

"What about Aunt Hattie?"

"Aunt Hattie has been free for over thirty years. My father released her when his own father died, and she is paid just as any other servant, although she is far more important than any employee, and she has stayed on even when Mother is only able to pay her partial wages."

Margaret closed her eyes for a moment, her trembling hand rising softly to her mouth as Ashton continued packing. He was against slavery, she repeated over and over again in her mind. Although she disagreed with his notions of states' rights, she now knew she had married a man who viewed slavery as the vile institution it was. Aunt Hattie was not a possession.

At last she opened her eyes, able now to concentrate on her husband, on the man she loved. She watched his every movement, etching his brisk motions in her memory, in case this would be the last time they would have together.

There was a timeless feeling to the scene, a wife watching her warrior husband prepare for the brutal uncertainty of war. This had been happening for centuries and would be repeated in the centuries to come, yet still there was a dreamlike quality to the occasion. The simple motions were so mundane, but the implications were staggering. Countless others had left just the same way, packing the clothes, making sure everything fit into the bag. And countless others had never returned.

He glanced at her occasionally, and she averted her eyes, unwilling to have him see the apprehension and fear there. All of his faculties needed to be focused on his military duties, not on the bride he left behind.

How much longer did he have? Perhaps the pattern of events would remain the same, and he would be killed by a sharpshooter on a dusty road in Atlanta the following July. Then again, perhaps the course of history would be altered, and he would have less time. Maybe he would not survive to see his next birthday. Everything had changed. She had changed everything.

With her head turned away, Margaret wasn't able to observe the expression on his face. His usual hard features softened when he turned to her, the piercing eyes that usually saw with such savage clarity clouded, and he was consumed with the unnerving sensation of not being able to see at all. He was only able to feel, not only his own overwhelming sensations but her changing emotions as well. They were as clear to him as though coursing through wires.

"Margaret." His voice was so low she almost didn't hear him. On the lawn outside were the sounds of his scouts waiting, soft conversation and laughter, respectful but still impatient.

Ashton stood in front of an open window, the bright sunlight tumbling over his shoulder, making his features indistinct. It was almost a silhouette, and she thought of the framed cutout silhouette of the little boy holding a ball. His arms were open now, ready to receive her, and she at once flew to him, to be enveloped in his warm embrace.

His strong hands ran over her back and upper arms, as if to imprint her in his mind, to carry the feel of her with him forever. Her eyes were closed, and he hungrily raked over her with his sharp gaze, her hair, the crest of her eyebrows, the long dark lashes, and her smooth nose. Always he would return to her mouth, soft and parted.

She floated her hands over his back, the knotted muscles under the fine gray uniform. Then his mouth bent down to hers, and her feet seemed to lift above the ground. Gently he kissed her at first, a sweet farewell. Then his body seemed to clench, and the kiss became savage, demanding, more intimate than anything she had experienced before. His hand was at her throat, an almost primitive gesture. With any other man the pressure at her throat would have felt threatening, but his touch was protective, fervent, heartbreakingly tender.

They began rocking gently back and forth, a soothing motion that neither remembered initiating. In their swaying embrace the kiss softened, and Margaret opened her eyes, coming again to her senses, wanting to see her husband's face.

He was watching her already with a gaze of such feverish intensity that she felt a jolt shudder through her.

"General," came a voice from outside. "We're ready now, sir."

Ashton smiled, his focus never wavering from her eyes. "They make it sound as if they've been keeping me waiting." His voice was gravelly and soft.

An uncomfortable knot welled in her throat, and she tried to swallow it away, but it wouldn't leave. Instead, a sob escaped her lips.

"Shush, love." His finger crooked under her chin. "I'll be back soon. I always am." His rough thumbs smoothed the tears from her cheeks.

"For your birthday?" Her voice was strangled, and he brushed a light kiss on her forehead before strapping on his sword and pistol and reaching over for his saddlebags. She wasn't sure if he heard her, so she repeated the question.

"Perhaps." His answer was distracted. She realized that in a very real sense, he had already left her.

Now she was alone at The Oaks.

Of course the house was brimming with people, strange faces she was supposed to know, her new relatives by marriage. Only Lizzie seemed comfortable to be with, her easy banter was reassuring and light, as if there were nothing wrong in the world.

Everyone else was friendly, but Eddie seemed to treat her with grinding civility. His words were polite, but there was an underlying distance that he seemed eager to preserve. With Lizzie he was playful, trying to trip her skirts as she walked ahead of him, telling her some of the repeatable jokes he had heard from other soldiers. But when Margaret joined in the laughter,

Eddie's face would become impassive, and he would change the topic.

Within hours of Ashton's departure, she felt the full crush of loneliness. She wandered in and out of the rooms where he had grown up, perusing books in the library, trying to decipher the signatures on some of the landscapes in the hallway.

She was looking at an old map of Virginia when she heard voices and started toward the small parlor. She needed cheering up, and there was the welcome sound of Lizzie's giggle wafting from the room. Then she heard Eddie's voice, and hesitated. She didn't want to spoil their fun, and Eddie would certainly view her company as a most unwelcome addition.

"Tell me, Eddie," pleaded Lizzie, her voice teasing.

"Well, I'm not so sure if Ash wants everyone to know . . ."

"Oh, come on, you goose. He told me about the last one. Sort of."

Eddie cleared his throat. "Very well. Do you remember that scout named Ethan?"

"Of course I do."

"He is not just a scout, not by a long shot. Before the war he studied the telegraph at Samuel Morse's school in Washington City. Did you see that funny round pocketknife of his?"

There was silence, and Margaret assumed Lizzie was either nodding or shaking her head. Then Eddie continued. "It's his special design, an instrument for cutting into telegraph wires. He's able to slice into the wire without interrupting the current, so no one on either end knows he's in on their conversation. So you see, it's like eavesdropping on old Abe Lincoln himself. Ethan and Ash have discovered some Union wires, and that's not all."

"What else?" Her voice was excited.

"Ethan can mimic the taps of other telegraph operators. He was telling me just this morning that every operator has a distinctive style; it marks a man every bit as well as a voice or a face. Well, Ethan and Ash have rerouted a few of Mr. Lincoln's men in blue. Ethan pretends to be, say, the operator at a Maryland station, and orders General So-and-So to some distant place."

"Go on!"

"Remember last spring, when McClellan just sat with his troops, whittling away time? Our own Ash made the poor sod believe there were hundreds of thousands of angry Rebels just waiting to take aim on his men. Ash called it a bloodless victory, or something along those lines. McClellan got the sack because of Ash and Ethan."

"So what is Ash going to do next?"

Margaret could hear the grin in his voice. "He's going to take a few nips at General Grant now. Says he's been enjoying southern hospitality altogether too long for his liking. If anyone can run circles around Grant, it's Ash. He'll do his old trick of coming out of nowhere, taking a couple hundred prisoners, some horses and rifles, then he'll vanish. Grant will never know what hit him."

"How does Grant measure up to the other Yankee generals?" Lizzie sounded more pensive now.

"Well, he's a far sight better than the other ones. He must have Bobby Lee worried, because he wants him out as soon as possible. Ash is going to try his darnedest to make Grant look like the biggest fool on the face of the planet."

Eddie's easy knowledge of Ashton's movements infuriated Margaret. Of all people, she should know where he was. Not only was she his wife—she was the only person who knew the basic sweep of both armies.

She alone could keep him from wandering into the enemy's clutches.

The enemy. She thought of the Union Army now in terms of the enemy. She swallowed hard, trying to dismiss a terrible thought. If her husband was successful in his mission, and General U.S. Grant—who, teamed with Sherman, would bring the Confederacy to its knees—was indeed disgraced and dismissed, the South could very well win the war.

"I want him to bring me some Union jackboots like his. Did you notice them? His other boots got torn up at Gettysburg . . ."

Margaret no longer heard Eddie's voice. She closed her eyes and pressed against the cool wall.

"Why, Mag! You poor dear, you're as pale as a ghost." It was Aunt Eppes, fluttering a black-edged handkerchief in front of Margaret's face. "Eddie and Lizzie, you two take care of your cousin Mag."

In spite of her misery about Ashton's mission, Margaret's eyes widened. "Cousins? We're cousins? Ashton and I are related by blood?"

"Why, of course, Mag. You're second cousins once removed, I believe. Isn't that right, Eddie?"

Eddie and Lizzie exited the small parlor stiffly. Eddie's face was flushed red; Lizzie looked like a rabbit caught in car headlights, startled and frozen. They said nothing.

"Now, you two help poor Mag up to her room. I'm sure she misses her Ashton, as we all do. My own Mr. Giles passed away five years ago, and I do believe I miss him as much as ever."

Lizzie rolled her eyes. "Mother, please. It's not as if Ashton's dead." Her eyes flicked to Margaret, apologetic. "I'm sorry. But Ash will be back—he always comes back."

Eddie and Lizzie each took hold of one of Margaret's shoulders, Eddie using a little more pressure than absolutely necessary. They marched her up the stairs and into her room, the room she had shared with her husband just hours before.

A sudden, absurd thought sprang into Margaret's mind, fueled by exhaustion and her aching need for Ashton. She thought of penning a letter to an advice columnist. In her mind she could envision the column, typeset into a newspaper from a hundred and thirty years in the future.

Dear Abby,

I have enjoyed your column for years and can't believe I am actually writing you now. I have a problem I have never seen addressed by you. Perhaps other readers are in the same situation.

You see, some time ago I time-traveled back to the American Civil War. The good part is that I now inhabit the body of a beautiful southern belle and am married to the most magnificent man I could ever imagine. The bad news is that he is a Confederate general and I am a Yankee. Also, Dear Abby, he is a very good general. If he succeeds, if he even survives this war, there is a good chance the United States will be destroyed. I can probably help him defeat the Union troops he is facing and save his life. The cost would be the eventual end of the United States. That would be placing my own selfish happiness above that of the entire world. Can you imagine what would have happened in World Wars I and II without the United States? Can this marriage be saved?

M.J.
The Oaks
Amelia Station
(near Petersburg, Virginia)
1863

P.S. I have also just learned my husband and I are cousins. Will our children have webbed feet?

Just before Eddie closed the door to her bedroom, he saw a brief smile flit across Margaret's lovely mouth.

"Damn," he muttered to Lizzie in the hallway. "Ash is going to have my hide over this one."

He paused, a brilliant idea forming in his mind. He would simply tell his commanding officer the entire situation, and cross his fingers that his colonel would understand how important it was to the cause to post a man at The Oaks. His new sister-in-law needed to be watched. Carefully.

Ashton's men were delighted to see him. Some of the other high-ranking officers offered him some gentle ribbing on his marriage to the beauteous Mag, careful not to cross over the lines of ribald impropriety.

Their campsite was close enough to the Federals that they could hear the enemy's bugler at night. The Confederate pickets shouted over to the Union counterparts, issuing song requests, swapping gossip about women, asking to trade their plentiful tobacco for Union food and real coffee beans.

Ashton's aide-de-camp entered his tent with a crisp salute. "Sir," Sam Walker began, "the scouts have located the Yankees' main storage area. It is lightly guarded at the present time, and the men were wondering if you still plan on a midnight raid. The men are anxious for an answer, sir."

The bright-eyed eagerness of the youth made Ashton grin, and he stood and put a hand on Sam's shoulder. "You tell them to get a few hours' rest. The raid is on, just as we mapped out."

"Yes, sir!" Sam began to leave the tent and paused,

his hand holding the flap open. "Oh, and sir?" Ashton glanced at the younger man. "May I tell you how very pleased we all are to have you back. Everyone's morale was sinking mighty low, and you have cheered them up faster than a Christmas turkey. If you understand my meaning, sir."

"I thank you, Sam." Ashton frowned slightly as his aide left. How would his men react if they knew he'd give just about anything in the world to have this cursed war over? And the fearful part was, he was getting to the point where he didn't give a damn who was victorious. He simply wanted to see an end to the slaughter.

Waffles, Ashton's horse, tapped the ground with his front hooves, ears flat against his sleek head. Ashton patted the animal as he peered through the field glass to the camp just beyond the creek. Even in the darkness he could sense his men waiting in the foliage, horses primed and trained.

This had to work. The blow to the Federal supplies had to be swift and certain; there was no time for indecision. Once he issued the command, there would be no turning back.

The time was just about right. A memory kept flitting in and out of his consciousness, of Margaret, her eyes moist with tears. Damn. He had to push the thought away.

The first thing he had done when he returned to his command was to order one of his best scouts back to The Oaks. For his own peace of mind, he needed to know that his wife was not a spy. How would she feel, knowing that her own husband trusted her so little that he would spare one of his precious scouts to prevent her from spying?

But part of him did trust her. He trusted her with his heart and soul, opened himself to her as he had never imagined possible. He had always felt secure in the knowledge that he was in love with Mag. Yet what he felt now, the way he found it hard to breathe when she was near, told him how wrong he had been.

It was only since she became so ill and recovered that he knew the true meaning of the word love.

A branch snapped, and Ashton turned angrily to the sound, his hand raised for silence. A few more clumsy noises like that, and they would all be guests of the United States Army. If they were lucky.

His mind returned to Margaret. Her smile, the way she fumbled with her hair. She hadn't done that before, it was a new habit and, as with everything about her, he found it enchanting. Again, he pushed her from his mind.

He held the field glass to his eye. The time was right. He felt the peculiar sensation of his heart turning over, it happened every time before a raid. The excitement. The fear. His hand raised higher, and he sensed his men positioning themselves. This had to work.

"Now!" he rasped, and from all sides there was a thundering of horses' hooves pounding the damp grass, the hollow clump when they passed over stone. Each man knew his target, each man thoroughly understood his specific duty in this raid.

There was a blur of flashing rifles in the dark, the shouts of his own men, and the gasps of the startled Federals. Everything was going as planned. Some of his men were already leading dozens of Union soldiers, some clad only in their long johns, over the hill where more of his men were waiting to receive the prisoners.

Three of his raiders hurriedly stockpiled clothing, shoes and jackets and hats and as much underwear and blankets as they could carry. His men desperately needed the items. A barefoot cavalry would hardly spark fear in the enemy.

Others watched for the onslaught of Union troops that would sweep the area the instant they discovered what was happening. Ashton patrolled as the raid concluded, wandering behind a trio of tents, searching for any signs of trouble.

And within moments, he found it.

Even above the din of his own men and their activities, he heard the clattering of another cavalry just over the hill. The Yankees were on their way.

Ashton whirled Waffles around and galloped to the center of his frantic men. He whistled twice, the predetermined signal for the raid to conclude and for the party to dash as swiftly as possible to their own lines. Three extra lines of Confederate pickets were crouched in the bushes, readying as they heard the distinctive whistle.

The mounted men swiftly began their retreat, and Ashton took one look around the camp before he himself escaped. There, right beside a dying campfire, he saw Wade Corbett, one of his newest recruits, struggling with a Union soldier. Corbett's horse was nowhere to be seen, and even in the darkness of the night Ashton could see the wild fear in young Corbett's eyes.

Ashton aimed his pistol, but the men were rolling around so much that he could not fix his target without his own man coming into the sight.

He could hear the voices of the Feds now, hissing in anger, and knew his time had evaporated. With a galloping sweep, he bent down and pulled Corbett into his own saddle, praying that the extra weight wouldn't slow Waffles down enough to cause their capture.

Corbett was unconscious now, and Ashton used his

elbow to hold him in place, the same arm that held the reins.

But it was too late for escape. He was now surrounded by bluecoats, all pointing rifles at his head.

A single, frantic thought entered his mind: Margaret. He couldn't leave her, not like this. There was so much to say, so much needed to be made clear between them.

With a speed that stunned the approaching Federals, Ashton leaned in his saddle, still balancing Corbett, and scooped up the Union soldier who had struggled with the young man. Gripping the pistol, he rode slowly to an opening in the lines, using the startled Union soldier as a human shield.

Waffles stumbled once under the weight of the three men, but the horse seemed to understand the urgency of the situation and recovered his footing. Ashton thought, distractedly, that the Union man needed a bath.

Within a few moments they were almost to the edge of the forest. Soon his own pickets could cover for him.

The Federals, mounted and armed, stood in openmouthed wonder, still not believing the audacity of the man holding one of their own men.

"Sir?" It was the Union soldier Ashton was gripping.

"Yes, soldier," Ashton replied gruffly.

"I believe I am going to be sick." The man had a faint Irish accent.

"Soldier, please. I will let you go as soon as I reach my own lines, and my own men will cover your return. I vouch for that. But I beg of you, please do not soil this uniform . . ."

The man moaned, and Ashton, realizing he was almost safe, gently lowered him to the ground. He heard the click of rifles, and shouted.

"Hold fire, men. Let this soldier return to his camp. He has just saved my life."

And finally, Ashton and his rescued soldier were safe. Once back at camp, the men reveled in their success, telling and retelling the story of their general and his escape. Ashton himself sat with his men for a while, enduring the painfully lavish praise, slightly embarrassed.

It was a relief when at last he could return to his own tent and, just as the orange sun rose over the trees, he wrote a letter to Margaret.

CHAPTER
12

Margaret first noticed the man skulking about The Oaks four days after Ashton's departure. A linen towel, damp after her morning washing, was still in her hands as she glanced out the window of her room. From the corner of her eye she saw something move, a rustling in the distant trees, and she paused, wondering who in the world would be rattling the bushes at this early hour.

Instinctively, she stepped away from the window and continued to watch from the cover of a partially closed shutter. The man looked vaguely familiar, even at the distance of some four hundred yards. She rubbed her eyes, and it came to her who the man was.

It was one of Ashton's scouts.

For an instant she felt a surge of pure joy. Was Ashton coming home? Then the scout, perhaps aware that he had been seen, disappeared. She waited for him to reappear, for his bright red hair to again flash

178

within range, but it never did. It was as if he had vanished.

Carefully folding the towel and placing it on the wooden rack, her mind worked frantically, trying to determine why the scout may have returned. Clearly it wasn't to retrieve an extra pair of socks.

Then it hit her. The scout was on surveillance duty. Suddenly bits of extraneous information lined themselves up and presented a vivid picture to her. The hostility she had seen in everyone from Mrs. Thaw to Eddie, the tail-end glances she would catch when she spoke, Ashton's reluctance to tell her of his own whereabouts.

The plain truth was painfully obvious. Everyone, including her own husband, thought she was a spy.

Before anger could replace the raw hurt, Margaret noticed another movement about a dozen yards from the spot where Ashton's scout had been hiding.

"What the . . ." she whispered to herself, stunned by the sight of another furtive man in the shrubbery. This one wore a slouchy gray kepi and seemed to be following Ashton's scout. Margaret pulled up a straight-back chair to her hidden spot. This was rapidly becoming a most fascinating show.

Finally the two scouts, circling around each other, moved out of her line of vision. Unless she stuck her head out of the window, she would be unable to follow their path until they returned.

She bent down to lace up her half boots, gaiters, she heard them called, her eyes still focused outside. There was another movement, and her mouth dropped open. From where the rustling was, this would have to be a third man. He was placed a little further back than the twirling pair, his gaze intent on both of them.

Were they all Confederates? She was fairly certain

that Ashton's scout was there to watch her. But who sent the other men?

She stood up in clear sight of the three men, exposed fully in the open window. She squelched the almost overwhelming desire to wave at them, perhaps applaud. Instead she pretended to be simply stretching in the crisp autumn air.

All movement stopped. There was absolutely no indication that three grown men were lurking in the bushes.

"Thank you," she muttered in their general direction. For without their unintended help, she would not know exactly what the members of her new family thought of her.

And without their aid, she would have been able to convince herself that Ashton trusted her completely.

Breakfast at The Oaks, Margaret was rapidly learning, offered a very good argument for staying in bed. Although food in general was scarce, it was most apparent at the day's first meal. Traditional breakfast fare—eggs, bacon, cornmeal pancakes—was almost nonexistent. When it was found, when one of the scrawny hens gave up an egg, or a precious hog went to its final reward, Aunt Hattie invariably held the treat until supper. It was too special to waste on breakfast.

The entire household, as with every meal, would dutifully gather around the massive dining room table. There were special china breakfast plates, and a plainly patterned set of silverware, as if the war had not reduced the menu to cornmeal gruel. An ornate coffeepot, made of china but covered with a metallic glaze called lusterware, proudly held a brew made of everything from corn husks to peanut shells.

Ashton's mother remained distant. At first Margaret felt she simply didn't like her new daughter-in-law, but after a while she realized that Eliza Johnson seemed to be operating in a state of permanent despair. Only her sister Eppes seemed capable of bringing a smile to her thin face, usually by making some sort of silly, strange comment.

One morning Aunt Eppes declared that it was the Yankee women who started the war, for it was well known in the upper circles of Washington that the southern hostess, particularly the Virginia hostess, was far and away the most delightful breed in the world. The northern women, jealous of the attention and praise lavished by their husbands on the charm of southern women, planted the idea of war into their husbands' minds in order to free themselves of the competition. Another morning Aunt Eppes stated that General Quarles should have done the honorable thing by marrying her daughter Lizzie.

"Oh, Mother." Lizzie sighed. "Please. Let us not bring up that tired subject again. You know full well that it was I who broke the engagement with the general, not he. I was not in love with him, Mother. And by mutual consent, after I explained my feelings, we decided not to marry."

"But your cousin Sam Jones says . . ." began Aunt Eppes.

"Sam is also a general now, Mother, and has little enough time to bother with gossip." Eppes drew a hurt expression, her forehead dissolving into deep lines, and Lizzie winked at Margaret. "I am sorry, Mother."

But Ashton's mother smiled, and Eppes, upon seeing her sister's face, gracefully changed the subject.

This morning, however, the four women remained silent, each involved in her own contemplation. Margaret wondered if she should mention the men outside and decided against it, for fear of sending Aunt Eppes swooning. Perhaps she could confide in Lizzie.

"I've been thinking," Lizzie announced, causing the other women's heads to snap up.

"Very good, my dear," said Aunt Eppes.

Lizzie grinned at Margaret, who returned the smile before Lizzie continued. Then her face became serious, all traces of the impish grin vanished. "Mother, Aunt Eliza, and Mag—I really want you to hear what I have to say."

Margaret was curious now and put down her spoon.

"With Eddie and Ashton away, so gallantly serving the cause, it seems to me that we should do more than knit socks and save lint to make bandages."

Aunt Eppes was about to speak when Lizzie continued. "I believe we should turn The Oaks into a hospital and nurse soldiers right here."

Both Eppes and Eliza gasped, but Margaret felt the stirrings of excitement. For days she had done nothing but mope about aimlessly, certainly no good to the household or Ashton, and positively no good to herself. Even the scouts would soon grow weary of watching Margaret pace in circles.

This would give her purpose, direction—not to mention she would be of genuine help to men who desperately needed aid.

"Oh, Lizzie," exclaimed Margaret. "What a terrific idea! When I rode here last week, we passed homes with wounded soldiers on lawns and under trees. Surely we can . . ."

"No!" cried Eliza. "We will be ruined, I tell you. Four women alone in a household with strange men! Think of our reputations, Lizzie. Mag, too. Why, it simply isn't proper."

Lizzie had been prepared for this exact response from the older women and had even expected it from Mag. But strangely enough, Ashton's wife seemed eager to help. Lizzie cleared her throat before she began speaking again in calm, deliberate tones.

"Aunt Eliza, before the war it would, indeed, have been unseemly. But this is a different time and circumstance. The hospitals are overflowing, the nurses there are worked to exhaustion." She waited a moment, then spoke in a softer, less strident voice. "I'll ask my friend from Richmond to come here. She's helped arrange several hospitals, and she'll show us exactly what we need to do."

Eppes had regained her voice. "Lizzie, your aunt Eliza is right. It would be most indelicate. It is absolutely out of the question."

Margaret gathered the nerve to speak. "If Ashton or Eddie is wounded, I certainly hope any woman nearby, Yankee or Confederate, doesn't feel it's indelicate to nurse him."

There was a silence, and Eliza turned slowly and stared at Margaret as if for the first time. Margaret met her gaze unflinchingly, and she saw a slight softening around Eliza's mouth.

"You are right." She swallowed, her eyes suddenly moist. "Lizzie, make whatever arrangements you must. I'm sure Eppes and I will be happy to do our part."

Eppes was about to speak when Eliza's firm voice stated, "As I said, Eppes and I will do our part." And Eppes simply shook her head and returned to eating her breakfast.

Lizzie had written to her friend, an apparent human tornado named Mary B. Cox who had organized a half dozen hospitals in Richmond. A letter came to Lizzie by return mail, stating that while she was unable to leave Richmond at the moment, Lizzie and Margaret were welcome to travel there and see firsthand the workings of a hospital.

While Lizzie was busy with their travel plans, Margaret sat alone in her room, reading and rereading a pair of letters she had just received from Ashton.

Margaret was amazed to have the letters in her hand two days after the postmark indicated they had been mailed. This was the Confederacy in the last year and a half of the Civil War, and the fragmented mail system was still more efficient than in computer-driven, peacetime twentieth-century New York.

His first letter vaguely indicated his whereabouts, somewhere on the Tennessee–North Carolina border. Yet other than a few scattered references to camp life, the letter could have been penned by a business traveler resting before his next call.

The second letter mentioned a raid, and Margaret was surprised and delighted that he confided in her. Then she realized that he was merely trying to deflect credit for his daring escape. Of course, she had heard all about his close brush with the enemy, the Petersburg and Richmond newspapers were filled with her husband's last-moment dash over enemy lines.

Upon hearing of his narrow escape, Margaret was unable to find joy in his audacious ingenuity. Instead she fought the urge to cry at the very danger everyone else seemed to applaud. What about the next time? she wanted to scream. So he was very clever and lucky. What did it matter if he was caught or killed in the end?

She also knew that this event had not happened before, the first time history played itself out. This was a new twist. Surely she would have read about this exploit in her studies. It was exactly the sort of tidbit that scholars relish—the little anecdote that would illustrate how spunky the Confederates were and how very amusing history could be.

All things considered, she couldn't wait to reach Richmond. Anything was better than sitting in enforced idleness, waiting for precious letters that may or may not arrive, and wondering what life-threat-

ening misery her husband was enduring at that precise moment.

"No, please," Ashton groaned, rubbing his flat
stomach in genuine pain.

Sam Walker looked up from his own plate and
grinned. "Real maple syrup, General. I didn't credit
the information as accurate, sir. But those Yankees
must eat well. I'm sure they don't mind sharing a little
with their southern brethren."

"That is a point they might debate, Sam." Ashton
watched in alarm as his aide reached for the platter
with four pancakes remaining. "Sam, I believe you
should rest. You have eaten over a dozen pancakes. I
would not want to see you ill."

"I beg your pardon, General, but I did win the
pancake-eating contest at Magnolia. This is nothing."

"You did win that contest." Ashton sighed. "But
this is perhaps the last full meal you have consumed
since then. Have a little restraint now, and you may
eat them later if you wish."

Sam's two-pronged fork was poised between his
mouth and the sticky plate. "Have no fear, General."
His mouth opened wide to receive the folded pancake,
and he chewed shamelessly, a trickle of syrup spilling
down his chin.

Suddenly his ruddy face became ashen, and he
stopped chewing, as if the very action was distasteful.
He swallowed the remaining morsel in his mouth and
rose swiftly from the planked table.

"Sir?" he moaned, his arms folded over his midsec-
tion.

"Yes, Sam. You are dismissed." Ashton didn't have
time to complete the sentence before Sam bolted from
the tent, tripping over a wooden stake and muttering a
few oaths before he reached a distant tree.

The tent flap was still open when Ashton's scout arrived, issuing a crisp salute, his eyes on the remaining pancakes. "General, I have news of Mrs. Johnson, sir."

Ashton straightened in his chair and raked a distracted hand through his hair. "Please, Ben, help yourself to the pancakes. But first tell me what you have."

The scout glanced at his general, hesitating for a moment. He did not want to give him the information now, in case he would be banished from the tent and unable to eat the flapjacks. They were covered in syrup, and Ben felt his mouth water in anticipation.

The general seemed to read his mind. "The pancakes are yours, Ben. No matter what. Just tell me what is happening at The Oaks."

"Well, sir," Ben began uneasily. "Mrs. General Johnson is no longer there."

"She what?" The scout jumped at Ashton's tone, and he made an effort to lower his voice. "Forgive me. Please explain." His hands were placed on the table, the fingertips touching, a pose of infinite calm.

"She has gone to Richmond, sir, with your cousin Miss Giles. They took a gray horse named Pretzels and hitched her to an old rig. The horse seemed mighty mad, if I may add, sir."

"Why in blazes was she going to Richmond?"

"From what I could gather, sir, from listening under the window at night, they are going to turn The Oaks into a hospital."

"I don't believe it," Ashton murmured under his breath. Mag working with the sick and wounded? Could she have changed so drastically? He shook his head in disbelief.

"If they are turning The Oaks into a hospital, what are they doing in Richmond?"

"You see, sir, Miss Lizzie Giles has a friend who

186

knows how to set up a hospital. They are going to bring the knowledge back with them. Also, they need to clear the idea with the president. As you know, sir, civilian hospitals have a poor record. They lose more men than they save. So President Davis will not allow a civilian to organize a hospital without his permission."

Ashton gestured toward the platter, and the scout wasted no time pulling up a chair and digging into the pancakes.

There was something wrong, Ashton thought, rubbing his hand over his mouth. There must be more to the story.

"Oh, sir," the scout mumbled with his mouth full. He chewed hurriedly and swallowed. "There are at least two other men watching The Oaks. And from what I could gather, they both have their eyes on Mrs. General Johnson."

Ashton looked up at the scout, and the young man continued. "I do not know if they are Yankees or not, but one of them wears a Confederate hat. That means nothing, sir. I do know they were all gathering information on your wife's activities."

"Did either of them speak to her or have any sort of contact?"

The scout shook his head. "No, sir. But she kept on looking out of the window, as if she was expecting someone."

"Damn." Ashton spat. The scout looked alarmed, and Ashton managed to smile at him. "Enjoy your breakfast. You've done well."

At that, the general left the tent. He needed to be alone now, to think, to go over the facts as he now knew them. His wife was in Richmond, and he wondered if it was really to gather information for a hospital.

Or was his wife gathering information for the enemy?

The stench was overwhelming, a sticky-sweet fragrance mingled with the odor of rotting meat.

Margaret held a handkerchief over her mouth and nose, and Lizzie—her face suddenly very pale—did the same. Lizzie's friend Miss Cox didn't seem to notice the scent as she lead them briskly up the marble stairs. A yellow flag billowed overhead, proclaiming this building to be a Confederate hospital.

When they reached the top of the steps, Miss Cox turned to the two young women. "The awful part is that after a while, it doesn't disturb you."

Margaret was about to ask what she meant, for the nurse spoke as if they had been in the middle of a conversation. Then she heard the voices, the moans, some garbled sounds. And Margaret realized Miss Cox meant that she was no longer bothered by the smells and sounds and, she presumed, the sights.

It was cold in Richmond, a chilly breeze whipped the hem of their skirts and hinted at the coming winter. But the breeze did nothing to defuse the sound and musk of suffering.

"Before we enter, I need to tell you a few things," began Miss Cox. She was a lovely young woman, with clear green eyes and dark lashes, unusually white teeth, and a complexion that suggested she spent more time outdoors than was strictly fashionable. Her hair, a chestnut brown, was shiny and simply dressed, pulled back into a knotted braid at the nape of her neck. There was an inner vitality about her, a sense that although her duties as a nurse were taken seriously, she could also be a great deal of fun. Margaret was impressed, and so, apparently, was Jefferson Davis, for he had granted her the commission of major in the

Confederacy to allow her the leverage she needed in providing for the wounded soldiers.

"The men inside are all suffering, some more than others," warned Miss Cox. Margaret could tell she was gauging their reactions, anticipating a dramatic swoon or perhaps a delicate fit of vapors. Margaret unconsciously jutted her chin, and Lizzie stood straighter. Miss Cox smiled. "It's easy to be strong out here. Inside, you may not be able to carry on as bravely as you might wish. And I want you both to understand that any reaction you may have is completely natural, but try not to show your distaste to the men. Along with physical ailments, these are young men in a most unnatural setting, certainly not of their choosing. Some were handsome and are now disfigured. One young man was the best dancer at cotillions in Baton Rouge, and now he's lost a leg. Most are away from home for the first time. As a nurse, your duties will be simply to make them as comfortable as possible, to read or just hold their hands if you have the time, to tend to them tenderly when you do not. There are several Yankee patients in there, and you are to treat them no differently than you would Robert E. Lee himself—those young men are even more frightened than the others."

She paused, waiting for her words to sink in. When neither Lizzie nor Margaret made any motions to leave, Miss Cox continued.

"Now, for the time being I am going to ask you two to simply bathe the men's faces with a cloth. You are not ready for anything else, and this will give you an idea of what the hospital is really like. Don't be embarrassed if you wish to vomit, simply go behind a curtain or leave the hospital entirely. Just don't let the men see you. Do you both understand?"

Both nodded. Miss Cox stared at the women,

wondering if they would go the way of so many gently bred, well-meaning young ladies who had offered to nurse the wounded. Some were seeking adventure, others were hungry for romance, or at least suitable male companionship. The war had robbed parlors all over the South of men from sixteen to sixty. There were young women who should have been married by now and, instead, could barely recall how to speak to a beau.

Most nurses lasted a half day, just long enough to realize there was nothing romantic about lice and gangrene, just long enough for the more sensible, coherent patients to fully understand why they left so quickly.

But some women did stay. The daintiest of ladies occasionally astonished her with an ability to assist with an amputation one moment and laugh gaily with a recovering soldier the next. Perhaps Lizzie would be able to withstand the rigors, both emotional and physical, of nursing the men. Miss Cox wasn't quite sure of the other woman, Mrs. Johnson. Before meeting her in person, she had merely heard that the general's new wife was a beauty and an accomplished flirt. There were also rumors that she was some sort of spy or courier for the Union, but everyone with a family member in the North was suspected of being a spy, especially if that person happened to be as dazzling in face and form as Mrs. Johnson.

"Excuse me, Miss Cox," began the general's wife.

"Please, call me Mary B.," said Miss Cox with a smile.

"Mary B.?" Margaret's question was forgotten.

Lizzie and Mary B. exchanged glances, as if they had heard the same line of questioning a hundred times. "It stands for my middle name, Barksdale," explained Mary B. "Most women in my family are named Mary, so we all use our middle name initials to differentiate."

Margaret nodded, slightly perplexed. In this day and age, it usually took years of close friendship to call another by a first name, and she had only just met Miss Cox. On the other hand, they would most certainly be working together closely in this crisis, and this was hardly a place where social niceties could be strictly observed.

Southerners during the Civil War, she concluded, were an altogether eccentric breed.

The three women entered the hospital together, a building, Margaret learned, which had once been used as a grain warehouse. There was not enough grain in the entire Confederacy now to warrant the space. There wasn't enough of *anything* except wounded and diseased soldiers, and those the South had in abundance.

The odor was overwhelming as her eyes adjusted to the dim light. Mary B. probably had them stand outside for so long to allow Lizzie and herself the chance to get used to the stench a little at a time.

The inside of the hospital was a sight unlike any Margaret could ever conjure. There were a few dozen cots; the rest of the men were spread on the floor in what appeared to be a haphazard fashion. For a moment it looked as if the floor itself were alive and crawling, but it was merely an optical illusion created by the writhing movements of some of the men.

From the doorway it was difficult to comprehend the men as individuals. One seemed identical to the next, with the sole distinguishing feature being a missing arm or a filthy bandage wrapped about the head. The clothing of all of the men was tattered and soiled, the original color or fabric dulled long ago by the grime of gunpowder and sweat and mud.

There were puddles on the floor; no area that was free of a human body was free of some sort of liquid. A slender, stoop-shouldered old man in what appeared to be a butcher's apron made his way down the aisle to the women, wiping his hands as he walked.

Mary B. greeted him warmly. "Dr. Parish, I have brought you two more nurses."

The doctor squinted at them and nodded. "I do hope, Miss Cox, that these ladies are able to withstand the rigors of this position better than that unfortunate duo you delivered to us last week."

Mary B.'s face remained frozen in a smile as she spoke to the doctor. "Thank you so much for reminding me, Dr. Parish."

At that the doctor raised his head, a scrawny bulb covered with downy white hair, and let out a raspy laugh. Suddenly Margaret was prepared to like him very much.

"The doctor," said Mary B., "has saved more lives than anyone can count. He's the main reason the men lucky enough to find their way to this hospital are given a fighting chance."

The doctor dismissed her flattery with a grunt. Mary B. made an open-palmed gesture, as if she was about to introduce the new nurses, when he abruptly turned his back and began creeping past them.

"Spare me the introductions, Miss Cox," he muttered. "If they stay any length of time, I'll make their acquaintance. If they leave, well . . ." His voice trailed off as he stopped to bend over a soldier, placing a hand on the young man's arm. He had mentally dismissed them.

"He's a dear, once you pass muster," whispered Mary B. She led them to a small wood shelf with chipped bowls stacked next to some dingy-looking rags and a half-full earthenware jug of water. After pouring some water into two of the bowls and handing them to Lizzie and Margaret, she pointed to the rags.

"Ladies, you are on your own now. I'll be here, of course, but don't call me unless it's an emergency. Bathe their faces, talk to them if they are awake. That is about all you can do today."

With that she left them. Lizzie stared at the bowl, then up at Margaret. "Mag," she said softly, "I'm not sure I can do this."

Margaret felt the exact same way, but refused to voice her fears. "We must, Lizzie." She grasped two rags and passed one to Lizzie. "Just imagine the soldiers are Ashton or Eddie."

"But some of them are Yankees."

"And as Mary B. said, they are even more frightened than the others. Let's not talk about it." Margaret picked up the hem of her skirt and gave Lizzie a wan smile of encouragement. "We have to do something, Lizzie. We must help them—it's only fair."

As Margaret walked away, Lizzie stood frozen for a few moments. Then, slowly, she walked to the other end of the aisle to begin her tour.

Margaret now poured her full attention into the job at hand. She began with the first man in the first row. He was young, perhaps in his late teens, and was lying motionless on a frayed blanket. A battered hat served as his pillow, and Margaret would have thought he was dead, but she saw the slow rise and fall of his chest as he breathed.

She bent over him and realized her hoops shot out behind her, right into the face of another patient. Mumbling a few choice words, she tried to adjust herself, but the space was too narrow.

"The hoops will have to go, ma'am." It was the young soldier, a faint grin on his face as he watched her struggle. With his eyes opened he appeared even more youthful, an unlined face with good-natured humor etched on the corners of his mouth.

Margaret returned the smile. "I'm glad," she confided. "I've been dying for an excuse to get rid of the hoops."

"If you don't mind some advice, ma'am, you can just pull the drawstring at your waist, and the hoop will collapse at your feet faster than an old dog on a hot day. I beg your pardon."

With her eyes wide in feigned shock, she placed the bowl and rag on the floor and, with one finger, reached into the waistband of the tartan plaid skirt and released the crinoline. It came to the ground with a whoosh, and the soldier's mouth dropped to his chest.

"I didn't mean right here, ma'am!"

"Well, never mind. I thank you for the advice." She unceremoniously stepped out of the petticoat and whisked it around the corner, propped against a wall. Now she was able to kneel by the soldier, whose expression of surprise had given way to a hoarse chuckle.

Dipping the rag into the bowl, she gently wrung out the excess water and was about to wash his face. But she halted when she saw the young man's sudden frown.

"Don't you want me to wash your face?"

"Well, ma'am," he answered slowly, biting his lower lip when he paused. "It's not that, exactly."

"Please, tell me what's wrong," Margaret urged.

"It's just that . . . well, begging your pardon, ma'am, but this will be the eighth time today my face has been bathed by some fancy lady. I don't know how much longer my skin will last at this rate."

They stared at each other for a few moments, and suddenly Margaret began to giggle. The soldier, relieved that he hadn't offended her, joined her, never taking his eyes off her extraordinary face.

"As you can probably tell, I'm new at this," she confided.

"I get all the new ones, ma'am, being the first man in the first row and all. Sometimes they leave after me, other times they get as far as Jeb Thompson down yonder."

"Well," Margaret said defiantly, "I intend to stay as long as I'm needed." She put the bowl aside and smiled at the soldier. "Is there anything I can do for you?"

He shrugged weakly. "I could use a little company, if you don't mind. I have four sisters at home, and I sure miss female talk."

"Four sisters? So that's how you knew how to remove a petticoat."

His sudden blush was his only answer, so she changed the topic. "Where are you from?"

"Tullahoma, Tennessee, ma'am," he answered.

Her mind worked to think of something else to say. She thought of asking if he missed his home and decided immediately against such a stupid question. He seemed shy, so she didn't want to ask if he had a sweetheart back home.

"It's muddy there," the soldier said.

"Excuse me?"

"In Tullahoma. It gets real muddy this time of year and in the spring, too. They say Tullahoma is an old Indian word."

"Really?" Margaret shifted slightly. "What does it mean?"

"Well, 'tulla' is Indian for mud. And 'homa' is Indian for 'more mud.'"

It took a few moments for Margaret to realize the joke, and when she did, she looked down to see the young man staring expectantly at her. When she began to laugh, he grinned, pleased with himself.

"Allow me to introduce myself, ma'am. I'm Private Spence Pender, although I don't get much 'private' anything since I've been here." He reached up and she clasped his hand.

"It's wonderful to meet you, Private Spence Pender of Mud, More Mud, Tennessee. I'm Margaret Johnson of, let's see, Petersburg, Virginia."

The grin faded from his face. "Johnson of Petersburg? Are you any kin to General or Major Johnson?"

Apprehensively, she nodded.

"Why, it's a real honor to meet you. A real honor. My cousin James says Major Johnson is some wizard of an engineer. He designed a bridge in no time flat, and an entire brigade was able to get over it before the Yankees knew what had happened. And the general, well . . ."

Margaret said nothing, but her expression must have encouraged him. "The general is something else, ma'am. I'd rather have one General Johnson on our side than a hundred Meades, that's for sure. Did you hear about what happened last week? He fought off a whole swarm of Yankees using one of their own men as a shield! I'm sure you knew that, being kin and all. Are you a cousin?"

"No, well. Actually, I think I am, but primarily I'm his wife."

"Mrs. General Johnson? Blazes! Wait till I tell James that Mrs. General Johnson washed my face!"

"Wait until I tell him," she whispered, "that you told me how to remove my petticoat."

Private Pender blanched until he saw that Margaret was trying to keep from chuckling. "Well, Private," she began. "I don't want to make a liar of you."

He gave her a perplexed look, and she placed the damp cloth on his forehead. "Do you suppose your skin can take it?"

The soldier nodded stoically, and for the first time in two weeks, he forgot all about the bullet in his thigh.

CHAPTER
13

~~~

After three months of nursing the soldiers, of picking up the hems of her skirts heavy with blood and water, holding hands with wounded boys too young to leave their mothers and men too old to fight, of the constant stench of death and the sight of raw flesh and continuous suffering, Lizzie Giles had to leave Richmond. She knew she was becoming a liability; her increasing discomfort was obvious to all who saw her. It was time for her to go home, back to The Oaks, where she would face nothing more than the usual wartime difficulties and the occasional outbursts of her mother bemoaning her broken engagement to General Quarles.

Gone were her dreams of becoming a nurse or of turning The Oaks into a civilian-run hospital. She now understood why Mary B. had insisted that they come to Richmond. It was easy to send one nurse home but nearly impossible to ask wounded soldiers to find a new place to recover. Had she turned The

Oaks into a hospital, it would have been an absolute disaster.

"I feel so guilty, leaving you here like this," she confessed to Margaret as she tightened the strap of her trunk. The management of the bustling Spotswood Hotel was delighted at the prospect of a free room. Margaret was staying, doubling up with Mary B., to nurse as long as she was needed.

No one was more surprised than Margaret herself at her ability to comfort the men, at her instinctive knowledge of what to say and, more importantly, what not to say to the patients. Of course she had the advantage of twentieth-century pop psychology. In the back of her mind were all of the articles on post-traumatic stress syndrome, studies that began during World War I on the fragile emotions of men who had been exposed to the horrendous sights and dangers of warfare.

On the other hand, she had to temper her knowledge with a healthy dose of ignorance. This was a vastly different age from her own. These were God-fearing rural folk with no set notions of human rights. There was no Geneva Convention, no firm convictions that one should protest a war you didn't believe in. She had to respect their unshakable belief in honor and duty and God. It was an alien foundation to her, and she made every effort to understand these men.

"Don't feel guilty," soothed Margaret. "You're needed at The Oaks. And you tried, Lizzie. You did more than most people would have. You were brave and did more good than you'll ever imagine."

"I also threw up on several patients."

"Ah, but they were honored," she answered with a grin. "One of the men said it was a far sight better than having Dr. Parish bend over with his whiskey breath."

Lizzie smiled, and stared at Margaret for a few moments. "I never would have believed it, Mag. You are absolutely selfless with those men, even the vulgar ones. Ashton is right, you have changed."

"More than you know." Margaret thoughtfully patted a strand of hair that had escaped her prim snood. "Actually, this is the first thing I have ever done to really help others. All of my studying and schooling before was an escape from the world, from having to deal with real people and their imperfections and frailties. I was afraid before, but now, I think because of Ash, I am learning to be less judgmental, not to form snap conclusions about people based on their appearances or their accents." She glanced at Lizzie and shrugged apologetically. "Sorry."

"No need." She leaned over and hugged Margaret. "Are you sure you'll be all right sharing a room with Mary B.?"

Returning the embrace, Margaret nodded. She would genuinely miss Lizzie in the brief moments she had to herself. And the even briefer moments she wasn't writing to Ashton.

She hadn't received a letter from him in over ten days, and she tried not to dwell on the reasons she hadn't heard from him. The last letter had been extra long and pensive, filled with warmth and humor. Again, there had been no mention of his exact whereabouts, but Margaret suspected he was somewhere in the vicinity of Chattanooga.

His birthday had come and gone weeks ago, and still no word. She welcomed the numb exhaustion each night, the dreamless sleep that overtook her before she was able to imagine him ill or wounded, before her mind could substitute one of the scores of dying men she was nursing for Ashton, lying in torment on a cold, hard floor.

Suddenly the door of the small room flew open. It

was Mary B., breathless and disheveled—she'd been working since five that morning, scraping together breakfast for the men. She didn't even look at Lizzie.

"Mag," she gasped. "Dr. Parish told me to get you—it's Private Pender."

"No! He's been doing so well . . ." She grabbed her shawl and turned to Lizzie.

"Go," urged Lizzie with a wave. "I'll write from home."

But Margaret was already running down the hallway with Mary B.

"What happened?" She clutched the banister, her full blue skirts in the other fist. She was wearing the same indigo dress, a gown she would hate with a passion if she was able to spare the time or the emotion. Over the dress was an apron made of a rough greenish cotton, the only spare fabric around. Its wide-yoked bib and loose skirt covered her dress, and the large pockets were stuffed with clean cloths and pencils and paper, whatever she might need when with the patients.

"Dr. Parish suspects part of the thigh bone was grazed by the ball. We thought he was so lucky, but apparently a bone fragment has sliced an artery."

"My God. Will the doctor operate?" They were on Main Street now, heedless of the stares of well-heeled pedestrians, ignoring the gray-clad officers who turned down the street just as the women scurried up Seventh Street to the hospital steps. Their flattened skirts and aprons immediately identified them as nurses to everyone, the lack of hoops a sure sign of their devotion to the cause.

The tallest soldier fixed a hazel gaze on the woman in the familiar blue dress, startled by both her dark-haired beauty and her alarmed expression. His gray wool cape was dusty, a tumble of wavy auburn hair brushed his shoulders, and the wide-brimmed felt cavalry hat was at a rakish angle, but the other officers eyed him with awe.

"General?" Sam Walker asked.

Ashton said nothing, simply followed his wife into the building.

Margaret tried to contain her panic as she entered the ward and saw the commotion around the first bed in the first row. In the past few months Spence Pender and Margaret had become genuine friends, and she had grown to rely on him to help her through the grueling moments, cheering her with a wink and a gentle word, praising her growing skills as she passed the rank of face washer and was given more responsibility. Dr. Parish now knew her name, as did every man in the ward, and Mary B. had become a friend as well as her overseer, but Spence was special.

He was soon to go home, back to Mud, More Mud, as he said, and she was planning a small party. Spence did have a sweetheart back home, Lydia. He thought okra tasted like soap and his mother's buttermilk biscuits were so light they could float away.

Earlier in the week he had gestured toward the next blanket where a wounded Yankee lay, and said, "I can't figure out this war. Here's the nicest guy in the world, but because he's from up North, some other guy shot him. For all I know, I could have been the one to fire on him. There's a war going on, but when you meet the other soldiers, all we understand is that we're trying to kill each other, and nobody's mad."

Dr. Parish was leaning over him, and blood was everywhere. Spence was lying pale and motionless, his eyes closed. The doctor saw Margaret and shook his head softly, and she tried not to cry. There would be time later on for that.

"Mrs. Johnson," said the doctor. "Could you please hold your hand here?" She eased over Spence and placed her finger on the inside of his thigh, and the doctor backed away.

Spence opened his eyes and smiled at Margaret. "I'm so glad you are here," he whispered.

"Private Pender," began the doctor with more tenderness than Margaret had ever seen him display. "Listen to me carefully. There is no hope for you, son. When Mrs. Johnson removes her finger, you will bleed to death. Do you understand?"

There was no response, and Dr. Parish was about to repeat his statement when Spence grasped Margaret's free hand. "I'm so scared." His voice tore from his throat, harsh and broken.

"I'm here, Spence." Margaret leaned close to his ear, careful not to move her finger from his thigh. "Dr. Parish." She turned to see the doctor moving to another patient. "Can't you do something?"

Even as she spoke she realized the futility of the plea. This was the medical Middle Ages. The patients and even Dr. Parish thought she was addled for washing her hands before attending a wound and trying to boil the rags before they were reused as bandages. What did she expect the doctor to do—perform microsurgery at a time when hundreds of people died from contaminated water?

"I will stay here forever," she whispered into Spence's ear, hoping he missed the waver in her voice. Unexpectedly, he smiled.

"Now, Mrs. Johnson, what on earth would the general say about that?"

"I don't suppose he would be surprised, especially when he discovers that you are the one who ordered me to drop my petticoats." She was perilously close to losing complete control, and for the very first time in her life she felt as if she might faint. Spence made a motion that Margaret assumed was a silent laugh, and she took a deep, steadying breath.

"Have you received a letter from him today?" Spence's tone was almost conversational. She couldn't believe he had just been given a death sentence, and he was asking her about the mail.

"No. Maybe tomorrow." And she realized that for Spence, there would be no tomorrow.

"I want you to write Lydia and my folks, if you don't mind. Tell them how much I love them, and tell my mom that I believe I was ready to meet the Almighty. Could you do that?"

"Spence." Margaret was unable to say anything else. She swallowed hard. "Of course I'll write them."

His hand tightened in her grasp. Everything became very quiet, the usual din fell away. With her eyes closed, Margaret leaned her forehead on their clasped hands. "Our Father, who art in heaven," she whispered. She hadn't prayed since she was a child, but somehow it seemed to be the only thing for her to do.

Spence joined her. "Hallowed be thy name. Thy kingdom come, thy will be done . . ."

As they recited the Lord's Prayer, Margaret imagined she heard Ashton's voice, soft and distant, and the notion was strangely comforting.

Standing away, his hat in his hands, Ashton watched his wife and the young soldier with cascading emotions. He was suddenly humbled by her and ashamed by his own actions of posting a scout to watch her. Her letters had emphasized her weariness, her longing to see him, but he interpreted her words as exaggeration. Now he saw her, and in spite of her exhaustion and paleness, she was more beautiful than ever.

He had seen lady nurses before, bored wives or eager young women seeking excitement and romance. They made little secret of their dislike of the more mundane duties.

His scout informed him that Margaret had thrown herself into nursing with a rare fervor, and the scout had been right. What Margaret was doing now, her hands trickling with blood, was beyond what most hardened men could bear.

The prayer was over, and Margaret kissed the private's hand. The young man smiled. "Mrs. Johnson." His voice was low. "I want you to know, I mean, I have never met a lady like you before. You sure are pretty, but even if you had a face like a hunk of pickled meat, I do believe any man could love you."

His voice trailed off, and Margaret pressed harder on his thigh. It didn't seem to be working anymore, she couldn't stop the blood, warm and sticky on her hands. She leaned close to him. "And I do believe, Spence Pender, that any woman would love you."

Spence took a deep breath, and his unfocused eyes turned to her. "I'm not scared anymore." He swallowed once. "You can let go now."

"No."

"Please. If you don't do it now, I might get scared again. Let go."

A pair of strong gloved hands gripped her shoulders, and she instinctively rested her cheek against one. The hands were gently pulling her away, and, with her eyes wide but unseeing, she slowly removed her hand from his thigh. Blood shot out in great spurts, gradually lessening, and within a few moments it had stopped altogether.

Margaret turned, and her eyes met Ashton's, and only a small moan passed her lips before she went limp in her husband's arms.

The brisk December air stung her cheeks, and with the groggy veil of unconsciousness slipping away, she pulled an unsteady hand over her eyes. Ashton was speaking to someone, his voice a low rumble next to her ear, and the wool of his greatcoat seemed to envelop her.

This was not how she had imagined their reunion. In her mind it would be a romantic meeting, Margaret prepared and looking her very best, Ashton perhaps a little hasty and battle-worn. In the idyllic scene she pictured, Margaret would not mention the men who had been watching her. She would wait for a day or so, for their love to be rekindled before she asked him, gently, of course, who the men could possibly be.

This was not at all what she had imagined.

"Margaret, can you hear me?"

Reluctantly, she opened her eyes, not quite ready to face the world. Spence Pender was dead, a fact she could scarcely comprehend. A few moments ago he was alive and speaking to her, now he was gone.

Ashton held her in his lap on the front steps of the hospital, his broad back shielding her from the stares of the curious citizens of Richmond. His hair was longer, his face seemed harder than before, but still he was magnificent.

"You jerk," she muttered.

He looked perplexed, then apologetic. "I'm sorry if I jerked you, love. I just wanted to get you away from the sickness inside and into the fresh air, so I . . ."

"No, you are the jerk, the rotten husband who . . ."

"Lieutenant, I believe I can handle this." Ashton's head snapped up to the young officer standing uncomfortably by their side. The officer needed no other prodding. In two strides he had escaped around the corner, where the other men stood.

"I'm delighted to see you feeling so much better." He lifted her to her feet, and she grasped his powerful arms for support.

"You have been spying on me this whole time." Her

voice was flat, and Ashton's eyes immediately softened.

"Inside, Margaret, you were extraordinary. I had heard that you were wonderful with the patients, but I . . ."

"From your spy? Did he give you the details?"

"No, damn it. From Lizzie, and, well, other sources."

"The spy."

Ashton pulled her close, and the gray cape encircled her. She tried to duck away, but he held her to his side.

"What was I supposed to do, Mag? There are rumors that you do help your brother. I posted a man to watch you to clear your name as much as anything else."

"Oh, no problem," she bit. "Nothing like a little marital trust, is there? Is this going to become a regular pattern? Everytime you suspect I'm doing something you don't particularly like, I'll see three men lurking around, just waiting to report to the boss?"

"Who are the other men," he whispered. It wasn't a question, it was a demand.

"I have no idea. Don't you?"

He said nothing, his piercing gaze holding her close. Finally he let out a thick sigh. "No."

Margaret suddenly felt completely drained. Ashton looked every bit as exhausted as she felt. Tears blurred her vision, and she reached up and placed her hand on his cheek, slightly scratchy with a light growth of whiskers.

"Ash," she breathed. He was alive and with her, and she had done nothing to show him how exquisite it was to see him. "Happy birthday."

He glanced down, and a small smile tugged on his mouth. "Ah, Margaret. I've envisioned our reunion many times. Somehow, no matter how many versions I dreamed of, it was never like this."

They remained silent for a few moments, heedless of the bustling street sounds behind them, the grinding carriage wheels, the squeaking springs below passenger rigs, hooves clamping with gaits as individual as the riders. They walked slowly down the steps, Margaret relying heavily on his arm for support. At the bottom of the stairs, on a narrow wooden sidewalk, Ashton leaned against a hitching post and shook his head.

"So you really have no idea who the other two men watching you are?" He adjusted the shawl over her shoulders, and she shook her head. He still wore his gloves, soft buff yellow with large, bell-like cuffs.

"Nope. But I suggest next time you choose a scout, make sure his hair isn't bright red. Your guy is hard to miss."

"I was hoping he would have blended in with the autumn foliage." He laughed. "I wanted to get one more mission out of him before the first snow. You put him against a white background, and you might as well have a brass band announcing your arrival."

Margaret looked up at him, squinting against the dull sun. "How are you? I mean, how are you feeling, how have the missions gone, have you been hurt?"

"I'm fine." He reached for her hand. "But I'm better now."

"What are you doing here?"

There was a slight hesitation before he answered, and a surge of anger made Margaret pull away.

"I am not a spy, Ashton. I have no recollection of events here until I was ill, and in case you haven't noticed, I, too, have been rather busy. There are very few military secrets to be had in a hospital filled mostly with privates." She turned swiftly and began walking back to the Spotswood Hotel.

A small crowd had gathered to watch them, the famous general and his lovely wife. Ashton followed her, very aware of the attention they were attracting.

"Margaret, come here," he said between clenched teeth.

She stopped, her back to him for several long seconds, her heel tapping angrily on the walk before she pivoted to face him. "For your own information, General, if I did happen to be a spy, you would never know. Unlike Belle Boyd or Rose Greenhow, I would not feel a compulsion to tell the world of my exploits. The secret would go to the ground with me."

With that she turned sharply. Unfortunately for her graceful retreat, the toe of her boot caught on the long hem of her dress, and Margaret fell face forward onto the slatted wooden sidewalk. Her hands had been clutching the shawl, so nothing was able to soften her fall.

There was a stunned silence, a gentle gasp from a woman in an oversize green bonnet. Margaret lay for a moment with her face on the filthy wood, waiting for Ashton to come over and help her to her feet.

He didn't come.

Instead he crossed his arms, waiting to see how much longer she would remain in that awkward position. The crowd glanced from Margaret's prone form to her husband's, the shock dissolving into grins of amusement. The men were especially entertained, most of the women cringed softly.

Slowly, she rose to her knees, her hair falling loose, one hand covering her nose.

"Um, Ash?" Her voice was pleading. "I think it's broken."

His eyebrows arched and he went to her side, raising her to her feet.

"My nose." Her voice was muffled behind cupped hands. "I think my nose is broken."

"If it is," he whispered, "it's no more than you deserve."

With a swift motion he removed his gloves and placed them in his pocket, then tenderly removed her hands from her face. The crowd was moving on now. There wasn't much to see; the excitement was over.

Her eyes were brimming with tears, and her nose was painfully red. Ashton winced but soon smiled. "It's not broken, Margaret. It will be fine for the ball."

"What ball?"

"For the ball at the Davises. I'm seeing the president tomorrow, so he suggested I come a day early and take you to their ball tonight."

"Great," she moaned miserably, taking the arm he offered, her other hand still cradling her nose. Sniffing once, she realized it was beginning to bleed.

"Wait a moment, Mag." He tilted her head back, reaching into another pocket for a handkerchief. "It should stop in a while."

The sound of footsteps clattered behind Ashton, and Margaret saw the outraged expression on his aide-de-camp's face. "General, sir," he stated sharply. "I had heard that you and your wife had some harsh words, but never, sir, and I repeat, never would I imagine you to be the type of man to actually strike a woman!"

Ashton opened his mouth to explain, when his eyes caught Margaret's, and for the first time since they had been reunited, they were both able to laugh.

The lock of hair was sand-colored with a slight curl. Margaret touched the ends, watching them spring back into place.

Both of the letters Spence had asked her to write were completed, to his mother and to his sweetheart, Lydia. Mary B. had clipped a large swatch of his hair, and she divided the lock between the two letters, securing them with threads pulled from her apron.

The letter to Spence's mother was tucked into a package containing his watch, a small pocketknife, and the letters his mother had sent him since he entered the army eight months earlier.

Her hands felt clumsy using the thick pen, having to dip it back into the ink bottle after a few words. The first word formed with a newly dipped pen was invariably splotched, then it became easier as the ink ran out, finally leaving nothing but a light scratch on the paper. She had never thought of the technology behind a ballpoint pen, or even a fountain pen, but now she would have appreciated one more than she could have ever imagined. The letters were difficult to write in content alone; the last thing she wanted to worry about was the finicky pen.

Ashton walked into the room, a bulky package under his arm. The desk clerk at the Spotswood, beaming at the thought of having the famous General Johnson as an unexpected guest, had been able to procure a room for them.

"How does your nose feel?" The package slid onto the bed and, without taking his eyes from her, he pulled off his gloves.

"Like Karl Malden's," she replied absently, her attention still focused on the letters she had just written, and of the overwhelming sadness she felt over Spence Pender's death.

"Who is Karl Malden?"

Margaret turned to her husband, and his breath caught in his throat. Had she always been this beautiful? The strange, almost violet-colored eyes, her hair so black that the light reflected off the smooth surface as easily as off a mirror, the skin glowing with a translucent luster, iridescent as a rare pearl.

"He's an actor with a hat who tells people not to leave home without their American Express cards."

It took a moment for Ashton to respond to her answer. She had been making strange comments lately, odd remarks that he couldn't quite follow. Before he had attributed her unusual observations to her illness. An officer of his had behaved in a similar fashion after losing an arm at Malvern Hill—he insisted that his missing limb had gone on without him, and his eyes searched about constantly for the arm, waiting to meet up with it around every next corner, each new bend in the road. He spoke with such conviction that Ashton actually caught himself looking for a lone arm. After that Ashton had the man discharged, concerned that his entire brigade would soon be following orders of the phantom limb.

With Margaret, he had assumed the odd comments and her inability to recall past events seemed to be linked. He would have tried to help her, to gently prod her memory and ask her to clarify her strange remarks, but the overall change in her personality had been so extraordinary, he was afraid to alter a single aspect.

Once she had been a vain, emotionally selfish woman whom he had loved in spite of her obvious flaws. Now she was slightly scatterbrained and delightfully unpredictable, but there was a gentleness about her, a kindness that would be rare enough in any person and unheard of in a woman with her striking beauty. This new Mag was unafraid of fighting, of risking reputation for the sake of nursing soldiers, of showing the entire world her likes and dislikes. And above all, this new Mag seemed to love him. It was certainly worth putting up with the multitude of quirks for that one thing alone.

He walked to where she was sitting, her nose slightly red, her slender white fingers spotted with black ink.

After today he did not believe she was ever a spy. But one worry gnawed at the back of his mind: How did her outburst appear to the dozens of people who saw her on the street? With the war turning so suddenly against the Confederacy, everyone was searching for some place—or some person—on which to place the blame. Her words today could easily be twisted and misconstrued. Hell, even taken verbatim, without the embellishments every witness would most certainly add, her impromptu speech could sound like a blatant admission of guilt.

"Have you ever gotten used to writing these?" Her voice was so soft he leaned forward to listen. She gestured weakly to the letters for Spence Pender's family.

"No," he admitted, his hand on the back of her neck, gently kneading the tension from her muscles. "Every time I have to write a mother or a wife, I think to myself—this is the worst thing I have ever had to do. And then, all too soon, I find myself writing to another man's mother or wife, the same words attached to different names. The more you know the person, the more difficult it is. But one thing might make it a little easier, Margaret."

"What?" Her eyes were very large, searching.

Without removing his hand from her nape, he pulled up a chair and sat down, their eyes almost level now. "Just remember how very much your words will mean to the person receiving the letter. No matter how difficult it is for you to write, it will be infinitely more difficult to be the one reading the words for the first time. But everything you can add, each personal recollection or special memory, will be something the bereaved ones will cling to as they recover. Your letter will be cherished as a final link. The sooner you can send the letters off, the sooner his family can begin to recover from the loss."

They remained silent for a long moment, a comfortable silence of shared companionship. Then she looked at him, his eyes creased in the corners, a slow, sweet smile forming on his lips. "Thank you," she whispered.

He pulled back, the smile soon dissolving. "You're exhausted," he stated, pulling her over to the soft, inviting bed.

With a single nod, she sat on the bed, her shoulders slumping. "We have a few hours before we're due at the Executive Mansion." He was already unbuttoning her blue dress. "Why don't you take a nap?"

Instead of slipping the dress over her head, Margaret shrugged her shoulders, sending it crumpling into a circular heap at her feet. She was wearing a simple camisole and lightly laced drawers, and Ashton swallowed hard, feeling like a lecherous monster for the thoughts that were rampaging in his mind. If he had any decency, he would simply tuck her in bed and then read a book, but he was unable to avert his gaze. Never had he wanted a woman the way he wanted Margaret.

Her eyes were closed, and her head was tilted back, exposing the gentle column of her throat, smooth and white. He reached out, intending to brush a strand of hair from her neck, but she sighed heavily.

"Oh, Ash, I have missed you so." She was thinking of all the awful sights and smells she had experienced in the past few weeks, of the strange feel of a patient's arms, the dirt and filth that assaulted her daily. Ashton was clean and familiar, his scent welcome, the feel of his body comforting. He alone could banish the horrors from her soul.

"Margaret." His mouth was upon hers, bruising, impossibly sweet.

And Margaret suddenly realized that she needed

him far more desperately than she needed a few hours of sleep.

The Confederate Executive Mansion was vastly different from its counterpart in Washington City. A private home before Jefferson Davis and his wife and children took residence, it was smaller and lacked the sprawling landscaping of the White House. Still, Margaret couldn't help but be impressed. The square home was gloriously lit that evening, casting an orange glow down Clay Street.

Margaret stood motionless, her arm hooked through Ashton's, watching the scene inside unfold. Behind the panes of glass Margaret could see the slightly distorted figures, women draped in satin and silk, men in gray uniforms or stiff frock coats. All took on a spectral luster under the gas jets, a slightly garish gleam on fabrics, brilliant stabs of light flickering from some of the jewels clasped about white throats and tucked above small gloved hands.

Her eyes flicked to a balcony on the first floor in the rear, barely visible from their spot slightly to the left of the main entrance.

"Is that where the little boy fell?" she asked Ashton in a hushed tone.

"What little boy?"

"The little Davis child," she replied.

Ashton looked down at his wife, an uncomfortable chill spreading down his spine. She was behaving strangely tonight, and he wondered if perhaps the strains of nursing were too much for her to manage.

Earlier that night, following an afternoon of glorious lovemaking, he had presented her with a package. It was one of her own gowns, a delicate creation of pale silks with a scalloped hem fixed with satin flowers of pinks and lavenders. Last year she had spoken of little else but the gown, reporting in detail every bit of progress, from procuring the fabric from a Havana-based blockade runner to commissioning a French-born seamstress to sew it. He had had it sent from Magnolia, posted by his gardener there, stunned that she had left it behind.

When she opened the brown paper wrapping, she was clearly delighted, and she just as clearly had no memory of the dress. She held it up to her slender form, twirling in the mirror, asking him how on earth did he buy it when simple bread was fetching five dollars a loaf.

At first he thought she was having fun at his expense. Then he realized she was completely sincere. Margaret, who had spent the better part of six months obsessed with the silly gown, had never seen the damn thing before. Although he applauded her common sense in not becoming obsessed with a handful of cloth, he was, indeed, alarmed at her complete lack of recollection.

Maybe she should have rested back at the Spotswood. Maybe he should have let her sleep instead of waking her up to help her dress.

On the other hand, she created such a luscious vision tonight, it would be a shame to keep her hidden. Nobody would remember exactly what she said once they saw her wrapped in the ambrosial gown of silk pastels, made more alluring by her simply dressed raven hair and the utter perfection of her delicate features. Her eyes sparkled even in the muted evening light outside, bright and dark-lashed, a more brilliant color than the violet hue of the gown.

He shook his head, ridding his mind of her intoxicating beauty, trying to concentrate on her words. Like the physical impact she had on him, her train of thought seemed nearly incomprehensible.

"I believe the little boy's name was Joseph," she stated.

"Margaret, when did this happen? Little Joseph is but four or five, and I know the rascal well. I have heard nothing of such a tragedy, and surely I would have known by now."

She closed her eyes and rubbed the bridge of her nose, less red but still painful from earlier in the day. When did the balcony accident occur? A sudden thought slammed into her mind. It hadn't happened yet. The little boy died in the winter of 1864, and it was now December of 1863.

Ashton steadied her as she grew pale. "I'm sorry," she stammered. "I must be thinking of someone else."

"Another Confederate president who happens to have a son named Joseph?"

She was about to ask to leave when a masculine voice, mellow but commanding, called from just behind a white column on the tiny front porch. The house was so close to the street that the dirt from the unpaved road slipped over the porch, making it one with the street.

The figure stepped forward, a slender man with military bearing, an unusually long torso on rather short legs. But it was his hair, a startling white with a graceful white beard, that proclaimed his identity.

"General Lee, sir," greeted Ashton, turning to his wife. "Now, Mag, I don't want you upsetting anyone with predictions of death or defeat. Promise me you won't tell Varina Davis what you just . . . ."

"Of course not!" She gave him an indignant nudge, and he grinned.

Robert E. Lee took one step toward them, clapping Ashton on the shoulder as soon as he could reach him. His stern face betrayed genuine delight at seeing the younger man.

"Ashton, how are you?" He then turned toward Margaret with a slight, stiff-waisted bow. "Madame, I hope you fare well. If mere appearance is an indication, you seem to be thriving in your newly married state."

"Yes, General. Thank you, sir." She understood the devotion his men felt toward their general now; she felt the power radiating from his every movement. This was a good man, she realized. He was doing his very best against staggering odds, but his very best was, unfortunately, leading to hundreds of thousands of deaths. If he wasn't such an aggressive leader, the war would have ended a year ago.

After the war, Henry Adams would make a comment about Lee that she thoroughly agreed with: "It's always the good men who do the most harm in the world."

As she held on to Ashton's arm, she realized, with a visible shudder, that the exact same statement applied to her husband.

General Lee caught her shiver and smiled affectionately at Ashton. "Son, you'd best get your beautiful wife indoors. I feel winter will be with us soon."

Ashton and Lee shook hands, and it wasn't until they were inside the foyer that Margaret realized that not a single word had passed between the two concerning the war. If their brief conversation had been plucked from the air, it could be inserted almost anywhere at almost any time without revealing the identity or circumstance of the speakers.

Inside, a gracious warmth spread down her arms as Ashton handed her dark green cloak to a stoic black man dressed in ridiculous satin knickers. Ashton, handing his own greatcoat to the butler, smiled at the man.

"Martin, is that you under the white wig?"

The man tried unsuccessfully not to chuckle. "Yes, sir, General Johnson. This isn't my idea, no sir."

"I'm glad to hear it. This, Martin, is my wife."

Margaret extended her hand, and Martin's eyebrows lifted high enough to disappear under the hairline of the snowy wig. "It's good to meet you, Martin." She shook his hand vigorously, and Ashton —as well as several of the other guests—gaped in astonishment.

As if nothing unusual had occurred, Margaret turned to Ashton. "You look exceptionally handsome tonight, General," she whispered.

His answer was a gentle squeeze of her hand, and she gazed up at him, his hair shining in the artificial light, his uniform elegant and crisp. With her free hand she patted the absurd hoops under her gown, hoping she didn't collide with another woman like an out-of-control bumper car.

There was a large room, furniture cleared to the sides, and a small orchestra composed of very old men seated in a semicircle about to start another song. They must have just returned from a short break, for there had been no musical sounds wafting outside.

Then a hush fell over the gathering as General Lee entered with a tall, fine-boned man and a rather plump, dark-complexioned woman. It was Jefferson Davis, austere and dignified, and his strong-willed wife. The president nodded to gentle applause and polite smiles, then gestured for the band to play.

"My dear." Ashton gave a mock bow. "Would you afford me the pleasure of this dance?"

"Ash," she hissed, "I don't remember how. The last real dance I attended was a disco and . . ."

Without wasting another moment, Ashton led his wife to the floor and gave her a lifetime's worth of dancing lessons.

CHAPTER

14

⤜❦⤛

Margaret had never experienced the romantic exhilaration of the waltz. Although she had taken ballroom dancing lessons in junior high school, she had always towered over her partners, eventually sitting out the slower numbers drinking red fruit punch and trying not to spill on her white gloves. The gloves were mandatory, to keep the already reluctant and outnumbered male members of the class from having to hold perspiring hands. Both partners had sweaty palms, but with the gloves they could pretend, at least for a while, that it wasn't a terrifying experience to close-dance with a member of the opposite sex.

As Margaret flew in Ashton's arms, wide circles following his skillful lead, she finally understood why such dancing would withstand over a hundred years of incompetent, bifocaled instructors and endless vats of lukewarm punch. With the right partner, the experience was absolutely sublime, the feeling of his hands on her skin, even through layers of filmy fabric, was intoxicating.

Others in the room watched the couple; the women, many of whom had been Ashton's partners in the past, heaved discreet sighs at the expression on his face. He stared at his bride with undiluted ardor, smiling his lightning-fast smile at something she said, bending his head close to utter words into her ear. He had always been a figure of dash and excitement, even his tenure as a college professor had not dimmed the electric aura he projected as a young West Point cadet.

But now, with his fame growing with every audacious exploit, his stature had been inflated to almost legendary proportions. The South needed Ashton Johnson almost as much as it needed Robert E. Lee, for after the death of Stonewall Jackson, a universal despondency seemed to settle over the Confederacy like an unwelcome mist. Lee was revered, but as a distant marble figure. They craved a flesh-and-blood hero, with daring and humor and even a touch of sexual charm. Ashton was the man, and stories of him were told and retold as eagerly as outrageous tales of Confederate victories.

The one disconcerting aspect of General Johnson's character that had truly alarmed most southern men, and even most women, was his inability to resolve his courtship with Mag. She seemed to dominate him, played him the fool on countless occasions, a situation that would be considered amusing with almost any other man, but a glaring weak spot in a mighty general.

Everyone on the dance floor was startled at the change in Mag, delighted that Ashton Johnson may have tamed the wild-eyed beauty.

"I still think she's a spy," muttered a black-swathed dowager from behind a pair of silver-framed spectacles.

"Mother," said her daughter, a spinster of thirty-five who had once danced with Ashton at a ball in Washington City, "I refuse to believe that the general would ever marry someone who could be so dangerous to the cause."

"Well, I understand she all but admitted to being a spy right in front of the Spotswood this very afternoon. The general punched her in the nose, and that was the end of that. But mark my words, she will be found a spy, and I hope she'll hang for it."

"Mother!"

"Oh, Lavinia," sighed the mother. "Why couldn't you have married him?"

Jefferson Davis also watched the couple swirl on the polished floor. His wife returned from their private quarters upstairs and tucked her arm in his.

"The children are finally asleep," she murmured, and then she, too, focused on the stunning couple. "My, but they are graceful together, the general and his bride."

Her husband said nothing but continued to watch the pair as Ashton laughed, whispered something to Mrs. Johnson, and she, too, laughed.

"I understand she has become something of a marvel in the hospital," continued Varina Davis, accustomed to her husband's more disagreeable habit of silence. "Why, Mary B. Cox herself vouches for her skill and devotion in the wards. Jeff, will General Johnson be staying here all winter?"

"That's the plan," he said distractedly.

"Perhaps I'll have Mrs. Johnson over to tea along with Mrs. Chesnut."

He gave no indication of hearing his wife. "Varina, do you believe she's a spy?"

The First Lady of the Confederacy considered the question for a moment, watching as Margaret reached up and brushed an invisible speck from her husband's expansive shoulder. A slight smile played on her lips as Ashton gazed at her, a wordless understanding passing between the two.

"No, Jeff. I do not believe any woman who looks at her husband with such an expression of love could be capable of causing him harm."

Her husband said nothing, and staring straight ahead, he missed the expression of infinite love that crossed over his own wife's generous features.

He had just made a decision. For the sake of the Confederacy, as well as for the sake of his favorite general besides Lee, he would post a discreet guard to make sure Mrs. Johnson didn't pass any information to any suspicious characters. With that decision complete, he turned to his wife.

"Dear, would you like to . . ."

Before he could finish his question, Varina gave a slight incline of her head, smiled, and began gliding to the dance floor. "Why, Mr. President, I thought you would never ask."

Margaret awoke in the middle of the night, gasping for air, her heart slamming against her ribs. After delightfully langorous lovemaking, she had fallen asleep in the heavy comfort of Ashton's arms, unable to determine what it was in the back of her mind that kept on bothering her.

The ball had been a tremendous thrill, the heady feeling of dancing with her husband, of actually meeting Jefferson Davis and Robert E. Lee and General Longstreet. It was like having a Confederate wax museum come to life.

She had been surprised at Jefferson Davis. At first he had been exactly what she expected, taciturn and blandly rigid. But when they were finally introduced, he was friendly, even displaying flashes of wit and a smile that transformed his stiffly composed visage into a delightfully accessible and pleasant face. Ashton had explained the transformation when they again approached the dance floor.

"He is distant, even threatened by those he considers his equal, namely wealthy white males." Ashton held his wife closer than the other dancers. "But he's always magnanimous with women and dogs and children and slaves."

Margaret was shocked. "Is he? How very kind of him." She was unable to keep the acid from her voice. "So I am an underling?"

Ashton simply admired the sudden spark in her eyes.

"Then why is he so standoffish with his wife?" she asked.

"Ah, Varina." Ashton grinned. "She is in a different class, you see. He's scared to death of his wife, even though she is a woman. He actually left her once, but he came trotting back as soon as he could. She acts the part of the dutiful wife in public, but in private I believe he is the dutiful husband."

Margaret was thoughtful for a moment, then arched her eyebrows. "Remind me to ask Varina Davis how she does it."

The entire room paused when Ashton's explosive laugh rose above the music, and everyone smiled at his obvious happiness.

But even then, Margaret had felt slightly off balance, a little out of kilter.

Calming herself, she looked down at Ashton, his face gently illuminated by the moonlight streaming in the window. His chest rose and fell slowly in deep slumber, and she wondered if he was able to sleep this soundly during campaigns. Gently, careful not to wake him, she removed his arm from around her waist and slid out of bed.

The Battle of Lookout Mountain in Chattanooga would soon begin. Then it hit her: She could not remember the exact dates.

"My God," she whispered, her mind tumbling from shock. This would be the real beginning of Grant's ascent, plant the foundation for Sherman's march through Georgia and, ultimately, the end of the war. But it all seemed hazy to her, the dates uncertain, the events cloudy, as if she had imagined the whole conclusion of the war.

Yet the past was as vivid as it had always been. Even without Ashton as a reminder, she knew that Gettysburg had taken place on the first three days of July, several months earlier, and Lincoln delivered the address a few weeks ago to commemorate the opening of a Union cemetery there. Every date from Fort Sumter to the present autumn were etched completely and unshakably in her consciousness. But what next?

Leaning over a small writing desk, her arms braced on the back of a chair, she closed her eyes. The future was uncertain because of her.

Every event from now on had a potentially different ending.

She softly opened a drawer and removed a thick piece of paper and a pen, uncorking a bottle of ink. Sliding into the chair, she began writing furiously before she even sat down.

The pen scratched as she wrote, and she spilled out every fact she could recall as quickly as she possibly could. She needed to get the facts committed to paper before she forgot every bit of information she possessed, before she became as helpless as any other woman in the Confederacy.

The paper filled up with remarkable speed.

"Sherman's March, November 1864. Battle of Atlanta, summer–early fall, 1864. Sherman wages war on civilians to end war. Appomattox Court House, Lee surrenders to Grant, April 1865. Lincoln reelected in 1864, then assassinated by Booth in April 1865. ASHTON KILLED ON LICK SKILLET ROAD on July 28th, 1864."

She tapped the pen and wrote some other dates, other events, finally concluding. "World War I—U.S. enters 1916, Allies win 1918. Treaty of Versailles, 1919. Stock market crash, worldwide depression, 1929. Hitler. World War II—1941–45, Korea—???, Vietnam—???, Kennedy assassinated—1966? Teenage Mutant Ninja Turtles, the Beatles, Woody and Mia, TV and Sam Malone on "Cheers," civil rights, Martin Luther King. Who are Bill and Hillary Clinton? Madonna? Robert De Niro? Bart Simpson?"

Her hand was trembling. She dipped the pen into the ink to write more, and the nib snapped. The farther into the future she reached, the less she remembered. Her own life was still clear, learning to drive a car, taking SAT exams, her family's death, her first week of classes at Columbia . . . right until her brief days at Magnolia. But events on a grander scheme eluded her.

She folded the paper, heedless that some of the ink was still damp, and shoved it back into the drawer. Perhaps in the morning she would remember more. Maybe then her mind would clear and relax, and the information would come rushing back to her.

For a while she sat at the desk, staring but not seeing out of the window.

Ashton watched his wife, the frantic writing done now, the paper hastily pushed into the drawer. Even when she returned to the bed, her soft arm closing around him, he was unable to find sleep. He knew with absolute certainty that he would not be able to sleep at all until he read what was written on that paper.

In the brightness of day, the Executive Mansion, formerly owned by the Brockenbrough family, seemed less magical than when illuminated for a ball. Its harsh lines seemed stark and cold, just another house on the corner of Twelfth and Clay.

Ashton paused for a moment as he passed. He hadn't meant to walk this way—he simply needed to clear his mind before facing the leaders of the Confederacy. A sleepy-looking guard was posted, the only indication that someone of importance was in residence. Upstairs he heard the voices of the Davis children, shrieks of delight, a call of "You're it!" as they engaged in a game of tag.

In his pocket was his own speedily drawn copy of the notes Margaret had made in the middle of the night. Just after daybreak she had donned the green apron and set off for the hospital, giving him ample opportunity to examine the paper.

The words were clear, their meaning, however, uncertain. The one lucid point, other than the approximate dates of recent battles, had jumped out at him. In bold letters, his wife had written: "ASHTON KILLED ON LICK SKILLET ROAD, July 28th, 1864."

Had that been a prediction, or was she informed by some enemy source that that was the plan?

He immediately dismissed the notion that this was some sort of scheme. Nobody, not even Lincoln himself, could point a finger and say with any certainty where a person would be on a day over six months in the future. The war was taking twists and turns that could not be anticipated even a week before. It might be waged in northern soil by then, or in the westernmost territory of Tennessee or the eastern coast of

Virginia. If England joined the war on the side of the Confederacy, the fighting could be in New York City—even St. Louis.

The words were probably the result of a dream. Or perhaps she felt some sort of psychic vision, the kind Queen Victoria had made popular ever since the death of her husband Albert two years earlier. Communication with the departed was all the rage, and since most of Margaret's family was now dead, she would certainly have more than her fair share of sources "on the other side."

Yet he was still bothered by the inked words. How could she know about those events? And the broken phrases that seemed to indicate a southern surrender were completely baffling. Of course the war was not going well for the Confederacy, but history was filled with instances of victory pulled from the jaws of defeat.

Then the note deteriorated into a jumble of strange babble, meaningless strings of words such as World War I and TV. He wasn't sure whether or not these were the product of some sort of hallucination. He immediately thought of the small amount of laudanum he had given her at Rebel's Retreat, but shrugged off that notion. The few drops had not been significant, and she had been acting strangely before that.

Next he wondered if she had perhaps been sneaking some sort of mind-altering elixir from the hospital. He instantly became ashamed at the very thought—his wife had bitterly complained of the fact that there was nothing in the hospital to dull the pain of the wounded men, nothing to lessen their agony. His spy had even told him that she was gently reprimanded by Dr. Parish for trying to locate his brandy stash to give to a wounded Yankee. The doctor said he appreciated her effort and understood her desire to help the men, but the ones who would survive would do so without his brandy, and they all needed the doctor. Without the liquor to brace him, he would be unable to treat the patients.

What he needed was time alone with Margaret, a real honeymoon, days to spend getting to know each other. In truth, he knew very little of his wife. The war was playing havoc with romance, shattering whatever security a newly married couple might attempt to create.

Ashton straightened his shoulders and headed toward the old U.S. Customs House on Main Street between Tenth and Eleventh. His mind flashed to the meeting he would soon be attending in the second-floor office the president shared with the Confederate State Department. The reason for the conference was to discuss the Union's U.S. Grant, a general they had been hoping would remain in obscurity.

An arm grabbed Ashton, and he turned to see the bearded face of General Longstreet, "Pete" to his friends.

"Morning, Ash," said the older man with a swift nod. His worn uniform had a fresh stain on the lapel, and Ashton shook his hand.

"Morning, Pete. You going to the meeting?"

"Yep." Together they marched to the Customs House, Longstreet, never much of a talker, typically silent.

"You know him, don't you?" Ashton asked. He didn't have to explain that he was speaking of General Grant.

Longstreet nodded, a faint smile coming to his face at the memory of his old friend. "I was the best man at Sam's wedding," he said at last, referring to Grant by his nickname.

"Do you think he's going to be a problem?"

Ashton's question was, by now, purely rhetorical. Everyone in the Confederate Army knew damn well that U.S. Grant posed a serious threat.

Longstreet didn't answer. Instead, he looked Ashton directly in the eye. "Do you know what? When Sam first came to West Point, he was mortified by the fancy luggage his father had given him. His initials were embossed in gold, and not many people know this, but his real name is Hiram Ulysses Grant. So here he was, entering the military academy, with a big trunk with the word HUG emblazoned across the top."

Ashton gave an exaggerated cringe, knowing full well how mercilessly any incoming cadet would be taunted with such a trunk. "What did he do?"

Now Longstreet chuckled once, a rare sound, especially since his three children had perished in a fever epidemic the previous spring. "Well, first he made the leather store switch the first two letters, so that it read UHG. And then the registrar at the Point was kind enough to jumble the name further, making him Ulysses Sampson Grant. To me, he's been Sam ever since."

The guard at the Customs House snapped to attention and opened the door for the two generals. Just before they entered the president's office on the second floor, Longstreet turned to Ashton.

"You can bet on it. Old Sam is going to give us a hell of a lot of trouble."

Margaret was surprised at how much easier it was to treat the patients when she knew she would be seeing Ashton in a few hours. Every job, from the tedious duty of foraging for food to writing dictated letters home for the patients, even changing the gruesome bandages was more pleasant for Margaret.

The soldiers noticed her quiet happiness and gently

teased her. Behind her back they all whispered about the gallant General Johnson and how very fortunate he was to have married Margaret. Any mention of her earlier reputation, of being a spy or even her formerly flirtatious air, was swiftly hushed. They appreciated her for her warmth and humor and dedication, ignoring the unjust gossip from the previous year.

Mary B. was especially delighted with her new nurse. Other women, no matter how selfless their original intentions, were simply unable to withstand the emotional strain of the work. Usually they withdrew their services in less than a week, amid tearful apologies and ladylike sniffs.

She glanced up from a young private and saw Margaret smoothing the brow of a soldier whose face had been disfigured by an exploding shell. Everyone else around him had been killed instantly, and even more alarming than his terrible wounds had been his prolonged silence, expressing nothing but a heartfelt yearning to join his dead companions. Margaret had spent extra time with the soldier, speaking in soothing tones, patiently but persistently urging him to recover.

After ten days her persistence paid off, and he mumbled for her to leave him alone. Margaret redoubled her efforts, deciding that if she could truly irritate the man, he might recover simply to be able to leave her.

It worked. Instead of wallowing in miserable self-pity, he began to complain bitterly about the nurse who was always at his side, continuously telling bad jokes, always quoting some trite homily. Soon his fever was down, and he was sitting up in bed, watching the nurse glide from bed to bed. By the time he realized what she had done, he, too, had become a devoted admirer.

There was a commotion up front, but Margaret had learned to ignore the sounds of new arrivals until she was asked to help. Otherwise, she would simply be in the way.

Dr. Parish and Mary B. were in deep discussion, nodding in agreement, swift decisions that could alter a man's chances of recovery.

"Margaret, an officer has just been brought in." Mary B. stood over her, a strange expression on her face.

"Really? How odd. We don't usually treat officers." Margaret returned to her patient, but Mary B. did not move. She looked up, a sudden terror coursing through her. "No, it's not Ashton?" she uttered.

"No," reassured Mary B. quickly. "No, please. It's not your husband, but it is your brother-in-law."

"Eddie?"

Mary B. nodded as Margaret rose to her feet. "Where is . . ."

"Right in front," she answered.

"Could someone tell Ashton? He's in a meeting with—"

Again, Mary B. answered before Margaret could complete the sentence. "We've already sent someone."

Margaret hesitated for a moment. "What are his wounds?"

"He's been shot in the left shoulder. Dr. Parish is looking at him now."

Eddie was there, wounded just like any other soldier. But any other soldier would be grateful for her help, for her attention, even for her touch. Eddie hated her. No matter how Lizzie or Ashton tried to reword it, under the benign guise of simple brotherly concern or youthful passion, he hated her.

"Margaret, what on earth is wrong?" Mary B. had pulled her aside, her green eyes questioning.

Margaret's gaze darted restlessly to her folded hands. "He honestly despises me," she whispered.

"My presence would not help him, and I might even do more damage by simply showing my face. Does he know I'm here?"

"No," Mary B. replied, wanting to ask more but not wanting to make her friend uncomfortable. "I'll look after him. But I will say this, he must not have much in the judgment department."

Margaret shrugged as Mary B. picked up her skirts and stepped down the aisle to Eddie. Feeling an uncomfortable sense of defeat, Margaret turned in the opposite direction to get as far away as possible from her brother-in-law. Maybe one day they could be friends. But certainly not today.

Ashton sat in the president's office, wondering if anyone besides General Longstreet truly understood how difficult the next phase of the war would be. Lee exuded an air of absolute confidence, and President Davis seemed to cling to that bravado, perhaps with the notion that wishing it vehemently could make it come true.

At this point they were no longer making plans to invade northern soil. After Gettysburg, they had simply tried to foil an all-out northern invasion of the South. Should Richmond or Atlanta fall like Vicksburg, they all knew—as did everyone in the Confederacy—that the war would be lost.

"So are we agreed, gentlemen?" Davis tapped his foot on the carpet, the only visible sign of his agitation. "Our first priority is to block both Sherman and Grant. The seasons are on our side. But by spring we must put an end to these two generals."

Lee nodded distractedly, ideas already forming in his mind. Ashton was silent for a moment, unsure if what he was about to say would be taken seriously.

In the two hours since this conference began, it was as if he could suddenly see the entire situation clearly, perhaps for the first time. Their position now was obvious—the numbers of men in both armies, the success of the Yankee blockade that had been keeping food and vital materials from the Confederacy. He took a deep breath, knowing how his thoughts would be received. But, for his own peace of mind, they needed to be said.

"The losses have been horrendous, President. On both sides. What will we do if we are able to prevent the Union army from invading?"

"What do you mean, General?" Davis had stopped tapping his foot.

"We will be exactly where we are right now, sir. Only with fewer men and a weaker morale. The Yankees, however, will keep on coming. Have you seen how well equipped they are? Even the privates are better dressed and fed than our officers."

"Just what are you implying, General Johnson?" Davis was using his frosty, imperious tone, but Ashton was not intimidated. Lee's eyes snapped to his, a warning look there, but Ashton continued.

"It has just occurred to me, looking at this map," Ashton's hand swept over the detailed parchment, "that even if we manage to repulse the Union Army on our most vulnerable fronts, we still must actually invade and conquer all of this," he gestured to the vast northern and western states, "if we are to win."

There was a brittle silence as Ashton persevered. "Unless England truly sides with us, I fear we are doomed to fail."

"That, sir, is treason," spat Davis.

"No. What I believe, I trust, will go no farther than these walls." Ashton pushed back an errant strand of hair. "I will fight, to my death if necessary. But I needed to tell you what I believe."

There was a gentle knock on the door, and a burly guard entered the room.

"I beg your pardon, gentlemen." The guard was clearly distressed at having to enter a room filled with the nation's most powerful men. "I have a message for General Johnson. His brother, Major Edward Branch Johnson, has been wounded, and has just been brought to the hospital."

"Chimborazo?" Ashton asked standing up, naming the largest hospital in Richmond.

"No, sir. He's at Miss Cox's hospital."

Ashton turned to the three men, leaning down to collect his gloves and hat. "Gentlemen? May I please . . ."

"Of course, General." Davis was a trifle less angry as he dismissed Ashton. Lee also rose to his feet.

"Ash, let me know as soon as possible how Eddie is faring." Lee grasped the younger man's arm.

"Yes, sir. Thank you."

As he pivoted to leave, a small piece of paper fluttered to the carpet. Longstreet was about to stop him, but Lee held up his hand. "No, Pete. I'll give it to him later. He needs to get to Eddie."

President Davis picked up the paper when his eyes unconsciously raked the side with Ashton's distinctive handwriting. A phrase caught his attention, and he read the note.

"President Davis," murmured Longstreet, "I hardly think you should . . ."

The expression on his face quelled him. The president cleared his throat and handed the note to Lee.

"General, I believe you should look at this." His voice was weak, and as Lee scanned the paper, Davis walked to the door and closed it softly.

"My God," rasped General Lee, feeling behind him for a chair. He sat down heavily, his eyes darting over the paper.

"What is it, sir?" asked Longstreet, baffled by the strange behavior of his commanders.

Lee remained silent, and President Davis was the first to answer. "The paper, General Longstreet, appears to be some sort of cipher. But from what I can gather from General Lee's reaction, he too has reached the same conclusion. Ashton Johnson is a spy."

CHAPTER
15

They were going to amputate Eddie's left arm.

Margaret paced from bed to bed, glancing over at the small circle—Dr. Parish, Mary B., and the soldiers who had brought Eddie to the hospital. She didn't dare approach her brother-in-law, for fear that the anger and frustration and pain he must be feeling would be hurled at her. She wasn't being a coward, her mind rationalized, she simply didn't want him to expend the energy he would so desperately need in order to recover.

Perhaps it would do him some good to scream at her, for as the details were emerging of how he had been wounded, she realized that Eddie was going to have to direct his fury at some point other than the enemy. He had been shot by one of his own men, a young skirmisher who aimed his uncertain carbine at the first noise he heard. In the dull light of the morning, Eddie and his five soldiers had been mistaken for a Yankee patrol.

A respectful silence settled over the room, as if someone very important had entered the ward, but Margaret didn't bother to see who it was. Instead she busied herself with sorting clean rags by size. A large hand rested on her arm, and she turned around, knowing immediately that it was Ashton.

She didn't wait for him to ask. "He was shot in the left shoulder," she said quietly, staring into his somber visage. There was a gentleness there, a slight vulnerability, that made her place her hand over his. Very few people, she realized, had ever seen this facet of him.

"Ash, he was wounded by his own men, a case of mistaken identity." Her mouth felt dry, and she licked her lips, trying to phrase the next piece of information as delicately as possible. "Dr. Parish believes it is necessary to amputate."

The only perceivable reaction Ashton displayed was a convulsive clench of his fist, and Margaret, with her hand covering his, was the only one who was aware of it. He took a deep breath, and she felt an overwhelming need to touch him, to cradle him against her, but they were being watched. The most she could do was tighten her hold on his fist.

"No," he whispered.

At first she thought he was denying the severity of the wound, rejecting the idea of his brother being so seriously injured.

"I will not let them amputate," he said, his eyes meeting hers.

"Perhaps you had better speak to Dr. Parish . . ."

"Margaret, the only cure doctors seem able to attempt is amputation. They wanted to hack off my leg at Gettysburg, remember?"

"And do you remember Spence Pender?" she countered. "He would probably be alive right now, teasing me about one thing or another, if his leg had been taken off. Ash, it might be the same thing with Eddie."

Ashton was silent for a few moments, weighing her words. At last he gave her a wan smile. "Maybe I should consult my brother and the doctor before I make any medical decisions."

"I believe they would both appreciate that," she replied, reaching up to run her fingers softly over his face.

A strange expression crossed over his brow. "Margaret, I need to tell you something—"

"General?" Dr. Parish had no qualms about interrupting anyone, no matter what their status. In the hospital, his domain, he outranked them all.

"Your brother has a ball lodged in his left shoulder. I believe it has shattered the bone, and the best solution, in my opinion, would be to amputate." The doctor glared unflinchingly at Ashton.

"What does my brother say?"

Dr. Parish gave a dismissive grunt. "He says what they all say, that he would rather die than lose his arm. Believe me, General, most young men change their minds mighty fast when they realize they might actually die."

"I'll speak to him," said Ashton, pushing his hand through his hair as he started to walk to his brother.

"Ash," Margaret whispered. "Shall I contact your mother?"

He stopped, and with a genuine smile, shook his head. "Not yet, Mag. We have enough problems just now."

He did not urge her to accompany him to Eddie, and she realized that he, too, felt that would be a mistake. She watched him walk away, the broad shoulders squared, the expressions of awe on the faces of the patients as he passed. Even the Union men stared in fascination, and one actually saluted. But Ashton didn't see them; his eyes were already ahead, on Eddie.

Margaret returned to the rags, stacking neat piles of torn cloth as if it were the most enthralling task imaginable. Her mind whirled, trying to recall what paltry medical facts she could, wondering if some other treatment besides amputation could help Eddie.

So absorbed in her own thoughts was she, mechanically folding bandages, that she wasn't aware of the hushed confusion that suddenly overtook the hall.

The patients knew something was wrong as soon as the four large Confederate soldiers entered the ward. One remained at the front door, the only open exit. The other three marched toward Ashton, who was speaking to Eddie.

"General Johnson, you are to come with us."

Ashton's eyes snapped up, disbelieving.

"I am busy at the moment, soldier," he said with an unmistakable edge to his voice, then he returned his full attention to Eddie.

His brother swallowed, looking up at the soldiers looming over his bed. Even through the gauzy pain, he recognized something was very wrong.

"Ash." He closed his eyes. "Better see what they want."

Impatiently, Ashton stood up, and the soldier who spoke whispered something into his ear. Ashton's face was impassive as he reached into the pocket that had earlier held the parchment. It was gone.

Ashton glanced over at Margaret, her back turned, graceful arms moving as she worked on the bandages. He needed to speak to her, to explain what had happened, to ask her what the scribbled words meant.

"Sir, you are to come with us immediately," repeated the soldier.

Margaret stopped working, an uncomfortable prickle creeping up her arms. She stiffened, trying to figure out what was wrong. Then she noticed the eerie quiet of the hospital, a sense that she was being watched, that something urgent and compelling was occurring.

Without thinking, she dropped the rags, heedless as they fell to the filthy floor, and spun around.

Ashton, flanked by two enormous soldiers bearing rifles, was being ushered from the hospital. Another soldier was behind them, as if to prevent him from escaping their escort.

"Ashton!" Her voice was shrill and unnatural, startling to her own ears, but she was vaguely aware that no one else seemed surprised by her shout.

Ashton turned to her, his face blank, but a betraying look caused her hand to fly to her mouth. His eyes seemed unnaturally bright as he stared at her. Then he mouthed a simple sentence.

"I love you."

Before she could react, the soldier to the rear placed his hand on her husband's shoulder and guided him forward. Ashton did not resist.

The air hung heavy with a strained silence. Margaret realized that her hand, still over her mouth, was trembling.

Never had she seen Ashton, or any officer, virtually shoved through a door by mere privates.

Something was terribly, awfully wrong.

The knowledge that Eddie disliked her didn't even enter her consciousness as she raced to his bedside. She didn't hesitate a moment, and grabbed her skirts the instant the front doors swung shut.

"Eddie," she uttered as she knelt by her brother-in-law. For the first time since she met him, he turned to her with eyes clear of malice.

"What are you doing here?" His voice was harsh in

pain and confusion. She reached for a tin mug filled with clear water and carefully tilted it toward his lips, cupping his head with her hand. His eyes, a gray-blue, she realized for the first time, flicked to her with a brief spark of gratitude, and he sipped the water.

Eddie Johnson, Margaret noticed, was quite handsome.

"I work here. Lizzie left for The Oaks, but I'm staying on." She then switched back into her nurse mode. "How are you feeling?" His uniform was splashed with blood and cut away at the left arm. The bandage was already stained, and even under the caked dust Margaret could tell his face was pale.

"The hell with me, Mag. What happened to Ash?"

Margaret looked up to see who was listening, but the soldiers who had come with Eddie seemed to be staring at the closed front door, muttering to themselves. "I don't know. Did you hear what the soldier said to him before they took him away?"

"I'm not sure." Eddie closed his eyes for a moment before continuing. "I think I heard something about a piece of paper."

"A piece of paper?" She dipped a corner of a clean rag into the water and gently wiped his face. "How could a piece of paper cause them to force him out the door?"

As she spoke, a tiny kernel of understanding seemed to plant itself in her consciousness. A piece of paper. Last night she scribbled sketchy information from the future about battles and Ashton's death and television. Could Ashton have somehow taken that paper?

"Mag, what's wrong?"

"I had, uh, dreams last night about the future and the war. I scribbled the stuff down so that I wouldn't forget it. Could that be the paper . . ."

"What kind of dreams?" The weariness seemed to be leaving his voice.

She hesitated. "You wouldn't understand."

"What kind of dreams," he repeated, only this time it wasn't a question.

"About the war, about other wars to come. Television . . ."

"What about the war, Mag?"

"This war?"

He rolled his eyes, exasperated, then nodded.

"Well, I wrote about Gettysburg and, I think, the battle of Lookout Mountain and Sherman's march . . ."

"A song?"

"Excuse me?"

"You said 'Sherman's march,' and I asked you if that was a song."

"No. Well, later it will be, but first it's an event."

"An event you dreamed?"

"No," she said softly, leaning close to his ear. "It will really happen next November after the fall of Atlanta."

"The what!" His good hand clamped over her forearm and pulled her close. She was surprised by his strength. He was about to say something, when his eyes focused just beyond her. Margaret turned to see Mary B. hovering over them.

"Well," she said in her briskly efficient tone. "I'm delighted to see the two of you getting along so well, although excessive hand-holding is strictly against Dr. Parish's bylaws."

Eddie immediately dropped her wrist, but a slight smile played on his lips. "Mary B. Cox," he rumbled, "I heard you had taken up nursing with a vengeance. Tell me, have you killed any ducks lately?"

Margaret gave a perplexed sigh, and Mary B. reached over and grabbed Eddie's hand, the side of her thumb moving expertly over the pulse point at his wrist.

"I did not kill your duckling, Eddie Johnson," she murmured. "You did, by giving him that chunk of ham. He choked to death, I was simply trying to save him."

"By turning him upside down and swatting him?"

Mary B. said nothing for a few moments, then placed his wrist gently onto the frayed blanket that covered him. "He would have died of old age by now anyway. That was over fifteen years ago."

There was an amused silence between the two, his smile fading as he looked up at the nurse.

"Do you know where they took my husband?" Margaret asked Mary B., in spite of her fascination with the recent exchange between her brother-in-law and Mary B. There was a tension between the two, not unpleasant, but vibrantly charged.

"I have no idea, nor does Dr. Parish. Go after him, Margaret. I'll watch over Eddie . . ."

"Mag, you have to find out," urged Eddie, the suspicion gone from his expression. "I can't do anything until I get better. But the way they fetched Ash, it seems to me that it was much more than another meeting."

Margaret stood immediately. Grabbing her shawl, she rushed out of the door, not sure where she was going. Why hadn't she followed him and the guards? She had been too stunned, she realized, to follow. And the guards wouldn't have allowed it.

The streets were already teeming with pedestrians and carriages, the dust of the streets hovering in a constant, billowing swirl. A few of the passersby stared at Margaret, aware of who she was, or simply caught off guard by the sudden appearance of such beauty amid the everyday hustle.

A beige cloud of dirt puffed into her face as an open rig rattled by, and she closed her eyes reflexively. But she wasn't fast enough, and a speck of grit lodged in her right eye. With both hands covering her eye, she backed away from the street.

"Mrs. Johnson?"

A young man steered her to safety, and with her clear eye she could see it was Sam Walker, Ashton's aide-de-camp.

"Lieutenant Walker." Her eyes were tearing, but she felt the particle leave her eye. Blinking, she looked up at the young man. "Thank you. I might have been trampled."

He shrugged, his face reddening, and she looked around to make sure they were not being heard. "Where is my husband?"

At once the lieutenant sobered. "I was just coming to ask you the same question, ma'am. I was to meet him later today, but just now I saw him walking with four of the meanest looking men I've ever seen. I tried to speak to him, but he shook his head and said 'Later.' I hate to say this, but he sure looked to me like a man under arrest."

"Which direction is he headed in?"

"They just went into the old Customs House, and I—"

Margaret didn't hear the rest of what he said; she simply waved a distracted farewell and ran to the Spotswood to see if the paper was still there.

No matter what, she was sure of only one thing: Ashton had somehow gotten himself into more trouble than a brigade of Yankees.

How odd, Ashton thought, surrounded by the men he had seen barely an hour before conferring as equals on the fate of the Confederacy. Now the three men— Lee, Davis, and Longstreet—eyed him with suspicion. He was no longer one of them. No matter what the outcome of this conference, the delicate balance of their relationship had been altered, and he would always be an outsider.

"I repeat the question, General," Davis said crisply. "What is the meaning of this paper?"

On the elegant mahogany desk was his version of Margaret's note. He looked Jefferson Davis straight in the eye and answered as truthfully as possible. "I honestly don't know, President."

"Ash, please." General Lee shook his head with a weary sigh. "This is in your handwriting. Just tell us the meaning of the odd words, and I am most certain we will be satisfied."

There was a hopeful, almost pleading tone to his voice that Ashton found touching. But he could never betray Margaret, no matter what the words signified. He had violated her privacy by reading the paper in the first place, and compounded the offense by copying the words himself. His own carelessness had led him into this situation, and he would die before he allowed Margaret to suffer because of his actions.

Ashton said nothing.

At once their attention was turned to a scuffling outside, the sounds of a woman and a man engaged in some sort of disagreement. A look of irritation passed over President Davis's face, for ever since the bread riots, starving housewives and mothers had been clamoring for food. His initial pity was fast dissolving into annoyance. How was he to run the Confederacy if he was constantly badgered by irate females?

The heavy door flew open, and Margaret stumbled into the room, as if she had elbowed the door, not expecting it to actually give way.

Two guards pointed their bayonets halfheartedly in Margaret's direction, their confused expressions belying their aggressive stance.

Ashton knew he should have been surprised and

should have been able to muster an angry glare in her direction. But one thing he had learned from Margaret was to never be surprised by her behavior. And another thing he discovered was that he was always glad to see her, no matter how dire the circumstances.

"Ash." She had begun to walk toward her husband when the guards stopped her with their menacing weapons, crossed and gleaming.

A sudden fury welled in Ashton. "Soldiers," he said tightly, "please allow my wife to pass."

They did not respond but looked to the president instead. Davis gave a swift nod, and the men left the room.

The guards had failed to obey Ashton. They had clearly been ordered to disregard his commands.

Ashton was in very big trouble indeed.

Margaret felt a tightening in her chest and struggled to make the feeling go away. Panic would overtake her if she wasn't careful. She was frightened, not for herself, but for Ashton.

"Mrs. Johnson," began Jefferson Davis with a tight smile, "we are conducting important business here. Please allow us to continue without interruption."

The expressions on the men's faces betrayed nothing, the bland faces of men in power. Her eyes darted around the room and rested on the paper on the president's desk. She recognized it immediately as the makeshift stationery of the Spotswood, less fine than the management would have wished, but still an unheard of luxury in these war times.

She reached for it, and before anyone could prevent her, snatched it up, and quickly scanned the contents. With a gasp, she realized what it was.

"Ash?" Her voice was weak, questioning.

His jaw was set in a hard line, impassive, unreadable.

"Mrs. Johnson." The president's tone was cajoling.

"I fear this little slip of paper, undeniably penned in your husband's hand, indicates he is guilty of treason against the Confederate States of America."

"No!" She tried to catch her breath, but it was as if an iron vise was clamped around her chest.

"Margaret." Ashton stepped forward, alarm in his amber eyes.

"General, stop!" The command was from the president.

"For God's sake, let him be," ordered Lee, and although the president technically outranked the general, when Robert E. Lee issued an order, it was generally obeyed. Davis allowed Ashton to attend his wife.

His arms wrapped around her, drawing her fragile body in his strong embrace. She closed her eyes, battling the rush of fear, concentrating instead on a neutral image. With his powerful, vital presence surrounding her, she was able to imagine that they were back at the Spotswood, not swirling in danger but reveling in each other's love.

The telltale wheezing began to lessen, and only then did Margaret realize that he had been murmuring sweet, broken words into her ear to soothe her. Then she was aware of his scent, so comforting and clean and familiar, and she inhaled deeply, leaning into his welcoming shoulder.

There was an unsettling quiet as Lee and Longstreet and Davis watched the scene, the striking couple so oblivious to the presence of others. After a few moments, Ashton gently kissed the top of Margaret's head, and she glanced up at him in response. Although no words passed between the two, they seemed to share volumes of communication. His eyebrows rose slightly, questioningly, and she smiled and nodded before turning to the other men.

Only Lee, who had witnessed Ashton's one-sided gentleness with Mag ever since they were both children, was himself virtually speechless. For as everyone in the room now knew with absolute certainty, Mag Johnson was terribly in love with her husband.

"I'm sorry, gentlemen," she rushed to explain, her face still pale, her hand—a little unsteady—still resting on the crook of her husband's arm. She then reached into the oversize pocket of the pea green hospital apron and withdrew her own copy of the paper. "You see, I wrote down some things last night, events that I had seen as if in a dream. Ashton, I mean General Johnson, must have copied them down. He's a very curious person, you see, and wanted to figure them out. There was nothing sinister, I assure you, about either of our actions."

"Margaret, no . . ." began Ashton.

She glanced up at him, her eyes twinkling, and he felt his heart turn over. Was she really so innocent as to think that would save him? He gave her a sad smile, resisting the urge to gather her into his arms again.

"Sir," said Longstreet. Margaret jumped—she had not heard his voice since entering the room. "That is the most despicable show of cowardice I have ever beheld. To involve your own wife in your schemes, to plant evidence on an innocent woman. Why, sir, everyone believed your wife to be a spy, when in truth it was you all along! She has shown her true colors in her nursing, while you, sir, have shown your true colors here in this room. When I . . ." Longstreet sputtered, his words spinning into an incoherent babble.

"No!" she cried. "You have it all wrong! Ashton is absolutely loyal to the cause, even though I'm not. If anyone's a spy, it's me! I can tell you all sorts of things . . ."

"General Johnson," snapped the president, "please tell us, did you plant that paper on your wife just now, under the pretense of an ardent embrace?"

Ashton looked at his wife, her eyes wide in panic, and gave her a gentle smile. It no longer mattered what was on that paper, what her scribblings might have meant. It was now in his power to save her from further suspicion.

"Yes," he answered, his voice firm.

"Guards!" The president clapped, and the two men reappeared in the room, gripping their weapons and eager to follow orders. "Take General Johnson to the antechamber below, and take care not to make too much of a commotion."

The men moved with stunning speed, prodding Ashton with the bayonets.

"This is a mistake!" Margaret tried to throw her arms around her husband's waist, as if that could somehow reverse the hideous events. Someone pried her away, and she realized it was Longstreet and Ashton himself. He did not look at her as he was led out of the door.

She turned to the men in the room, her fists clenched. "This is a mistake! He is innocent, I swear it. How can I prove it to you?"

General Lee gazed at her with tenderness. "My dear child," he said softly, shaking his head.

Margaret looked into their faces. Their minds were already made up—Ashton was guilty. She stiffened, determined to ignore the absolute terror rioting through her body, and left the room.

She waited until she was back at the Spotswood to completely give way to her uncontrollable sobs.

"Well," said President Davis, now holding both pieces of paper, "what do we do now?"

All three men were silent, still reeling from the

scene they had just witnessed. Ashton Johnson, one of their most trusted, admired generals—the jewel of the South, one newspaper had called him—was actually a spy!

"What transpired in here," said Longstreet, his voice gruff, "must not become common knowledge."

"And why not?" snapped Davis.

"Pete is right," said Lee, seeming very old and brittle. "Ashton is a beloved figure, the very image of manhood for both the North and the South. This could destroy us from within. Who can fight if the most admired leader believed in the other side all along? I tell you, gentlemen, I cannot believe it."

The president cleared his throat. "I have just put a scout on duty to watch her. It's early, but my scout claims there are other men following her, perhaps Federal agents. Who knows . . ."

"President." Lee glanced up at his superior. "I, too, placed a man on surveillance duty to watch Ashton's wife. He also reported seeing two other men. One, a young man with red hair, vanished abruptly."

"Doesn't Ashton, uh, General Johnson have a redheaded scout? My God—could he have placed a scout on duty to watch his own wife?" Longstreet's voice was incredulous, and he stood abruptly and paced to the window, his hands clasped behind him as if in an effort to restrain himself.

"Do you think it's possible that she was telling the truth? Perhaps General Johnson did simply copy her writing."

President Davis shrugged. "Does it really matter? He all but confessed by admitting that he placed the other slip of paper in her pocket."

"Maybe he was just trying to protect her," mumbled Lee, with a small trace of a smile now. "That boy has spent twenty years trying to protect Mag. Until today, I never really understood why."

Again, they lapsed into silence.

"We must keep this a secret," said Davis at last. "I will speak to the guards myself. No one must know that General Ashton Johnson is a prisoner. Agreed?"

The two men nodded, each still lost in private thoughts. This war, they all realized, was exacting a higher toll than they could have ever imagined.

CHAPTER
16

It was only two o'clock in the afternoon, and Margaret was completely exhausted, drained by her unrelenting, racking tears. She lay on her back, trying to think, but unable to conjure anything except the picture of her husband being led away by guards.

She flipped onto her stomach, the mattress bouncing slightly, her face buried in the smooth bedspread of the Spotswood. What was Ashton experiencing now, she wondered, the thought jolting her into an upright position. She had to help him, to prove him absolutely innocent. The question was how.

Finally she slid to her feet, thoroughly disgusted with herself for wallowing in despair for so long. Of all things she could not afford to squander, the most precious was time.

Giving her skirts a brisk shake with one hand, she grabbed the increasingly tattered shawl and left the room, trying not to dwell obsessively on Ashton. She resisted the urge to reach into his saddlebag, thrown casually over a chair, and hold his clothing to her face. That would seem like an admission that he was gone, and she refused to even act the part of the grieving widow. She *would* get Ashton out of this mess.

Without really thinking of her destination, she walked to the hospital, her face set in determination, her strides longer than usual.

"Did you learn anything?" It was Mary B., a large bowl of bloody water swishing in her arms. Both women ignored it.

Margaret nodded, her eyes searching for Eddie. He was propped up by a chipped column, his face cleaned, no doubt, by one of the new lady nurses who would be gone by evening. His eyes snapped to hers, questioning, and she hurried to his side.

Before speaking a word, she glanced around his blanket, making sure there was no one else listening to their conversation.

"It was that piece of paper," she whispered. "Ashton copied it, I suppose, to figure out its meaning. Lee, Davis, and Longstreet saw it, and now they think Ash is a spy."

"Bloody hell," he spat. But his anger wasn't directed toward Margaret, and she continued.

"We have to figure out a way to get him out of there. He's in a room at the Old Customs House, guarded by a pair of gorillas. How can we help him escape?"

Eddie was about to speak, a sudden spark in his eyes, when he fell back, as if in exhaustion or pain.

"Oh, Eddie, forgive me." She placed a hand over his good arm. "How are you feeling?" When he didn't reply, she began to babble. "You need to rest, not to hear the rantings of a demented sister-in-law. I should not have bothered you . . ."

An unexpected smile touched his lips. "No, Mag, I

truly feel better, and Dr. Parish thinks his original diagnosis may have been in error, and perhaps the bone is not shattered. I'm just thinking that I may have been very wrong about you." The smile vanished as he spoke. "But Mag—listen to me. We cannot help Ashton escape."

For a moment Margaret was speechless as Eddie watched her closely, the emotions so clearly played out on her features. "Do you mean because of your arm? Well, of course I realize you won't be able to scale walls or anything. If you could help me come up with ideas, help me plan his escape, that's all I need. I'll do anything, Eddie. Don't even consider my safety, because they wouldn't bother with a female. Look at Belle Boyd—the North had absolute proof of her guilt, and they gave her a simple slap on the wrist and sent her back South. What would the Confederacy do with me? Why, the same I imagine, only send me up North. But if Ash is safe, well, it would be more than worth it."

As she paused for breath Eddie interrupted. "Think, Mag. You know Ashton as well as I do, maybe better in some respects. Would he ever escape from anything if his honor was still in question?"

Her mouth was about to open with a response when the meaning of his words penetrated. Eddie was right. Ashton would never escape, never slink away from the Confederacy. That to him would be worse than death.

"Bloody hell," she moaned.

The two sat in miserable silence. Every time Margaret thought of an idea, she realized that Ashton would never agree with the plan.

Wild thoughts popped into her mind, of electrocuting the guards, of somehow using a crude camera obscura and projecting a phantom image on a wall, then grabbing the guards' keys while they ogled the ghostly vision. She thought of dressing up as a man, forgetting for a moment that she was no longer six feet tall. Also forgetting that dressing up as a man would do little to free Ashton. Then she wondered about the lock, if she could pick it with a hairpin or jiggle it with a piece of wire.

But every idea dead-ended when she thought of Ashton. They could blast a hole the size of Kentucky in the side of the building—another one of her unformed plots—and Ashton would still refuse to escape.

They were so absorbed in their own dismal musings that Mary B. cleared her throat several times before attracting their attention. Eddie frowned, but she was not put off.

"I just asked you, Edward, if you would care for a bowl of soup. It's not quite as elegant as the fare at The Oaks, but believe me, it's a far sight better than army rations."

Still receiving no response, Mary B. turned to Margaret. "I do hope you realize, Mag, that your skirt is on fire and your hair has just turned blue."

Margaret gave her a distracted nod and again tried thinking of ways to help her husband.

"Excuse me." She raised her voice a notch higher, shifting her weight to the other foot. "If I am interrupting anything, please just let me know. I can take a hint."

Margaret glanced up, her eyes flying to Eddie's. "Should we tell her?"

Eddie's face was wary. "I don't know . . ."

"Tell me what?" Mary B. leaned closer to the two.

Margaret swallowed, and Eddie finally gave a weak one-shoulder shrug. "We need help, Mary B., but first you must promise not to tell a soul what we're about to tell you."

Suddenly serious, catching the somber mood of Eddie and Margaret, she nodded. Swiftly, in little more than a barely audible hiss, Margaret and Eddie revealed the situation Ashton was in.

"Bloody hell," she murmured, joining the two in contemplative silence.

"Maybe," she said softly, and Eddie and Margaret turned to her, hope daring to flicker in their eyes. Then she shook her head, as if dismissing her fledgling idea as hopeless.

"Anything," said Margaret. "Please, any ideas at all. Time is running out. My guess, from the look on everyone's face this morning in the president's office, is that they want this matter resolved and out of the way as soon as possible. They are going to execute him." Eddie started to speak, but Margaret hushed him. "They think they have to—they will shoot him quietly, then announce in the press that he died from his wounds at Gettysburg or that he banged his head or fell down a flight of stairs. You both know it—it makes sense. So anything at all, Mary B., no matter how silly, please tell us."

Margaret wasn't aware that she was crying, or that her fists were clenched as she rubbed her nose. Eddie saw the desperation there and was suddenly ashamed for all of the awful things he had thought and said about her.

"I was just thinking," Mary B. began, "whatever the plan is, we can't let Ashton know. Not only will he refuse, but the less he knows, the better for his sake in case the plan should fail."

"Right." Margaret waved her on impatiently, not bothering to mention that if the plan should fail, Ashton would be killed anyway.

"Dr. Parish has a book on botany." She looked up, just to make sure their conversation was not overheard. "It's very old. He keeps it in his corner over there, under the more current medical books."

Eddie was about to ask her what aid a botany book could offer when Mary B. gave him a withering glare and continued. "There are poisons there, some lethal, others temporary. I'm not sure if something like this exists, but what if there was a plant-based drug to put him to sleep? We could say he's dead and pretend to bury him."

For the first time that day, Margaret felt a swell of genuine hope. "And we could build the rest of the plan on the drug itself, tailor it to whatever we need! We could get him out of there in a hurry in a box or a trunk, and before they knew what happened, we would be long gone."

"No," said Eddie, his excitement obvious. "We could pretend he is dead, somehow, and get him out of there in a casket."

An involuntary shudder ran through Margaret. "I hate to think of him in a casket. What if he wakes up?"

"I'd rather have him alive in a casket than dead in one," muttered Eddie, and Margaret grew silent.

"How can we get to the book without Dr. Parish finding us?" Margaret's arms were wrapped around her, as if warding off a chill.

"Dr. Parish goes home at seven each evening for dinner and a few shots of brandy. He'll return at nine o'clock for one last tour of the ward. That should give us enough time." Mary B. reached into the large pocket of her apron and pulled out a man's pocket watch. "We have a little less than four hours." She snapped the watch shut and slipped it back into the pocket.

"I should try to see Ashton." Margaret stood up.

The other two nodded, a charged expectancy coursing through the air.

"Don't mention this conversation, Mag," said Eddie with a Cheshire cat grin. "Tell him I'm much better, and that I'm even beginning to warm to my new sister-in-law under her expert nursing."

She returned the smile. "This *must* work," she added softly as she began to leave. But they all understood perfectly before she uttered the words.

The guards readily, even graciously, agreed to let her see Ashton, as if they had been given a crash course in jailer etiquette. One was actually posted inside his room, another was just outside the window, and the same two husky guards stood at the door.

When she entered, carrying a tin can containing some of Mary B.'s soup and a loaf of day-old bread baked at another hospital, she found Ashton reading a stack of old *Harper's Weekly* magazines and a *Frank Leslie's Illustrated Newspaper*.

He looked up at her, a slow, welcoming smile spread across his face, as if she had just bumped into him in a peaceful living room. Other than the guards, there were no obvious signs of his imprisonment, nothing that marked him as a man who had lost his freedom.

The room was airy, almost spacious, with a built-in bookshelf filled with leather-bound titles, and a heavy table set up like a dining room, with a half dozen comfortable-looking chairs surrounding the table. There were several framed prints on the white walls, and simple molding bordering the ceiling.

Clad in a white linen shirt and dark gray trousers, there was also no evidence of his rank in the army.

"Hello," she said self-consciously, very aware of the guard's watchful gaze.

In one movement Ashton stood up and reached her side. "Margaret," he murmured, wanting to say much more, but somehow unable to form the words. His hand cupped her elbow, and he noticed her slight trembling.

"Excuse me, Private Burdell," he said to the guard in a conversational tone. "Do you mind leaving my wife and me for a few moments? We would most certainly leave ourselves, but I have developed a peculiar fondness for this room."

The guard nodded. "Yes, sir." He stiffened. "Just as long as Mrs. Johnson has nothing, uh, well, nothing that might help you . . ."

"Escape?" offered Ashton.

The man flushed. "Yes, sir."

Margaret held up the tin can for his inspection and pulled away part of the cloth covering the bread. "Here, you may take a look at these, and I have nothing on me that could in any way be valuable in such an endeavor. I don't even have hoops. . . ."

As she began to lift her skirts, the guard's mouth dropped open, and he exited as quickly as possible, slamming the door behind him. Ashton's soft chuckle seemed to echo in the bare room.

Raising her head to see him, Margaret tried to smile but only managed to keep her mouth from turning downward. There was a nightmare quality to the moment, a fragile veneer of normalcy to conceal how horrendous the situation really was. Her husband was touching her, his body so close she could feel his warmth, but in a matter of hours he could be dead.

"Have they decided anything?" Her voice had a tinny quality, as if someone else was doing the speaking, and her emotions were not behind each syllable. She mechanically placed the soup and bread on the heavy table.

Her flat intonation did not fool Ashton. He inhaled deeply, gently pulling her toward him. He simply could not look at her face while he spoke the next words. As she nestled in his embrace, her arms circling his waist, he could feel the moist warmth of her breath on his chest.

"My love, you need to be strong." He felt her stiffen, and softly rubbed her back. "I must apologize for violating your privacy. You never intended that slip of paper for eyes other than your own. I should never have read what you dreamed. I had no right."

She was about to speak when he interrupted her. "Please let me finish. I just want you to know that I do trust you absolutely. I don't always understand you, but I trust you implicitly.

"Now you must listen to me. Go back to The Oaks, Margaret, as soon as possible. My mother and Aunt Eppes, for all of their idiosyncrasies, will take care of you . . ."

"But what about—"

"Margaret, listen to me." His arms tightened around her until it was almost painful, but she barely noticed. "Please bear no bitterness. We have been blessed with some hours of rare joy, but I do not want you to hate anyone or to blame anyone for what will come to pass. It is my fault, everything, and I bear full responsibility. Everyone else is just reacting as they must for what they earnestly believe to be the good of the Confederacy."

"What is . . ." But her voice gave out before she could continue.

"I have not been told yet, but my guess is that I am to be shot tomorrow morning."

Dazed, she shook her head, as if that would alter what he had just said. "No," she choked.

"Listen to me." His words were barely audible. "Do you know the best part of my life has been with you? I feel remarkably lucky, Mag. Not many men have given their love so shamelessly to a woman only to have it returned tenfold when he needed it most." He continued as if he were alone in the room, his own silent reflections suddenly given voice. "I used to regret that you didn't love me, but now I understand what a magnificent purpose that served. Your love is all the more precious because I understand its value, how rare it is, how rare you are. The most important war I waged was for your heart, and I finally won."

"No," she repeated, her entire body trembling.

"Margaret, you must find happiness—I need to know this before tomorrow. The president will issue a statement that I died of natural causes—you must not contradict this to anyone. I am telling you simply because you know what transpired today in the president's office. You are too intelligent to believe I suddenly died. You would never forgive me, and you would never forgive yourself. You need to realize that this was not your fault but mine. Are you listening?"

She started to back away, unable to look in his face, unable to hold on to him until she could come up with a solution.

Ashton reached out for her, but she eluded his grasp, and his hand dropped to his side. There was an expression on her face, pale and blank yet full of sheer panic, that alarmed him.

"Margaret," he began, but she was already at the door. "For God's sake, don't do anything foolish."

"No, no, I won't," she muttered. "I'll be back as soon as possible, I promise. I have to do something."

"This is the only way," he said softly. "Margaret, this will preserve my honor. Please listen to me—it will also preserve you in the end. Tomorrow's, eh, event, will lay the foundation for your future happiness. Don't you see?"

He truly believed what he was saying, she marveled.

"I'll be back." She glanced at him, then looked

away, unable to bear the sight of his posture, so straight yet alone, his palm open to her. Somehow she managed a smile. "Please eat your soup. I'll be back."

Her hand was shaking, splashing dots of hot wax all over Dr. Parish's botany text. The illustrations were beautiful, detailed, yet preserving the sense of freshness that the plants possess in nature.

"Careful," warned Mary B., her eyes searching the room for signs of the doctor's return. "I still don't understand why this couldn't wait until later, when the doctor will be gone for two hours."

It was late afternoon, but winter darkness already called for the extravagant use of a candle. Dr. Parish had only stepped out for a moment to supervise the distribution of some new patients.

"Hurry," urged Mary B., her toe tapping anxiously under her skirts.

"Here's something," whispered Margaret. "It's called Jamestown Weed and causes unconsciousness and, if you're not careful, death."

"That's not exactly what we want." Mary B. peered toward the door but could tell that the doctor was still out, otherwise she would hear him and see him bending over patients. "Does it grow here at this time of year?"

"Let's see." Her finger ran down the column. "Would you call this a warm climate?"

"Not exactly," she replied, rubbing her hands together to ward off chill.

"Damn. Most of these are native to South America or Asia. Let's see here, how about a savin shrub? The botanical name is *Juniperus sabina.* It says here that a nonfatal dose would cause a coma. Does that sound good to you?"

Mary B. shook her head. "No." She turned her

attention to the green bush pictured in the book. "Comas are too tricky, a fine line between life and death. We want him unconscious, not dead."

"Well, ladies, that is certainly a comfort." Dr. Parish folded his arms over his chest, eyeing his two best nurses. He was aware that they had not seen him enter from the back door, which was usually locked. "If you wish to usurp me, be my guest. Only don't poison me. I'll go willingly enough."

"Dr. Parish," Margaret uttered.

"It seems you ladies would like me to perish." He leaned over the text. "Good God! You two can't be serious?"

"Oh, don't worry, Doctor. This isn't for you. It's for, well . . ." Mary B. looked up at the high ceiling, barely visible in the dim light. "It's for rats," she said triumphantly, unable to resist giving Margaret a satisfied nod.

"How kind you ladies are, not wishing to actually kill a rodent, merely wishing to render him unconscious." He was unable to repress a thin smile. "And, Miss Cox, I am especially impressed that you fear a coma would be too dangerous for a rat. My question is, what will you do with the unconscious rat. Deport him? Send him up North?"

"No, it's not for a rat." Margaret swallowed hard, realizing that the doctor could very well turn her in and end her chance of saving Ashton. But instinct told her he might help. "It's for my husband."

The smile turned into a stern frown. "Young lady, I understand you and General Johnson have had some arguments, but I assure you, poisoning him is not the answer. . . ."

"It's my only hope," she moaned. "Dr. Parish, through a terrible series of accidents, the Confederate government mistakenly believes Ashton to be a spy. He is not. I swear to you on my life that neither of us is guilty. But that doesn't matter—they are going to execute him tomorrow morning."

Mary B. gasped, but Dr. Parish became very calm. "Never, my dear." He patted her hand with his dry, spotted one. "I'm sure you are simply overwrought and imagining such horrible things. They would never dare to execute General Johnson—"

"They are, and they are going to say he died of something else!" Squeezing her eyes shut in an effort to control her voice, she took a deep breath and continued. "He would never even attempt to escape, Doctor. He has such high ideals of honor and duty. So I was hoping to give him something, an herb or whatever I can find. Then I'll say he's dead and carry him out in a coffin."

"What then?"

She shrugged. "I hadn't really thought that far ahead. I just want to get him out of there."

There was a silence. The muffled sounds of the soldiers coughing in the next room seemed very remote.

"Are you absolutely sure?" There was an intensity to his expression that she had never seen. She nodded.

"I have heard strange rumors," he admitted. "This war is full of strange rumors, but I did see the general escorted out of here this morning, and I did notice that he hasn't returned to visit his brother or his wife—uncharacteristic of the man, from what I hear."

He absentmindedly rubbed his chin, a scratchy sandpaper sound as he thought. "I'm beginning to feel like Friar Lawrence," he mumbled, referring to the monk who gave Shakespeare's Juliet a sleeping potion.

"Then you'll help!" Margaret squeezed his hand, and he nodded.

"I was married once, you know." His eyes focused just beyond the women, as if a vision seen only by himself had been aroused. "We were very young, my wife and I, and I believe we could have been content together. Lord, how I missed her the first year after she died." He looked directly at Margaret. "I would have done anything to save her, anything at all. But I wasn't given the chance. Perhaps you, my dear, will be more fortunate."

The softness in his eyes vanished, and again he was the cranky old doctor, no longer the soulful young man who had lost his love. "First, put that book away," he ordered. "Where you found it—not on the top." As he spoke he opened a cabinet and pulled out a small teakwood box. It was an old tea caddy, and he reached into another cabinet for a tiny silver key.

"I do have something in here, collected a long time ago when I was a medical student. I am not sure if it has lost any of its potency, and God help us if the potency has increased over the years."

Opening the box, a strange, musty scent wafted through the dank air of the little corner. It was strangely sweet, and they all stared at it. Pandora's box.

He plucked out a small glass vial stuffed with dried brownish leaves and handed it to Margaret.

"This is monkshood. Take a large leaf or two small ones and make it into a weakish-looking tea. Your husband will probably drink it, even though it doesn't taste very good, because he's become accustomed to drinking coffee made from bark and corncobs and just about anything else under the sun. Plus he's young and foolish enough to drink anything his pretty wife offers.

"Now listen to me. This can be a fatal poison—he will most certainly die if you are not very careful. After he drinks the tea, he will complain of a headache in a matter of minutes, perhaps seconds. He will perspire, suffer from blurred vision, and probably be forced to lie down. Make sure others witness this—it will lend credibility to the story of his presumed illness and death later on."

Margaret and Mary B. stared at the vial, the leaves appearing as innocent as a dried rose from a girl's diary. The doctor continued.

"Soon he will begin breathing rapidly, and his pulse rate will become so fast it will almost be uncountable. Within a half hour, all functions will slow down. His breathing will be shallow, the heart reduced to a few weak beats per minute. In addition, his skin will take on an icy feel. For about an hour, he will truly seem dead—no pulse will be detected.

"Somehow you must get him alone, get his body moving to work the poison out of his system. Then, if you are very careful, you may give him more. . . ."

"More?" Margaret's eyes were wide with dread.

"Until he's safe, until no one can see that he's alive. As long as you manage to get him out of the stupor, return his vital signs to almost normal, you can repeat the procedure several times. But you must wake him up. Do not let him remain in the fully inert phase for too long or he will, indeed, die. Monkshood works by paralyzing the muscles, including the heart. Give him strong coffee, if you can find some, or continue moving him. Just don't allow him to succumb."

Her hand rubbed her temples, the weight of the responsibility making her head pound.

"One more thing," the doctor added. "He will remain fully conscious, mentally alert, no matter how he appears. He will understand everything that's happening around him, every word you say, every action."

Her fingers folded around the vial. "Thank you, both of you. I must go now."

Without another word, she left.

Dr. Parish watched her walk purposefully down the aisle, and finally through the door.

He turned to Mary B., still staring at the closed door. "Why do I have a terrible feeling that something awful will come of this?"

There was a single cot in Ashton's room with a pillow and a neatly folded blanket. He was seated at the table, a crystal ink bottle uncapped before him, writing with swift, bold strokes.

It was dark now; the evening shadows spread their murky darkness over everything in the dimly lit room. The guards allowed her to pass without her having to ask, an expression of regret on the youngest man's face. The moment she entered, the guard inside the room slipped through the door.

Ashton glanced up, part of his hair ruffled where he had clearly passed a hurried hand through. He put down the pen and smiled.

"The soup and bread were wonderful. Thank you."

Margaret didn't reply. Instead she simply stepped over to him. Before he could rise to his feet, she was in his arms, and he sat back down, cradling her on his lap.

"What are you writing?" she murmured into his ear.

"Letters to my mother and Eddie." He paused, brushing a rebellious curl from her smooth neck. ". . . and to you."

His hand rested there, his thumb stroking the hollow of her throat. "But you don't need to write to me," she replied, and he could feel her swallow. "I'm right here."

"It's for later . . ." His voice trailed off as he pressed his lips just below her ear.

Suddenly she straightened, aware that if she became

lost in his embrace, if she returned his passion, she would be unable to concentrate. It was vital that she keep a clear head. This was going to be the most difficult, and by far the most important, night of her life.

"Did I tell you that Eddie's doing much better? Dr. Parish thinks the ball missed the bone after all, and unless the arm becomes badly diseased, he should—" she gasped as his hand slipped over her breast. "Ashton!"

A lazy, insolent grin caressed his mouth, and she jumped to her feet.

"Aren't you freezing in here?" Her voice sounded as if she had inhaled helium.

"Not any more . . ." He pulled her back into his lap, his mouth over hers, soft at first, then harsher. She felt herself spin luxuriously out of control, her hands roaming over his thickly muscled back.

"No," she moaned unconvincingly, trying to pull away. He held her so close she was unable to get much leverage.

"No," she repeated, and this time he heard, and he backed away, confusion mingled with bold desire in his eyes.

"Tea," she said huskily. "I would love a cup of tea."

Shaking his head in confusion, he gestured to a covered tray on one of the chairs. "I believe there might be some water still hot in the pot over there."

"Wonderful." She hopped off his lap and lifted the cloth. There were several dishes covered with food, all untouched, more food than she had seen in the entire Confederacy. Biting her lip, she realized the lavish spread was probably intended as a last meal.

The water wasn't scalding, but it was certainly hot enough to make tea. There was a smaller pot, and she opened it—absolutely delighted.

Coffee—real, genuine, caffeine-filled coffee, dark

and rich, and probably worth a small fortune on the black market. Whatever the cost, it was priceless to her—she could use it later to revive him.

"Here," she said in the most conversational tone she could muster. "I'll make you a nice cup of tea."

"No, thank you." He sighed.

She hadn't anticipated any trouble this early in the plan. Keeping her voice light, she reached into her pocket where she had already separated two small monkshood leaves. Placing them in the bottom of a cup, she poured water over the leaves.

Soon the brew was a pale gray, not particularly appetizing. On the other hand, it looked a far sight better than peanut shell coffee.

"Here, Ash. A nice cup of tea." She brought it over to him, careful not to spill a drop. He waved her away.

"Margaret, I'm really not in the mood for tea. I'm in the mood for you."

Raising the cup to her face, she inhaled deeply and smiled. "This has the most marvelous flavor. All right, Ashton." She raised her eyebrows slightly. "I'll make a deal with you. If you drink this tea, I'm yours to do with you as please."

His eyes lit up and he reached for the cup. "Anything?"

"Anything at all," she confirmed.

He sipped the tea and frowned. "This is terrible." Then he looked up, his eyes gleaming over the rim. "But I would drink hemlock if you were in the bargain."

You're not far off, she thought, pierced by a stab of guilt as he drank the tea. She took the empty cup and placed it back on the tray, right next to the tepid coffee.

She turned to him, a panic beginning to rise in her throat. He looked so handsome, his hair slightly tousled, his eyes bright, the rugged even features she had grown to love.

He held out his arms for her, and she immediately flew to him. His mouth came down on hers with a fierce possession, and she wondered if she, too, might be affected by the poison on his lips. Suddenly he stopped, his hand flying to his forehead.

"Is anything wrong?"

He tried to smile, but a flash of pain must have shot through his head. Margaret put her hand over her mouth. Why hadn't Dr. Parish mentioned how much he would suffer?

"I don't . . ." He was unable to finish the words, and Margaret realized he was breathing rapidly, and perspiration dotted his forehead.

Slipping an arm around his waist, she led him unsteadily to the cot. Her ear pressed to his chest as they walked, she heard his heart pounding frantically, unnaturally and unevenly. Had she given him too much?

"Guard!" she cried, loosening his shirt. He was struggling for every breath, completely covered with a sheen of perspiration.

The guard stepped into the room, his eyes immediately landing on Ashton. "What—blazes! What happened?"

"Please send for a doctor." A sudden thought came to her mind. "Send for Dr. Parish at Miss Cox's hospital—now!"

"I have to get permission . . ."

"Then get it fast. Can't you see how ill he is?"

She was aware of shouts, of footsteps up and down the marble staircase. Pulling up a chair to the cot, she held his large hand in both of hers. "Ashton, I'm so sorry," she whispered. "Hang on, love. It will be over soon."

Dr. Parish entered the room, with Jefferson Davis leaning in from the door. The doctor's expression was blank, his eyes on Ashton.

"Mrs. Johnson," he said as he opened a battered leather satchel, "can you describe the events leading to this?"

"Well, we were talking to each other, and he was overcome with a sudden headache. His condition then became worse," she added lamely.

A feeling of total helplessness swept over her as she watched the doctor work on Ashton. He removed a listening tube from his bag and placed one end on Ashton's chest, the other in his ear. His eyes snapped to hers, then down at the patient.

"Doctor, can you identify the malady?" The president's expression was full of concern over a man he was planning to have executed the next morning.

"I will tell you the truth." The doctor put the listening tube back into the bag and looked up at the president. "This may be an unusual fever or the result of one of his wounds becoming diseased, but as you can see for yourself, this is a very sick man."

Margaret tightened her hold on Ashton's hand.

The doctor shook his head as he continued. "I would guess his pulse rate is somewhere around three hundred per minute, and no man can survive that for long." He turned to Margaret, his voice gentle. Was he playing along with the ruse or trying to tell her that she had just killed her husband?

"I am afraid he will not live through the night, my dear."

Just as Margaret was about to fall to her knees in anguish, Dr. Parish slipped her the biggest, broadest, most exaggerated wink she had ever seen.

There was a stillness to the darkened room, lit by a single flickering candle, that should have been eerie, but to Margaret, it was reassuring. It was proof that the farfetched scheme to save her husband's life was just crazy enough to work.

The usual early morning sounds, of carriage wheels and horses' hooves and good-natured greetings, were subdued, unnaturally muffled. Outside the Old Customs House, the Capitol Building of the Confederacy, small clusters of the curious and mournful were forming, gazing toward the window where the fallen cavalier was rumored to have sickened. The horrible news was just beginning to spread through the streets of Richmond.

General Ashton Johnson, the nation's most dashing hero, was dead.

Margaret sat by the cot where her husband lay motionless, his body cold to the touch.

"Please, Ash," she whispered into his ear. "I really

had no choice. It was between the monkshood and the firing squad, and I thought you stood a better chance with the monkshood."

Linking her fingers through his, she moved closer, brushing a strand of hair from his forehead with her free hand. There were no signs of life, at least not at first glance. If you studied the body for long enough, you might detect the shallow, infrequent breaths. If you felt for a pulse at the wrist, you would feel nothing, but Dr. Parish had assured her that was typical of the drug.

"So it's as if his body is in suspended animation?" she had asked the doctor in private.

He frowned for a moment, then smiled. "What an apt phrase, 'suspended animation,'" he repeated, rolling the words over his tongue, savoring their feel. "Yes, that is it precisely. You must stay by him, however—cause a distraction if he starts to wake up. No one will find it the least bit odd that a distressed young widow would refuse to let her husband's body out of her sight."

Everyone had backed away respectfully, hats held in sorrowful hands, allowing her to remain with him in solitude.

It was easy for her to be with him as long as she kept up her one-sided banter. "The next step will be to get you out of here in a casket, but don't worry. I've ordered one with nice padding and a satin pillow. It will cost the Confederacy plenty, but it's all their fault, so don't feel guilty."

Hollow footsteps echoed just outside the door, and she turned to see if anyone would enter. They did not. Whoever it was paused at the door, then continued down the hall, heels clicking measured paces on the smooth marble.

Ashton's skin had a strange, waxy feel. She tried to

ignore how truly lifeless he appeared. Slowly and gingerly, she lifted one of his eyelids the way Dr. Parish had earlier. For some reason what he saw there caused him to chuckle, a reaction he neatly transformed into a hacking cough for the benefit of the president, the secretary of war, and a cluster of misty-eyed soldiers, all craning to get a last look at General Johnson.

His eyelid moved back easily under her touch, and she reached for the candle to get a better look at his wonderful amber eyes. It was the most furious, murderous glare she had ever seen. Trembling, she put the candlestick down and pulled away from him, folding her hands on her lap.

"So you're mad, eh?" she hissed. "Well, this is the last time I try to save your neck, pal."

With an exasperated sigh, she looked up at the ceiling, then back to her husband, the anger defused. "I'm sorry. This isn't much fun for me, either, you know. You have the easy part."

A discreet cough behind her caused her to turn around. Standing in the doorway, dressed in a crisp uniform, was Robert E. Lee.

"I just heard, my dear." He walked slowly toward Margaret, but his eyes were on Ashton, an expression of fragile sorrow there. "Oh, my poor, poor boy," he mumbled to himself.

He reached out and brushed his hand over Ashton's icy cheek. "You are right, Mrs. Johnson. It is by far the hardest trial to be left behind. You husband is at rest now, and he does indeed have the easy part, as you said."

They both looked down at Ashton. Margaret's mind was churning to think of something appropriate to say, when she saw Ashton's thumb move.

"Oh," she gasped, throwing herself over Ashton's

torso. With one swift but awkward movement, she covered most of his body with her skirts.

"Mrs. Johnson, please, my dear," said General Lee with compassion. "We must not get overly distraught. Perhaps this was really the best way, after all . . ."

Ashton's arm began to flex.

"No! You stop it this instant!" she cried to Ashton.

"I am sorry," replied Lee. "Perhaps this is not the best time to offer . . ."

A deep groan escaped Ashton's mouth. "Please be quiet," she said harshly to her husband, who was clearly coming out of the stupor.

"Yes, my dear Mrs. Johnson." General Lee backed away. "I will speak to you later, then."

When the general left the room, Ashton stopped all movement. A charged panic shot through her—what if he was really dead?

Swallowing hard, she lifted the eyelid again. There was a distinct glare in his eye.

He was, without a doubt, furious.

Dr. Parish stood beside Margaret, an avuncular hand on her shoulder. She couldn't help wringing her hands in concern, and even the doctor's comforting words did little to lessen her apprehension.

"Mrs. Johnson, I assure you this reaction is perfectly normal. It was necessary to give him an additional drop or two of monkshood. You said yourself he was beginning to stir, and even the most passionate of mourners would no doubt notice if the body sat up and cursed."

Margaret nodded, understanding the need for more poison, but dreading the risk. "I just want him to be well," she uttered quietly.

"I will say this," the doctor said in a light tone. "Those Johnson boys are a strapping lot. I don't believe many men could have survived the dose of monkshood you initially gave Ashton." He ignored her expression of guilt. "And I surely don't believe many men could have rallied from their wounds the way both Ashton and his younger brother have."

"Eddie?" Margaret's gaze shot to the doctor's. "I haven't told him about the monkshood! He knew we were planning something, but . . . oh, Doctor, I had better tell him before he hears that Ashton is dead. He might think he was executed and that the government is promoting the story of . . ."

Dr. Parish waved his hand. "Mrs. Johnson, your brother-in-law is fully aware of the scheme. Miss Cox told him everything, and he is absolutely delighted. In fact, the news of Ashton's suposed death was the best possible tonic for young Major Johnson's shoulder."

A staccato knock on the door startled both of them. Margaret threw a worried glance at Ashton, who was perspiring heavily after the last jolt of monkshood.

"I'll take care of whoever it is." The doctor sighed. "You should sit by the general and make sure nobody sees his face."

Margaret positioned herself at the head of the cot, and she tenderly wiped the dampness from his forehead and cheeks. "Oh, Ash," she murmured. "Please forgive me."

Dr. Parish opened the door, a scowl already set firmly on his lined face. "Yes?" he demanded curtly of the visitor.

It was a young man with a wispy attempt of a beard, so sparse that his pink skin shone through in naked patches. He was rather short, but formally attired in a dark suit and a stiff white collar with painful-looking points.

"Is this where General Johnson is resting?" The young man carried a large tin bucket and several lengths of rubber hose coiled in the bucket.

"Yes it is, young man," he snapped. "But as her physician, I have insisted that Mrs. Johnson be allowed to remain alone with her husband. She is of a rather nervous disposition, and for the sake of her health, she must be allowed these moments for a final farewell. I bid you good day."

The doctor began to close the door when the young man wedged a foot in the door to prevent his dismissal.

"Sir, I am Grover Sharpe, of Sharpe and Foote, undertakers. I have been sent by President Davis to offer a complimentary embalming of the esteemed General Johnson." Grover Sharpe squared his narrow shoulders, as if he had just issued a mighty command.

From inside the room, Margaret blanched, stifling an urge to cry. She delicately raised Ashton's eyelid, hoping her poor husband had not heard.

Again, he seemed to be livid with anger, yet enjoying her discomfort.

"I'm glad you find this so amusing," she whispered into his ear.

But her voice carried to the young undertaker, whose jaw suddenly went slack with surprise. "Is she speaking to the deceased?" He leaned close to Dr. Parish, his tone one of professional curiosity.

"Yes, as a matter of fact," replied the doctor sadly. "She is showing symptoms of hysterical delusions, very common given the circumstance. The only hope is if she is allowed to remain with her husband. Eventually she will realize that he is not responding to her, and she will understand that he is dead. Otherwise, her sanity may never be restored."

Grover Sharpe stared in morbid fascination at the lovely young widow with tousled hair and flashing eyes. Then he regained his businesslike composure. "I understand, sir. And I must insist that you allow me to perform my work. To be perfectly blunt, sir, she will not find it pleasant to be with her husband for much longer unless he is embalmed, if you understand my meaning, sir."

For a moment Dr. Parish was speechless, and he glanced over his shoulder at Margaret and Ashton. Then a burst of gratified, silent elation passed through him, although he managed to speak in a sad, withered tone. "Ah, Mr. Sharpe." Dr. Parish nodded sagely. "That, you see, is part of the cure. Not only must she realize that he is dead by his inability to speak, but she must understand the rather distasteful changes in her husband in order to banish all of her romantic notions."

The undertaker shifted his weight uncomfortably, his hand still clutching the bucket and hose.

"Well, sir," he shrugged, wrinkling his pointed nose as he again tried to see over the doctor's shoulders. "Do you think you could explain that to President Davis? I might still be able to bill him, I beg your pardon, if he understands that I was willing to perform my trade."

"I will inform the president," the doctor said dryly.

"Thank you, sir." Grover Sharpe turned to leave, then paused. "Uh, it's a real shame about the general. I mean, even when I thought I might get a little extra business out of the incident, I was mighty sad. I saw him once with his men. Absolutely glorious, Doctor. A true inspiration." After a thoughtful pause, Grover Sharpe shook his head and left.

"Mrs. Johnson," said the doctor the moment he closed the door. "I suggest we get this thing over with as soon as possible. Perhaps we can hold the funeral this evening."

"Oh, no," moaned Margaret. "What will we do about the burial?"

A smile of genuine satisfaction appeared on the doctor's face. "I believe I have a plan, Mrs. Johnson."

With a delighted, hushed voice, he explained his complete scheme.

"Do you think it will really work?" Margaret asked.

"To tell you the truth, we don't have much of a choice," he responded as he examined the motionless figure of the general. "The longer he remains here, the more Grover Sharpes will flock to have the honor of embalming him."

Margaret looked directly into the old doctor's pale eyes. "Dr. Parish, I don't believe I can ever thank you enough for all you have done." She glanced back at her husband, a man who now had a real chance of growing old.

The doctor waved her thanks away, a gruff motion to hide his own feelings, deeper than he would like anyone to suspect. "It has been a rare pleasure, Mrs. Johnson. I see so much death every day. I see so many noble youths suffer hideously before they are allowed to go on to the next world, that it is a something of a restorative for me to help a deserving couple live happily ever after."

"Why, Dr. Parish." Margaret smiled. "I believe you are a genuine romantic."

He huffed in annoyance. "No, ma'am. I am a realist who only happens to dabble in romance." Then he winked. "And if you tell anyone that, I will never forgive you."

The casket was roomy and well-padded, comfortable by anyone's standards, but Margaret was unable to watch as two of the burly guards lowered Ashton into it. The scene simply looked too final, too realistic.

She had requested that holes be punched in the lid so that she could still speak to her husband when he was at last in his final resting place, and the carpenter shrugged and bored the holes. It didn't matter to him one way or another, and in his day he had heard stranger requests.

General Lee returned, along with other dignitaries, to pay their official respects to Margaret. She stood by the coffin, clad now in a black damask gown borrowed from Varina Davis.

"General Lee," said Margaret in a suitably hushed voice. "I must apologize for my behavior earlier. I am sure Ashton would be ashamed if he had seen me behave so poorly."

The general smiled sadly. "There is certainly no need to apologize. It is I who intruded upon you, and I most certainly should have waited until a more suitable hour."

There was an awkward afternoon, the drawn-out visitation, as men she had never seen before nodded to her or pressed heartfelt sympathy damply into her increasingly sore hand. She tried several times to work her way back to General Lee, but she was always detained by some member of the Confederate Senate or Congress.

Finally, just as Lee was about to depart, Margaret was able to reach him. "Sir?" she asked.

He paused and smiled warmly. "Yes, Mrs. Johnson."

"Excuse me, but I need to speak to you about Ashton's burial." Her voice wavered, as if with emotion. In truth she was terrified, for if this conversation did not go as she hoped, Ashton might very well be buried alive.

"Of course. I understand that President Davis has commissioned a magnificent monument, and the general's remains will be interred in Hollywood Cemetery, right over on Cherry Street."

"Well, General Lee, sir," she said, her eyes flying to Ashton, who was looking very handsome indeed in the open coffin. "I would really rather have him buried someplace peaceful, somewhere away from the war."

"Richmond is safe, Mrs. Johnson. He will not be bothered here." The general began to leave.

"No, sir." Her knees were beginning to feel like water. How dare she defy General Lee!

He stopped, startled by her rebellious tone. "You see, sir," she continued, "Ashton always wanted to be buried in England."

"England!"

"Yes, sir. I was wondering if I could just take him over there and bury him in some nice, quiet little patch of land, far away from the ugliness and sorrow of this conflict."

A group of men now gathered to watch Margaret and General Lee, some amused by her audacity, others furious that she would put the gallant General Lee in such an ungraceful position in front of so many other people.

"It is winter, my dear." He was not unfriendly, just a little stiff. "And there is, indeed, a war going on. We do not have a ship to spare to send you over to England, and even if we did, the danger from those people's armed ships would be too great. You would be risking not only yourself but the entire crew. No, Mrs. Johnson, I regret to say that I cannot allow you to bury him abroad."

Again, he started to leave. This was her last chance. "Flag of truce," she shouted, a little louder than she intended.

The general halted.

"I know mail sometimes passes through the flag of truce," she stammered. "This is a compassionate request, General Lee. Do you think the Yankees would prevent a grieving widow from carrying out her husband's last wish? They wouldn't dare. In fact, Ash has many friends up North, some in powerful positions. I would guess his old West Point friends would be glad to help us out, maybe even in a Yankee ship. It would be good public relations, sir. And good public relations is something the North badly needs right now."

A Mississippi senator spoke up. "Mrs. Johnson, why on earth would we wish to give the United States any favorable press?"

"Ah." She smiled, turning on all the charm she could muster. "Don't you see, sir, that both sides would benefit? The North would seem a little kinder to their own people, and we, the noble Confederate States of America, would seem positively saintly. Imagine if those scores of women grumbling for bread were told that their government thinks well enough of women to help a poor widow bury her husband."

There was a murmur among the men in the room, and Margaret knew Ashton could hear every word.

"And in England I could do a little work myself, trying to raise humanitarian aid for our cause. We would be a stronger nation if we had more food and a few extra blankets for the soldiers and civilians. I could be a sort of good will ambassador."

With a grudging nod, General Lee took Margaret's hand. "My dear Mrs. Johnson, I had no idea how much you loved your husband. Are you truly willing to leave your home indefinitely, risk your own life for this journey?"

"Without a second thought," she answered, looking him straight in the eye.

"I will see what I can do, my dear. Perhaps we could raise the necessary funds. I will speak to the president myself." And with that, General Lee left the chamber.

Within thirty minutes, the Richmond gossips were enjoying the best tidbit of the year. General Johnson's grief-torn widow had managed to challenge both the

military and the civilian powers of the Confederacy.
And from all accounts, the passionate Mrs. Johnson
had emerged triumphant.

The farewells were hasty, stuck between the frantic
preparations for the journey, the packing and the
letter-writing, and constantly watching Ashton.

When she was forced to leave his side, she insisted
that Mary B. or Dr. Parish or a rapidly recovering
Eddie watch over his open casket. She managed to get
a note to Ashton's mother, alluding to the plan. Eliza
traveled to Richmond to help with Margaret's last-
minute plans and to see both of her sons.

Although Eliza was not overly thrilled with the
thought of dosing her son with poison, Eddie had
convinced her of its necessity.

Margaret's last morning in Richmond was hectic
and more than a little terrifying. Here she had allies,
friends who knew exactly what was happening to
Ashton. She drew often on their moral support, a
funny word from Mary B., a slightly off-color joke
from Eddie, a comforting pat on the back from Dr.
Parish. Once she was on the ship, she would be alone.
The success or failure of the plan would depend
entirely on Margaret.

In a very real sense, Margaret would be completely
responsible for her husband's life.

She had one last letter to write, one vital slip of
paper that just might ensure Ashton's happiness for
the rest of his life. With unusual care, she wrote and
rewrote the letter, choosing the words painstakingly,
making sure the meaning of each sentence was unmistakable. There could be absolutely no doubt as to the
content of this letter, no part could be open to
speculation.

With ink on her hands, she threw the badly
splotched or imperfect copies into the fire grate,

watching as each piece of paper darkened, illuminated on the edges with a red glow, and finally burned into a darkened pile of ash.

She then addressed the letter—"To General Robert E. Lee. Do not open until January 1, 1868"—and hand-delivered it on her way to the ship.

Of all the men in the Confederacy, she knew that General Lee alone would save that letter for four years and never once be tempted to open it.

CHAPTER
18

London was especially cold, a chilly mist wrapping itself around everyone, penetrating clothes and carriages, making it impossible to get warm.

The patrons of the Maiden's Arms tavern were doing their best to forget the nasty weather blowing outside. A few mugs of ale seemed the best remedy, comforting the body and making the world seem a far more hospitable place indeed.

The rough oak door flew open, and there were the usual good-natured grumbles from patrons complaining of the sudden gust. But when the loudest complainer realized who the visitor was, his face melted into a welcoming grin.

"Why, look who it is, mates!" he bellowed. "It's Bertram Butler of that noble ship the *North Star!* Maiden, an extra special pint for my friend here."

The bartender, a surly man with arms the size of Highland sheep, glared at the request but sullenly pulled the tap and poured a glass of murky, room-temperature ale.

"So, tell me, Bertram, how are your travels?"

Bertram Butler, short and stout, with a nose that attested to his former career as a failed pugilist, did not speak until he had drained almost half of his mug. He wiped his mouth with the back of his arm, but a thick line of beige foam remained on his full upper lip.

"I tell you, I'm a free man. I couldn't take it anymore, and I'm well out of it."

"You left the missus?" offered one patron.

"You cut the ball and chain?" added another with delight.

"No, no," he said in a gravelly voice, not offended in the least. "Me job. I've left me job."

A stunned silence hushed the crowd, the only sounds to pierce the air were the shuffling of patrons to get a better seat for the tale sure to ensue. A few men took eager slurps of their beer, storing up the drink so they wouldn't feel a sudden thirst during the narrative.

"Tell us, Bertram," coaxed an older man with his left ear wrapped in a filthy bandage.

"This last crossing was the worst of me life, the worst ever, I might add." He drained the contents of his mug, and with a snap, another ale was poured. "Going over was fine, the usual band of crazies, but in my thirty years at sea I have become used to all the strange goings-on. Nothing, I thought, could make my eyes pop out. I've seen it all."

He cleared his throat, biding his time until his next mug was handed to him. He then continued, enjoying the undivided attention of every patron there. "Well, you have heard of the war going on over in the colonies, haven't you? A bloody, terrible affair it is, I might add."

"They should never have left us," spat the man with the bandage. "They thought they were so blooming smart, and look at them. Shame."

Bertram shot the man an irritated look, and then went on. "Anyway, this general, a young man, bravest man you've ever heard of, up and died a few weeks ago. Just up and died."

"Shame," tsked another patron.

"This here general was a southerner, a Confederate, mind you . . ."

"They're the ones like us," stated the man with the bandage, with a voice of authority.

"Right. Well, this Confederate general had lots of friends up North, in the United States proper. And he also had the most beautiful tidbit I've ever seen as his wife, a regular dainty tidbit she is. So this little lady wants her dead husband to be buried over here in England, if you please."

"A woman of rare taste." The man with the bandaged head nodded.

"So everyone, both sides, mind you, want this lovely lady to have her way. She is to get the nicest room on the *North Star,* and yours truly is to see to the lady's comfort."

"Coo! Lucky man!"

"Well, that's what I think, too, when I first see her, all white and pale. What do you think is the first thing the lady asks for?"

"Gin?"

"A pack of cards?"

"Bubble and squeak?"

"Wrong," Bertram announced in exultation, reaching for his third ale. "Wrong as wrong can be, every one of you. She wants the body of the husband to be put in her stateroom."

"No!"

"She wants a stiff in her room?"

"That's what I said. So I says, 'Ma'am, the usual procedure is for the deceased to be placed below. That arrangement, we find, is more comfortable for everyone.' Well, this lady will have none of it. And since I was told to give her what she wants, I bring up this big casket. The general must have weighed sixteen stone if he weighed an ounce."

"Don't stiffs get lighter as they ripen?"

"Not this one." He held up a hand with dramatic flare, silencing the sympathetic murmurs. "It gets worse. So here I am, helping her settle the coffin in her room. What does she want next?"

"Gin?"

"A pack of cards?"

"No," Bertram scoffed at the suggestions. "She wants me to put her husband to bed."

"To bed?"

He nodded. "She wants me to take him out of the coffin and tuck him into her bed, nice and gentlelike, so her hubby can be snug as a swaddled babe."

"I've heard of that!" shouted a patron from the back of the room. "It's called necra-something. I heard a fancy gentleman in my hack talk about it once."

Bertram waved an impatient hand. "Naw. That's not it. You see, she's so nice and pretty, well, I did it for her."

"You picked up the stiff?"

"I did. And he wasn't stiff at all, just sort of pale. And you know what? Even dead, this fellow was better looking than the lot of you. I felt sort of sorry for her, you know, the way she took care of this big guy. But I tell you, things got stranger and stranger.

"She asks for coffee, and I bring her some, but I forgot the sugar. Well, I come back a few minutes later, and knock once before I enter. Do you know what she's doing? She's holding a cup to the stiff's mouth, talking to him all sweet and nice, asking him how he likes the taste of real coffee and whatnot."

"Poor lady. She's as cracked as a ginger jar," murmured someone, and others muttered in agreement.

"Then she talks to him all the time. Once she opened his eyes like this." Bertram poked two stubby fingers over his eyelids, revealing a pop-eyed stare. "And she goes, 'So, are you still mad at me? My, you can certainly hold a grudge.'"

"So the stiff was mad at her for something?"

"I suppose. But she sure wasn't mad at him. Another time I walked in and she was giving him a shave."

"No!"

"I hear that dead people grow hair and whiskers and that if you want a dead body to look nice, you have to groom it," offered the hack driver.

"Well, maybe," said Bertram. "But are you supposed to take a dead body for a walk?" There was a harsh, collective gasp—just the reaction he had been hoping for. "She did, perambulating all over the place, chatting away with this great hulk of a dead general. Only in her room, of course."

"What else did she do?"

"She kissed him."

"What?"

Bertram grinned. "She kissed him on the mouth. More than once I saw her whisper something to him and kiss him. I caught her brushing his teeth another day."

"Mayhaps that was so that she could kiss him?"

Bertram glared, not wanting additional editorial comments. "And one time, when the seas were particularly rough, she lay right next to him. Said she didn't want him to roll off the bed and get hurt."

There was a universal silence. Even men with empty

mugs stood in contemplation, trying to make sense of the odd tale they had just been told.

"So, gentlemen, I quit my job. This is enough. No more. I can't take another chance of meeting up with a lady like that."

The man with the bandaged head clicked his tongue.

"So, Bertram," he asked. "How's the wife?"

February 1864

Margaret closed the window against the frigid winter breeze. Her arms clasped together, she shivered, wondering if she would ever again feel warm. And the chill wasn't simply physical.

She glanced at the chair where Ashton had spent most of his recovery, gradually regaining his strength with the help of a wonderful physician. The stronger he became physically, the wider the wedge between the two of them grew.

He simply did not understand.

For a while she kept up the one-sided conversations that had become her trademark. She watched in sheer joy as the color returned to his cheeks, as he filled out on the meals prepared downstairs and sent up in a pulley. She wondered if he had lost the ability to speak and hear, for he ignored her completely, but he was talkative enough with Dr. McCoy. And when he was well enough, he began spending time at a men's club.

Ashton, the handsome, mysterious southerner, became the most desirable addition to every social activity in London. Most assumed the gallant foreigner to be unwed, for he never mentioned a wife or spoke of his past at any length. He did express a desire to return to the Confederacy. That was all that could be determined about Ashton Johnson.

Since his manners and deeply rooted charm, and his obvious education, were so gently displayed, everyone also assumed that he was a man of great wealth. The cut of his clothes indicated the best London tailors, although they were all a little too new to be completely fashionable. His address, just off Hyde Park, was correct enough to allow mothers of unmarried daughters to dream of their own darling Elizabeth or Sally or Gwendolyne becoming the future Mrs. Ashton Powell Johnson.

Margaret walked toward the dining table, the scene of some of their more painful arguments. But they weren't really arguments. She could not get him to acknowledge her in any way, shape, or form. He was polite, but never spoke more meaningful words than "Pass the salt" or "I'm going out."

And when she called breakfast that morning their "Citizen Kane phase," he didn't bother to glance up from his plate.

She was losing him, and there wasn't a damn thing she could do about it.

At least he was alive, she told herself. She would be just as alone if he had been killed. Here she could see that he was well-fed, healthy if not happy. Thanks to the generosity of patrons, they could live in this style indefinitely. She had received enough checks from sources both North and South for them to live in comfort for years.

That is, if she didn't kill him first.

Intellectually, she understood his fury. Yet she honestly thought that by now he would have seen things her way, would understand that she did what she had to out of her love for him.

There was a soft knock on the door, and Margaret answered it herself. Their sumptuous flat boasted a maid's room, but Margaret didn't need a maid. After all, she was by herself most of the time, and the meals were prepared. She needed no one. Ashton slept in the maid's room.

"Dr. McCoy." She smiled, opening the door wide for him to enter. "How wonderful to see you. You seem to be my only friend here in London."

"He's gone out again?" Dr. McCoy asked sharply.

"Yes, he has." Margaret shrugged, not wanting to dwell on the topic. "Would you like some tea?"

"Mrs. Johnson, I've come to ask if he knows yet." Margaret swallowed and shook her head.

The doctor's eyes softened. "He must be told, Mrs. Johnson. He has a right to know that his wife is expecting a child."

"I suppose," she answered uncomfortably. "But I don't think that would matter to him. He wants to go back as soon as he is well enough."

"To face almost certain death? Is he mad?"

"No," she replied. "He's a Confederate."

The doctor seemed puzzled, then gave Margaret an appraising look. "Have you been able to keep anything down?"

"A little." She smiled, and Dr. McCoy was struck anew at how lovely this young American woman was. "To tell you the truth, some of your British dishes are a little tough to get used to. Kippered herring and kidneys are not my idea of appetizing."

He chuckled and reached for her wrist, checking her pulse against his gold pocket watch. "Mrs. Johnson, you are not my strongest patient. I do not wish to frighten you, but you are not going to have an easy time of it. You need to tell your husband."

"Oh, I will," she answered noncommittally.

"Well, then I must be off." The doctor offered her a reassuring pat. "He'll come around, Mrs. Johnson. He is a proud man, and until very recently he was a very ill man. Sometimes illness can alter a man's perspective on life."

"Sometimes," she said softly.

When the doctor left, she felt more alone than ever, as if she were the only person alive on the face of the earth. She stared out of the window for a few moments, watching the carriages driving through Hyde Park. The English seemed remarkably immune to their own weather.

Just as she turned to go over to the desk to write a few letters, she felt a stabbing pain in her lower abdomen. Like a giant, twisting knot, it tightened, doubling her over with the force of the burning sensation.

"No," she moaned, just before her knees folded under her and her head struck a sharp-edged table.

Ashton had mechanically eaten the lavish meal at Lord and Lady Trendome's, not truly tasting the expertly prepared dishes or distinguishing one fine vintage from the next. His unusual silence was duly noted by Lucy, the Trendomes' twenty-three-year-old daughter. She did her best to captivate the fascinating Ashton Johnson, and although his responses were correct and well-phrased, his eyes—a most intriguing blend of golds and greens—betrayed his lack of interest.

He glanced down at her, barely noticing the sumptuous parade of jewels clustered at her throat and up her bare arms. Seeing the display of gems reminded him of Margaret, of how she managed to shine at the Davises' ball without a single piece of jewelry other than her wedding band.

Lucy Trendome shot her mother an exasperated look, her smooth brow becoming lined with irritation. Lady Trendome responded by fixing a broad smile on her own face and turning toward Ashton.

"So, Mr. Johnson," she said with a practiced tilt of her head. Countless hours before her mirror had confirmed that it was a most becoming angle. "What do you think of our English women? Do you not think they are the most beautiful in the world?"

"Why, Lady Trendome." He flashed his smile, bright teeth glaring in the tiered candlelight. "I daresay I have never seen such lovely women." It was difficult to hold his smile, for all he could think of was his wife, the artless grace she so fully possessed, her flawless beauty. Above all, her kindness, her wit, and the way she loved him.

He did not doubt for an instant that she loved him. But she had gone too far. She dared to enter a man's world, to play with the very powers of the Confederacy.

She went too far, damn it.

"My dear wife is fishing for compliments." Lord Trendome laughed, his dark hair slicked over his smooth skull like the pelt of a wet otter.

Ashton smiled in response and looked down at the sorbet on his plate. When had it arrived? Raising a spoon, he ate the ice, heedless of the brilliantly fresh flavor.

Margaret.

How could she have done what she did? She had all but destroyed him, leaving his pride in tatters. Everyone back in the States had heard all about his wife's exploits. Everything that was so vital to him, the whole ideal of honor that had always defined his life, had been taken away from him.

But then . . .

His mind wandered to some of the comments she had made, her earnest chatter while he was confined to that cursed box. The casket. An unexpected grin appeared as he thought of her on the ship, oblivious to the startled responses of the poor steward.

She had said some strange things about the Confederacy. At one point she called Ashton a victim of "group psychology." He had been too close to the leaders, especially Lee, to see the situation clearly. Had he but looked objectively at a map, he would realize how hopeless their cause had been.

That had struck a nerve, for although she did not realize it, Ashton had seen a map in just such an objective way on the very morning of his arrest. And for that, even before the discovery of the paper in his pocket, he had been branded a traitor by the president.

The usual conversation at the silver-laden table continued to buzz, aimless prattle like so many annoying insects. At least insects found constructive ways to occupy their time.

Margaret.

This morning she had blanched at the sight of kippers, causing him to act like a child by devouring every single one on the platter. Had she eaten anything at all? In truth, she had grown even more slender since arriving in London.

It dawned on him in a horrifying instant—she was ill. He had been too furious to notice, but now he recalled the times she left the table, a napkin over her mouth. Her alabaster skin was unnaturally pale. The entire time he was recovering his robust health, she was growing sicker each day. And Dr. McCoy had been dwelling on her, watching her from under his tangled black eyebrows.

Ashton's hand clenched on the table. He had to leave now, as soon as possible. He had to get home to Margaret.

"I say, Mr. Johnson, that is a tragedy. An utter tragedy."

Ashton looked blankly at the speaker, a monocled gentleman in a dark green frock coat.

"Excuse me?"

"I said," the man repeated with irritation, "the death of your president's little boy."

Ashton said nothing, his mind in complete shock.

"What? Where?" he said stupidly. "Lincoln?"

"The little boy in Richmond, the Davis child. He fell off a balcony of some sort at the Executive Mansion. I understand he was only a little tyke, only about . . ."

"Five." Ashton was beginning to feel ill himself. This was everything Margaret had said, everything she had predicted or dreamed. And for that he had turned his back on her, called her a spy. "Joseph was five."

When had he last seen the little boy? Giggling under his father's desk, managing to coax a smile from his stern father with a silly poem. And now that child was dead. Ashton began to finish his meal, and he stopped. What the hell was he doing?

"Please forgive me, Lord and Lady Trendome. I thank you for a magnificent meal, but I just remembered that I have a prior engagement . . ." Before anyone could reply, Ashton was on his way out the door.

"Well, he was not completely taken with my charms tonight," complained Lucy to her mother as the men retired to their brandy and cigars.

"My dear daughter, you are too hard. Why do you say he was not attentive?"

"In case you failed to notice, Mother," she said petulantly, "as he said his abrupt good-bye, he drank the finger bowl."

"Margaret!" Ashton called as he entered the parlor.

Although it was just past nine o'clock, the place was dark. She usually read, keeping the lamps lit until eleven or so.

God, how he had missed her!

The entire way home from the Trendomes he had thought of her, of why she felt it necessary to ply him with monkshood on their bizarre escape from the Confederacy. Just as he began to cross Hyde Park, on foot because he lacked the patience to seek a hack, he realized that had the positions been reversed, he would have done the exact same thing. He would have stopped at nothing to preserve her life.

The uneasy feeling that had been plaguing him since that afternoon was no doubt caused by the confoundedly unnatural way he had been treating her. Without speaking to her, without sharing his feelings, he had managed to stall their healing.

His heartless treatment of her was unforgivable. Margaret risked everything to save his life, and he treated her with less civility than a hated enemy. Ashton had caused a one-sided civil war between them.

There was a small scraping sound, and it took a moment for his eyes to adjust to the darkened room. A feminine figure was leaning over the carpet by the writing desk.

"Mag?" he asked, but even as the name was out, he realized it was not his wife. It was one of the women who worked here, who silently scurried away whenever he appeared. She was busy with a stain on the floor and did not look up.

Ashton couldn't help but smile. Margaret had mentioned that she would feel uncomfortable with a maid. Something had clearly changed her mind.

"Excuse me, miss," he said softly. His own accent sounded strange after the rounded British tones. "Do you know where my wife is?"

The woman kept on scrubbing, but he knew she had heard him. There was a straightening of her back, a self-consciousness that hadn't been there before. He repeated the question, moving closer to the woman, looking down at the carpet as he spoke.

Blood.

She was scrubbing blood from the carpet. He had seen enough blood in the past four years to be able to identify it in every imaginable form, on every possible surface. The door to the bedroom opened, and Dr. McCoy emerged, his face set in barely restrained anger. Ashton was about to speak when the doctor silenced him with a brutal glare and motioned to the other end of the room, closing the door behind him.

Ashton's mouth was suddenly dry, as a fear more potent than any he had experienced in battle ran up his spine.

"What happened?" he managed to say harshly.

The doctor straightened and looked Ashton in the eye. "The baby is fine for now, in case you happen to be curious."

"The baby?"

"Damn it, that's what I said," Dr. McCoy spat, watching Ashton's reaction.

With an unsteady hand he reached behind him, feeling for a chair. The doctor guided him to an uncomfortable-looking carved thronelike seat, clearly not intended for someone of Ashton's size or weight. But the doctor was satisfied.

"What happened?" Ashton said again, wondering if he had slipped into some sort of nightmare.

"I believe she fainted and hit her head on that table over there." Dr. McCoy gestured toward the maid, who stood to leave, bobbing to the men as she exited with her clanking bucket.

"Is the blood . . ." Ashton began, not really wanting an answer.

"It's from a rather nasty gash on her right temple.

Head wounds always bleed excessively." The doctor poured Ashton a large glass of brandy and handed it to him before he poured one for himself.

Ashton's hand began to shake, and he quickly placed the tumbler of brandy on a table. "May I see her?"

"That depends," the doctor replied after a healthy gulp of liquor. "She knows all about what you've been doing here, you know. You haven't exactly made a secret of your stunning nightlife."

Receiving no response, he continued. "She also knows that you plan on returning to the Confederacy as soon as possible. You are well enough to travel, sir."

Ashton said nothing for several painful moments, staring straight ahead at the closed bedroom door, but not really seeing.

"Well, Doctor," he said at last, his voice unusually quiet. "Have you ever known a man to destroy his life so completely?"

Dr. McCoy almost smiled, but curbed the urge. "She loves you. Against all reason, I might add. She's alive. Given those two facts, I should think you have a good enough chance. I'd bet a pound that if you stop this ridiculous behavior, things can be mended."

Again, there was a strained silence. "How is she, Dr. McCoy? Is she strong enough to carry a child?"

"Ah, so you do have eyes." The doctor drained his glass. "To tell you the truth, it might have been better if she lost the babe today. The further along she progresses, the more difficult it will become. A lot will depend on simple will, how strong her desire to live is. And right now, she doesn't seem to care one way or another."

Ashton took a deep breath and rubbed his eyes. "How did you find her?" He asked the question with weary concern.

"I decided to take her up on her offer of afternoon

tea. When she failed to answer the door, I obtained the keys and found her over there."

"I can never thank you enough." Ashton's eyes were suddenly bright. "But I have no money, at least I don't think so. She's been handling the finances. I've been too angry to discuss anything with her. I don't know if I can pay for . . ."

"I have been paid."

"By whom?"

The doctor stood up. "I'll be back in the morning. She should be fine, just watch her carefully. And please, treat her kindly. No matter what your ultimate plans, she needs you now."

He began to leave, when Ashton stopped him. "Excuse me, Dr. McCoy. Who is paying you?"

With an enigmatic tip of his worn hat, the doctor left without another word.

Everything felt heavy. Her arms and legs, her head, even her hair, falling loosely over her shoulders, seemed to weigh an extraordinary amount. Her head pounded as if it had been struck; still she couldn't remember exactly what happened.

It was an oppressive drowsiness, with no pleasant stupor to erase the nightmare of the last few weeks. Although her limbs felt weighed down, her mind was alert, repeating every furious look and angry glance she had received from Ashton. The most vivid image in her mind was his perpetual absence, an emptiness from her life that seemed to speak eloquently of how he detested her.

Slowly, she moved her hand over her body, pausing to rest as she worked her way to the throbbing temple. Her eyes remained closed, partly because she lacked the energy to force them open, partly because there was no reason to look around the huge bedroom in which she had spent so many solitary hours. She knew every corner by heart, each piece of furniture as if she herself had carved it; even the cluttered bric-a-brac shelf was achingly familiar.

Margaret also knew what she would not see. She would not see Ashton.

Memories of the day before began to return, hazy at first, then a little clearer as she went over them again. As if it had happened to someone else, Margaret remembered Dr. McCoy placing her gently on the massive bed she shared with no one. He had been kind, reassuring her that her baby was fine; she had simply hit her head. He left abruptly, mumbling about another patient. Before drifting off to sleep, she had heard him speaking to someone in the next room, probably a maid.

A soreness in her throat made it difficult to swallow, and she recalled crying at some point, although she could not remember exactly what caused such an avalanche of tears. But it really didn't matter. She cried easily lately, set off by the near certain knowledge that Ashton was leaving her. The numbness she experienced at first, when she realized he would return to Richmond, was replaced by an emptiness that even the prospect of a baby failed to lessen.

Soon she would be alone in this strange place in a very strange time. She was just getting used to boots and layers of undergarments, hoops, and corsets, and music only when she herself clanked "Chopsticks" on a piano or when she happened to hear someone else play. The physical limitations were nothing compared to the social restraints placed on women. A lady was expected to be delicate and discreet, worshipful of her husband, devoted only to her children. A female with an opinion on politics or science was taken as seriously as a talking parrot.

As long as she had been with Ashton, the sense of being an utter alien in this century hadn't seemed to make so much of a difference. Now the prospect of raising a child in this era of infectious diseases and limited medical knowledge was absolutely terrifying. And before she could follow that hazardous path, she had to actually survive pregnancy and childbirth.

With a heavy sigh, she reached up and touched her head, wincing as she felt the stiffened wound, wondering if the doctor had stitched it closed.

"Does it hurt?"

She stopped. Was she hearing voices? Had she imagined Ashton's question, full of tenderness? Opening her eyes, she turned in the direction of the voice.

It was Ashton.

A feeling of panic rushed over her. Was he telling her that he was leaving today? Is that why he was wearing such formal attire? Torturing herself, she kept her eyes on him, realizing that he was more handsome than ever. Gone was the slightly wild look of the renegade cavalry general. In its place was the smooth aristocrat, still devastatingly masculine, slightly more polished. His hair, which once skirted past his broad shoulders, was collar-length, brushed off his face. The mustache had been trimmed, making the sensual mouth more visible.

He had been slouched in a chair, and from the rumpled state of his clothing, that was where he had slept. He rose slowly, his gaze never leaving hers, and he frowned slightly at her expression. With a terrible pang of recognition, he realized it was fear.

"Margaret," he whispered. "May I sit down?"

She nodded, and instead of pulling a chair up to the side of the bed, he settled directly on the mattress.

The nearness of his body unnerved her, his thigh so close to hers. She cleared her throat and fumbled with her hands, clasping and reclasping them over the cover. "So," she said with a valiant attempt at light chatter. "Do you come here often?"

He did not smile. Instead, he reached over to her, resting his large hand on her shoulder, his thumb stroking her softly. "Not often enough."

The compassion in his voice was her undoing. Margaret tried to bite her lower lip to prevent it from trembling, hoping that she would not dissolve into a puddle of sloppy tears. At least she could maintain her pride, hang on to a hollow feeling of self-respect once he was gone.

Instead, she burst into tears.

Her reaction caught them both by surprise, Ashton not knowing quite what to do, Margaret suddenly sobbing uncontrollably. They were fleshy, thick sobs, the kind that consume all energy and thought. The kind of tears that lead to hiccups and red-nosed embarrassment.

Through her tears she saw his confusion, not quite sure where to place his hands, fumbling with words of comfort.

"Oh, Margaret, well, come now . . ."

With a part moan, part wail, she flipped the covers over her head, not wanting him to see her like this. The moment she was under the blanket, she realized that she looked more ridiculous than ever, like an emotionally unstable linen closet. So she stopped crying—which was easier to do with Ashton out of sight—the sobs dwindling to infrequent sniffs, and sat very still.

Ashton did his best not to laugh, looking down at his shoes, trying to conjure horrific images of battle. But the very thought of Margaret sitting stock-still under the blanket, as if it was the most normal position in the world, and trying to begin what promised to be the most difficult conversation of his life, wore down his brittle defenses.

At first it was a quiet, contained chuckle, and Margaret felt the bed shake slightly. She assumed he was shifting his weight and remained under the blanket, trying to think of a graceful way out of the position. Then she noticed the vibrating motion was increasing, and a sound very much like a mirthful snort escaped from the direction of her husband. Surprised, she turned her head toward him, which, under the cover, reminded Ashton of a startled bird, and a full-fledged guffaw overtook him.

Curious and more than a little irritated, Margaret emerged from the blanket, peeking out cautiously at first, then pulling the covers down completely as she realized he wasn't even looking at her.

Reluctantly, she smiled, suddenly realizing how much she had missed his wonderful, rich laugh. His eyes were glistening with hilarity, and he glanced at her, sharing the warmth of his laughter.

"Ah, Mag," he finally sighed, wiping a tear from under an eye. "I do hope our child has a sense of humor. Otherwise, life will be pretty rough for the poor thing with us as parents."

Margaret was speechless for a moment, allowing the meaning of his words to filter through her apprehension.

"You know?" she stammered, her fists clenching the blanket.

Sobering, he nodded and placed both of his hands over hers. "And the notion has me torn in two." Before she could read any sinister meaning behind his simple words, he elaborated. "The idea of you having our child delights me, Mag. But I'm terrified that something may happen to you, that I may lose you." Unconsciously his eyes focused on the L-shaped laceration that was partially hidden in her hairline.

A cool thrill passed through her; a sudden lightness like a warm spring breeze seemed to lift her soul. All of the darkness receded as she threw her arms around his neck. Without hesitation, he drew her closer, his face buried in her silken tresses, inhaling her familiar fragrance.

"Ash," she murmured, her voice husky. "I'm so . . ."

"So . . . what, my love?" he coaxed.

"I'm so hungry," she sighed. "Is there anything to eat around here?"

She was instantly rewarded with a deep kiss followed by a five-course breakfast.

"Will you please let me get out of bed now?" she pleaded, as a sprightly red-haired chambermaid scurried away with the breakfast dishes.

"You heard Dr. McCoy. You are to remain in bed until you regain all of your strength." Ashton had shaved and changed into fresh clothes, looking impossibly rejuvenated for a man who had stayed up all night.

The past two hours had been pleasant, their chatter confined to nothing more personal than the weather. It was as if they both understood that this fragile truce was only a temporary fix, that they needed to find a way to restore their shattered faith in each other.

Margaret would glance at him, so happy to have him by her side, yet wondering where he had been all those evenings, and ultimately why he had felt the need to desert her. He still seemed remote, infinitely polite and considerate, yet a barrier stood between them. It separated them as effectively as a physical block.

Quite simply, she knew it was their vastly different ideas that put such a distance between them. Of course, she intellectually understood his belief in honor and pride, but to her they were little more than hollow words and certainly less precious than his life.

JUDITH O'BRIEN

He smiled in agreement at some comment of hers about the weather; yet he was wondering how on earth he was ever to fathom the workings of her mind. Margaret had done things no woman he had ever known could be capable of—from the gruesome duty of nursing to plotting the outrageous hoax of his death. His air of casual friendliness masked a thousand questions that demanded answers, wrenching discussions that had to be completed before they could resume their marriage.

She leaned forward at his gentle prodding, allowing him to straighten the pillows behind her back. "Ugh," she said, settling into the fluffed cushions. "I believe I ate everything on those plates. I feel like a human vacuum cleaner."

Ashton paused, a perplexed expression crossing his face. "What on earth is a 'vacuum cleaner'? By its very definition, a vacuum is nothing—a total void. Why on earth would you need to clean a void?"

Margaret closed her eyes. "We need to talk," she said softly.

He sat by her on the bed, not touching her.

"I know," he agreed. "I need also to get a few things straightened out." She nodded, and he continued.

"I will not allow you to interfere in my life." He stood suddenly, as he was no longer able to contain his energy. "You played with my life as if I were a puppet, yours to manipulate at will."

She started to speak, and he stopped her. "Be quiet." His voice was low. Had it been anyone else with her in that bedroom, she would have felt physically threatened. "I have tried very hard to understand what you did, why you felt compelled to make me a laughingstock. And don't you dare refute the facts, Mag. To half of the people back home, I am a traitor. To the other half, a buffoon."

"Stop it." Her voice was louder and more shrill

308

than she had intended, furious herself at his anger. "I am sorry if I made your life unbearable. But without my actions, you would have no life."

"At this point, my dear, that is an attractive alternative. For I have no future, no honor . . ."

"Honor? Is that what this is about?" She took a deep breath, trying to calm herself down. "Ashton, this is very difficult for me, but I can no longer stand by quietly as you talk about honor and all of that nobility fluff, because there is one simple fact I must state. Please forgive me, but as a Confederate, you're on the wrong side."

"What the—"

"Shut up and listen to me." Her fury startled him, and before he could think of a retort, she continued. "The Confederacy will not win the war. You know it and I know it, and soon the whole world will know it. Your goddamn cause is a lost cause."

Had she been a man, she felt certain Ashton would have struck her by now. As painful as it was for her to utter the cruel words, she knew that he had to hear them, and they were all the more painful because he must be aware that they were true.

"Margaret, I will not have you curse," he responded, his hands clenched at his sides.

"Is that the only problem you have with what I just said?" Her mouth was partially opened in astonishment, for she had expected a passionate defense of the Confederacy.

For a long moment he stared at her, and she could see the tumult of emotions playing in his eyes. At last he looked away, his shoulders slightly slumped, and paced to the window. With a deep sigh he parted the curtains, staring down at the park.

"I have nothing." There was no self-pity in his tone; it was just a statement of fact.

She had been able to handle his anger, ready to

match his rage with her own. But she was not prepared for the total hopelessness of his voice.

Without thinking, she slipped out of bed, her feet bare and cold on the carpet, and walked over to him. He seemed physically larger than before, but there was something missing, a spark in his soul that had vanished.

"Ash?" she asked, her hand resting on his powerful arm. He did not look at her, and she wasn't sure if he was aware that she was beside him at the window.

"All my life I have tried to live a certain way, tried to behave and think as I had been taught." He swallowed before continuing, his voice hollow. "Honor was vital to me, always honor and duty had gone together. Now it makes no difference, not to me, not to anyone. I can never return home, I cannot remain here. There are very few choices left to me."

He smiled, but it was without a trace of humor. "Ironic, isn't it? I used to lead men, they used to believe in me. And now I realize I simply forced ignorant youths into battle, the same way I used to force them to learn lessons. I convinced them that we could win the damn war. Hell, I even convinced myself. How many hundreds of boys were slaughtered because of me? Because they believed in me, because I believed in a useless cause . . ."

"Stop! I will not hear you speak like this," she cried, her fist clutching convulsively on his sleeve.

"No, Margaret. You are right—it was a lost cause all along, an army of fools and dreamers, and I was one of the leaders."

"This war had to be fought, don't you see?" She leaned on his arm for support, and he instinctively pulled her closer. "I've never realized the inevitability of this conflict before. Everything I read, all of the documents I studied, were slanted toward the North. Of course they were, because the victors controlled the press after the war. But this had to happen, Ashton. Sooner or later this war of ideals would have erupted. The end result will be a stronger Union, the most powerful country on earth." She rested her head on his arm, her knees beginning to tremble. "Perhaps you can help with the healing, write exactly what you feel, try to make sense of it all. And when you've finished, perhaps the country will be stronger, and we'll be stronger, too."

He looked down at her and was about to speak when he realized she was out of bed. "Margaret," he said softly, sweeping her into his arms and carrying her back to bed.

"Think about it, Ash." Her eyes were sparkling, and he nodded, placing her on the soft mattress, pushing a heavy strand of hair off her slender shoulder.

He sat by her on the bed, concentrating, it seemed, on her hair, raking his hand through the silken length. Finally he looked at her, and she held her breath. It had been weeks since he had looked at her with such an expression of openness.

"You poisoned me and stuffed me into a coffin," he said at last.

Cringing, she nodded. "I know," she admitted, "but they were going to shoot you."

He returned his attention to her hair. "They had every right to shoot me."

"Even though you were not a spy? The whole reason they were going to execute you was because of me . . ."

"No, it wasn't," he said.

"Excuse me?"

"They knew that I was already having doubts about our ability to win the war." His hand caught on a knot in her hair, and she winced. "Sorry." He continued. "The material they found on me, the stuff of your dreams, was just the final blow. But eventually they

311

would have been forced to do something about me. A general cannot be plagued by doubts. It shows, and the men turn mutinous and rebel."

She caught his wrist in her hand. "I just wanted you to live." She looked directly into his eyes.

"I know that, Mag." A slight smile lit his face, "But I can never go home again. I have a choice of remaining here, an alive fugitive, or returning home a cowardly traitor."

"No, Ash. I honestly think I fixed all of that." There was something in the smug squaring of her shoulders that made him repress a smile.

"God help me," he muttered.

"I wrote a letter to General Lee," she stated with satisfaction.

"The last time General Lee saw something you wrote, it failed to do me much good."

"I know." Margaret leaned closer, her head tilted slightly so she could see directly into his eyes. "Would you please listen to what I am about to say? I mean really listen to me with an open mind."

"My mind's nothing if not open."

"I was born in 1963," she began, her voice steady and deliberate. "My family was from outside of Boston, which is where I was raised. When I graduated from high school in 1981 my family—my parents and brother and sister and I—went on a trip to Martha's Vineyard, where they all died in a boating accident. Except, of course, me. I survived and went to college and to graduate school at Columbia University in New York City. I hold two doctoral degrees, one in American history—specifically, the Civil War. I wrote my first thesis on Sherman's march, very sympathetic to Sherman, I might add."

"Sherman's march?" Ashton asked. "A song?" With one splayed hand he raked a thatch of her hair through his fingers, admiring the lustrous shine.

Margaret let out an exasperated sigh. "No, but it will be. Anyway, my second doctoral degree was in English literature. Then I went down to Magnolia University to teach, and that's when I met you."

"Ah," he replied absentmindedly. "But they have no women teachers. No female students, in fact."

"They will in 1993," she stated, realizing he was not paying much attention. "What would you say if I told you I used to be six feet tall?"

"I would say you've been shrinking."

"Ashton," she said sharply. "You are not taking me seriously, are you? It's true—I am from the future, and I know things that . . ."

With a start he straightened, the dreamy expression vanished. "Mag, I almost forgot—Joseph Davis died. Exactly the way you said he would—from a balcony. How did you know that would happen?"

"That is what I have been trying to tell you," she said, her voice full of frustration. "Months ago when you came to me at Magnolia, I became a different person. I believe Mag died, and I somehow took over. Haven't you noticed a difference in me?"

"But you were different before that, Mag." His tone was gentle but firm. "I sensed a change in your letters . . ."

"Ah, but I am the one who wrote those letters!"

With infinite patience, Ashton nodded in agreement. "Of course, you did. That very change, the sensitivity you now possess, came shining through. That is what brought me to your side."

Margaret was getting nowhere, so she changed her tack. "Ash, listen to me. My family died—"

"I know, love."

"No you don't! You're thinking of another family, one from this time. I mean my family, people not even born yet."

Her voice trailed off as a thought came to her mind.

"Wait a minute," she mumbled to herself. "They went to Martha's Vineyard solely because of me, their youngest daughter. I am the reason my brother and sister returned for that vacation." A blissful smile lit her face. "This is wonderful! Don't you understand? If I am here in 1864, then my family will not go to the Vineyard in 1981. They will live, with two children instead of three."

Ashton patted her hand. "Margaret, wherever they are, I am sure they are happy."

Her eyes were filled with tears. "For so long I have felt nothing but guilt for their deaths. It was difficult for me to think of them, for I would always be reminded that they died giving me a silly graduation gift. But now everything's been fixed."

"I know you have always found it difficult to discuss your family, Mag. Remember? I was at their funeral. I held your hand."

Margaret heard his words, but her mind was tumbling with her thoughts. "I think I know what has happened," she said at last, her voice full of wonder.

Without waiting for a response from Ashton, she continued. "I was somehow born out of sequence. This is truly where I belong, not as a six-foot-tall Ph.D. in 1993, but here, in this time, as your wife. My family will live long, full lives. And you, Ashton." She faced him, and he was startled by the translucent light in her eyes, brilliant yet not quite natural. "You, too, will live. Don't you see? You won't die on Lick Skillet Road on July 28th. But if I had not arrived here to shake up your life, you would have been killed. I needed that knowledge from the future, knowledge, I might add, that I seem to be losing rapidly, I could have done nothing to help you. Instead, you'll . . ."

"I've been meaning to ask you about that. Where on earth is Lick Skillet Road? And how do you manage to guess where the war will be fought months from now?"

She waved her hand dismissively, as if he had just mentioned a second-rate play. "Oh, that. Easy—a date straight from my history books. You are supposed to be killed by a sniper, or as you all call them, a sharpshooter. But instead, you'll be here with me. I don't believe even Sherman's men have a rifle that would range over the Atlantic Ocean."

"Of course not." Ashton stood slowly. He shouldn't have asked. "Margaret, I do believe you need to get some rest."

She did not answer him; she simply smiled happily and snuggled into the pillows.

"This is absolutely fabulous." She sighed as she closed her eyes. Ashton shook his head, hoping her joy would last but that her delusions would eventually vanish. He would speak to the doctor about them as soon as possible.

"I'll be right in the next room," he whispered, quietly closing the curtains.

"Mmmmm," she replied, slumber gently falling over her.

He tiptoed to the door, turning back to catch one last glimpse of her before he let her sleep. An exhilaration surged through him, a rush of pure joy unlike anything he had ever experienced. His future was uncertain, his life was in shambles. A few minutes earlier he had, for the first time in his life, experienced genuine despair, nothing but empty black before him. Now he realized there would be Margaret and their child, far more compelling than any single cause. And he knew, with an absolute certainty, that no matter what lay before them, Margaret would remain by his side.

She had given him the gift of hope.

"I love you," he whispered, his own voice startling him by its resplendent emotion.

He had turned to leave, when he heard Margaret stir. Her voice was broken, but her arms slowly reached for him. "Oh, Ash. I love you, too."

They stared at each other for a moment in the dim light, then, from across the room, they both smiled. He did not go to her then. He didn't need to.

"You need to sleep," he said, and she dropped her arms and sighed, again settling into the sweet cocoon of bed. For the first time in weeks, she actually slept.

September 1864
Seven Months Later

Ashton put down his pen, hand cramped from the twenty pages he had already written since breakfast. The windows were thrown open, and a delightful September breeze ruffled his hair.

So far, London had been almost idyllic for both Ashton and Margaret. He had been making a decent living by writing editorials for the *London Times* on the American Civil War, and his pieces had been picked up by newspapers on the other side of the Atlantic, North and South.

His perspective on the war had changed since being away, and he finally understood Margaret's odd phrase "group psychology." In fact, it had been almost impossible for him to comprehend exactly what he had been fighting for. There was a loose notion of rights, a vague idea of each state's presumed freedom to leave the Union. Other than a secessionist manifesto, he could find no unifying ideal for the Confederacy.

He leaned back in the large leather chair, linking his

hands behind his head. The whole process of writing the editorials had been cathartic for him, healing in a way he never imagined possible. It had been Margaret's idea for him to simply put down on paper his train of thought concerning the war, as well as his feelings about the way he was forced to come to London, shipped in a casket by his wife.

Without his knowledge, Margaret bundled his jottings over to the office of the *London Times*. Delighted with the content, the newspaper ran the first three installments on the front page. The reader response had been tremendous, and the end result was that not only was he earning money hand over fist but he and Margaret had become celebrities in their own right. Only her condition, now obvious to all who saw her rounded figure, prevented them from receiving a dozen invitations for each evening. As it was, only six or so arrived with the morning mail.

Although he was vastly uncomfortable with his role of expert on all things American, and Confederate specifically, he was able to pay back some of the people who had been supporting them in England. He was shocked when Margaret reluctantly handed him a list of patrons, both Union and Confederate, who had raised money for them. At first the funds were for a lonely widow, but when news of Ashton being alive and well began to filter back to America, the checks became larger and more frequent.

"I suppose they truly don't want me to come back," he mumbled one morning, opening another package of checks.

"It's actually a compliment," Margaret had replied, rising from her breakfast to stand beside him, her hand resting on his shoulder. "The Yankees think you're too good. It's much easier to pay you to stay here than risk having you against them again. I also believe they genuinely like you. This is sort of a peace offering for when the war finally ends."

"How do you explain the Confederate money? For God's sake, Mag, they have barely enough to eat, and yet they have sent us hundreds of dollars."

"That is even more of a compliment, Ash. You're doing more good over here through your articles and, indirectly, through your diplomatic work. It may not be formal, but goodness knows, the English and other sympathetic Europeans are sending scads of aid—not military, but humanitarian—to the Confederacy."

She had then kissed the top of his head and pulled the checks from his hand. He was unable to think of anything else to say, other than make the simple comment that no one, as far as he could remember, had ever kissed him on the top of his head before.

Shaking his weary hand in the air in hope of restoring circulation so he could finish the piece he was working on, he grinned, thinking of Margaret. The feeling of hopelessness that had threatened to consume him a few months ago now seemed as remote as his patriotic Confederate fervor. The center of his life had shifted from intangible ideals to his very tangible wife. She was still delightfully unpredictable, and more than a little odd at times, but he wouldn't have had her any other way.

Mrs. Thaw stepped brusquely into Ashton's study, a feather duster poking from the large pocket of her apron.

"May I get you anything, General?" She asked, smiling with satisfaction as she straightened a bookshelf. She had come over as soon as Eliza Johnson explained the whole peculiar situation to her, that the general was indeed alive, but that Margaret was having a rather tough time with her pregnancy. Mrs. Thaw, with both her husband and only son dead, was delighted to be sent with all haste. Eliza herself would have crossed over to London, but she wanted to be near Eddie, who had rejoined the Confederate ranks.

She also wanted to help Mary B. with her wedding preparations. For Eddie, the consummate prankster, had finally fallen in love with his nurse.

Ashton blinked, shaken out of his musings by Mrs. Thaw's question. He frowned for a moment, then turned to her. "Have you happened to see my wife?"

Mrs. Thaw shook her head. "I will only answer that question, General, when you answer mine. I asked, sir, if you would like anything."

With a grin he stretched. "I would like to know where my wife is."

"She is once again making the rounds of charitable organizations to convince them to donate medical supplies and food to the Confederacy," Mrs. Thaw stated with approval. "She's managed to find some daredevils to try to run the blockade, and has wisely decided that medicine and food are what the Confederacy need most."

The smile faded from his face as he leaned forward. "How do you think she is feeling, Mrs. Thaw?" He recapped the inkwell and blotted the last page he had written. "Does she seem well to you?"

Her hands dropped from her hips, and she stepped closer to Ashton, her tone a little lower than before. "I can't tell, General. But she does seem more than a little tired these days."

Ashton nodded in agreement. "She refuses to make any concessions to her condition, always mentioning a promise she made to General Lee to help out. And she accuses me of placing too much value on the notion of honor." He smiled.

The front door opened and Margaret, a stack of papers in her hand, rushed through the door.

"Mrs. Thaw." Her voice was slightly breathless as she pulled off her bonnet with one gloved hand. "A letter for you—I met the post at the door."

Ashton stood and walked over to his wife as she handed Mrs. Thaw the letter. In spite of her slightly awkward form, she looked radiantly beautiful. He paused at a table and poured her a glass of water, which she gratefully accepted. In exchange, she handed him an eight-week-old newspaper from Richmond.

Mrs. Thaw's hand was trembling as she ran her calloused thumb under the rim of the envelope, loosening the seal. Her eyes scanned the letter, and then she gasped, tears springing to her eyes.

"It's my son," she choked. "He's alive in a Yankee prison in Illinois. . . ."

Margaret immediately passed her the water, accidentally sloshing it on the floor, and Ashton eased her into a chair. His eyes were fixed on the front page of the paper, and he glanced at Margaret, with an expression of astonishment on his face. Mrs. Thaw murmured, her eyes glazed as she again read the letter. "This letter is from a soldier who knows him in Blue Island Prison. Poor Osborn's been sick, and this friend wanted me to know that he's finally getting better. My son is alive."

"I'm so happy for you, Mrs. Thaw." Margaret was about to give the older woman a hug when a savage pain shot through her, gripping her middle like a tourniquet.

Ashton was still staring at the newspaper, only vaguely aware of Mrs. Thaw mentioning something faraway in Illinois, when he caught a glimpse of his wife.

"Mag?"

She shot him a tight smile and nodded. "I think it's

time, Ash," she said, her knuckles growing white from clutching the back of a chair.

Immediately, Mrs. Thaw snapped to her feet. "I'll send for the doctor," she said briskly, folding the letter and slipping it back into the envelope. "General, you take Mrs. Johnson into the bedroom. Don't let her lie down, prop her up with those pillows I have stacked over in the corner chest."

Ashton mutely followed her commands, leading his wife into the bedroom, allowing the newspaper to slip from his hands, forgotten for the time being. On the front page of the old paper was news of a fierce battle near a place called Ezra Church and a slaughter of Confederates on an obscure country path near Atlanta with a strange name.

Lick Skillet Road.

The door to the Maiden's Arms tavern swung open on its ancient hinges, alerting the patrons to the entrance of another customer. Enthusiastic "Hellos" and "Good days" greeted the newcomer as he threw a whip on the bar.

"Bertram Butler—how are you!" slurred a man with a bandage on his nose.

"I've had all I can take, mates," he grumbled. "I'm a free man."

"So you've finally left the wife?" The man with the bandage grinned.

"Lost the old ball and chain?" Another patron chuckled.

"No, no," growled Bertram Butler. "I quit the job."

"Again?" a disappointed voice spat. "You already did that months ago. . . ."

"Last winter," agreed another. "I remember because the ale was particularly flat that month."

"No, it's another job I've quit." Bertram glared at the barkeep. "Give me a whiskey."

The patrons exchanged astonished looks. No one ordered whiskey unless they had a few extra bob or were truly in need of strong drink.

After tossing back a small glass of whiskey in a cloudy tumbler, he motioned for another. "Well," he began at last, addressing the assembled audience, "you all know old Tom got me a position driving a hack after my misfortune on the *North Star."* There was a general nodding motion. Yes, everyone there remembered well.

"So I think, this is the top, driving a hack around the city of London. Wonderful, I thinks to myself. And for a few months it has been grand."

"What happened?"

"T'was my last customer, that's who."

All inside the tavern were silent, respectfully awaiting the next words. "You will never in a million years guess who my last customer was."

"Queen Victoria?"

"Jenny Lind?"

"Nah." Bertram paused. "The stiff who drove me off the *North Star,* that's who."

"No!"

"You mean the dead Yank with the pretty wife?"

"He wasn't a Yank," added another. "He was a southerner. They are just like us."

"Bertram, is that the one?"

He nodded sadly. "The very one."

"That chap gets around for a stiff, eh?" commented the man with the bandage on his nose.

"Now, Bertram," said a burly character wearing a slouchy tweed cap. "How can you expect us to believe that? Are you sure it was the stiff?"

"Positive. He remembered me, he did, and slipped me a quid and a cigar when he got out."

"A quid and a cigar? Was he still in the box?"

"Nah. He was alone, standing as straight as you

please, dressed like a real gent, and he said his wife just had a babe, and he thanked me for being so kind and all on the ship."

"Where was he going?"

"He had a stack of papers, and I let him off at the *Times* office. That's all I know."

"His wife had a little one," cooed the burly man. "Think the little one's a stiff, too?"

Bertram reached for his next glass. "I didn't ask. But the chap is right as rain now. I tell you, I can't take this any more. I quit."

Everyone nodded in sympathetic agreement. Finally, the man in the bandaged nose turned to Bertram.

"So, mate," he said. "How's the wife?"

CHAPTER

20

Lexington, Virginia
January 1868

The distant, familiar sounds of early morning drill
drifted through the closed windows of Robert E. Lee's
sturdy office. A thick shawl was draped around his
shoulders, warding off the winter chill. The green
blotter on his desk was stacked high with correspon-
dence, some personal, some pertaining to his job as
president of Washington College.

He glanced outside, through the frosted panes, and
saw the young men marching on the frozen grass.
These were the first boys to emerge since the war, the
ones mercifully too young to participate in the conflict. There was a satisfaction to this work, he thought,
as he reached for an unopened letter. He was preparing men for life, not for death. With luck, the boys on
the field would be facing nothing more treacherous
than an oversupply of young women.

The sealing wax, red and splotchy, gave way easily
under his careful thumb. The letter had been with him

for four years, ever since Ashton Johnson's wife pulled him aside and pressed the sealed letter into his pocket.

Weeks later he had heard rumors of Ashton being alive in England, and he clung to the tale, praying that it was true. When at last Ashton's articles began to trickle back to the Confederacy, Lee had savored every word, somehow not surprised when he read of Margaret Johnson's shocking plot, drugging her husband and playing the part of the sorrowing widow.

His lined face held a vague smile, and he wondered if his own wife would have gone to such lengths to save him. Perhaps, he thought, when they were young, and he was the gallant fresh officer.

He pulled the shawl tighter about his shoulders. Mary had made him the shawl with her own hands, in spite of her painful arthritis. Mary, his wife, a grand-daughter of George Washington.

On second thought, Mary would do anything to save him, even now. They were old, and still she loved him. He considered himself a lucky man indeed.

The letter was now open to him, and he saw Margaret Johnson's handwriting, remarkably sloppy, as if she had never before held a pen. There were drips and smears scattered throughout the note, like a child's first letter.

Reaching for his gold-rimmed reading glasses, Lee paused, his eyes resting on a thick, handsomely bound leather volume. The lettering on the spine was gold, and the book had been selling, as one Richmond dealer so vividly put it, "like hotcakes."

The title of the book was simple—*Reflections on a Civil War,* by General Ashton P. Johnson, C.S.A.— and it had been published within a month of Appomattox.

Lee had read and reread the book, stunned by the author's clarity of thinking and his vivid appraisal of the war. Without a trace of bitterness or hostility, he had managed to explain the emotions of the Confederate leaders, examine dispassionately what they had been seeking, and why, ultimately, their quest had been doomed to fail. At first he had been unable to read the book, especially when it became apparent that the victors up North in Washington City were all babbling about the greatness of the work.

But it soon became apparent that Ashton's book was smoothing over the rough patches in the new Union. Fire-breathing Yankee politicians became more reasonable after reading the book, finally able to see what the Confederacy was trying to accomplish. And the more radical Yankees soon found themselves without their congressional or Senate seats, undone and outvoted by more compassionate constituents who had read Ashton's book.

Many disagreed with his opinions, and there were spirited arguments all over the newly united nation about what had torn the country apart. More often than not, the arguments were settled peacefully, without rancor. Ashton's book had paved the way for discussion in a country that was heartily sick of bloodshed.

Lee's thoughts returned to the letter in his hand. He began to read, and with a start, he shook his head and read again the first line. Was it possible? He rubbed his eyes, trying to make sense of the impossible.

Dear General Lee,

I do hope you are enjoying your tenure at Washington College, where you are now in your third year as its president.

At the moment I am getting ready to sail to England. It is late 1863, and I know you will not be reading these words until January of 1868.

I am trying to tell you, General, that my husband is absolutely innocent of the crime of treason. For reasons I do not fully understand myself, I know the future. It is a gift I fear I am losing, so I wrote down what I could remember. Ashton, trying to decipher the meaning of my strange words, merely copied them. If he is guilty of anything, it is of trusting me. No man has served the Confederate States of America more nobly or more completely.

To prove that I have foresight, perhaps I should mention a few other events that will be history by the time you read this: In 1864, Lincoln will be reelected to the presidency for a second term with Andrew Johnson as his vice president. In May you and Grant will fight the Battle of the Wilderness, and Sherman will move toward Atlanta. Johnston manages to delay Sherman, who will be defeated in the Battle of Kennesaw Mountain, but Sherman presses on to Atlanta. President Davis will replace Johnston with Hood.

By September, Hood will abandon Atlanta, and in spite of early Confederate success, the siege of Petersburg will begin. Sherman begins his destructive "March to the Sea."

In early 1865, Hood will resign, Beauregard takes over. Sherman will burn Columbia, S.C., and your friend A.P. Hill will be killed in Petersburg. And on April 9th, Palm Sunday, you will surrender to Grant at Appomattox Court House, in Wilmer McLean's front parlor. You may have noticed a young, blond-haired Union general, George Custer, sneak away with the table you and Grant used to sign the peace document. Five days later, President Lincoln will be assassinated at Ford's Theatre in Washington while watching a production of *Our American Cousin,* featuring the actress Laura

Keene. The assassin, John Wilkes Booth, is the brother of actor Edwin Booth.

Strange details fill my mind although there are large blanks in my knowledge. Another event I recall, only indirectly linked to the war, is that a steamship called the *Sultana,* packed with recently released Union prisoners of war, will explode on the river in Arkansas on April 26th or 27th, killing close to two thousand men.

I cannot explain how I know this, General. I simply plead my case, and ask you to help Ashton. He was never guilty.

I hope this letter finds you in good health, and that you have recovered from your recent illness. Actually, I know you have.

Thank you for your time.

Sincerely,
Margaret Johnson

Robert E. Lee had no idea how long he had been sitting motionless in his office. The letter was in his hand, he had read it a dozen times. The facts were all accurate, and no parlor game could account for the letter. He had carried the letter with him since Margaret Johnson slipped it to him—the seal was unbroken.

Ashton Johnson's wife was a psychic. He had heard of such things, inexplicable events that could only be attributed to the mystic and unknown.

He stood slowly, wondering how Ashton's wife, four years earlier, had known he would be ill. Crumpling the letter, he tossed it into the fire grate, watching the red glow creep across the rim of the paper, leaving gray and brittle ash in its wake. No other eyes would see what he had just read. No one would know what he had just learned about Margaret Johnson.

Slowly he paced to the door, opening it a fraction of

an inch. A young man, his secretary, jumped to his feet.

"Sir?" he asked eagerly.

"Yes, Mr. Pointer." The general opened the door a little further. "I would like you to take a letter," he began. Then he stopped. "No," he amended. "Just find an address, an old friend of mine. Ashton Johnson."

"The writer, sir?"

General Lee smiled. "Yes. The writer."

"I believe he lives in London, sir."

"Very well. I would like it as soon as possible. And I thank you."

The general returned to his office and pulled out a sheet of stationery, fine stuff, with his name and title embossed in elegant lettering.

What could he possibly say? His thoughts were too complex to commit to paper. It was grandly ironic. Margaret Johnson clearly felt her husband would return if only granted the forgiveness of Lee, forgiveness for the crime of treason against the Confederacy. Yet Lee himself had been called a traitor on countless occasions, a traitor against the United States. He had lost his citizenship, as had Jeff Davis.

The truth was startling. Had Ashton appealed directly to the President of the United States, he would instantly be welcomed with open arms. That is, if he had, indeed, been a traitor to the Confederacy. The very fact that he remained in England, still considering himself a Confederate, was proof that Ashton had never been a Yankee spy, had never harbored treasonous thoughts, other than the painful doubts they all suffered toward the end of the war. Ashton simply felt those doubts sooner than the rest.

Thank God for Margaret Johnson. There had been enough needless death in the conflict without adding

Ashton's name to the sorry list. Had they executed Ashton, Lee would have had to carry the guilt for the rest of his life. As it was, he carried more than enough guilt for five lifetimes.

He dipped the pen in the inkwell, tapping it lightly to remove the excess. He wanted this brief note to be neat, to show no hesitation. The words he wrote were simple.

> Dear Ashton,
>
> Come home as soon as possible. I will meet your ship.
>
> > Yours,
> > R. E. Lee

With deliberate movements he blotted the ink and carefully folded the letter, allowing the shawl to slip from his shoulders. Somehow, the room wasn't nearly as chilly as it had been before.

The windows at Rebel's Retreat were thrown open, embracing the warm breeze and the fragrance of the late summer blooms. The leaves were just beginning to turn, a few trees had patches of vivid orange and scarlet tucked into the lush green foliage.

Margaret was exhausted, her hand still clutching a filthy rag, her hair covered with dust and paint flakes. The house had been nailed shut for over five years, and the accumulation of dirt and grime seemed to be embedded in every nook and cranny. Even with Mrs. Thaw's invaluable help, the task of reopening Rebel's Retreat had been daunting.

She stretched luxuriously before returning her attention to the mirror frame, removing as much thick dust as possible from the bawdy figures. The mirror still made her smile, and she leaned closer, rubbing the leg of one of the bar scene characters with the cloth dipped in beeswax.

"Nice job," commented Ashton from behind her left ear, his voice full of relaxed humor.

Margaret jumped, her hand immediately flying to her throat. "Don't do that again!" she cried, unable to keep from laughing. "You frightened me out of my wits."

"As if that would take much," he whispered, bending down to plant a soft kiss on her neck. She closed her eyes and leaned against him, ignoring the hard metal of his gold watch fob, barely visible from under his jacket.

Even in a simple brown suit and vest, Ashton carried the energetic dash of a cavalry officer. She reached up behind her and touched his face, the beginnings of a raspy beard defying his morning shave. At her request he had shaved his mustache, and she had been stunned by how handsome he was without whiskers.

He lifted her wrist to his mouth and kissed it, and she sighed.

Suddenly she pulled away. "Ash, how did it go? I mean, how many students do you have?"

Their eyes met in the mirror, and she saw the brilliant sparkle in his gaze, an excitement she had seen frequently since their return to Magnolia University.

"We have ninety-seven so far." He grinned. "And all but a few have paid in full."

"Why, that's wonderful!"

"The ninety-eighth will matriculate this afternoon —Osborn Biddle Thaw."

She spun around, her own eyes matching his in brilliance. "Mrs. Thaw's son Osborn! Oh, Ash, he'll be a wonderful student, I just know it."

Ashton nodded. "It may take him a while to catch

up with the others, and he's older than the rest of the boys, but he deserves a chance. I thought I could help him out with his studies if he needs it. He was going to work in the kitchen, but I have a feeling there's a real scholar lurking under that apron."

"Mrs. Thaw is going to be so proud," Margaret said softly. She didn't need to add that she knew all about feeling flushed with pride. Ashton saw it in her eyes.

"Where are the children?" His voice was unusually rough as he gently brushed some dust out of her hair.

"Ash is over tormenting Eddie and Mary B., and Lisa is upstairs taking a nap." She raised her eyebrows mischievously. "By the way, how is Professor Edward Johnson reacting to the academic life?"

"I'm not sure." Ashton glanced just over her head in thought. "I will say one thing, engineering will never be quite the same. He wants to teach the first-year students how to blow up a Yankee bridge."

"Isn't that more the realm of the physics department?"

"I've been trying to explain that to him, but he's convinced he's right."

"He's always convinced he's right," Margaret added under her breath, and Ashton threw his head back and laughed, lifting her slightly into the air.

A sound from upstairs quieted them both, the stirrings of their eighteen-month-old daughter. "Now look what you've done," Margaret scolded, her hand reaching up to his face.

In an instant his mouth descended upon hers, sweetly and hungrily. But the upstairs murmurs soon became a genuine wail, and Margaret reluctantly pulled away.

"I'd better go up." She sighed, her eyes lingering over his familiar form. It seemed impossible, but he was even more dashing than before, a new confidence radiating from him, a relaxed joy that didn't depend on a battle's success or military accomplishment. His rare appeal emanated from within, an inner glow that caused men to like him immediately and women to swoon. She straightened his tie. "I'm just glad Magnolia doesn't admit females yet."

"Females? Here?" Ashton said in mock indignation. "Never, Madame!"

"Ha!" She smiled, holding her skirts as she skipped up the stairs. "Just you wait."

Ashton remained at the foot of the steps, watching his wife until she turned into the children's room.

How lucky he had been.

The smile faded from his face as he recalled how close he had come to losing her, first by his own stubbornness, then by the birth of their son. After that he realized how stark his life would be without her, how aimless and dim.

Without Margaret, he would not be alive. He would have died on Lick Skillet Road; he was convinced of that now. She had ceased talking about coming from the future, just as Dr. McCoy said she would, especially after the children began to consume so much of her time in London.

The popularity of his writing was still a source of astonishment to him, and he had been able to support his family well, if not lavishly, even during the disastrous first year after the war; and he had repaid—with interest—those who had supported them in London.

He walked into the parlor, or, as Margaret always called it, the living room. There were stacks of newspapers there, some documenting his return to the United States, being greeted at the dock by General Lee and President Davis, as well as General Sherman and Margaret's brother Tom. She had not recognized him at first, and after the first half hour, Tom—his old friend—had pulled him aside.

"You have a delightful wife," he had said, an odd expression passing over his face.

Ashton had said nothing, then Tom added, "I sure as hell don't remember my own sister being anything like that woman over there, but you have a delightful wife, whoever the hell she is."

Tom had left soon afterward, muttering about getting back to Boston. It had been a strange homecoming, the awkward moments smoothed over by Margaret's cheerful chatter.

Ashton moved a pile of papers, the dust puffing up in his face. When would this house be ready for real living? he wondered with a chuckle. They needed to add another two bedrooms, perhaps next spring. He wiped the dust from his eyes and looked about the cluttered room.

There was a single stack of papers in the corner, just under one of his footed chairs. The shape was oddly regular, unlike the scattered newspapers piled throughout the house. He picked them up, curious now, and read the top paper.

It was written in a neat, thin-lined hand, rounded and without so much as a single swirl.

Dr. Margaret Garnett
English Survey 101
September 3, 1993

With disbelieving eyes, he read the first essay, a badly spelled paper on the importance of *Beowulf.* They were all on *Beowulf,* all fairly intelligent, some mentioning something called television and PBS.

He could hear Margaret upstairs, singing softly, and more than a little off-key, to their child. She had told him she was from the future, a professor. He swallowed, holding the papers, wondering what to do. She had been right.

Margaret Garnett was from the future. Something brought her here to him. He saw the cold fireplace grate, and without hesitation, he brought the stack of papers to the fireplace, dumped them in, opened the creaky flue, and set the papers on fire.

He now believed her. Perhaps part of him always had. But the actual papers terrified him—a visceral fear that if she laid eyes on them, she would be thrust back into the future.

A few moments later, Margaret entered the room, a perplexed frown on her face. "Ash? Why are you lighting a fire? It's at least eighty degrees out, and—"

But she was unable to complete the sentence. Her husband had hastened to her side and pulled her close in a crushing embrace.

"I adore you," he whispered, "and I believe you—about everything."

Margaret, bewildered but unwilling to let the moment pass, tightened her arms around his waist. "Ash, I . . ."

"Do you know what we have to do?" His voice held the barely contained excitement again.

"No," she sighed, unable to keep up with his mercurial moods.

"We have to make this the best university in the nation. We need the best professors, the best students, the best—"

"Well, we already have the best president in you," she stated complacently, snuggling closer.

"Margaret." His voice seemed faraway. "How would you like to teach here, perhaps an English Survey 101 course? Perhaps your students could write an essay on—"

"Beowulf." She froze, then her eyes snapped to the fireplace just as the last paper withered and crumpled, licked by thin orange flames. For a moment she stared ahead, and Ashton watched the wonderment on her

face. "Ash," she said suddenly. "How were they? The essays, I mean. Did you read them?"

"They were fair," he answered as he brushed a bit of dust from her cheekbone with his gentle knuckles. "The spelling was atrocious, but some of the ideas expressed were quite interesting."

"But with help, they could have been much better?"

He nodded. "Absolutely. All they needed was a good professor."

Their eyes met, and slowly they both smiled.

"My dear," he whispered. "I do believe we have our work cut out for us."

EPILOGUE

Johnson University
September 1993

There was a general commotion among the faculty members of prestigious Johnson University as the president of the school, Dr. Osborn Biddle Thaw VII, tried to regain the podium.

"Ladies and gentlemen," he pleaded into the microphone, which responded with a painful ring of feedback, "please take your seats, and I will try to explain further."

The buzz of conversation began to ebb as the sounds of metal chairs scraping the floor signaled a return to order. Dr. Thaw, whose great-grandfather was in the first postwar graduating class of Johnson University—then called by the ridiculous name of Magnolia—stood a little straighter. One professor puffed eagerly on a pipe, another sat with folded hands, simply glaring at Dr. Thaw. Behind him was a large square object, clearly a painting, covered with a white cloth.

337

"I ask you once again, sir," said an older man in the back of the room. "How on earth did you come across a previously unknown portrait of General Johnson and his wife?"

"If you all will be quiet, as I have said a half dozen times, I will tell you." The sound of clicks permeated the hall, bouncing off the marble floor and high ceiling of Johnson Hall. "Will the media and press please refrain from taking photographs for a few moments? I assure you all, there will be ample opportunity for you to complete your jobs later. And if you can all behave, I believe cookies and milk will be provided later." There were a few scattered chuckles, and the hushed murmurings gradually died away.

"Thank you," said Dr. Thaw with satisfaction. His slight British intonation struck some as a blatant affectation, others saw it as a byproduct of his years studying at Oxford as a Rhodes scholar. "As I am sure most of you know, I am here at this podium because of Ashton Johnson. . . ."

"Oh, come on," spat the professor with a pipe. "We are all here because of him and his wife. They made this into the great institution it is today."

There was a round of enthusiastic applause and a few scattered cries of "Here here." Dr. Thaw nodded. "I agree with you, of course. But my great-great grandmother was actually the general's housekeeper. He and his wife allowed my great-grandfather to be educated here—they used him as an educational guinea pig, so to speak."

"Enough about you, Thaw," shouted a reporter from the rear of the hall. "Let's see the portrait!"

The voices of assent were thundering; those who weren't clapping their hands were shouting to see the picture.

Dr. Thaw shook his head, still slightly surprised at the attention his find had created. He reached into his briefcase and plucked a notecard containing a few carefully typed paragraphs. A cellophane bag rattled as he closed the case, and he hoped no one had seen the remains of his midmorning snack.

"I found this portrait in the attic of Rebel's Retreat. It was covered with soot, and I almost threw it out as trash, when it caught the light and I saw the tracings of two figures under the grime. Realizing that this might be an important find, I called upon a friend of mine who is an art expert in New York. By careful research, and a lot of luck, we have learned that the portrait was commissioned by Mrs. Johnson in 1870 and was painted by one of the general's former scouts, who by then was a well-known portrait painter." Dr. Thaw glanced up from the card, and grinned. He now had their full attention.

"The most unusual aspect of the work is the subjects themselves. The experts in New York all agreed that the rendering of both the general and his wife is most extraordinary, their eyes are especially expressive. And their pose, given the usual staid positioning of Victorian-era portraits, is, eh, well, unique."

"Let's see it!"

"Come on, Dr. Thaw!"

This was the moment he had been waiting for. He nodded once, the room grew quiet, save for one woman with a cough, who was hushed by several others. With a dramatic flair, Dr. Thaw stepped over to the covered object, grasped a corner of the white tarp, and, with one bold whoosh, yanked off the fabric.

There was a universal gasp, a collective silence. And then, one by one, the people in the room, professors and reporters and photographers and the plain curious, began to applaud, as the fresh portrait of the general and his wife seemed to come alive.

The portrait was stunning.

It was Ashton Johnson, looking as vibrant and magnetic as a Hollywood leading man. Unlike the other portraits that lined the hall, including several of the general himself, this showed Ashton Johnson smiling, revealing strong white teeth and a face that seemed to light up the room. In his arms, an intimate moment frozen in time, was his wife. She was seen in profile, laughing, her head tipped toward him, her hair loose and flowing down her back. Their eyes were locked, an intensity that seemed both awed and carnal at the same time. They were the most radiant, beautiful couple anyone had ever seen.

"My God," sputtered the professor with the pipe. "Is this quite decent? I mean, this is the man who helped reunite the Union . . ."

"He never did take the oath of allegiance to the United States, you know," added another. "Lee did, Longstreet did, but Johnson said he never felt comfortable with the oath."

"My God," repeated the professor with the pipe. "It's like seeing a picture of George Washington in bed with Martha! Look at their expressions! Is it decent?"

Several workmen, clad in clean gray jumpsuits, emerged from the back of the room and lifted the portrait high into the air. At first there was a wave of disappointment as the people thought the picture was to be removed from their sight. But the workmen walked carefully over to a large, vacant wall and raised the picture high, securing it on the wall. Immediately, track lights that no one had noticed before flicked on, and the photographers pushed their way to the front, eagerly snapping away.

Osborn Biddle Thaw smiled with satisfaction and grabbed his briefcase. Leave it to the general and his wife, he mused, to still cause a commotion.

One of the photographers, concentrating on the amazing picture, almost slipped on a crumpled cellophane bag that had fallen out of Dr. Thaw's briefcase.

"What the heck?" he murmured, as he picked up the empty bag of Uncle Bo's Bar-be-que Flavor Pork Rinds.

AUTHOR'S NOTE

The real Ashton Powell Johnson, C.S.A., was killed by a single bullet to his head on July 28, 1864, on a country path called Lick Skillet Road just outside of Atlanta.

Unlike his fictitious counterpart, Ashton never had a chance to reach adulthood. Only eighteen when he was killed, his commander, General Quarles, had already pushed through the paperwork to promote him from lieutenant to captain.

The Ashton I created, however, is true to the character of the real Ashton. His brief adventure in the Confederate Army is chronicled in the scores of letters he wrote, as well as their responses, which were found in his saddlebags still attached to his horse, Waffles, after his death. The letters were saved from certain destruction by my aunt, Grace Johnson Stewart, his niece. To her he remained alive, just as he remains alive today to anyone who reads his wonderfully rich and warm letters.

The names of most of the characters in this book are true. Their letters, along with Ashton's often humorous responses, rest in musty volumes not three yards from where I sit now. Eddie, only sixteen at the time of his brother's death, longed to follow his "Bro. Ash" in Quarles's brigade as soon as he completed his engineering degree at Lexington College. He fought during the siege of Richmond, which caused his mother, Eliza Branch Johnson, and his slightly hysterical aunt, Eppes Branch Giles—both at The Oaks— no small amount of grief. They worried about Ashton, of course, but somehow he seemed beyond harm. He had seen his mother and aunt through so much death, the loss of so many other children, that the thought of Ashton not surviving was quite simply inconceivable.

General Quarles himself, in his letters to Ashton's mother, vowed to protect her son, admitting that although he first grew fond of Ashton "because of another," he soon became attached to the young aide "on his own account." Ashton was most attractive to women as well, for the general mentioned that "lately I have worked him so hard he hasn't had time to break many hearts." Ultimately, Quarles grew to love Ashton almost as a son, and hoped that "before the war is over he will be, I trust, one of our most intelligent and efficient officers." The day Ashton was killed, Quarles, sensing the skirmish on Lick Skillet Road would soon become bloody, tried to send his young aide a mile or two behind the lines to hasten ammunition. Ashton insisted that a courier be sent, for he felt it his duty to fight and would not have the other men, veterans he now outranked, cast aspersions on his honor and courage.

Lizzie Giles, Ashton's adored cousin, broke her engagement to General Quarles, but they remained cordial for Ashton's sake. She did, indeed, smuggle her Paris-bought trousseau from St. Louis to The

Oaks. Lizzie is mentioned in Mary Chesnut's diary and was part of a small circle of friends that included Mrs. Chesnut and Varina Davis. Ashton teasingly called her "the belle of Petersburg," and from all accounts, she was.

Mary B. Cox is alive and well and never nursed a soldier in her life. She was my roommate at the University of the South in Sewanee, Tennessee, one of the most beautiful places on earth.

And the real Ashton Powell Johnson, in spite of his flirtations with women from Mobile to Atlanta, was in love with his cousin Mag Garnett from Seven Pines. Only one of her letters survives, written on the back of one of Eliza's letters when Mag was visiting The Oaks. She rushed to say that the rumor of her engagement to another was not true, and she was terribly upset that he had been told such a falsehood.

The photograph of Ashton used to frighten me as a child, a young man of startling good looks with eyes of such a pale hue that the St. Louis photographer had to touch them up.

I used to turn away, reminded of his untimely death, and the fact that he had suffered nightmares about being shot in the head just before he was killed. He told several people that he could survive anything but that.

Now I see the photograph and think of his short life, and how he touched so many people with his spirit. There are scores of condolence notes following the awful telegram from the Confederate States of America. Some were sent under flag of truce, others smuggled from up North through Havana. Most are from fellow Confederates, then questioning, as did Ashton, a war that could lead to such a loss.

The photograph of Ashton sits above my desk at this very moment. He has the Branch eyes, deep-set and slightly downturned. My grandmother had those eyes, as does my own mother, and from photographs it is clear that Eddie and Lizzie and Eliza and Aunt Eppes had them, too. So do I, as does my five-year-old son.

I was worried about this book, concerned that somehow, wherever he is, Ashton might be upset to find himself promoted to the rank of general. Painfully honest, his letters are free of the usual soldierly bragging. The last thing I wanted to do was embarrass him.

Yet I also believe, from the beauty of his letters, that he might have become a writer, and he was always telling his little brothers (in reality, there were three) to study so that "perhaps you might one day be kind enough to appoint me to *your* staff." To have him end up as a writer and a college professor was not an unlikely stretch.

This afternoon, as the sun fades and the cheerful shouts of children playing outside fill the room, I see his expressive face in the sepia-toned photograph. My own is reflected on the computer screen. And Ashton, just a few inches away, seems to have a small smile crinkling the corners of his Branch eyes.